SUBJECT—MURDER

SUBJECT—MURDER

A Novel of Detection
By
CLIFFORD WITTING

GALILEO PUBLISHERS, CAMBRIDGE

Galileo Publishers
16 Woodlands Road, Great Shelford, Cambridge
CB22 5LW UK
www.galileopublishing.co.uk

Distributed in the USA by SCB Distributors
15608 S. New Century Drive Gardena,
CA 90248-2129, USA

Australia: Peribo Pty Limited
58 Beaumont Road
Mount Kuring-Gai, NSW 2080
Australia

ISBN 978-1-912916-99-3

First published 1945 by Hodder & Stoughton
This edition © 2023
All rights reserved.

Cover illustration © A. Batov
by kind permission of Zvezda LLC

Series consultant Richard Reynolds

Printed in the EU

DEDICATED

In Friendship and Affection

To

EDWARD SEYMOUR

My Battery Sergeant-Major

At the Time

This Book Was Written

By the same author and available as reissues from Galileo:

Catt out of the Bag
Dead on Time
Let X be the Murderer
Measure for Murder
Midsummer Murder
Murder in Blue

CONTENTS

PROLOGUE

Subject—R.I.P.

M OST of us at Battery headquarters had certainly considered the possibility on more than one occasion, yet, for all that, it came as rather a shock when somebody did murder the Sergeant-major.

Cruel Yule ... I forget who in the Battery first called him that, but the epithet fitted, for Battery Sergeant-major William George Yule, of the Royal Regiment of Artillery, was the cruellest man I ever met. Not that his was the straightforward brutality, the healthy gall, of the Army bully. It was more of the cat-and-mouse type. He liked to see others in pain or distress, particularly if he himself had been the agent of their suffering. Dr. Freud would have been most interested in him; and so would that misunderstood, thoughtlessly reviled student of the human emotions, that "mild, gentle, rather bald and grey-haired person," de Sade.

At the time of his death, Yule was in his thirty-first year; was no more than five feet eight in height, with a solidity of build that would have matured, had not Nemesis intervened, into grossness. His healthily coloured face, with the beginnings of a double chin, might have led the casual observer to sum him up as a jovial, hail-fellow-well-met kind of a chap; but the dead-cod eyes and the cruel lines on each side of his mouth would have warned the discerning against so charitable a judgment.

Yule was a Londoner, though one would not have guessed it from his accent. Some inherent disability gave his voice a thick, guttural tone with a sort of click in it, as if—which was not really the case—he wore a very loosely fitting top set of false teeth.

In Civvy Street, he had been a factory foreman. In pre-war days, the firm had run its own Territorial unit; and, as is the usual way with such affairs, military appointments had been governed by civilian standing, so that the chairman's son became major, the vice-chairman's nephew became captain, the remaining pips became distributed among the departmental heads, and William George Yule, bless his little heart, became sergeant-major. When, in the summer of 1939, the unit was drafted *en bloc* into the regular Army, he went with it, still in his old rank. How he managed to hang on to it for over four years was little short of a miracle, for he was no soldier; and judging from his negligible administrative abilities and his complete disregard for the welfare of the men under his control, he could have been no works foreman either.

He had a wife somewhere in south-east London. He very seldom mentioned her and, as far as my own observation went, never wrote her a single line.

That, then, was cruel Yule. An unkindly picture, but a faithful one. In his life there was nothing to commend him; and in his passing there was neither manliness nor honour, but merely the harsh, brutal justice of the Dark Ages.

For his death—if one can believe an anonymous biographer—was similar, in its ghastly indignity, to the death of Lopez de Gonzala, Marquis of Santagena, over four hundred years ago.

PART I

Subject—P.T.C.

CHAPTER ONE

I

MY name is Peter Bradfield. Before I became a soldier I was a policeman—or, to be more precise, a detective-constable. Glancing through the various cases of Inspector Charlton, who was the Big White Chief of my pre-Army days, I have found myself mentioned here and there in what is known in the world of entertainment as a small supporting role. In one place there is a whole paragraph devoted to me, so, with no little trepidation, I am going to copy it out. At least it will be less of a shock to sensitive minds than a photograph facing page nine.

"Detective-constable Peter Bradfield," it runs, "was young, energetic and very likeable. If he had followed the suggestion of his father, who was a solicitor in Hampstead, he would have entered into the same profession; but Bradfield Junior had no taste for it. He preferred something a little more exciting and chose the Police Force, not realizing that nothing, on occasions, can be less exciting, than the Police Force. Again, if he had followed his father's suggestion, he would have entered the Police College at Hendon and been passed out, in due course, as a junior station inspector; but Peter elected to start at the bottom and work his way up. That he had not yet gained more advancement than the right to wear his own well-cut clothes on duty did not in the least discourage him or cloud his sunny disposition. Nobody would have called him handsome—his nose was too wide and flat—but he was a great favourite of those young persons known as The Girls."

Reading that again, I very nearly crossed it out, but further consideration has persuaded me that, if I have to write this story, I must first of all describe myself, for fear some people might envisage me with a squint, a wooden leg, and a wife in Birmingham. And if I have left in the complimentary parts of the passage, I have, on the other hand, included an offensive reference to my nose. I submit that "wide and flat" would be better used to depict the Sahara Desert. As for my so-called sunny disposition and the concession I won to wear civilian clothes on duty, the famous Bradfield cheerfulness is none the better for many months of Home Forces soldiering; and no amount of argument would induce the War House moguls to agree that my regulation battledress should be laid aside in favour of a civvy suit, however natty.

So much for that. Now I can go on to describe the day—sixteen months before the death of Sergeant-major Yule—that I joined the armed forces of the Crown—and let it be said now, before this book is tossed aside as "just another rookie's war-diary," that these first chapters are not to be random military recollections, but the opening scenes of a comedy-drama that ended in tragedy—and very nearly in something far worse.

II

On the 2nd July, 1942, my career as a soldier began. It would have begun long before if I had had my way, but there had been those in a position to decide otherwise.

My calling-up papers directed me to a far-flung outpost of Empire in North Wales, where, a thousand miles—well, a mile and a half—from the nearest civilization, was the –th Primary Training Centre.

At the London terminus I bought *Lilliput* and *Men Only* to while away the journey, but after the train started, even the illustrations failed to claim my attention for long, for my eyes kept drifting from the—er—illustrations to the countryside through which we ran. Not that I took in much more of the changing scene than an occasional group of children who waved grubby hands at us, as is the way with children, and an equally occasional herd of cows that took no notice of us, as is the way with cows. At every level-crossing was a middle-aged woman holding a bicycle with a wicker-basket attached to the handlebars. It is, perhaps, worth adding that, in all my travelling experience, I do not recall a single occasion when there was not.

Yes, in that express from Paddington, there were so many things for me to think about. I was entering on a new life. Let me say hastily that I was no green youth torn ruthlessly from the bosom of his adoring family. No tears welled up in my eyes. I did not whistle, inaudibly but bravely, between my teeth. I did not try to over-wind my wrist-watch every couple of minutes. I did not yawn, as is the weakness of shy young men when suffering from nervous disturbance. I did not even gulp.

Quitting the aged parents meant very little to me. I was very fond of them, of course, but it was some years since, with weak little wings, I had first flown from the nest. In 1942, parting was not such sweet sorrow as it had been in 1937, in which year I had been first transferred from the uniformed branch to the C.I.D. and had been sent to assist Inspector Charlton to stamp out crime in the neighbourhood administered by Superintendent Kingsley's Division of the Downshire County Constabulary.

I had had some good times—and some exciting ones—with Inspector Charlton and that grand old fellow with the sandy hair, that plain-speaking stalwart from Camberwell, that finest of all sharers of a tight corner, Detective-sergeant Bert Martin. Soldiering was going to be different from police work. It did not promise to be particularly pleasant, especially at first. Reveille at 5.45, I had heard, and Lights Out at 10.15. I was not afraid of a spot of early rising and retiring. During the few previous years I had been accustomed to sleep when I had got the chance, day or night. No, it was the regularity of it that frightened me—the way they had in the Army of ordering your life through every moment of the day. It was definitely not the ideal existence for the sort of bloke that Shelley had in mind when he wrote of "a pard-like spirit, beautiful and swift." It was going to be so dull at first, learning new things. . . . Tedious things like arms-drill and square-bashing. . . . How would that pard-like spirit have reacted, I wondered, to arms-drill and square-bashing? . . . Then there was the business of settling down in unfamiliar surroundings and an uncomfortable way of life. . . . Making new friends. . . .

At that point my mind stopped wandering in the past and future, and came sharply back to the present. I was being smiled at.

He was sitting opposite to me: a slight, ginger-headed, freckled young man of twenty-five or six, in a Home Guard uniform with a collar far too large for his thin neck. A small leather-covered book was held open by his slender, sensitive fingers. And he was smiling at me.

I smiled back. It was the least I could do.

"Lovely morning," he said.

"Marvellous," I agreed.

"Going my way?" he asked pleasantly.

"Depends which way that is," I grinned. His smile was infectious.

"I haven't got the hang of pronouncing it yet," he admitted, "but it begins with C-W-M and ends with a hiccough."

I glanced at the travellers in the other corners: a youth of sixteen chewing spearmint, with a tattered, folded penny-dreadful held much too close to his busy eyes; and a bareheaded young woman in dark blue trousers, high-heeled shoes and a short coat as scarlet as her lips. Neither of them looked like an enemy agent. That, in itself, should have prompted caution; nevertheless, I took a chance. If the length of the war is increased by five minutes because of my indiscretion, I am truly sorry.

Leaning towards my red-polled *vis-à-vis*—who might also have been one of Hitler's young men—I murmured in my best Celtic:

"Cwmsamfach?"

"That's the spot," he nodded. "Sounds a bit heathen, doesn't it? I think we're both on the same jolly errand, aren't we?"

"Looks like it," I agreed. "How did you guess?"

"It was written all over you!" he laughed, showing his white irregular teeth. "The tendency to smooth down the hair. The glances at the attaché-case on the rack. The glazed eye—"

"No bravely repressed tears?" I threw in anxiously.

"Not a sign," was his solemn assurance. "*My* weakness is yawning."

"Funny you should mention that. I was thinking along those very lines when you brought me back to earth just now. I'm glad to have got to know you, anyway. My name's Bradfield—Peter Bradfield. I've a second Christian name, but I keep it dark."

"Mine's John Fieldhouse. I like to be called 'Johnny,' but most people insist on 'Ginger'." He paused before adding sadly, "I don't see why."

Mata Hari, on the same side of the compartment as he, turned her head from the window to have a look.

"It's certainly rather obscure," I said, gravely eyeing his fiery summit.

"Because my hair's not ginger. It's auburn. Don't think I'm vain. I wouldn't mind much if my hair was a bright green. But I can't stand loose descriptions. Auburn is a definite colour and ginger is another: They're entirely different. Ginger is a light reddish yellow. Is my hair a light reddish yellow?"

It was a light reddish yellow. It was unequivocally ginger. Mata Hari was smiling openly. But it was a pity to smash up a friendship so newly begun, so I fished out a flabby war-time packet and offered him a bent cigarette.

"Been in the Home Guard long?" I enquired after we had lighted up.

"Since it started. I was one of the original L.D.Vs. All the uniform we had in those days was an arm-band, which fitted me much better than this darned thing. I finished up as a lance-corporal, but took the tapes off last night. I wouldn't have come in fancy-dress if I hadn't been ordered to. I've heard that if the Army N.C.Os. get to know you were in the Home Guard, they beef you for it. So if you've done any of it, take my tip and keep your mouth shut. Know nothing until they tell you themselves; and furthermore"— he drew a deep breath—"volunteer for—"

"That's an old Army motto," I interrupted quickly, with an apprehensive glance towards the beautiful spy. "No, I've not been in the Home Guard. As a matter of fact, I'm in the C.I.D."

"What, at Scotland Yard?"

I laughed at his awestruck tone.

"Not exactly *at* it," I told him. "I was attached to the Downshire Police. Tracking down missing bicycles, questioning small criminals about the seventeen apples found in their pockets, and similar responsible work."

I had really done a bit more than that, but we Bradfields are no braggarts.

"But isn't the C.I.D. on the list of reserved occupations?"

"At Flodden, Agincourt and Crécy," I said, "when the battle was at its height, invariably the cry went up: 'A Bradfield! A Bradfield!'"

"And where were you?" he asked with interest.

"I wasn't there personally at any of the scraps, but there's been a Bradfield on most battle fronts. The family chronicles have it that had not Sir Jasper Bradfield missed the troop-train at Carlisle, Bannockburn might have ended very differently. So, you see, no list of reserved occupations, however comprehensive, is going to keep a Bradfield out of the present little party."

Johnny Fieldhouse's eyes had been dancing at this lively exchange, but now his face clouded and it was mournfully that he said:

"I'll never make a soldier. I'm the man with two left feet. I only got my Home Guard stripe because they made me platoon-clerk—paying out subsistence money, buying the tea and so forth." He shook his head. "But the military juggernaut got me in the end. Heaven knows what it'll do with me."

He went on to tell me of his employment in the Head Office of one of the big banks. We chatted idly for twenty miles or so, then went back to our reading, I to *Lilliput* and he to his little leather-bound book. Soon he slipped it away in the breast-pocket of his battledress, but ten minutes later it was out again.

"Poetry?" I asked him.

He raised his eyes from the page and looked at me dubiously, like a man invited to admit that he is running two homes.

"Yes," he acknowledged eventually.

"'Awake! for morning in the bowl of night ...'" I murmured. "You know it?"

"Who doesn't?" I smiled at his eager tone.

"Just a moment," he said. "You quoted from it. How did you know it was the *Rubaiyat*? You couldn't have seen the name on the cover, because I purposely kept my hand over it." Gently I took my revenge.

"Young men who yawn when they're nervous," I told him, "always take refuge in Omar. The delightful old reprobate helps to restore their ebbing courage. 'Nothing really matters,' is his message; and they believe him, the poor little devils."

Johnny put the book back in his pocket and rebuttoned the flap.

"You know," he said, "I'm going to like you."

CHAPTER TWO

THE train stopped at a station and, without seeming to transfer even a fraction of his attention from his reading, the boy with the spearmint felt for the door-catch and got out. He set off along the platform with the thriller within six inches of his nose. Whether he knew where he was, or why he had come there, and whether he finished his story before becoming involved in a fatal accident, I have never known.

There is a curious thing about railway travelling. When four persons, strangers to each other, occupy the corner seats in a compartment, they may travel for a hundred miles without exchanging a word. But should one of the four alight at a station, the remaining three will invariably start a conversation. With the departure of the fourth traveller the atmosphere becomes, in some way, more chummy, as if none of them cared for the looks of Number 4 and they are mutually glad of the riddance.

So it was in our compartment that brilliant summer's morning. Admitted that Johnny and I, by previously fraternizing, had not run to type, but Mata Hari—except for her fleeting smile over Johnny—had been determinedly unsociable. Yet as soon as the young bookworm had left us, she began to unbend. I do not mean that she spoke to us, but she did what amounted to the same thing: she took a packet of cigarettes from her handbag, then produced that finest of all ice-breakers, the-cigarette-lighter-that-doesn't-work. Many times in my gregarious career have I met that type of lighter; many times has my stronger self laid a restraining hand on the arm of his weaker brother: and many times has that hand been impatiently shaken off.

Now it happened once again. With one of those courteous grunts that are the modern equivalent of, "Allow me," I pulled out my own lighter, stepped across to her, flicked a flame and held it to the end of her cigarette. She thanked me with a smile and said that her own lighter must need refuelling. What more natural than that I should sit down opposite her, the more comfortably to discuss the many things that can go wrong with a petrol-lighter?

She was a bright, pleasant lassie, in spite of her dreadful taste in clothes, and we got on splendidly. From petrol, flints and wicks, the chat flitted from the weather to rationing, from rationing to Income Tax and from Income Tax to Bob Hope. Johnny Fieldhouse took no part in our small-talk; he had picked up one of the magazines and was reading it defensively, as if defying all comers to interrupt him. When Mata Hari and I had discussed the chances of the war being over before Christmas, she said:

"You're both going to Cwmsamfach Camp, aren't you?" When I did not immediately reply, she smiled. She had rather a nice smile, I noticed.

"You needn't answer!" she went on. "I couldn't help hearing you and your friend talking about it. I know a lot about Cwmsamfach. My brother did his training there in 1939. Then he went through Dunkirk and now he's back again at Cwmsamfach. Ever so funny they should send him back there, wasn't it? They've made him a sergeant-instructor."

"Really?" I said. "that's his speciality?"

"Oh, he teaches everything except P.T. He's ever so clever."

I suggested: "Maybe we shall come across him."

"Yes; and if you do, give him my love, will you? Say it was Edie. Oh, and tell him he hasn't written home for over three weeks and Mum's getting anxious."

"Yes, of course I will. I shall probably bump into him. What's his name?"

"Sergeant Thomson—without a 'P.' Everybody puts a 'P' in it. Funny, isn't it?"

"How does he like the place?"

"He says it's ever so dull. Miles from any life. They've a camp cinema and there's an Ensa show nearly every week, but

Bill—that's my brother—he likes something with a bit more go in it. Even when he was at school. . . ."

She went on to describe, in some detail, the early years, boyhood and adolescence of her brother. Eventually I managed to lead her back to the subject of the –th Primary Training Centre, of which I wanted to learn as much in advance as possible. When I glanced across at Johnny Fieldhouse, his expression denoted so much concentration on his reading that I knew that he, too, was listening hard.

Miss Thomson's news was disquieting. Things seemed to be run on strictly military lines at Cwmsamfach. The C.O. was a colonel in a Guards Regiment famous for spit-and-polish, the officers were martinets and the N.C.Os. were swaggering emperors—and, reading between the lines of her encomium (for she thought him marvellous), Sgt. Bill Thomson was the worst of the bunch.

"Ever such a fine soldier, he is," she enthused, "and always insists on things being done in the way he wants, just like when he was no taller than *that.*"

But I was not inclined to take so fervently partisan a view. Bill Thomson sounded poison to me. I made a mental note to keep out of his way.

Our conversation drifted to other matters, until the train began to slow down.

"This'll be my station," she said.

She trod out her cigarette-end on the floor. The train drew into the station. I opened the door for her to get out.

"Well, bye-bye," she said from the platform. "Hope you both get on all right."

"Thanks very much," I smiled down at her. "I expect we shall soon find our feet."

The guard waved his flag.

"And don't forget, if you see Bill," she said, "to say I sent him a big kiss."

We began to move.

"And tell him to write, 'cause Mum's getting worried."

"I will," I called back to her.

I stayed with my head out of the window as we gathered speed, watching her walk back towards the barrier. If women only knew, I reflected, how they looked from the rear when they wore high heels with trousers they would never wear high heels again. I could not suggest they should never wear trousers again, for trousers for women, alas! are like Eliza; they have come to stay.

On that sombre note, I withdrew my head into the compartment and went back to sit opposite Johnny Fieldhouse.

He dropped the magazine on the seat and looked at me.

"Disgraceful," he said.

"Oh, I wouldn't say that!" I protested. "With these air-raids, they're much easier to slip on quickly in the middle of the—"

"What are you talking about?" Johnny demanded.

"Women's trousers," I told him.

"Well, I'm not!" he retorted. "Goodness knows I'm broadminded, but for you to open a conversation with a member of the opposite sex—a complete stranger—and then to—to wave goodbye to her . . ."

He left the sentence unfinished. His face was as stern as such a good-natured, freckled little face could be.

"Don't be a silly ass," I said lightly, and opened *Men Only*.

"You hadn't even been introduced," he went on hotly.

"It's a pretty bad state of affairs when a young woman can't travel alone without being . . . without being accosted."

I tried to detect a twinkle in his eyes, but they stared at me very gravely.

"You don't expect me to take you seriously, do you?" I asked.

"Certainly I do. Women should be honoured and respected, not treated like"—again he had to search for a word—"like chattels."

"My dear, good fellow," I said with heavy humour, "even your keen and critical young eyes did not see me treat Miss Thomson-without-a-'P' as if she were an item of movable property such as you mention. As for honour and respect, I do not recall that I did more than exchange a few casual and entirely decorous remarks with the young lady. There is not much dishonour or disrespect in that, I think? In other words, don't be a damn fool!"

It was my turn to take up a defensive position behind a magazine. The heir to the Bradfield estates was somewhat hot under the collar.

The North Wales train rattled onward. In one compartment there was silence for quite a while. Then Johnny Fieldhouse's voice broke it.

"I'm sorry," he said quietly.

The admission pleased me, not so much because I wanted or expected an apology, as because I cannot stand on my dignity for long, without wanting to laugh.

"That's all right," I smiled forgiveness. "A storm in a teacup, anyway."

"I shouldn't have spoken to you like that," he said. "Our friendship's not old enough for us to be rude to each other. It was—well, I suppose it was because I'm not used to that sort of thing. . . . I mean, casually striking up an acquaintance with a girl and then waving goodbye to her, as if you'd known her all your life, instead of half an hour! No decently brought up girl likes that kind of treatment."

"This one did!" I grinned. "Johnny, from the way you talk, anyone would think that I behaved like the villain of the piece and that Edie Thomson should have leapt screaming for the communication-cord. I only chatted with her on general subjects, just as a fellow-traveller—nothing more. As for waving to her, it was only a little wave. Nothing behind it but the Bradfield *bonhomie*. I'm a matey bloke, Johnny, I'll gossip with anybody—man, woman or child. Part of my training as a 'busy', I suppose." I got another cigarette going.

"It's a curious thing," I went on, "I don't know what there is about me, but as soon as a woman claps eyes on me, she always gets the urge to take a run at me and sob out her little secrets on my shoulder. I must have that Big Brother look. . . . *I* didn't begin the Edie Thomson incident—*she* did. She used the dud-lighter routine—and if you've never seen it before, it's as well to beware of it. Take a good look at the filly before getting out the Bryant & Mays."

Johnny wrinkled his brows thoughtfully.

"I suppose it's the war," he said. "It's made everybody realize the existence of his neighbour. We all take a much friendlier view of the people around us; and we're not nearly so critical as we were in peace-time. Yet," he went on, feeling for his words, "although we've gained something, I think we've lost something even more important. It's a creditable enough policy to look on every man as your brother, but"— he smiled quaintly—"you can't very well look on every woman as your sister, can you? Old Mother Nature wouldn't stand for it. . . . There's a great deal to be said, Peter—you don't mind if I call you Peter?—there's a very great deal to be said for the segregation of the sexes. Take the women of the East: the mystery, the all-enveloping robes, the *yashmak* veiling everything but the alluring eyes. . . . Wasn't it Keats who said something about 'lovely modesty and virtues rare'? I ask you, Peter, did you detect any lovely modesty in Miss Edie Thomson?"

I opened my mouth to answer, but it seemed that his question was rhetorical, for he swept on:

"'But when I see thee meek and kind and tender'—I'm still quoting from the same poem—

> But when I see thee meek and kind and tender,
> Heavens! how desperately do I adore
> Thy winning graces;—to be thy defender
> I hotly burn—to be a Calidore—
> A very Red Cross Knight—a stout Leander—
> Might I be loved by thee like these of yore."

He paused for breath before adding:

"But why should I bore you with all this?"

"Go on," I urged him. "I'm interested."

And I was. It was not every day that one met a twenty-five-year-old Keats-quoting Puritan who denied the colour of his own hair.

"Nobody nowadays," he accepted my invitation, "wants to be a Red Cross Knight. Women have made themselves too cheap, too accessible, for the chivalry of the Crusades and the Round Table. . . . Camelot has become a *Palais de Danse.*

Would you joust against Sir Lancelot du Lac to win a smile and a word from Edie Thomson? Of course you wouldn't! And why not? Because you could get them both without working for them—without risking your life to gain them. In consequence, they mean nothing to you, do they?"

This time he clearly expected a reply.

"Times have changed," I hedged. "In any case, all you hear about the ancient chivalry and derring-do is mostly poppycock. And those women with the seductive eyes behind the *yashmaks;* those mystical, enigmatic daughters of the Orient: I bet most of them badly need a bath. Give me Edie Thomson every time—trousers, high heels and all."

Johnny tried to say something, but it was my turn to sweep on.

"Those lines of Keats: 'But when I see thee meek,' etc. *Notice the* operative word, Johnny. The operative word is 'But.'"

"I don't follow you," he confessed.

"Stop me if I'm wrong," I said in the tones of one who knows jolly well that he isn't, "but that same poem begins—and don't look so surprised at my erudition; I learnt the thing during my last term at the reformatory—it begins:

> Woman! when I behold thee flippant, vain,
> Inconstant, childish, proud and full of fancies;
> Without that modest softening that enhances
> The downcast eye—

"You see that even in Keats's day, the feminine idol was showing signs of clay feet—definite traces of a few friendly frailties. You can't put a woman on a pedestal and worship from afar, even though your rose-tinted spectacles do have telescopic sights."

"There I can't agree with you," said Johnny, with an impatient shake of his ginger head. "True worship can only be from a distance. Then you don't see the flippancy and the vanity, but only the lovely modesty that I mentioned just now."

"And what good does that do you?" I demanded crudely.

"You keep your dreams."

He said it with such simplicity that I could not smile.

To bridge an awkward silence, I glanced at my watch and remarked that we were getting along. Johnny, however, elected not to change the subject. He gave an ironic laugh.

"You keep your dreams," he repeated. "What a phrase! What footling nonsense! There seems no end to my talent for self-deception. I don't want to put women on a pedestal. I don't want to worship from afar. The fact of the matter is, Peter, that I'm dead scared of them—and I bolster up my self-esteem with a lot of high-falutin' nonsense. I'm as shy of women as a cat is of water."

He brooded for a moment or two.

"What made me leap at your throat? Was it the outraged feelings of a prim-souled anchorite? No, it was envy."

He looked at me with morbid eyes.

"Nothing more, nothing finer, Peter, than envy. Green, naked envy. You're tall, good-looking and devil-may-care. I'm small, scraggy, and freckled. You did what I'd give almost anything to be able to do. Calmly, casually, without awkwardness or effort, you strolled into her life—"

"And out of it again, don't forget," I threw in. "That was the fiendish master-stroke, Johnny. It's far, far easier to stroll into a woman's life than out of it."

"I'd risk that," said Johnny.

CHAPTER THREE

I

"INTAKE all out!"

That was the welcome we received as our train drew into Cwmsamfach station. It was uttered by strident voices all along the platform and it began some time before the train came to a stop. It was not unlikely that the reception committee had started to shout while we had been at the previous station, twenty miles back.

It is a rule in the Army that all orders will be carried out instantly and without question, yet I decided not to take those noisy exhortations too literally; we might have been killed. So Johnny and I waited until the train came to a complete standstill, then made a sedate descent on to the platform—right, as it were, at the feet of one of the Stentors.

I noticed that he was young, large and healthy, and that he was wearing three stripes.

"Come on, you two!" he yelled at us. "Wake your ideas up!"

I knew enough to hold my peace, but Johnny answered in that clear, decisive voice of his:

"We couldn't get out before the train stopped."

The lordly one shoved a bent arm towards him.

"What d'yer think those are, Ginger—bars of chocolate? When you address me, stand to attention and call me 'Sergeant.' Now fall in with the intake outside."

I turned towards the station exit.

"Get on with it!" said Stentor. "You ought to be there by now!"

Johnny would have stayed for further parley, but I got hold of his arm and shepherded him towards the barrier, through which a file of men, of all ages and sizes—and each with his little attaché-case or brown-paper parcel—was passing, under the watchful and not very friendly eyes of a couple of tall, red-capped C.M.Ps.[1]

"But he shouldn't talk to us like that!" Johnny protested as I urged him along the platform. " The man was quite rude. He didn't expect us to leap out of the train like a couple of circus acrobats, did he? And he called me Ginger!"

"My son," I said paternally, "you must get used to answering to Ginger. It is your destiny. You and I know that your hair is a rich, glorious auburn, but what are we two amongst so many? And don't argue with N.C.Os. The more you argue, the worse you make it for yourself. Take no notice of the angry bellowing of corporals and the primitive sarcasm of sergeants. All that play-acting comes under the general heading of Bullsh."

"Bullsh?" Johnny asked, looking up at me. "What's Bullsh?"

I endeavoured to enlighten him.

"According to friends of mine already in the Army," I said, "Bullsh is a military purgative, compounded of equal parts of blanco and bluster. It is administered whenever the patient shows signs of recovering. If he is wise, he will not refuse the dose, but will swallow it with a grain of salt."

We drew near to the barrier.

"Now," I advised him, "march smartly past the redcaps—and don't stop to reason with them if they call you Ginger."

We passed without incident between Scylla and Charybdis and were among the last off the platform. When we emerged into the station yard, fifty or sixty men were already lined up in three extremely untidy ranks. Encompassing them, like vigilant collies around a flock of sheep, were loud-voiced sergeants and, by reason of their lesser rank, even louder-voiced corporals. Presumably they were there to see that no one got away alive.

As Johnny and I came out into the yard, the nearest corporal bawled out at us:

---

[1] For glossary of abbreviations, etc., see end of book.

"Get fell in!"

I attached myself to the ragged end of the front rank. Johnny took up his position behind me, and in a few moments we were marching off to our new home. I say "marching," but "proceeding on foot" would better describe the progress of the doleful cavalcade. No two adjacent men were in step, unless by the merest coincidence; and as we made our way along the streets of Cwmsamfach, the inhabitants of that sleepy little Welsh town watched us from pavements, doorways and windows. More than one of them called out to us as we slouched unhappily by with our cases and parcels:

"Italianos?"

Whether these were genuine enquiries or just sardonic commentaries on our woe-begone appearance, I cannot tell.

It was a mile and a half from the town to the camp. Our road lay uphill most of the way and the day was hot. I, for one, was glad when we reached our objective, which we had glimpsed with horror on breasting the hill.

The more I witness of the Army and its works, the more I am reminded of the phrase in the old missionary hymn, "Though every prospect pleases, and only man is vile." The –th Primary Training Centre—or Borstal, Mark II, as we came to call it—lay in a valley; as ugly a cluster of human habitations as I ever wish to see. It was a great, irregular collection of huts, some of wood, others of corrugated-iron (the dreaded Nissen), all surrounded by an intimidating fence of coiled barbed-wire. Here and there were parade-grounds, of which we were to see overmuch during the coming weeks, and, also within the boundaries of the wire, sports-fields.

We turned off the Cwmsamfach road into the short, newly concreted stretch that led to the gap in the wire that was the camp's only means of ingress, egress and—as, with an eye to the future, they always cautiously add in legal documents—regress. A private with "R.P." on his armlet stood guard at the heavy gates that were bolted fast at night, but were now fixed back, just like the entrance to a rat-trap—and with the same ominous implications.

As we went past the guard-room, a solid, brick-built structure, immediately inside the gates, Johnny murmured to me.

"'All hope abandon, ye who enter here.'"

We marched past numerous huts set in staggered formation, went along the side of a parade-ground, past more huts and finally, by the combined and vociferous efforts of our fighter escort, came to a shuffling, uneasy halt.

"Fall out on the grass!" was the next order.

It was the first humane command that we had so far received and we were only too ready to comply. But it was a modified concession, for as we flung ourselves on the grass in question, a sparsely covered bank running alongside the concreted roadway, the sergeant who had met Johnny and me at the station roared direfully:

"Fall *out,* I said, not *down,* you gutless jellyfish! Sit up straight! You're soldiers now, not lovely judies on beds of—roses! Hey, Ginger! Who d'yer think you are—the sultan's favourite concubine?"

Grudgingly Johnny raised himself from his back and sat more or less upright, muttering as he did so:

"I don't think I like that red-faced butcher's boy."

The big young sergeant took four swift paces, to stand glaring down at Johnny.

"What was that?" he demanded.

I took a hand. Johnny's tongue was likely to get him into trouble. I said:

"He said, 'Yes, Sergeant.'"

"I wasn't talking to you, Pugnose," he snarled at me. "As for you, you ginger-nobbed little runt, any more of your back-chat and you'll find yourself on a charge."

With which impressive threat, he stalked away.

"Did he hear what I said?" Johnny whispered eagerly into my ear.

"It doesn't matter greatly if he did," I answered with bitterness. "You couldn't do much more damage than you've done already. Why don't you keep your mouth shut?"

"Well," persisted Johnny, unrepentant, "he does look like an overgrown butcher's boy. Probably the chief assistant in the pig-slaughtering department and happy at his work."

I smiled in spite of myself; Johnny's word-pictures were pleasingly clear-cut.

"That's no reason why you should tell him so," I admonished. "You'll land yourself in a sticky mess before you're finished—and then expect me to get you out of it."

Which was, though I little guessed it then, prophetic.

II

Opposite the verge on which we squatted with our hand-luggage was the entrance to a long wooden hut. The double doors were closed. In front of them, under the scorching July sun, were two trestle tables, side by side, with a couple of chairs at each. I presumed that, before long, certain military personages would emerge from the hut, take their seats at the tables, summon us one by one—or four by four—question us, check us, number us, sort us out, then draw us into the hungry maw of the –th P.T.C.

"We'll probably get separated," I warned Johnny.

The N.C.Os. who had brought us from the station had all drifted away, except one corporal, who was sitting apart from us. The assumption was that he had been left in charge of us, although the aloof manner in which he smoked his Woodbine gave the impression that he wished to disassociate himself from us as much as possible, in case any of his frivolous friends passed that way.

Half an hour went by. We lost our rigidity of pose and lapsed into less military, though more natural attitudes. Johnny was not long in reassuming his role of the Fairest Flower of

22

the Harem. Now and again, parties of men marched past us, each with a lance-corporal and each showing a different stage in the early training of a soldier. The first to go by were still in civvies or Home Guard uniform. They marched like Benedict Arnold's rabble-in-arms, having arrived that same day, but by an earlier train than ours. Every face wore an expression of deepest gloom, arms hung limply at sides and nervous hands held newly issued white china mugs and those three other necessities, knife, fork and spoon. By their dejected demeanour, one might have thought they were being led off to Tyburn, instead of to their first Army dinner.

Johnny raised himself on one elbow.

"Beginning to feel peckish myself," he announced before dropping back.

The next party to pass us looked slightly, but only slightly, happier. They all wore battledress that went to confirm reports I had heard that uniforms are issued in two sizes only: too large and too small. Their badgeless "fore-and-afts"—officially Caps, F.S.—were pulled down firmly on their heads, so that tops became flattened and buttons were dead central over the nose instead of the right eye. Their faces had the pallor of civilian life; and it was with a conscious effort that they swung their arms—"in line," as their lance-corporal kept on reminding them, "with the shoulder."

The third platoon were seasoned soldiers, with all the hallmarks of a fortnight's service. They were as brown as berries. Their denim trousers were buttoned round the ankles and held up by webbing straps from their equipment. The sleeves of their collar-less, open-necked, khaki shirts were rolled above the elbows in the regulation width of fold. They swung their arms as if they enjoyed it and the sharp warnings of their lance jack failed to keep a song from their lips. I wondered if I should ever become so brisk and carefree a soldier. I was just going to pass on the thought to Johnny when our corporal suddenly jumped into life.

"On your feet!" he shouted. "Cigarettes out!"

We scrambled up. The doors of the long hut had opened at last.

We were about to be drawn into the maw.

CHAPTER FOUR

I

A N assurance was given early in this book that it was
not to be just another rookie's war-diary, yet now that I
have set out to recount the beginning of my friendship with
Johnny Fieldhouse, recollections of our first weeks together
crowd in so fast upon me that it is difficult to prevent my eager
pen—or, more exactly, the Battery Office typewriter—from
running away with me. I could, with the greatest ease in the
world, devote the whole of the book to those long, scorching,
un-ending days of primary training at Borstal, Mark II, when
Johnny and I—and Chris Wilkinson—still lived in happy
ignorance of the detestable Yule. But after Cwmsamfach, there
came Burntash, Boxford, firing-camp, Stalcote-on-Sea and
then—miracle of miracles!—Lulverton, the hunting-ground
of my old C.I.D. days. The Odyssey began at Cwmsamfach,
but at Burntash, Boxford, the firing-camp and Stalcote-on-
Sea there were incidents, that must have their place in the
tale before I can come to the climax at Lulverton, under the
kindly shadow of the South Downs, in the November of 1943.

So I must not tarry overlong at Borstal, Mark II.

II

Johnny and I were duly drawn into the maw of the –th
Primary Training Centre. Our identity-cards and ration
books were taken away from us by the shirt-sleeved sergeants
who came from the hut to sit in the sunshine at the tables. I
wondered whether one of them was Edie Thomson's brother.
We answered many questions of which we felt the military
authorities should already have the answers. We announced
our religion as Church of England, which was short-sighted of
us, for C. of E. parades were held in the camp, while all other

25

denominations were allowed to attend their own churches outside. It was whispered that few of them ever got further than the W.V.S. Canteen in Cwmsamfach.

I was the first of the two to be called to the tables. When my catechism was over, I was directed to one of the three groups into which our train-load was being systematically split. I gathered that we were "C" Company and that the other two were "A" and "B." Johnny's name was one of the last to be called. I waited in some suspense for him to leave the table. The odds were against his joining me in "C" Company, and I was loath to lose him so soon.

The questioning ended—and my hopes were dashed by the pointing finger of the sergeant. Johnny obviously shared my disappointment, for it was a sad little figure in a misfit battle dress that dragged unwilling feet towards the other recruits for "B" Company.

The last of the sixty was summoned to the Inquisition, was interrogated and sent to us. After one glance at his thickly greased and crinkly hair, his deep side-whiskers, his soiled flannel trousers and his pointed patent-leather shoes, I felt that we could have done very well without him.

There was a pause while the four N.C.Os. sorted out their papers. Then one sergeant spoke across to his *confrère* at the other table. The second man referred to a sheet. I caught Johnny's lost-soul gaze in my direction. He reminded me of Dives looking yearningly up at Lazarus in the bosom of Abraham; and I tried to keep from my face the slightly smug smile that Lazarus, being human, must surely have given him.

The second sergeant looked up and nodded. The other shouted:

"Private Fieldhouse!"

Johnny stood uncertainly for a moment, as if not quite sure of his own name—a curious affliction that invariably attacks the new soldier. Then he braced himself, stepped forward—and left the "B" bunch for ever. When he was dismissed from the reception table, he marched smartly across to us, with his white, uneven teeth showing in a radiant smile and even his freckles seeming to dance for joy.

"That," he grinned up at me as he took his place beside me, "was an eleventh-hour reprieve!"

"I fixed it for you," I told him without a blush.

III

A trio of lance-corporals appeared as if from nowhere, got each Company's intake into something approaching military formation, marched us along to the quartermaster's store, to draw pint-mugs and eating-irons, then to the vast dining-hall for roast beef, baked potatoes, cabbage and Yorkshire pudding.

Johnny said across the table:

"I thought they always had stew in the Army."

I was trying to get my knife and fork somewhere near my plate. When I had managed to free my elbows from my neighbours, by a ju-jutsu trick once taught me by a grateful Chinese whose life I had saved in Wapping, I replied:

"They always feed you well at Training Centres, to stop you from dying on them." After a generous mouthful, I added; "They don't always succeed."

Sultana pudding followed. I began to feel much better. We returned our plates to the counter at the end of the hall, on the walls of which were painted such slogans as "No SMOKING" and "DON'T WASTE FOOD" and chummy little reminders about the strict disciplinary action that would follow non-observance.

Johnny and I fought our way through the exit and rinsed our cutlery in the wash-tub of tepid water that stood outside the dining-hall. From the colour of the water and the questionable things that our stirring raised from its coagulated depths, we decided that it would have been better to have lunched at an earlier sitting.

27

Other recruits for "C" Coy.—I was getting to know their faces—began to collect around us. The raw levies for "A" and "B" were also bunching, but separately. Already each Company was tending to keep itself to itself, for even at that very early stage in our soldiering we were becoming unit-conscious—and unit-consciousness is the most deep-rooted instinct in the British fighting-man.

We of "C" Coy. looked at each other rather helplessly.

Johnny asked: "Where do we go from here?"

The question was answered, not by any of us, but by one of those ubiquitous and hard-working men who are the very backbone of a Training Centre; the men who are never far away, yet do all the running about; the men who have to know everything, from stripping an L.M.G. to darning a sock; the men who act as male nurse, mother, sister and brother to half a hundred defenceless and dependent conscripts, and messenger boys to the sergeants; the men who are clung to from below and shot at from above; the men who always take back the can: the lance-corporals.

This one, who had marched us to dinner, had sat at the top of the table and served out sixteen joints-and-two-veges before taking a mouthful himself, now said:

"You can get a cup of Rosie Lee at the Naafi, along there, on the right. The entrance is round the other side. But I want you all back outside the Q. stores by two o'clock, to draw biscuits and blankets."

We thanked him and set off for the Naafi, Johnny and I in front and the others trailing behind. When we turned the corner of the building we faltered in our stride.

"You can," the lance-corporal had said, "get a cup of Rosie Lee at the Naafi." I do not seek to dispute this statement, for tea and other refreshments were undoubtedly obtainable at the Naafi. The drawback was that one could not get anywhere near them; they were like the clear water and luscious fruits that always remained just beyond the reach of poor young Tantalus.

The queue that met our eyes when we rounded the corner must have been a couple of hundred strong; and after twenty minutes we were still almost as far from a cup of Rosie Lee as when we started. I shall always remember the Naafi at Cwmsamfach. Over its ever-distant door were the welcoming words, *Servitor Servientium.* From far away, day after day, we slowly shook our heads and sadly answered *Non Possumus.*

IV

By three minutes to two, Rosie Lee-less and unrefreshed, we were gathered outside the quartermaster's store. There, within half an hour, we were issued with blankets, straw-filled pillows and three biscuits apiece. These biscuits were not, as some of us had imagined, eatables, but square, flat cushions, which, placed in a row on our bunks, formed a prodigiously uncomfortable mattress. During the day-time they were piled neatly on top of each other at the head of the bunk, thus forming a basis for folded blankets and laid-out kit. After our first night, Johnny reminded us that the word "biscuit" meant "twice-baked," adding that his three had been left a bit too long in the oven.

Each man carrying his bedding as best he could, we were conducted by our lance-corporal from the Q. stores, all the way to the north-west corner of the camp, where "C" Coy.'s lines were situated. The hut into which he led us was furnished with a central wooden table and, with their heads to the wall, twenty double-tier bunks, some of which had already been allocated.

"You'll bed down in here tonight," the lance-corporal told us. "Tomorrow you'll be split up. There's three platoons in the Company and some of you will go to each. You may have to shift your bedding, so don't get too dug in."

"This time," Johnny murmured to me, "we probably *shall* get separated, or"—he shot me a sly glance—"have you fixed that, too?"

29

I did not answer, for I had noticed a movement among our fellow conscripts. They were staking their claims on the lower bunks by dumping their bedding on them. Not anxious to risk the perils of an upper berth, I darted for the nearest ground-floor accommodation. Johnny was not so lucky and had to be satisfied with the bunk above mine.

"Why should I have the top one?" he grumbled, throwing back his head to gaze up at his eyrie. "You're taller."

"And you're lighter," I retorted. "In the middle of the night, I might crash through on you."

"I'll toss you for it," he suggested, feeling for a coin.

"Oh, no, you won't!" I laughed. "The motto of the Bradfields is *Sauve qui peut*."

Ours was not the only dispute in progress. The single non-participant in the general rumpus was the man next to me, who had stacked his biscuits and blankets at the head of the bunk and, using them as a back-rest, had stretched his legs out comfortably on the curved plywood base of the bunk and was now placidly smoking his pipe. I put him somewhere in the late thirties or early forties; a solidly made fellow, with a heavy sandy moustache clipped clear of his mouth, gold-framed spectacles and observant, twinkling eyes.

The lance-corporal called us to order.

"Get moving!" he shouted good-humouredly. "You've still to draw uniforms and kit. Fall in in three ranks outside."

We did as he ordered and he marched us back to the quartermaster's store. When we later emerged from that vast and fully stocked military warehouse, each of us was loaded to the point of collapse with suits of battledress, greatcoat, gas-cape, steel helmet, respirator, kit-bag, large pack, small pack, webbing equipment, belt, shaving kit, toothbrush, P.T. shorts, vests, shirts, towels, boots, scaling-ladders and a Valentine tank. I am open to correction on the last two items, but by the time we got back to the hut I was convinced that I had something of the kind tucked away somewhere about me.

If, before, there had been disorder in the hut, there was now utter chaos. The place became a riotous tangle of clothing, footwear and accoutrements. The din we made was terrific, with anguished cries of:

"That's mine!"

"No, it isn't!"

"Where's my tin hat?"

"I'm an ear-plug short."

Those of us who had grabbed the lower bunks found them to be not unmixed blessings, for those scourges of all communal dwellings, "the people upstairs," claimed the right, by virtue of the inaccessibility of their own sleeping quarters, to sort out their kit on our bunks. Need I describe the confusion that ensued? The only beneficial result, as far as I myself was concerned, was that I came into possession of a greatcoat that fitted much better than my official issue. But we Bradfields have always been opportunists.

At last the tumult and the shouting died. There were no captains and kings to depart, but we, the rag, tag and bobtail, fell in in three ranks outside with our mugs and eating-irons and were marched off to tea.

CHAPTER FIVE

I

IT is a curious fact about Education For War that some of the most important of the things one learns do not figure in any of the training programmes. They are taught by the example of more practised soldiers, by cruel experience and by the sheer harsh necessity of self-preservation. Not all of them are honourable; and that those in authority are not unaware of this is implicit in the award of long-service pay, the granting of which is contingent on a minimum period of undetected crime—the operative word being *undetected*. All that the common soldier does, and all that he possesses, must resemble, in one paramount particular, Mr. George Robey's celebrated egg, which, as it may be remembered, *looked* all right. Just as long as everything looks all right—that the façade, as it were, is impeccable—then all is well with Tommy Atkins. I myself have seen, during a barrack-room kit-inspection, the same hairbrush figuring among the laid-out kit of three different men. The deft manner in which it was passed from one end of the hut to the other, under the very nose of the inspecting officer, was pretty to watch.

The first precept that we learnt at Borstal, Mark II—one that had nothing to do with keeping up appearances—was: hang on to your knife, your fork, your spoon and, above all, your mug. Watch them like a cat; sleep with them under your pillow; defend them, if necessary, by force of arms. Your note-case, your War Savings book, your cigarettes, your chocolate ration—they were all safe enough, for new soldiers seldom pilfer; your other kit could be replaced; but cutlery and mugs—especially mugs— were in short supply at Cwmsamfach. If you lost any of them— well, the remedy was not to be found in any A.C.I.

The first warning came from our lance-corporal, before we set off for the dining-hall.

"Treat them mugs careful," he said. "You won't get another, not for love or money, and you can't drink tea straight from the cookhouse bucket. And when you're on the march, don't wave 'em about or you'll be banging 'em against the next feller's and be left with just the 'andle. Carry the mug in the left 'and against the small of the back, with the knife, fork and spoon held in the right 'and, not—repeat not—in the field-dressing pocket. Them's for field-dressings, not eating-irons or fag-ends. Party!—Party, shun!—Move to the left in threes—left turn!—By the left, quick march!"

II

After tea we drew an issue of brown-paper and string. Our civvy clothes and other odds and ends had to be packed up for despatch to our homes. Johnny had an easier job than I, for he had no suit to send. His Home Guard battledress had not been changed by the quartermaster. Certainly, it was a scandalous fit, but so was the other with which he had been issued that afternoon. Being more of a stock size, I was luckier.

We took the parcels and paper-covered attaché-cases down to the Q. stores, parted with them with a pang, as being our last link with the old life, and went from there to the camp shop, where we bought metal polish and the authorized shade of blanco, known as Khaki Green No. 3.

When our greatcoat buttons and G.S. cap-badges (identical with those on the forearms of a regimental sergeant-major) were polished to our satisfaction—but not, as we discovered next morning, to the satisfaction of the Platoon Sergeant—Johnny and I spent an hour wandering round the camp and getting our bearings. We located "C" Coy. Office, the Ablutions (bathroom in Civvy Street), the gym, the Garrison Theatre, the rifle-range and the football field. We also tried to get (a) into the Naafi, and (b) out of the camp, but failed in both attempts. The R.P. at the gate took pleasure in telling us that all intakes—which meant us—were C.B. for the first week after arrival. By the end of that time, he said, we would have learnt to salute properly and could be reasonably expected not to disgrace the -th Primary Training Centre in the eyes of the worthy citizens of Cwmsamfach.

"Besides," were the R.P.'s last words, "you ain't on yer summer 'olidays."

So we wandered back to Hut 7—our sleeping quarters—feeling somewhat sorry for ourselves. Already, although it was still early, some of our room-mates were in bed. Johnny and I decided to follow their example. It had been a long, trying day, and the Daily Orders pinned on the board outside Coy. Office had warned us that we should have to be up betimes in the morning.

Getting ready for bed, with Johnny fluttering round me like a half-fledged eaglet that had fallen from its high nest and was anxious to get back, I fell into conversation with my spectacled, moustached neighbour, who was sitting up in bed in his white flannel night-shirt, puffing at his pipe.

I told him my name, and he, in his turn, gave his own as Wilkinson. I tried to introduce Johnny, but a couple of blankets were doing their best to turn Johnny into a Bedouin chief and he took no notice.

Wilkinson—Chris, as I was afterwards to call him, and Grandad, as he was to be christened by his platoon—always reminded me of the wise old owl—

> A wise old owl lived in an oak;
>   The more he heard, the less he spoke;
> The less he spoke, the more he heard:
>   Let's emulate that wise old bird.

It was not that Chris had little to say, for in his slow, monotonous, rather woolly voice, he could be quite verbose and argumentative at times—especially on the subject of the

Small Trader. But he should unquestionably have lived in an oak. In fact, he should have had a top bunk in Hut 7. With his pipe, his twinkling eyes, his kindly smile and his white flannel night-shirt, there would have been something splendid, something celestial, about him up there.

There are men who can weather every storm of life by keeping their feet warm and their heads cool. Such a one was Christopher Wilkinson. He never stampeded; was always, even in the worst emergency, calm, collected and undismayed. Had the earth suddenly opened up in front of him, Chris would have sat down with his legs dangling over the crevasse, got his pipe going and genially surveyed the devastation through his gold-rimmed spectacles. But let it be noted that he was not a man of action, not the fellow with nerves of steel who automatically takes charge in a crisis. He would not have been frightened by that crevasse, but neither would he have got himself and his friends to safety on the other side. To change the picture, were he ever to fall into enemy hands and be warned that he was to face a firing-squad in five minutes, he would have talked without a tremor in his voice, but his talk would have been, not of escape, but of chrysanthemums.

He was married, with a son aged two, had his own grocery business at Catford, S.E., and was—thus making me something like ten years out in my guess—twenty-nine years of age. His hobby was gardening.

The substance of our chat that evening is of no importance now. The only remark of his—made with an upward jerk of his pipe towards Johnny, who was, by then, in bed—that seems worth recording was:

"Our young friend up there will have to watch out or he'll be getting himself into hot water."

"So I've told him," I agreed. "Once you get a black mark in the Army it follows you round like your own shadow. A regimental entry is as difficult to live down as..."

I sought for the appropriate thing.

"Cheating at Rummy," supplied Johnny's drowsy voice from above.

CHAPTER SIX

I

THERE was sweet music in my ears.... Someone was early with their radio.... I seemed to know the tune.... Some military programme, by the sound of it.... No, it wasn't. It was a bugler outside Hut 7, and he was blowing Reveille.

I pulled my arm from under the blankets and looked at my watch. It was 5.45 a.m. on Friday, the 3rd July, 1942.

The bugle was saying:

"Get out of bed! Get out of bed!"

The double bunk swayed and creaked and Johnny complained fretfully:

"Tell that infernal fellow to take his trumpet somewhere else!"

He turned over and went to sleep again.

All around me blankets were being pushed aside as men reached for their cigarettes. Until I joined the Army I never realized how many men smoke in bed. In a moment or two, they were all happily coughing their hearts up. Chris Wilkinson was already producing clouds of choking smoke from his pipe; it was not unlikely that he had slept with it in his mouth, with a matchbox handy for the very moment of wakening.

On the previous evening I had popped my head into the Ablutions shed, which was adjacent to Hut 7. I had counted twenty wash-basins. Now, even though still half asleep, I did a spot of swift mental arithmetic, decided that a hundred would not go into twenty with any comfort—and reached hurriedly for my trousers.

It was a wise and statesmanlike move. I was one of the first to get into the Ablutions. By the time I had finished shaving, under the fourfold handicap of cold water, inadequate lighting, a plugless wash-basin and no mirror, there was a queue of six men waiting behind me, muttering what our grandparents used to describe as imprecations. As I pushed my way out I noticed that Johnny, tousle-headed and bad-tempered, was seventh in another queue.

Still, we all managed to get our toilets finished in time for breakfast-parade at 6.45. Not that that was anything to be proud of; it was a whole hour since Reveille. Every morning after that we had to fold our blankets, place our kit on the bunk in the exact pattern prescribed by Standing Orders (there was a guide plan pasted on the wall) and thoroughly clean out the hut before we went to breakfast. We should have had to do still more, I imagine, if the powers that be could have devised anything.

II

We were not to know it when the bugle aroused us, but it was to be an easy day for us—easy, yet painful. After breakfast we returned to Hut 7 and, under the direction of our lance-corporal, put it to rights. We learnt the only official way to fold blankets; how boots, with soles blackened with polish and with no more—and no less—than thirteen studs in each, should be placed on the bunk; how the greatcoat should be folded into a small compass by undoing the belt at the back, crossing the two ends over and buttoning them at the front: and a dozen other little pranks in the Bullsh category.

At eight o'clock we paraded in shirt-sleeve order and were marched, with the remainder of the intake from the other huts in "C" Coy.'s lines, to an open stretch of grass, where we were given an address by the Company Commander, a tall young first-lieutenant.

We sat in a half-circle round him on the grass.

He welcomed us, he said, to the British Army. However much we disliked the idea of compulsory soldiering, and however much we would have preferred to stay at home, we were now, he said again, in the British Army. We were all in the war together. The war had got to be won. So we must see to it that it was won as soon as possible. He, together with the other officers and the permanent staff of N.C.O. instructors of the -th P.T.C. were there for one purpose and one purpose alone: to turn us into good soldiers in six weeks. Hitherto, it had taken considerably longer than six weeks to turn men into good soldiers, but now it had to be compressed into forty-two days. And it was going to be done in that short period, even if—though he did not put it quite so harshly—it killed us.

He then turned—and I felt, somehow, that this was the real reason for assembling us—to another matter. We had been taken, he said, from almost every walk of life, from every social plane. Some of us had worked for a weekly wage, others had been their own masters; and *all* of us, having been born and bred in a democratic community, had certain clearly defined ideas about the liberty of the subject. But the country was at war. Those cherished principles of freedom of action and speech had to be put aside for the time being, so that they might not perish for ever. We were now in the British Army (yes, he said it again); and in the British Army complete freedom of action for the individual was impossible....

He said quite a lot more on the same lines, but what it all boiled down to was simply this: the -th Primary Training Centre was prepared, in its austere, yet fundamentally benign fashion, to play ball; but as soon as we, the new intake, showed the slightest disinclination to play ball also, the -th P.T.C. would immediately cease to play ball.

And that was that. We had been warned.

III

We were marched back—there were something like a hundred of us—to the parade-ground outside "C" Coy. Office, where the business of splitting us into three platoons was proceeded with. Each platoon would be in charge of a sergeant, with a corporal and a lance-corporal to assist him. I noticed, with some disquiet, that one of the three sergeants was Johnny's red-faced butcher's boy and sent up a little prayer that, even if I were to come beneath his direct authority, Johnny, at least, would go through his primary training under a more benevolent eye.

My prayer was not answered. The butcher's boy was in charge of No. 3 Platoon; and for No. 3 Platoon were both Johnny and I selected. Chris Wilkinson went to No. 2.

This splitting up necessitated rearrangement of the sleeping accommodation, and the next task that morning was to transfer bedding and kits, so that Nos. 1, 2 and 3 Platoons occupied Huts 5, 6 and 7 respectively. In this, Johnny and I were lucky, for I was able to stay where I was, and Johnny, as soon as Chris Wilkinson moved out of his bunk next to mine, moved in. I was sorry to lose Chris, for with his quiet humour and matter-of-fact point-of-view, he had the makings of a good companion. The platoon-corporal and lance-corporal—the little fellow who had looked after us, whose name, by the way, was Hutchins—were to sleep in with us, one at each end of the hut. The Sergeant had his own quarters elsewhere.

"What's the platoon-sergeant's name?" I asked Hutchins.

"Sar'nt Thomson," he answered.

Edie's brother.... I had felt it in my bones. Just to make doubly sure, I said:

"With a 'P'?"

"No," he shook his head, "without."

Edie's brother.... Blood relation to the girl we had met on the train. Ever such a good soldier. Always insisted on things being done in the way he wanted....And I had made a mental note to keep out of his way! I turned to Johnny with a wry grimace, but he seemed quite undismayed. He shrugged his shoulders indifferently.

"Isn't this one of those times," he suggested, "when some idiot always says, 'It's a small world'?"

Further discussion on the immutable workings of. Providence were prevented by the noisy arrival of the platoon-corporal, a tall, skinny, self-important fellow by the name of Baker—subsequently nicknamed "Sunshine"—who was to irritate me exceedingly before my primary training had progressed very far; and who now kicked open the door of the hut to shout in at us:

"All into P.T. kit and outside in two minutes!"

Not for the first time—or the last—hell broke loose in Hut 7. We dived, as one man, for our kit-bags, like as many dogs after carefully hidden bones, for our blue shorts, singlets, gym-shoes and, deep down somewhere, the laces.

"Come on!" yelled the corporal. "You ought to be there by now!"

It was a stock phrase. They always treat you like that at a P.T.C. The theory is that it turns you into a smart soldier. In practice, it reduces you to a nervous wreck—if you let it.

We of No. 3 Platoon were new to things and did our very best to lace our shoes, struggle out of our clothes and into our P.T. kit within the stipulated two minutes. We failed, of course, but only by the narrow margin of a quarter of an hour.

IV

Outside Hut 7 the lance-corporal took charge of us. The orders he now gave were strange to us and given in a tone we hardly recognized as his. Physical Training has its own technique.

"Atten-*shon*!—With a jump, right *turn*!—Running—*begin*!" Keeping pace with us, though in trousers and boots, he took us from "C" Coy. lines back again to the centre of the camp, where, alongside the Q. stores, was the gymnasium, outside which he brought us to a halt. Other platoons from different companies were already lined up, and more followed us. All were in P.T. kit.

But we had not been brought to the gym to do physical jerks. Platoon by platoon, and in single file, the new intake passed into the building. After fully an hour, by which time we were getting bored and, despite the time of the year, rather chilled, our turn came.

The gym was set with a row of small tables, behind each of which stood a senior M.O. with his henchmen around him. Before we had entered, L/Cpl. Hutchins had handed out to us our medical-history sheets; and now, having removed our singlets, we passed in single file from one table to the next. The M.Os. were specialists, each one concerning himself with only a portion of our anatomies: eyes, ears, heart, feet and— so on. The last of them, a lantern-jawed old gentleman with grey hair, ended the proceedings by jabbing a damnably blunt syringe into our arms.

We surrendered our medical-history sheets at a table by the entrance door, answered a few questions and came out again into the open. Hutchins was waiting to run us back to "C" Coy. lines.

When we reached our home base, he said, before giving the order to fall out:

"Now you've 'ad your first T.A.B., you're excused duty for forty-eight hours. If you take my tip, you'll get your beds down before them arms o' yours begin to stiffen up. All men who refused inoculation will parade here for cookhouse fatigues at ten-hundred hours." His glance travelled along the ranks before he added dryly: "I've got their names."

On being dismissed we crowded into the hut, changed out of our P.T. kit and made our beds. The three who had rejected the attentions of the old gentleman with the syringe stood about and watched us with envious eyes. Maybe they were wondering whether, perhaps, they had paid too much heed to the horrid warnings of the Anti-Vaccination Boys.

V

It was an hour later and, snug in my bunk, I was beginning to feel pleasantly drowsy. Johnny, who could drop off at any time, was sound asleep.

Suddenly the peace of Hut 7 shattered. Employing his usual method of opening the door—by kicking it—Sunshine lurched in.

"All outside!" he shouted. "Best battledress. No gaiters."

The men nearest the door remonstrated gently with him. We had been given our first dose of T.A.B., they told him, and were off duty for forty-eight hours.

"It can't be helped," he replied, mildly for him. "The regimental tailor wants to make a fit of your best battledress. Most of 'em look like sacks, 'specially round the neck."

They certainly did, but we were quite prepared to wait for a couple of days. Still, as Sunshine went on to point out, them was the orders, so we crawled out of bed and inserted ourselves into best battledress—very gingerly, for arms were beginning to get painful. I noticed that Johnny was not looking at all well.

Once again we were marched down to the Q. stores. No. 2 Platoon had arrived before us and were being critically inspected by an elderly man in mufti, who took his tailor's chalk from man to man, from rank to rank, leaving the white marks of his craft on collars, sleeves and trousers.

Before the tailor had finished with No. 2 Platoon, Sgt. Thomson came from somewhere behind and began pacing up and down in front of us, with his cane—all the instructors at Borstal, Mark II carried canes—underneath his arm.

Johnny and I were in the middle of the front rank. The Sergeant paused in his walk, came to a stop in front of Johnny and looked him up and down, as if examining something faintly funny.

"Well, Ginger," he said good-humouredly, "what's your name?"

I was relieved when Johnny remembered to come to attention before answering:

"Fieldhouse, Sergeant."

Then he spoilt everything by adding, before standing at ease again:

"And I like people to use it."

No. 3 Platoon held its breath, but oddly enough, Sgt. Thomson allowed the remark to pass. He smiled in quite a friendly way as he said, taking in the rest of us with a glance:

"My name's Thomson. I'm your platoon-sergeant and you'll find that, if you behave yourselves, we shan't get on too badly. Only don't try any funny stuff, that's all."

I was favourably comparing this terse warning with the O.C.'s lengthy discourse on the same subject, when a voice said, "Sergeant." It was Johnny again, the young fathead.

Thomson turned to him and said, "Yes, what is it?"

"We've a message for you, Sergeant—"

I muttered out of the side of my mouth:

"Pipe down, you damn fool!"

But Johnny went stubbornly on:

"Your mother's getting worried. You haven't written home for three weeks and she's anxious about you. We were to say it was Edie, who sends a big kiss."

A delighted titter went through the ranks. This, thought No. 3 Platoon, was worth being got out of bed for. A man in the rear rank guffawed loudly. Sgt. Thomson's red face went even redder. I tried to look somewhere else.

"Shut your trap, you little ——!" he shouted, finishing with a word that men have died swiftly for using.

Johnny took one pace forward, stood smartly to attention in front of Thomson and said, calmly and clearly:

"You're an insolent, uneducated, ill-mannered lout."

He held himself rigid for a moment, then flopped into a pathetic little heap on the sanded asphalt.

The first T.A.B. had reclaimed its victim.

CHAPTER SEVEN

I

I OFTEN wondered afterwards whether that chance meeting with Edie Thomson in the train from Paddington had a calamitous effect on Johnny Fieldhouse's military career. Had I not offered her a light for her cigarette we should never have known her relationship with the Sergeant of No. 3 Platoon, and Johnny would not have committed the howling indiscretion that I have just described. On the other hand, Johnny had fallen foul of Thomson as soon as he had stepped out of the train at Cwmsamfach, and would doubtless have found another early opportunity to ensure that his own life was made a burden. Yet if Johnny's army life had not begun so badly, things might have turned out differently. I often wondered. ...

There was nothing complex about Johnny's character. He was fanatically loyal to his friends, honest and straightforward— yes, there was the rub: he was too straightforward. Everything for Johnny was either black or white. There were no intervening shades of grey. And, though he often mistook one colour for the other, he was always ready to stand by his decision in the face of the most intimidating opposition. Resenting and resisting any kind of authority, he lacked the great gift of reticence, which may have made things awkward for John Fieldhouse, Esq., but which was disastrous for Pte. Fieldhouse, J.

"Why, why," I demanded, sitting on his bunk in Hut 7 later that day, "*why* do you have to say these things? Will you *never* learn when to hold your tongue?"

"He called me something that I'll let nobody call me," Johnny answered serenely. "Decent people don't call each other a ———"

"Yes, yes," I waved his arguments aside, "and that's why you probably won't be put on a charge for calling a senior N.C.O.

a—what was it? ...An insolent, uneducated, ill-mannered lout. But just because he doesn't take it any further, he's not likely to forgive or forget. You're in for a pretty thin time, from now on. But that wasn't the cause of the trouble. The major *gaffe* was when you babbled out about Edie sending him a big kiss."

"Well, she did, didn't she? Those were her exact words and she was very insistent that he should be reminded that it's high time he wrote to his mother. And it jolly well is, too! The old lady may be in delicate health and a letter from her son might—"

"Stop!" I implored him. "For pity's sake stop! Leave his mother right out of it. Forget her. Concentrate instead on this one stark fact: this morning, on the barrack-square of the –th P.T.C. you, a private with a single day's service, turned a sergeant of the British Army into a figure of fun."

"I didn't mean to," said Johnny.

"You didn't *mean* to!" I snapped at him. "You didn't *mean* to, but for all that, you managed to do it! The story's going to spread round this camp like a forest fire, Thomson will be the laughing-stock of the sergeants' mess—and for the next six weeks he's going to give you hell!"

II

And so he did. No official action was taken over the exchange of compliments on the square, but, as I had prophesied, Sgt. William Thomson neither forgave nor forgot. All those whose business it is to educate or instruct are pleased to have a stooge, usually some poor fellow with less brains than the average, who can, by astute management, be made to look a bigger fool than he is; who can always be asked the tricky question; who can always be the first to be hauled out in front of the class, to name all the different parts of, for instance, a Bren gun, a few minutes after the instructor has introduced the weapon for the first time: and who can then be so slanged and ridiculed that he either breaks down, to the gratification of the instructor, or answers back, to the delight of the class. In either case, the instructor wins.

Johnny had not less, but decidedly more brains than the average, yet he became Sgt. Thomson's stooge; and, with the heart of a lion in his frail little body, he never broke down, but answered back with his ready, biting tongue. Consequently, he spent most of his spare time on cookhouse or sanitary fatigues. Sunshine, the lanky corporal, played up to his chief, though with less finesse, and when poor Johnny wasn't putting up with the sarcastic taunting of the sergeant, he was suffering the loud-voiced bullying of the corporal. Little L/Cpl. Hutchins was friendly enough towards him, but he counted for very little.

I have just stated that Johnny never broke down. That is not strictly true. He broke down once at Cwmsamfach, but it was neither an N.C.O. nor any other human being that caused it.

The incident happened one afternoon, about a month after our arrival. The whole Company—that is, Nos. 1, 2 and 3 Platoons—was engaged on a field exercise. We had been taken by lorries some miles away from camp; and, after the instructors had given a demonstration of concealment and taking advantage of natural cover, while we rookies sat on the grass, watching, smoking and basking in the sun, it was our turn to show what we could do.

No. 1 Platoon were selected as the holders of a hill, half a mile away from the starting-point, that commanded a good view of the intervening fields. For the purposes of the exercise, their job was not to defend the hill, but to detect as many as possible of the attacking force, Nos. 2 and 3 Platoons, as they crawled along the edge of a field or darted across a gap in a hedge. It was useful experience in the arts of war and quite good fun—at first. The only ones not interested were half a dozen horses in one of the fields, who went on with their grazing as if there were no war on.

With No. 2 Platoon leading the way, we started off, one by one, at intervals. Johnny went before me. Chris Wilkinson, towards the rear of his own platoon, was not far ahead of us, and well behind us, last of the file, was Cpl. Sunshine Baker.

All went well until we reached a point where we had to get down in a ditch that ran along the edge of a field, crawl through a tunnel-like hole in the thick-set hedge and make our cautious way along the ditch on the other side, which was under direct observation of the watchers on the hilltop.

Bending low, so as not to be seen above the hedge, I followed Johnny along the side of the first field and paused at the proper distance away, to give him time to negotiate the tunnel. I saw him get down on his chest in the ditch and begin to wriggle through the hole. But in a second or two, just as I was about to move forward, he backed out again. On his knees in the ditch, he turned to look at me—and there was terror in his eyes.

Instinctively I moved towards him.

"What's the matter?" I murmured.

"I daren't go through, Peter! It's standing just on the other side!"

"What is?"

His lip trembled as he answered tensely:

"A horse."

I smiled. "Well, it won't bite you. Get a move on or we'll have Sunshine wanting to know the reason why."

"But I can't do it, Peter! It's standing right on the edge of the ditch—a great grey brute, tearing up the grass with its wicked yellow teeth!"

I stopped smiling. This seemed no laughing matter.

I looked over my shoulder. We were holding up the procession. Dutifully keeping their intervals, the men behind us had come to a stop. We could not parley there much longer. I made up my mind quickly.

"Move to one side," I said, "and let the rest of the fellows get past us."

He scrambled out of the way and I waved the others on. Johnny sat on the edge of the ditch, trembling violently. I stood by him until Sunshine arrived.

"What do you two think you're playing at?" he wanted to know. "Get on through that hedge. This is an exercise, not a —— choir-outing."

"Fieldhouse isn't feeling too good, Corporal," I told him. "I think he's got a touch of the sun, and with all this crawling about, he's—"

"Touch of the sun, my ——!" snorted Sunshine. "He's bone lazy. That's his trouble—and there's a good medicine for it! Fieldhouse, if you're not down on yer belly and through that hedge in five seconds, I'll—"

"But I *can't!*" Johnny almost whimpered.

"Oh, you can't, can't you? Another one of yer funny little jokes, eh?"

"Leave him alone, Corporal!" I said sharply. "You can see he's not well. Let me take him back to—"

Sunshine turned on me.

"You keep out of this or I'll peg you as well!" he threatened. "Come on, *you!*"

Beyond the hedge the horse whinnied. Johnny's scream frightened me. In a flash, he was out of the ditch and running back the way we had come—running like one demented, as if something swift and horrible was at his heels.

Then he tripped and fell.

Without a word, I left the corporal to continue the remainder of the exercise without us, and hurried to help Johnny. He was lying on the grass with his little red head buried in his arms—and he was crying like a child.

III

Late that evening, filthy dirty and utterly exhausted from scrubbing every square inch of the vast floor of the gym—

Sunshine's answer to the afternoon's affair—Johnny and I got rid of the buckets and brushes and wandered off in our denims to the nearest open space, where we flopped on our backs and lay breathing in the cool evening air. For ten minutes neither of us spoke. Then:

"Sorry about this afternoon, Peter. I didn't want to get you into trouble. I'm getting used to scrubbing out the gym, but you've had no practice at it."

"You'd better go sick in the morning," I suggested. "They may be able to give you some tablets or something."

He raised himself on his elbow.

"Tablets?" he demanded. "What do I want with tablets? There's nothing wrong with me."

"They've been pushing you too hard. You're working up for a nervous breakdown, Johnny. The business of the horse ..."

"Oh, that."

He sank back on the grass and it was some time before he spoke again.

"I've always been like that over horses. I must be— what's the word?—allergic to them. Ever since I was a kid, the mere sight of a horse has been enough to bring me out in a muck-sweat. Sounds like a toddler who's frightened of Moggy-on-the-Coals, or an old spinster looking under the bed for burglars. ... No power on earth, Peter, would have got me through the hedge today, with *that* waiting on the other side. ... Horses. ... I'm terrified of their great bloodshot eyes and those dreadful decayed teeth. Fancy being bitten by a horse. ..."

I sensed his shudder of revulsion; and fully understood how he felt. Authorities on heredity insist that it has nothing to do with pre-natal influences. Be that as it may, most of us have an unaccountable horror of something. With me, it was toads; with Johnny, it was horses.

"Le cheval est un animal bien aimable," I murmured rather sleepily.

Johnny yawned in concert.

"The French are curious people," he said. "They also eat frogs."

Which made me jump. Whether Johnny had guessed my secret or not, the random shaft had found its mark.

IV

Six weeks. ... Forty-two days of training to be a killer. ... Long days. ... Endless hours. ... Square-bashing, arms-drill, anti-gas, bayonet practice, P.T., map-reading, rifle, Bren, anti-tank gun, fieldcraft, second T.A.B., route-marches, films— "Next of Kin," "Name, Rank and Number," "Platoon in Attack." ... Forty-two days. ... And always by my side—in the lecture-huts, the barrack-square, the open fields and roads—little freckled Johnny Fieldhouse. Bullied, bruised, foot-blistered, jankered, rapier-tongued, indomitable Johnny, frightened of nothing in earth or hell—nothing but the old grey mare. And women.

But time and the hour, if I may adapt the tag, breathe through the roughest six weeks of primary training. At length the end of the feverishly pursued syllabus of full-tilt cramming was reached, and the moment arrived for them to take stock of us, to decide which of us should go into the infantry, which into the engineers, which into the artillery. We underwent our T.O.E.T., to ascertain how much, if anything, we had learnt. Then those expert gentlemen known in most sections of the British Army as the "trick-cyclists" had a go at us. They prevailed upon us to work out little problems in arithmetic, commonsense and mechanics; they lured us into reassembling the parts of a bicycle-pump and a door-lock; they persuaded us to dash about the gym, transferring metal rings from one wooden post to another. They had a great time with us, did those psychiatrists. They were very serious about it all and were quite confident that their tests would show whether a man was suited for foot-slogging or clerking, sanitary duties or field-marshalship. Whether the Higher Ups took any notice of their findings, or just carried on quietly choosing their sappers, gunners, craftsmen and potential field-marshals by the old square-peg method, is not for me to question.

In Hut 7, during those last few evenings, there were only two topics of conversation: Who was going into what? and, Would we get leave before we went there? The second question was dealt with out of hand by L/Cpl. Hutchins. His answer was, "No." Nobody, of course, believed him. The first question opened up a limitless field of speculation. Men told how, during the five minutes' interview with an officer psychiatrist that every one of us had been granted, he had intimated that they were destined for big things in Intelligence, or were the very chaps needed for the four-figure jobs at the War Office. The impression one gained from their reports was that not one single man was earmarked for the infantry. Every half-hour or so, one or another of us popped along to Coy. Office to see if the posting details were yet on the notice-board.

There was more to it than natural curiosity. One makes friends more easily at a P.T.C. than anywhere else in the world. That, at any rate, was my experience. And one is reluctant to lose them, to think that one may never see them again. Johnny, for instance. We Bradfields draw back wincing at the slightest suggestion of sticky sentimentality. We pride ourselves on being men of the world. But I admit now, without shame, that Johnny had become rather important to me. I had got used to having him around. We laughed at the same things, while everyone else stayed stony-faced. We disagreed so exhilaratingly on almost every subject under the sun. If I was going to be a field-marshal, I wanted Johnny to be one, too.

Though neither of us said much about it, Johnny, I knew, felt much the same; and the evening before the eagerly awaited news appeared on the notice-board, he summed the matter up, as we lay on our backs side by side under the stars, by murmuring, half to himself, those simple, lovely lines:

They told me, Heraclitus, they told me you were dead;
They brought me bitter news to hear and bitter tears to
  shed.
I wept as I remembered how often you and I
Had tired the sun with talking and sent him down the
  sky.

V

The next morning we knew. We were not to be separated just yet. Both of us were to go to a place called Burntash, to be trained as anti-aircraft gunners.

Further down the list, amongst the W's, I saw, "Pte. Wilkinson, C."

PART II

Subject—L.A.A.

CHAPTER EIGHT

I

WE did not get leave, not even forty-eight hours. By 07.00 hours on the forty-second day, all the companies that had comprised the intake of the 2nd July were lined up on the main barrack-square, not in companies or platoons, but in parties, some large, some small, according to the arms of the service to which they had been allocated.

We had packed the night before. At 07.15 hours our kit-bags were on their way to the station in lorries; and at 07.30 hours the first party—in a perfection of F.S.M.O. that is rarely to be seen outside a training centre—moved off.

And thus, without sorrow or regret, we said goodbye to Borstal, Mark II. The first ordeal was over.

II

Burntash Light Anti-Aircraft Training Camp was in the beautiful heart of Surrey. To come from the high-speed Bullsh of Cwmsamfach to the—to us—easy-going life of Burntash was like being rescued off a raft. There were things at Burntash that took a lot of getting used to. For instance, we could get into the Naafi. Reveille was at 06.45 hours instead of 05.45. We did not have to clean the studs on our boots with metal-polish. We did not have to march with arms in line with the shoulder. We did not have to raise our left feet six inches from the ground when we came to attention. We had to remember that we were no longer

Privates, but Gunners; that we were now in a Battery, not a Company, a Troop, not a Platoon, a Detachment, not a Section. And above all things, we had to bear in mind that junior N.C.Os. in the Royal Artillery are not corporals, but bombardiers—or, if you knew them intimately enough, "Bomb."

I have very happy memories of the weeks we spent at Burntash. Everyone was so decent to us, which, alas! did not stop Johnny from being in trouble most of the time; but Johnny was such a stalwart upholder of the liberty of the subject that he would have got into trouble in any organized community, however moderate the control.

The camp was set among pine trees: comfortable wooden huts, with not an abominable Nissen amongst them. Half a mile away was the sizeable village of Frog's Green, where there were a couple of first-rate hostelries.

Our training was thorough, but without the "sick hurry" of a P.T.C. Although both in "B" Battery, Johnny and I saw much less of each other than we had at Borstal, Mark II. He was put in 9 Troop and I in 10 Troop, so that while I was on the gun-park he was doing P.T., and later in the morning, when it was my turn for P.T., he was dodging the column in the bushes behind the Aircraft-Recognition hut.

Chris Wilkinson also came to 10 Troop. He and I had the opportunity to improve the acquaintance that had begun in Hut 7. We fell into the almost nightly habit of walking to Frog's Green, discussing the day's doings and the world's affairs over a pint of wallop, then strolling back to camp. On the first two or three jaunts, Johnny joined us, but after that he let us go by ourselves. His excuse was that he did not share our fondness for beer. The real reason was that he and Chris did not get on too well together. Johnny was too mercurial for Chris; Chris too stodgy for Johnny. The arrangement did none of us any harm. Johnny and I continued firm friends.

III

It is possible that the Cwmsamfach trick-cyclists had detected in me the inborn qualities needed for a No. 1 in a Light Ack-Ack detachment. In any case, that was what the Troop Commander decided I should be; and the predictor, that uncanny box of tricks that pivots on a three-legged stand some yards from the gun and does everything but fire it, became my particular care. Chris was made a No. 4, the fellow who stands on the platform and, unless his mind happens to be on something else at the time, brings his Army boot down on the foot-pedal when No. 1 orders, "Fire!" Johnny, with his own troop, was a No. 9. He looked after the generator, which supplied electric current for gun and predictor. The generator is always placed some distance from the gun, an arrangement that has its advantages for No. 9, for the generator makes as much din as a motor-cycle and, by pretending to be Robinson Crusoe, with no other human being within five hundred miles, he can fix his abstracted gaze on anything but the gun and completely fail to hear the detachment commander's, "Switch off!" however loudly it is yelled. As this command occurs frequently in gun-drill and as, every time, the D.C. has to send a man with a message to No. 9 in his noisy solitude, an astute No. 9 can make himself an infernal nuisance on the gun-park. Johnny had the time of his life.

We found there was more in Ack-Ack gunnery than met the eye. Had any of us previously thought about it at all, we had probably imagined that the two fellows in the seats turned their handles until the barrel of the gun was pointing at the target and then a third fellow fired off the round; and that if the D.C. was not quite satisfied with their aim, he would say, "Up a bit, Bert! A shade to the left, Harry!"

This, we discovered, was far from the case. With a swift-moving target like an aeroplane, travelling in three-dimensional space, there is a lot of quick thinking to be done, to ensure that both round and target arrive at a given point at the same moment. It was not the present position of the target that was the point of aim; it was the position in which it would be by the time the round got up there.

So apart from drill on the gun-park, we were given many lectures on ballistics, trajectory and the like. We learnt the meaning of vertical deflection, muzzle velocity, quadrant elevation and course angle; and how to deal with direct approachers, crossing divers and other enemy pranks. We were taught how to take the gun to pieces and how to put it together again; and we were initiated into the deep mysteries of its mechanism. In addition to all this, we received instruction in aircraft-recognition, in order that we should never shoot down a Hurricane in mistake for a Heinkel III, or allow ourselves to be dive-bombed by a Ju. 87B in the blissful belief that it was a friendly Wellington. We became acquainted with the significance of such terms as leading-edge, trailing-edge, dihedral wings, spinners, dorsal turrets, nacelle, chord, and in-line engines.

I am reminded here of a little incident that will serve to introduce another man who was later to play some part in the events that led up to the death of B.S.M.Yule.

A familiar sight in the sky at Burntash was a captured enemy plane, an M.E. 110, that used to fly round. It was always accompanied by a couple of our fighters, to prevent over-eager ground defences from taking a pop at it. In our aircraft-recognition class one afternoon, the bombardier-instructor asked a soldier how he would recognize an M.E. 110. The reply was:

"By its Spitfire escort, Bomb."

The reactions of the instructor to this suggestion need not be recorded here, but the anecdote gives some insight into the character of little Gianella. With a brain of considerable alertness, he never missed a chance to seem a fool. In civilian life he had been a hairdresser. At Burntash he supplemented his Army pay by haircutting. Most of us were only too pleased to pay him a tanner to escape the rough attentions of the camp barbers, whose lightning technique was to leave the top of the head and remove the hair from sides and back with two fierce horizontal sweeps of their electric clippers.

Gianella was a very small, dapper man of about thirty. His dark hair was always perfectly kept and he had a moustache that was no more than a pair of thin curving streaks, the delicate elegance of which he accentuated with black boot-polish before going out in the evenings. He looked after himself; was always very smartly turned out. Even his denim trousers had a crease in them. His brown walking-out shoes were a brilliant example of dark-tan splendour. By descent he was Italian, but his father, and *his* father before him, had been born in Islington. His only accent when he spoke, which was often, was exactly the same as any other Londoner of his class. As an anti-aircraft gunner, he was utterly useless. He saw to that.

He was quite frank about it, too. Chris and I fell in with him one evening at the White Hart in Frog's Green.

"I never asked 'em to put me on the —— guns," he confided from the other side of a pint tankard, "and I'm taking good care that they don't. You've got to use yer loaf, you know, in the —— Army. No use being too good at anythink. They take advantage of it. They gives you a stripe and then it's curtains for you. You spend yer time carrying back the can for a lot of good-fer-nothink so-and-so's what've showed a sight more sense than what you 'ave. Act dumb. That's my motter till the victory bells ring aht. If they smacks a trick-cyclist test-paper in front of you, answer all the questions wrong. And when they shows you a Whitley and says what's that, tell 'em it's a Sunderland flying-boat. They can't touch you. What odds is another tanner a day proficiency pay as long as the Missus is in work?"

He took a swig at his beer.

"Catch me on them guns," he went on with a knowing wink. "Nasty dangerous things, them guns is. Let yer 'and slip off the jack while you're doing 'Halt Action'—and there's a broken wrist for yer. Bloke I know got 'is 'ead cracked open by the barrel when No. 10 was traversing. 'Orrible mess 'e was—and then never 'ad the —— brains to work 'is ticket with it. And look at the stags you 'ave ter do! Standing aht there in the rain all hours, waiting fer damn-all to 'appen! Oh, no! Mrs. Gianella's little boy is after something cushier, where 'e can make a bob or two on the side. Unit barber'd suit me— or officer's batman. It's the blokes 'oo are backward in coming forward what get the soft jobs in the Army. The bright boy what's always catching Teacher's eye—all 'e gets in the end is a bellyful of machine-gun bullets. And you've got the Army where you want 'em, see? 'cause they can't peg you fer not knowing no think, can they?"

Before I had time to sort out the negatives, he was off again.

"Look at it another way. Cousin o' mine was in the 'Eavy Ack-Ack. Liverpool. Full bombardier, 'e was. Wife, two kids and another one in the box. Gets friendly with a girl in Liverpool, goes a bit too far with 'er—and then what does 'e turn rahnd and do? 'E marries 'er, the silly——!

'Im with a wife turns rahnd and marries some other bit in Liverpool! What would you call im?"

"A bigamist?"

With a wave of his tankard, he swept my suggestion aside.

"I could er told you that," he said. "I mean, wouldn't you say 'e was barmy? Didn't use 'is loaf, see? You'll never get yerself nowhere if yer don't box clever. Fairly asking for it, 'e was, if you ask me."

He brooded over his beer. There was a welcome silence.

"What happened to him?" Chris Wilkinson asked at length.

"What 'appened? What d'yer think? Somebody shopped 'im, of course. One of 'is pals. First thing 'e done was turn rahnd and permit bigamy, then, as if *that* wasn't enough on 'is plate, 'e went and told the 'ole story to one of 'is pals! Probably did it when 'e was under the inference of alcohol.

This pal—what a pal!—considers it 'is dooty to tell the troop-sergeant and the troop-sergeant whispers the 'orrid scandal into the ear'ole of the B.S.M., 'oo, being of the friendly type, 'as a word with the O.C. And that was that."

"What did he get?" Chris wanted to know.

"No more'n what 'e deserved fer not keeping 'is trap shut: nine months over the wall. Still in there, as far as I know, and swearing on the gospel as 'e'll get the lot of 'em when 'e comes aht—B.S.M. and all. Probably 'ave a go at it, too. 'E's that sort. Got no sense. But it only just goes to show, don't it? Act dumb, watch points and play safe—and you won't go far wrong; but try the clever-Dick stuff, talk aht er yer turn, let somebody chivvy you into doing the big thing—and you'll finish up in the glasshouse or in Westminster Abbey. Same again?"

"Not a bad idea," I answered; and when Chris agreed, Gianella marched up to the counter with the three empty tankards.

While the little man was waiting in the queue for the refills, I said to Chris:

"I don't admire the moral arguments of our small and talkative friend, *or* his attitude towards the national war effort, but I certainly agree with his contention that a man who commits bigamy is asking for trouble."

Chris was always ready for an argument on social problems. Now he replied in his slow, woolly voice:

"He may be asking for it, but it doesn't necessarily follow that it comes to him. Getting married in this country is the easiest thing imaginable—as far as the legal side of it goes—and what's easy to do once is easy to do again. They can't keep a check on the legality of all marriages, and if Jack Jones wants to repeat the performance with another leading lady it's really only bad luck if he ever gets found out. You'd probably be surprised at the number of couples who've been living in happy bigamy for years. It's only the unfortunate few who get caught, and nearly always because, as Gianella said, somebody shops them."

"For all that," I said, "bigamy's a sordid, shabby business."

Chris relighted his pipe, blew out the match and dropped it in the ashtray.

"Take this case—a hypothetical case, naturally. A man—young, ambitious, anxious to settle down and raise a family—marries the wrong woman. Let's say it was in Leeds. This woman has money of her own. She makes his life a misery by—well, anything you like; it doesn't alter the argument. He sees his ambitions going down the drain; and one evening he leaves a note on the dining-room table and slips out of the house for ever. He knows she won't starve. It's probably he who'll do the starving, because he's run away from his job as well as from her. He goes to—where shall we say? London's a big place. Let's assume that he goes to London. He finds another job. He meets another woman—the girl of his dreams. Love ripens between them and, as the weeks go by, he finds himself less and less able to tell her that he's married. He sees that she is getting impatient; that something must be done. Dare he suggest that marriage is old-fashioned and that they should dispense with a ceremony? No, he daren't. The girl lives with her parents, a dear old couple. He's well aware that if she knew the truth, she would rather give him up than cause them pain. So what does he do? He marries the girl quietly at a registry office. Stimulated by her sweet encouragement, he goes on to achieve all the ambitions that continued existence with his legal wife would have made impossible. He settles down. His second wife adores him and is gloriously happy. The old people are content with their daughter's choice. The years pass. They raise a family and they all live happily ever after."

"Or until someone shops him," I said.

His laughing eyes gleamed through his spectacles.

"Most unlikely," he replied; and added as Gianella came back with the beer, "Don't forget it's a fairy story!"

CHAPTER NINE

I

JUST before afternoon parade, at the beginning of our fourth week at Burntash, Johnny Fieldhouse drew me on one side and asked:

"Can you give Grandad Wilkinson a miss this evening and take a little stroll with me?"

"Of course," I agreed readily.

"I'll call in your hut for you at seven o'clock, then. Don't let me down, will you, Peter? It's important."

My heart sank.

"Have you been getting yourself into serious trouble again?" I demanded. "I thought you'd learnt—"

"No, really!" he protested. "It's nothing like that, Peter. I just want to ask your advice about something. Nothing to do with the Army."

"Good," I said with a sigh of relief. "Seven o'clock, then." He smiled his thanks and ran off to join his troop for the fall-in.

At the appointed hour, he appeared in the doorway of my hut. I gave a final rub to my cap-badge and was ready.

We took one of the footpaths leading down through the trees to the Frog's Green road. That was one of the many things we had found difficult to get used to at Burntash: the ease with which we could get in and out of it. At Borstal, Mark II there had been one single gateway. The junior N.C.Os. on the permanent staff had boasted that there was another less official way in after Lights Out, but we had never discovered it. Somebody in Hut 7 had suggested that it took the form of a subterranean tunnel, coming up at one end in the corporals' mess and at the other in the cellar of the Roebuck Inn in Cwmsamfach. At Burntash the freedom was almost embarrassing. All roads and footpaths led eventually out of camp, with no fences, walls or wire to bar the way. There was a main gate, but no soldier off duty ever used it. The only place that was taboo after dusk was the gun-park, with its dozen practice guns tucked away for the night under their waterproof covers. The park was guarded by armed sentries from the ranks of the trainees and, as most of them were keen to hear what sort of a bang their rifles could make, their belated friends crept in some other way.

Johnny and I came out on to the road and turned towards Frog's Green. It was a marvellous evening. He did not immediately broach the important. matter to which he had referred earlier in the day. In any case, he was too busy keeping up with my longer legs to do much talking.

We passed on our left the solitary house that had been requisitioned as an Attery for the girls who did office work and cooking for the camp, and reached the bridge where the river Trim ran under the road.

"Shall we get down and go along the bank?" Johnny suggested.

"And be gnawed to death by gnats?" I answered.

"I'll get my pipe going. That'll keep them away."

I was inclined to agree with him. His pipe was new and much too inexpensive; and I had yet to discover the nature of the substance that he was using in lieu of tobacco.

We scrambled down the embankment and took to the towpath. Beside the slow-flowing Trim, which ran in the same general direction as the road and passed under it again through another bridge before they both reached Frog's Green, Johnny showed signs of tarrying. He finally lagged so much behind that I asked, somewhat sarcastically, if he wanted a rest. He shook his head and quickened his pace, but after fifty yards lapsed again into a crawl. I sensed his difficulty: he wanted to say something, yet lacked the courage to begin. With the river-at-eventide setting, I felt like a damsel about to be popped the question. So I stopped in my stride, slumped down on the sloping grass bank alongside the towpath, pulled out my cigarettes, lighted one and said briskly:

"Now, Johnny, out with it."

He sat down beside me, hesitated, then began in a rush:

"I want your advice, Peter. It's a sort of personal matter, really. ..." That was as far as he got in the first spurt. After a moment or two, he went on again: "Do you remember that first train journey together and what we talked about?"

"Yes," I agreed, "I remember."

"And you haven't forgotten the poem by Keats?"

It was manifest which way the conversation was being, somewhat clumsily, directed.

"What's her name?" I asked Johnny.

I glanced sideways at him. He had blushed a fine healthy red, yet he answered me coolly enough:

"Guessed it, have you? But don't rush me. I want to tell you in my own way. I was furious that morning on the train—not with you, but with myself; furious I'd never had the guts to do what you did; furious that I was so skinny and insignificant that any average girl would throw me to the cat. You were different. You had a manner. You wore your hat at a rake-helly angle. You were tall and broad-shouldered. You had good looks—of sorts."

"Thanks very much," I murmured gratefully.

"A galloping inferiority complex—that's what I was suffering from. No, it wasn't a complex; there was nothing involved about it. It was just a plain, straightforward feeling of—of worthlessness; of failure where women were concerned. When I used to go to parties, I never danced like the other fellows. I was the stooge who covered up his nervousness by winding up the gramophone and turning the records over. And years before that, Peter, at kids' birthday rallies, the postman knocked for every boy but me. Don't laugh, you hulking brute! ... You'd have thought I should have grown out of it, but I haven't. Put me anywhere near a woman—or a horse—and I panic. And now the whole thing's reached a crisis, because I've fallen in love with one."

"What, a horse?" I asked, but he did not smile.

"No, a woman—a girl, rather. She can't be more than nineteen or twenty. She's wonderful. Not too tall, dark, lovely brown eyes, a smile like a ray of—"

"Spare me the catalogue," I begged him. "What's her name? Where does she come from? Do I know her?"

"I haven't found out her name," he admitted. "She's an At in the Regimental Admin, office and even in that grotesque uniform—"

"Yes, yes," I threw in hastily, "and what would you like me to do about it: draft you out a dignified proposal of marriage?"

"I want you to tell me how I can get to know her. I've been hanging around the Admin Office a good deal lately. They don't finish work there till some time after we do. Although she's come out several times, I haven't had the gall to speak to her. I'm almost certain that she practically half-smiled at me on Monday."

"A good start," I approved. "What did she do on Tuesday?"

"She dashed out of the hut and ran like mad."

"That's bad," I sympathized. "Had you frightened her?"

"She didn't see me. I think she wanted to catch the post. But Peter, I can't go on haunting the Admin Office, can I? I'll be pegged for it if I make myself too noticeable."

"'In that he did ...'" I quoted sadly from Army Form O. 252. "Well, it seems quite easy to me, Johnny. At some moment during the early evening, she leaves Regimental Admin Office, walks out of the camp and proceeds to the Attery, which, as you may know, is about two hundred yards from the main camp-entrance, along towards Frog's Green. We passed it just now. All you have to do, Johnny, is to take up a position somewhere along that stretch and, when she comes tripping along, open a conversation with her—that's provided, of course, that she's alone. Her immediate reactions will tell you your fate. It'll be one of two things: either *Vous avez cliche* or *Vous n'avez pas cliche.* It's all the luck of the game."

Johnny savagely chewed a blade of grass.

"That's all very well," he said, "but how do I start this precious conversation of yours?"

"It should," I observed judicially, "present little difficulty. The main thing to remember is that the average girl does not much care for clever, sparkling dialogue. So your remarks must be simple. Should you be fortunate enough to discover, later in your acquaintanceship, that the young person is of more than customary intelligence, then a well-chosen epigram or two—preferably original—will not come amiss."

"Stop gagging," said Johnny. "I want advice, not a correspondence course."

"A case in point!" I instantly took him up. "'I want advice, not a correspondence course.' Far too sophisticated, my friend! To cite a smashing little blonde that I fell in with at Cwmsamfach, too *sarky*."

"A blonde?" Johnny said, creasing his brows. "I don't remember her."

"You were scrubbing out the gym at the time," I informed him sweetly. "So, as I said, be simple. Make your opening remark something like this: 'Hullo, Peggy!' Then she says, 'How did you know my name was Peggy?' You answer, 'A little bird—'"

"But her name may not be Peggy."

"All the better. Then she can reply, 'My name's not Peggy'; and you can flash back at her, 'Well, what is it?' She ripostes, 'Why do you want to know?'—and with the conversation so well and pleasantly advanced, you should have no further trouble."

He sighed despondently.

"It sounds so feeble."

"You try it."

He pondered for a while, then suddenly jumped to his feet.

"Dammit, I will!" he announced in a voice that sent a trio of ducks skimming across the Trim.

II

"The Junkers 87B, which was the original Stuka," I wrote, "is a dive-bomber. It has a single in-line engine, with a large radiator beneath it."

It was the following evening. I was in the camp writing-room, making a fair copy of the day's note-taking. I dipped my pen in the ink and resumed:

"The widespread under-carriage is not retractable and there are spats over the wheels. The tail-plane is wide and rectangular. The single fin and rudder—"

I stopped writing, for a familiar voice was speaking behind me.

"Don't forget the pointed nose," said Johnny.

I swung round in my chair.

"You shouldn't read over people's shoulders," I reproved him. "Still, you're perfectly right. I didn't know you knew anything about aircraft-recce. When did you learn it?"

"Between meals, old friend," he chuckled, "between meals."

He was looking so disgustingly pleased with himself that I guessed his love-making must have prospered.

"I don't want to hear about it," I told him flatly. "Go away to gloat somewhere else and leave me to get on with this."

He looked round at the other occupants of the writing-room and bent down to mutter hoarsely in my ear:

"I've got to tell somebody or I shall burst—and you're the only one there is I can tell."

There was something very touching about Johnny sometimes. I controlled the ridiculous lump that rose in my throat and gave a sigh of exaggerated resignation.

"We shall get the raspberry if we talk much more in here," I said, collecting my notes together. "You can give me the whole story in the Naafi—but not until you've bought me a cup of tea."

The tale did not take long to tell. Following my advice, Johnny had waylaid his charmer that evening between the camp and the Attery. She had been alone, and Johnny's opening speech—which I am sure he had previously repeated to himself over and over again; and am equally sure bore no resemblance to the one I had suggested—was wasted, for as she had drawn near to him, the girl had smiled and had wished him a good-evening. Johnny had been so taken by surprise by this frontal attack that his mind had been jerked forward to a point three-quarters of the way through their first chat, as he had planned it; and, without even responding to her greeting, he had blurted:

"Will you come for a walk with me tomorrow evening?"

The young lady seemed to know her own mind, for without hesitation she had said:

"I'd love to! I'll meet you by the bridge over the river at eight o'clock."

With which she had smiled once more and had continued on her way towards the Attery.

"Did you find out her name?" was my only question.

He shook his head. "I didn't remember to ask."

"Which says something," I told him, "for the 'Hullo, Peggy!' line of approach."

III

The third act in the little comedy, of which I was afterwards to be so poignantly reminded, was very short.

The following evening, Chris Wilkinson and I were taking our accustomed noggin in the White Hart, when Johnny pushed his way into the bar. He bought himself a half-pint shandy and came over with it, to sit at our table. I looked at him enquiringly.

"She didn't turn up," he grunted.

I glanced at the watch on my wrist. It was ten-past eight. I finished my beer.

"Chris," I said, "be a good chap and get a couple more stoups of ale."

He was an understanding fellow. He drained his own mug and went up to the counter, although it was my turn to pay.

"You didn't give the girl a chance," I muttered indignantly to Johnny. "It's a good eight minutes' walk from here to that bridge. Get back there at the double!"

My savage tone must have scared him, for he left his shandy untouched and was out of the bar before Chris came back with two fresh pints.

IV

I went round to see Johnny before turning in for the night. He was alone in the hut and already in bed.

"Well?" I queried.

"She wasn't there," he answered. "You know, Peter, I think there was some confusion. There's another bridge over the—"

"Yes," I interrupted, looking down at him, "and it's known as Pons Asinorum. Johnny, there's something *far* worse than a coward. It's a liar."

Without a word, he squirmed under his blankets and turned away from me, with his face to the wall.

The next morning he threatened a sergeant with post-war vengeance and was awarded seven days' C.B. and jankers.

CHAPTER TEN

I

SEPTEMBER, 1942, was a little over a week old and our stay at Burntash was coming to an end. Johnny and I had settled our difference. Neither of us had made further reference to the girl in Admin Office, so I supposed that, having failed to honour their first appointment, he had kept well away from her.

After morning parade, we of 9 and 10 Troops were marched round to one of the lecture-huts, where we were given a short talk by the officer commanding the two troops. He had news for us. Within forty-eight hours, some of us were to be transferred to another training-camp in the north of England; the rest would stay behind. He read out the names on the two lists. Johnny and Chris Wilkinson were scheduled to go north; I to remain at Burntash.

The troop-officer gave no reasons for these moves, but after he had left the hut the bombardier of 10 Troop threw out a few hints, from which we gathered that those who went north were destined for A.D.G.B., and the remainder for service overseas.

It looked like the parting of the ways for Johnny, Chris and me. The following afternoon, the A.D.G.B. list went up on the Battery notice-board. My two friends were to parade in F.S.M.O. at 07.00 hours the next day.

The three of us arranged to have a farewell drink together in the White Hart that evening. Chris and I arrived first; and found very little to say to each other. It had been much the same with Johnny and me at Cwmsamfach, before we had known that we were both to go to Burntash. Yet now there was a difference. At Cwmsamfach we had not been told; this time there was no doubt about the impending separation.

Chris and I exchanged addresses, promised to keep in touch with each other, went over some of the experiences we had

shared in North Wales and Surrey, drank a good deal of beer—
and waited for Johnny.

He was a long time coming. It was well after nine o'clock
before he put in an appearance. He was beaming with joy—a
much happier young gunner than when last he had joined us
in the White Hart. He bought us a pint of beer each before we
could show him our recently filled tankards.

"You're looking very pleased with yourself, Johnny," I
smiled, as he sat down at the table.

"So I jolly well ought to be!" he answered, and merrily sank
his half-pint shandy in one reckless go.

When he came up for air, he rattled on:

"I've made it up with her. I caught her outside the Attery
this evening, threw myself at her feet and begged forgiveness.
I got it, Peter, my boy, I got it! Full pardon. She's promised to
write to me. She lives in London and we're going to see each
other again after the war. Isn't that marvellous? And just to
think I've wasted days—"

A question from me stopped the flood of words.

"Did you take the precaution of asking her name?"

"Yes, it's Hazel. A lovely name for a girl. Hazel has always
been one of my favourite—"

"Any sort of surname?"

"Surname? Oh, yes. Hazel—I've forgotten it for the
moment. I wrote it down somewhere, if I haven't lost it."

He went through his pockets with mounting anxiety,
eventually finding the name scribbled on the next-of-kin page
of his A.B. 64.

"Here it is!" he said. "Hazel Marjoram."

"Sounds like a made-up moniker," grunted Chris, the doubter.

"Couldn't be," was Johnny's confident assertion. "A girl
like her couldn't possibly have any other name than Hazel
Marjoram. You might just as well say that an empty glass
shouldn't be called an empty glass."

The hint was of the broadest. I took it.

II

Next morning they left for the north—and Gianella went with them. I assisted them to finish off their packing. I rolled their gas-capes. I helped them on with their packs and equipment. I stood waiting with them for the fall-in. I shook them both by the hand with awkward, meaningless words. I watched them fall in on the marker. I listened as they answered to their names. I saw them fall out and pile into the waiting transport. I waved to them as their lorry jerked into motion; and went slowly back to my hut.

There was an envelope lying on my bunk. It was addressed to me. Inside it was Johnny's slim little leather-bound copy of the *Rubaiyat*. On the flyleaf, "John Fieldhouse, 1938" had been crossed out and below it had been written, "To Peter from Johnny, September, 1942. I have parted on the same day with my most cherished possession and a very dear friend."

With my mind elsewhere, I glanced through the book, until my attention was taken by a verse that had been bracketed in pencil:

> There was a Door to which I found no Key:
> There was a Veil past which I could not see:
> Some little Talk awhile of Me and Thee
> There seem'd—and then no more of Thee and Me.

The lines haunted me for the rest of the day. I wanted to know why Johnny had marked them—and when.

III

After the departure of the A.D.G.B. contingent we learnt that their destination was Boxford, a town in the Peak District, where their training was to be completed and they were to be formed into operational units for the air defence of this country.

We, the remnants of "B" Battery, were received into the depleted ranks of "C" Battery. I looked round for other friends with whom to while away my hours of leisure, but found no kindred spirits in my new troop. This threw me on my own resources more than I liked, because, as I have mentioned before, we Bradfields are of the chummy type. Maybe that accounted for what followed.

Johnny and Chris had been gone some days. The long hours on the gun-park, the assault course, in the gym and in the lecture-huts had dragged to an end. I had had my tea, changed out of my denims into my second-best battledress; and it was half-past seven.

With time on my hands, I went down one of the numerous footpaths between the trees, turned to the right and strolled along the road towards Frog's Green, with a view to sinking a solitary pint at the White Hart. The road took me past the camp's main gateway, just outside which was a public telephone-box, used chiefly by Army personnel. As I drew level with the box, the door of it was pushed open and held there by a small, smartly shod foot. A feminine hand with palm uppermost was stuck out and a bright, pleasant, but won't-take-no-for-an-answer little voice commanded:

"Lend me two pennies for a minute."

Luckily I had them. I produced them from my pocket and laid them on the outstretched, impatient palm, which instantly withdrew into the box, like a frog's tongue with a toothsome fly on the end of it. The foot and leg disappeared as well, which was a pity. I heard the coins pressed into the machine and Button "A" also pressed, and found myself faced with a ticklish problem. I wanted to hover round till she came out, yet did not wish it to appear that I was waiting for my twopence. A copper or two meant nothing to me—except on a Wednesday. This being Thursday, I would cheerfully have fed pennies into dainty hands, just for the devilment of it, without any thought of subsequent reimbursement. The first step, obviously, was to retire out of earshot. The box being, as I have said, used mainly by the Services, most of the glass panels were either missing or no longer intact. In such circumstances, one does not care to linger too near; not only is it discourteous, but it is also in one's own interest: other people's telephone conversations always seem such a waste of money. So I strolled on in the direction of Frog's Green, trying to walk just slowly enough not to be too far away when she hung up the receiver, and just fast enough not to be hanging round for my twopence.

Her chat, for a woman, was short. I had not gone fifty yards before I heard the slam of the call-box door and the detaining cry that she sent after me. I stopped in my stride, turned and walked back more quickly than I had come.

She was dressed as if for a dance. My natural leaning is towards blondes, but this bare-headed brunette sent me toppling over in the other direction. I will not go into details—I would as soon seek to describe a sunset or a liqueur brandy—but she was breathtaking. How such a vision from Civvy Street came to be wandering round borrowing two-pences and making telephone-calls in an essentially military locality, I neither knew nor cared.

"I was afraid you'd gone," she smiled as I drew near.

The darned twopence business cropped up again. I could hardly grin back, "You bet I hadn't!" So I just said:

"But not very far."

She unclipped her little handbag and pulled out a shilling.

"Have you change?" she asked.

"Those were my last coppers," I lied without remorse.

"Oh, dear!" she said. "Then what can we do?"

Well, there seems no need for me to repeat it all. It was only twopence, anyway—*and* Thursday. The upshot was that we spent the evening together. She had, she explained, arranged to go to a dance with a girl friend, but the friend had cried off at the last minute. She had rushed to the nearest phone to catch another girl friend, but she had already gone out. So there she was, as she told me with a pretty gesture of despair, all ready to go to a dance, yet with nobody to accompany her.

Need I record that not for the first time in the major emergencies of our country's splendid history, a Bradfield stepped in? What did I care if the sex of her otherwise occupied acquaintances had been tactfully changed for my benefit? Let the silly fellows get on with their fretwork or their post-war planning, I said. Let them regret it and phone her in the morning. Let them do what they liked tomorrow, so long as I took this glorious little creature out tonight!

The dance was in the Church Hall at Frog's Green. We had every dance together, except when some unprincipled scoundrel snatched her away from me in an "Excuse Me" foxtrot.

The last waltz merged into the strains of the National Anthem. She collected her wrap from the cloakroom and we went out of the oppressive, smoke-clouded atmosphere of the hall into the clean, healthy night.

At the first stile we came to, after Frog's Green had been left behind, we paused—it almost seemed with one accord. Two minutes later—or it may have been a trifle longer—I murmured:

"Why haven't we met before?"

"We ought to have done," she answered; "we're close neighbours."

"Are we? Where do you live?"

"In the Attery."

"But I thought you were a civvy!"

"Oh, no!" she laughed. "I got permission to wear a frock for the dance this evening. They let us, you know—it keeps up morale."

"Well, well," I said. "And now we're such old friends, won't you tell me your name?"

She answered, "Hazel."

IV

It was embarrassing, to say the least. My better self was up in arms at once.

"This must be stopped immediately," it announced sternly. "This girl is undoubtedly the beloved of Johnny Fieldhouse, one of your best friends. It would be deepest treachery to trifle further with her affections."

Then that robust ruffian, my baser self, took a hand.

"Don't talk nonsense, you pompous old fool!" it jeered. "He only took her out once. He's probably forgotten all about her by this time."

My better self was working on the rough draft of a devastating reply, when Hazel said:

"Don't you like it?"

"I think it's great!" I said with enthusiasm. "It suits you perfectly. I shouldn't dream of allowing you to be called anything else."

"There you go!" said my better self. "First you pinch his girl, then you borrow his patter!"

I sickened of the fellow and decided to follow the advice of my baser self. His suggestions were always so much more practical.

V

There followed five delirious evenings. Tuesday was the last of them, though we did not know, when we said good-night, that the ecstatic interlude was over.

That evening, for the first time, I made an indirect reference to Johnny.

"Yes," she laughed, "such a quaint little boy! He was fidgeting about near the Attery when I came back from the office to tea. He looked at me in such a funny, shy way that I said good-evening to him. Then, without sort of leading up to it, as most people would, he simply *hurled* an invitation at me to go for a walk with him the next evening. He looked so eager and lonely that I said I would. But though I kept the appointment, he didn't turn up."

"The dirty dog!" I exclaimed indignantly. "But go on...."

"The poor boy probably lost his nerve," she laughed indulgently. "I didn't wait more than ten minutes for him; and I didn't see him again until the evening before he was posted away. Then I found him waiting for me. He spoke very quickly, was very red and uncomfortable and apologetic. I told him that it didn't matter and—but why do you want to know all this?"

"I like to hear all about my rivals," I told her lightly.

"He said his name was John Fieldhouse and wanted to know mine. Then he fumbled in his pocket and brought out a postcard with his name and home address on it. It was written in beautifully neat copperplate and you could see where he hadn't quite rubbed out the pencil lines he'd ruled, to get all the letters the same size. He sort of—pushed it at me and asked me to write to him."

"Are you going to?"

Her answering laugh was gay and derisive.

"Of course not! He was only a nervous little scrap of a soldier. All he wanted was mothering. I only promised just to please him—and it did, too! He went off as happy as anything."

"When?"

"What do you mean, when?"

"You didn't... You didn't go places together?"

"Good heavens, no! He was far too shy for that! As soon as I'd said I'd write to him, he tried to raise the civvy hat he wasn't wearing, then turned and almost ran away."

Yet Johnny had been two hours late at the White Hart.

I was a long while getting to sleep that night. The painstaking tenderness of those rubbed-out lines made me feel that I had behaved extremely badly.

The next morning, at an hour's notice, they shot me off to Boxford.

PART III

Subject—B.S.M.

CHAPTER ELEVEN

I

THERE were only two of us to go to Boxford. Why those who decide such matters had changed their minds about us so suddenly was one of those many questions that will not find an answer until after the war, if then.

My travelling companion was tall, thin and brittle-seeming—so brittle-seeming that one wondered why he had not snapped long since. He was a good three inches taller than my own six feet, and I put his age at the middle twenties. The grim secret was not disclosed during our journey north, but he bore the almost incredible name of Postbechild. Although I was to learn his initials in due course, I never knew his Christian names; they were doubtless equally peculiar. In fact, everything about Postbechild was peculiar. He might have come straight out of *Alice in Wonderland*. The character that he most nearly approached was the White Knight, who, it will be recalled, said to Alice, "You're my prisoner," and fell off his horse.

Postbechild was habitually as pale as a ghost. His tow-coloured hair was always untidy. He walked with a shuffling stoop and never—even on the hottest summer's day—looked comfortably warm. I began to have some idea of his eccentric temperament quite early in our acquaintance, for soon after the train started he produced from somewhere about him a paper bag, from which four large cigars protruded. He held it towards me.

"Have a burn?" he asked mournfully.

I refused hastily, saying I much preferred a cigarette; and with a shrug of his narrow shoulders he prepared a cigar for himself with great care.

"Set me back four shillings apiece," he confided as he took off the band.

That, I was to find, was one of the many oddnesses of Gnr. Postbechild. Every week he would take his pay to the nearest shopping centre and spend the whole lot on something expensive, fantastic or useless. That week, it was cigars; the next week, it might be a hot-water bottle or a geranium in a pot. One never knew with Postbechild.

Having—to my horror—lighted the costly weed with a foul petrol-lighter that burnt and smelt like a rag soaked in paraffin, he went on in his sad, dispirited voice:

"I'm T.B., you know. They've put me down as A I in my pay-book, and the medical specialists said there's nothing wrong with me except I'm a bit bronchial. But they only do that to stop me from worrying about my——self." He took the cigar from his mouth in order to give a hollow laugh. "Cor starve a crow! They can't——kid me! Oh, no! They can't kid me any more over that than they can over my gastric ulcer. I wasn't born yesterday." He lowered at me with dull eyes. "Would you say I was A—— I, to look at me?"

"Well, you seem fit enough and if the medical specialist said—"

"Ho! You're the same as the rest of 'em, are you? 'There's nothing wrong with you,' they say. 'All you want is good food and plenty of exercise,' they say. 'Get out in the fresh air,' they say. Best thing I can do is——die on 'em."

"Not a bad plan," I agreed, "if you can get away with it."

In this fashion was I entertained all the way to Boxford. By the time we got there, I was beginning to speculate whether the medical board had kept something back from *me*.

II

There is a tale they tell in Boxford. Maybe it is a fable. It is about a man, called Finklestein by some of the narrators, Guggenheimer by others and just plain Cohen by still more. The story also concerns the Grand Wells, an hotel standing on the hill that crowns a town that is full of hotels, for Boxford is by way of being a spa—not so famous, perhaps, as Leamington, Bath, Buxton or Tunbridge Wells, but nevertheless a place of some importance to those whose Mecca is a medicinal spring.

Before the last war, while Boxford was flourishing and all the other hotels were doing big business, the Grand Wells fell on evil days. Visitors who came at regular intervals to take the waters and who, for twenty years, had stayed nowhere but at the Grand Wells, began to go elsewhere—to the Grosvenor, the Regent or even the Windermere. Nobody, it seemed, ever discovered the reason for this mass desertion, which did not happen suddenly, but extended over a considerable period of time, until finally, the proprietors found themselves faced with bankruptcy.

They tried, discreetly at first, to rid themselves of their 300-bedroomed white elephant—if such an untidy figure of speech is allowable—but a purchaser by private treaty was not to be found; there was a hoodoo on the Grand Wells and shrewd investors were unready even to look at it. Rapidly the owners lost their first caution and soon the daily and weekly press carried lavishly adjectived advertisements of this peerless hotel in its commanding, unrivalled position. A score of estate agents had it on their books; and their boards were stuck all round the property like flags on a war map. And still there were no takers.

Then, in the autumn of 1914, Mr. Finklestein (or Guggenheimer, or just plain Cohen) arrived on the scene and proved to be, for the distracted owners of the Grand Wells, a *deus ex machina*. For he was ready to talk turkey.

He bought the Grand Wells. Certainly he paid only a fraction of its real worth, yet, for all that, it was a considerable sum. The shrewd investors nudged each other with knowing winks and murmured something about one being born every minute. The gouty and the rheumatic continued to go to the Grosvenor, the Regent and even the Windermere. Nineteen disgruntled estate agents snatched their boards away, while the twentieth, whose name was Greenbaum—or it may have been Schultzberg—pasted across his, with his own fat hands, "SOLD BY." House-decorators, architects, plumbers and quantity surveyors from near and far, foreseeing extensive interior and exterior work and rich pickings for themselves wrote letters, telephoned, sent representatives or called personally. But Mr. Finklestein (or Guggenheimer, or just plain Cohen) had other plans.

He got rid of all the guests—a mere handful of fifty or so—by the simple expedient of telling them to get out and stop out. He dismissed the whole staff. He closed down the hotel. He put in a caretaker at fifteen shillings a week. And he waited.

He waited for six months. He had been prepared to wait a year. Then, one morning, in the spring of 1915, a letter was delivered to his palatial London home. The envelope was buff coloured and it was marked "O.H.M.S." When he had opened it and read its contents, Mr. Finklestein (or Guggenheimer, or just plain Cohen) smiled happily, to show the teeth that his enemies—whose name was Legion—cruelly compared with the Klondyke's richest seam. The Grand Wells had been requisitioned.

For nearly four years the Army authorities paid an enormous rental for the Grand Wells and when, at last, they moved out the claim for dilapidations ran into five figures. Again the house-decorators, architects, plumbers and quantity surveyors from near and far wrote letters, telephoned, sent representatives or called personally. But not a penny was spent on the great building. It was left exactly as it was, even to the rude pictures chalked by licentious soldiery on bedroom walls.

Mr. Finklestein (or Guggenheimer, or just plain Cohen) was waiting for another war.

III

It was to the Grand Wells that our joining instructions directed us. There was no transport to meet us at the station, so we had to shoulder our kit-bags and toil sweating up the hill under the broiling mid-afternoon sun.

The Grand Wells was much the same in appearance as most other large hotels. It stood, originally in lonely splendour, in its own extensive grounds, but by the year 1942 it had to share its acres with a mixed assortment of huts and gun-sheds. The entrance gates had disappeared long since and the griffins on the pillars were not the fine monsters of yore. The wide, once-gravelled, drive was now the north parade-ground. Along the back of the building ran a broad, stone-balustraded terrace, from which there was still, in spite of the Army and Mr. Finklestein (or Guggenheimer, or just plain Cohen), a magnificent view of the saw-toothed Kinder Scout. Below the terrace, green lawns had once pleased the eye of the visitor, but now the grass had given place to asphalt, and those on the terrace looked down on nothing more aesthetic than the south parade-ground-cum-gun-park, on which, day after day, as many as a dozen detachments at a time went through their gun-drill again and again, with N.C.Os. shouting themselves hoarse, and Ack-I.Gs. on the permanent staff dodging from gun to gun, advising, explaining, instructing and, more often than not, hindering. It is saddening to compare the old-time conversations over tea and toasted scones on that tranquil pleasance with the harsh phrases of total war. Who of that former sedate and placid company could have foreseen that one day there would be no reposeful small-talk on that spot, but instead, the ear-splitting, nerve-racking repetition of "Detachment—*rear*!" "Make safe!" "Gun out of phase!" "Halt—*action*!" and the perpetual staccato "Held!" of the No. 4s?

Postbechild and I walked across the front parade-ground and passed through the main central doorway into the marble-pillared reception-hall. With sighs of relief we allowed our kit-bags to slide off our shoulders. Almost before they had touched the floor, a particular nasty voice snarled:

"Nah yer c'n picker mup agine!"

This formal welcome to the Grand Wells was extended to us by a regimental-police wallah—a small, scraggy, sour-faced single-taper, who was on duty at the foot of the main staircase. We did as we were told; we had no option. I thought Postbechild really was going to snap in the middle as he heaved up the heavy load.

"No 'angin' abaht in this 'all," Cerberus went on.

"We're reporting to the Light Ack-Ack Training Regiment, Bombardier," I told him politely.

He jerked his head backwards.

"Admin Office, first floor."

I thanked him and we moved across the hall towards him. He remained planted in such a position that we had to go to our left of him to get on to the staircase. I had gone up four stairs, with Postbechild just to the rear, when Cerberus yelled at the top of his untuneful voice:

"Keep to the right, you—— ——s!"

When we had got round the second corner and were nearing the first floor, Postbechild, struggling along behind me, said:

"He stood there for the——purpose."

"Let him have his little hour," I answered soothingly over my shoulder. "Somebody will get him eventually."

Somebody did—and within the month. The R.Ps. at Boxford—a local body, not to be confused with the red-caps, the Corps of Military Police—were the worst handful of useless, brainless, browbeating jacks-in-office that I have ever encountered. After our Battery had left there, the news trickled through that one night some vengeful men from an outgoing unit had systematically sought them out and got them all. One of them nearly died. But that is by the way.

A small bunch of men was already assembled in the passage outside the Admin Office. Within half an hour they began to call us in, one by one. Postbechild and I were both instructed to report to XYZ Battery Office, on the third floor. (I should add here that "XYZ" is my own invention. For obvious reasons, the figures represented by those three letters cannot be published.) Postbechild waited to see what happened to me; and, when I came out of the Admin Office, we went up together to the third floor.

We found, at the end of a long corridor, a door that had once been painted white. It bore the notice: "XYZ Bty. Office. Knock & Wait." Postbechild knocked with a not too clean forefinger, but we did not have to wait. A voice instantly told us to come in. It did not shout; it merely told us to come in.

We had dumped our kit-bags against the wall. Postbechild opened the door and I followed him into the room. There was only one occupant. He was sitting at a plain deal table, facing the door. There was nothing on the table except an ink-pot with a pen sticking out of it, a tobacco tin lid used as an ashtray and a ragged sheet of blotting-paper. His hands were in his pockets, and the manner in which he was sprawled back in his chair suggested that he had nothing to do and did not care who knew it. A cigarette hung from his lips and he did not take it out before asking:

"What do you want?"

One of the battery clerks, I thought. His tone was indifferent rather than peremptory. His battledress bore all the evidence of a sedentary job. There was cigarette-ash on the front of the blouse; and a fountain-pen was clipped to an unbuttoned breast-pocket.

Postbechild, who was a pace in front, answered:

"Admin Office told us to report here."

Casually, as if easing his position, the man in the chair pulled his hands out of his pockets and rested his elbows on the table.

Postbechild sprang to attention—if one can say that he ever sprang—and added a smart:

"Sir."

I, too, had seen the crown-and-laurels on the forearms.

He was a thick-set man, this sergeant-major who did not shout at us. He was, in fact, the exact opposite of the buzzing little wasp who had greeted us downstairs. His ruddy face and general appearance gave the impression of a reasonably genial, easy-going, slightly slip-shod man, who would have been more at home in shirt-sleeves behind the bar of the Horse & Groom than in battledress in a Battery Office. Only two things were out of character: his voice and his eyes. His voice was not breezily Cockney, but thick and guttural, somewhat like that of an English actor playing the part of a U-boat commander. His eyes were dull and cold. I have already tried to describe him on an earlier page. His name was Yule.

With their task completed, he put his hands back into his pockets, and the arm-badges were hidden again by the table top.

"Wait outside in the passage till you're called," he said.

As we withdrew, half an inch of ash fell unheeded from his cigarette on to his battledress.

IV

From the day that he is called to the colours, the soldier must accustom himself to hanging about, for he will do more of it during his term of military service than during the rest of his days on earth. Postbechild and I had got used to it, so that it meant nothing to us that we might have to wait a couple of hours outside the door that was once white, at the end of the long corridor. We unbuttoned our belts, slipped out of our harness and sat down on our kit-bags, ready to jump up suddenly if the necessity arose. That is the worst feature of the Army brand of hanging about; there is in it no real relaxation, only a feeling of tenseness that is difficult to describe.

We had been there ten minutes when Postbechild muttered:
"Shall we risk a burn?"

"Not those cigars!" I warned him swiftly.

"What d'you——take me for?" was his cheerless retort.

He had no cigarettes, so I gave him one of mine. He pulled out his odorous brazier and worked on the wheel till the wick flamed smokily. I took a light from it eagerly, being more than ready for a smoke; but hardly had I taken a single, soothing draw, than the Sergeant-major said from the other side of the closed door:

"Put those cigarettes out!"

Gnr. Postbechild looked scandalized. He nipped out his Gold Flake, blew through it, thumbed it into his field-dressing pocket and leant towards me to whisper:

"The crafty——! Must have been looking through the—— keyhole!"

I thought not. Postbechild's lighter was a noisy machine to start. Besides, sergeant-majors do not ordinarily peek through keyholes—not of Battery Office, at any rate.

Five minutes later he came out, passed us without a glance and went off down the corridor. Before he had turned the corner at the end, Postbechild was fumbling in his field-dressing pocket.

The great building was full of many distant noises; voices shouting, doors banging, boots tramping: but where we were, at that particular hour of that late-September afternoon, was a quiet backwater. We had finished our first smoke and were half-way through another before we heard approaching footsteps.

"The——'s coming back," Postbechild announced moodily.

But it was not the Sergeant-major who appeared round the corner. It was a two-taper; a full bombardier. He was quite young, not more than twenty-two; of medium height, pale, dark-haired and thin-nosed. He, too, had a fountain-pen sticking from his breast-pocket, and he was wearing civilian shoes. As he came towards us, his pleasant, intellectual face wore a worried frown. In one hand he was carrying an untidy sheaf of papers and in the other a rifle.

Postbechild and I, together with our effects, took up most of the passage, but the young bombardier threaded his way through, like a spring poet wandering, aimless as a cloud, in a wood. When he reached the door of the Battery Office, he propped the rifle against the wall; then, with his hand on the door-knob, turned, as if suddenly realizing our presence.

"Are you two waiting for me?" he asked in a quiet, educated voice.

"Yes, Bombardier," I answered. "The Sergeant-major told us to wait here until we were wanted."

He smiled apologetically.

"So sorry to keep you waiting," he said. "I've been trying for an hour to get away from Admin Office."

It had happened. I knew it would, sooner or later. An N.C.O. had apologized to me.

I stole a glance at Postbechild, to see if he had noticed the wonder; but he was standing with his arms hanging and his face indifferently adroop. In repose—which was almost always—Postbechild gave the impression that he was suspended from a hook attached to the neck of his battledress.

We followed the bombardier into the office. While he put the rifle in a corner, I had time to notice that there were two other desks besides the Sergeant-major's in the room. One was seemingly not in use, except as a repository for Army pamphlets and booklets; the other was completely covered with letters, forms and soldiers' pay-books. He threw the papers he had brought up from the Admin Office on top of the others with a tired sigh. Some of them fluttered on to the floor. He left them there.

I produced the envelope with which I had been entrusted before leaving Burntash, and handed it over to him. He ripped it open, took out the documents—medical-history sheets, etc.—and added them to the pile. He asked for our pay-books, which went the same way. Then, without fumbling or hesitation, he pulled a foolscap sheet from somewhere in the middle of the *mélange*, consulted it for a moment and said:

"Postbechild, you'll be sleeping in Room 151. Bradfield in 152. There's one vacancy in each. Dump your kits there now, and draw blankets and bedding from the Q. stores after tea. Tea parade's at seventeen-hundred. Come back here at eighteen-hundred; the Battery Commander will see you then." He smiled as he added: "That's all, thank you."

I felt that the trifling affairs of Gnrs. Postbechild and Bradfield had been banished from his overburdened mind before we left the room.

V

The whole of XYZ Battery was housed on the third floor of the Grand Wells, in addition to the Battery Office and the quartermaster's store. Room 152 was not far away from the office. A gouty major or a rheumatic old lady would have complained in 1912 that it was far too cramped and poky for an adult, but in September, 1942, it was serving as a bedroom for seven men. I made an eighth; and when I opened the door and had a look in, it was clear that some of the others would have to move up a bit. There were no beds, straw-filled palliasses being laid on the floor.

Leaving my kit on the clear patch in the centre of the room—for the palliasses were folded back in the day-time, with blankets and kit on top of them—I called in next door for Postbechild; and, as it was nearing the time for tea parade, we walked along to the main staircase and went down in single file, taking care to hug the right-hand wall.

There were eighty-three stairs down to the ground floor and another twenty-five to the dining-hall in the basement. One hundred and eight stairs down and—for there are occasions when arithmetic is too precise—five thousand six hundred stairs up. I remember with a shudder the many times I had to make that climb during my fortnight at Boxford, with always some howling dervish in an "R.P." armlet pouring out instructions about keeping to the right, refraining from smoking and anything else that occurred to him in his frenzy of temporary dictatorship.

After a magnificent tea—the food at Boxford was the best Army fodder I have ever eaten and almost made up for all the discomforts of life in a requisitioned hotel—Postbechild and I toiled back to the third floor and sought out the Q. stores. A voice called, "Come in," when I knocked.

There was only one man in the room. He was on the other side of the counter, bending over a pile of underclothing. He spun round when I quietly greeted him with:

"Hullo, Johnny."

CHAPTER TWELVE

I

MENTION has been made in these pages of neuro-psychiatry as employed by the Army to sort out the square pegs from the conventional round ones. My own opinion is that, in a citizen army, *all* the pegs are square, and that the utmost to be hoped is that the majority of them will find eventually a hole which, though of a meticulously military circularity, will fit them well enough to serve the country's interests and their own comfort. My belief is that, whatever the findings of the psychiatrists may be, a soldier will finish up in the job for which he is best suited.

Johnny Fieldhouse was a case in point. Johnny was a square peg, if ever there was one. There was no real place in the Army for him. He was too much of an individualist; too prone to stand out against authority. He had to be ridden with a light rein, to get the best out of him. At Boxford, he had found his niche. He had been appointed quartermaster's storekeeper—the only quartermaster's storekeeper in the Battery. Not a position of any great social or military distinction, but just the job for Gnr. Fieldhouse, J. He was able to potter about among his piles of Vests, woollen; Drawers, cellular; and Boots, ankle; as happy as the managing director of a one-man band.

Later in the evening, he took me out to show me round the town, but before that, Postbechild and I were interviewed by the Battery Commander.

Major T. W. Mellis, R.A., was no longer young. To describe his appearance, I cannot do better than quote once again Gilles de Rais' pen-portrait of the Marquis de Sade: "a mild, gentle, rather bald and grey-haired person." He was small and clean-shaven, and if there is an adjective that fitted him better than another, it is, inoffensive. He had two pairs of horn-rimmed spectacles and was for ever changing one for the other. Even in those early days, so soon after the formation of XYZ Battery, he was known to the gunners, quite affectionately, as the Old Lady.

My first conversation with him was, at the time, unimportant. I have a particular reason for repeating it here, as nearly word for word as I can remember it.

"So you are..." He changed his spectacles to examine the papers in front of him. "You are Gunner Bradfield?"

"Yes, sir."

"You can stand easy, Bradfield. Which gun-number were you trained as?"

"Number I, sir."

"Feel pretty confident you could take over an operational gun?"

"Yes, sir."

"How long have you been in the Army?"

"Nearly three months, sir."

"Married?"

"No, sir."

"What was your civilian occupation?".

"I was in the Police, sir; plain-clothes constable."

"A detective, eh? We shall have to mind our step in this Battery! A detective.... Well, well. Where were you stationed, Bradfield?"

"I was attached to the Downshire County Police, sir. I was actually stationed at Lulverton."

"An ugly old town, if I remember rightly, smelling perpetually of hot rubber. Where were you educated?"

"Wraxham, sir."

"Cousin of mine went to Wraxham. Name of Bourne. A bit before your time, I expect. What sort of work did they give you in the Police?"

"Anything that cropped up, sir. One or two murders, but there's not much real crime in a country district like Downshire. Petty theft, a burglary now and again, pickpocketing on market days. Things like that."

"Do you know anything about criminal jurisprudence, Bradfield?"

"A smattering, sir."

"Well, what does the law have to say on the subject of—what shall it be?...What is the law about cruelty to animals?"

The interview was hardly proceeding as I had anticipated. It was like being psychiatrized all over again. I did my best to give him an intelligent reply. Perhaps I overdid it.

"Cruelty to animals, sir," I said, "is covered by the various Protection of Animals Acts. The principal one was in 1911. It provides that if any person illtreats an animal, or overloads it, or tortures it, or causes it any unnecessary suffering, he is liable, on summary conviction, to a fine of twenty-five pounds and three months' imprisonment. The chief offenders, in my experience, are those who overwork horses."

"How about vivisection?"

"The Act doesn't apply, sir, though, of course, vivisection can only be carried out under a licence from the Home Secretary."

"Thank you, Bradfield. Very interesting.... Twenty-five pounds and three months' imprisonment, eh? Too lenient, Bradfield—far too lenient. They should give the fellows ten years.... Well, that's about all I have to say to you, except one last word."

He removed his spectacles and laid them on the table.

"Every man in this Battery, Bradfield, has access to me, through the normal military channels. If for any reason— *any reason at all*—you want to see me—it may be official, it may be some little private worry—you will know what to do won't you?"

"Yes, sir," I said. "Thank you, sir."

They were conventional, those last phrases of his. All O.Cs. say the same thing. Yet this one, I felt, really meant it. There had been an odd gleam in his kindly grey eyes when he said the words that I have italicized.

"That is all, then. Please send in..." He replaced his spectacles and turned over the sheets on the table. "Please send in Gunner Postbechild. Upon my soul, what a singular name!"

"Very good, sir," I said, saluted and right-turned.

I reserved my judgment on the Sergeant-major, but about the O.C. I had made up my mind.

II

Johnny introduced me that evening to his most pleasant discovery in the interesting old town of Boxford: a quaint little eating-house, where, in spite of the rigours of food rationing, one could get a first-rate supper and some real coffee. The place was run by a married couple and their two grown-up daughters. It was on two floors, yet there were so many half-landings, partitions, alcoves, cubicles and "mind-the-steps" that one wondered how, having taken an order, the members of the family ever remembered exactly where to report back with the victuals.

We managed to get a little cubicle to ourselves. When they had taken away the plates and set coffee before us, I said:

"Now tell me how the world's been using you."

"Nothing very exciting's happened," Johnny replied. "I'd only been here a couple of days when they snatched me off the gun-park and pushed me into the Q. stores. I've never had such a good time since I first came into the Army. The Q.'s a good scout and he gives me a pretty free hand. He says I ought to get a stripe soon after we've left here. The whole Regiment—all four Batteries, XYW, XYX, XYY and XYZ— is going from here to firing-camp in a couple of weeks."

"No need to tell the world about it," I cautioned him.

"Oh, that's all right!" he answered airily. "I got that last bit of news from a tobacconist yesterday evening. The civvies here are much better informed about our future movements than we are."

"What's the Q. like?"

"Oh, he's a fine fellow. Tells you what he wants done and then leaves you to get on with it. I don't have to do everything by numbers like a jerking Robot; and if I feel like stopping work for a few minutes, in order to think about the cosmos or Dalton's Atomic Theory, he doesn't jump down my—"

"When I ask, what is he like, I mean, what does he *look* like?"

Johnny noticed that I had not used my sugar and helped himself to it from my saucer.

"You want a word-picture?" he said, dropping the lump in his own cup. "Well, first of all, his name is Ackroyd. Battery Quartermaster-sergeant Richard Ackroyd. He's got a wife who's—well, let's say she's neurotic, and a couple of kids. Two jolly little kids, a boy and a girl. He's got some photos that he took on his last leave and—"

I stopped him. I was not concerned with Mrs. Q. and all the little qs.

"Johnny," I said, "I asked you to describe the B.Q.M.S., so that I may recognize him when I meet him. However bonny his children may be, they will not enable me to say, as I pass him on the twenty-fourth floor of the Grand Wells, *that* is our quartermaster-sergeant."

"Still as impatient as ever, I see," said Johnny. "It's a sign of nerves. The Q. is about thirty-two or three. If you met him, you could immediately recognize him by one thing and one thing alone. His nose. It is a glorious nose, the emperor of all conks. I don't mean its colour; that's quite normal. But for size and shape it stands in a class by itself. In outline, it is superbly Roman, with a magnificent bridge. In size—well, it's huge, like Cyrano de Bergerac's or Robert Herrick, the fellow who wrote 'Fair daffodils, we weep to see—'"

I muttered something indelicate about daffodils.

Q. Ackroyd, Johnny went on, "is a smart-looking soldier when he's properly dressed. Jet-black curly hair. Rather gypsy-ish—the sort of face that goes well with a bandanna. He's taller than I am."

"That's not saying much."

"Well, he's nearly as tall as you, if you like that better. Been something of a sportsman in his time: steeplechasing and point-to-point. Played a lot of Soccer, too. He's Yorkshire and proud of it! Always says, 'I were' and 'aye' instead of 'yes.' He's awfully decent to me."

"You've already been into that rather thoroughly. Now tell me about the Sergeant-major."

He writhed his small body, and his lip curled with repugnance.

"Ugh! The mere sight of him gives me the shivers. He's like an affable slug with a nasty mind. Have you met him yet?"

"Yes—and I wasn't at all impressed. I didn't like the droop of his mouth. Or his eyes; there's something behind their deadness, something evil...."

Johnny leant forward across the table and his voice dropped to an undertone.

"I'll tell you something, Peter. Just now I said that nothing's happened. That wasn't true. There's been one incident and it was... disgusting."

He finished his coffee.

"The other evening," he went on, "I was in the stores with the Q. He was just going out to a cinema, but at the last minute couldn't find his cap. Then he remembered that he'd left it in the Sergeant-major's room when he'd popped in to have a word with him after tea. He sent me along the corridor to fetch it. He said that if the Sergeant-major wasn't in, I was to barge in and grab the cap, because he was in a hurry. I knocked on the B.S.M.'s door, but got no reply, so I went in. The B.S.M. was there, but he didn't take any notice of me.... He was sitting at the table, pressing a glass tumbler upside down on to a folded sheet of blotting-paper." Johnny moistened his lips with his tongue. "Under the glass was a little brown mouse.... He was watching it suffocate."

I pressed out my cigarette-end in the tray. Johnny went on haltingly:

"It was rolling over... weakly... on its back.... And with both hands holding the glass down, he was gloating over it.... You said his eyes were evil, Peter."

"What did you do?" I asked after a pause.

"He hadn't heard me come in. I think he was in a foul trance, beyond noticing anything outside the glass."

"What did you do?" I asked again.

Johnny looked at me doubtfully before saying:

"I flew at him. Wouldn't you have done the same?"

"Yes," I grunted, yet wondering if I should really have had his thoughtless courage.

"I leapt into the room, grabbed at his wrists and wrenched them off the glass, which fell off the table and got smashed. Then I shoved him out of the way, swept the mouse off the table and put the poor little devil out of its misery with my boot."

"What did the B.S.M. do?"

"Nothing. He just sat there looking at me. I found the Q.'s cap—and left him to clear up the mess. I had half a mind to tell the Q. about it when I got back to the stores. He's not afraid of the B.S.M. and would have told him what he thought of him. But I decided not to; it would only have stirred up a lot of unpleasantness."

"Have you heard nothing of it since?"

"Not a word. In fact, the B.S.M.'s gone out of his way to be nice to me. I think he's got the wind up and wants the affair kept as quiet as possible. I'm well aware that it's a serious crime to lay hands on a W.O. II, but he can't very well peg me for it, can he?"

I hoped not. With all my heart, I hoped not. Why, I asked myself despairingly, did these things always have to happen to Johnny?

III

We ordered some more coffee to take the taste of the Sergeant-major out of our mouths.

I asked Johnny for news of Chris Wilkinson.

"Oh, him," Johnny said without relish. "He's in XYZ, too—in 'C' Troop. He's still doing No. 4, but there's talk of his being brought into B.H.Q. They'll want a medical orderly in due course, and as Grandad has had a lot of First Aid experience, they think he's the man for the job."

From his tone, I took it that he did not agree with them. He added:

"He'll be made up to lance-bombardier, which'll give him a bigger idea of his own importance than ever."

"Chris Wilkinson is not like that," I protested. "He's a thoroughly decent, unassuming fellow. Dependable, too. You and he don't get on too well together because you're of such different temperaments. He's a trifle—well, stolid. He doesn't get worked up over things. You, Johnny, are just the opposite. You don't need much excuse to fly off the handle. You've got to make allowances, Johnny."

"He doesn't approve of me," he said sulkily; "and when a chap doesn't approve of me, I make a point of not approving of him. It maintains the *status quo*."

"All right," I said. "Be stubborn if you must; but you'll sing a different tune when your chest needs rubbing with camphorated oil."

"I'd get someone else to do it. Did the Old Lady grant you audience today?"

I raised my eyebrows. "Which old lady?"

"There's only one Old Lady in the Battery—the Major. That's what they call him."

"Yes, he had me in. We had quite a chummy little chat. He seems a nice old boy, but a bit negative."

"He makes an agreeable change from some of the officers we've had to put up with. He *will* listen to you. He saw from my docs. that I've been a stormy petrel; and when he interviewed me, he talked to me like a father. I think it was he who put me in the Q. stores. The Captain wouldn't. If the

Captain had his way, we'd all be on the guns. His theory is that the pen-pusher is the lowest form of human life and that the only soldier worth his salt is the one that pokes a bayonet into the intestines of the foe; or, failing that, practices all day on a sandbag, shouting rude remarks at it and scowling horribly. 'Fostering a spirit of hate,' he calls it. Yes, he's a real fire-eater, is Captain Fitzgerald. The only living thing he seems to care a hoot for is his Cairn terrier, Scottie. He oughtn't to be in Ack-Ack; he'd be much more in his element leading risky commando raids. He's a striking-looking blighter, still well on the right side of thirty; the type of man who can't look wrong, whatever he's dressed in, even denims. If you wanted to be unkind, you'd say he was too, *too* perfect to be anything but an Army tailor's dummy. But it wouldn't be true, Peter. He goes round the assault-course with the best of 'em, and they say that only the Q, can touch him at the half-mile. He's a thing of beauty to look at, with the heavy black moustache that 'Anton' is fond of for his Army pictures in *Punch*; but believe me, Peter, I'd rather be with him than against him in a rough-house. He's handsome dynamite."

"So he takes a poor view of military clerking?"

"Extremely. Even he doesn't say that a Battery can be run without an Admin section—it's like expecting a clock to work without a spring. But he argues that every man in the Battery—clerks, batmen and all—should be able to do any gun-number in an emergency and, in addition, be so highly trained that they can switch from pen to Bren at a moment's notice."

"There's something in it," I said.

"It's all right in theory, but not in practice. Take the case of Bombardier Morton. The Captain—"

"Who's Bombardier Morton?"

"Paul Morton? You saw him this afternoon, didn't you? He's the Battery clerk and I don't envy him the job! Captain Fitzgerald took it into his head that a spot of gun-drill wouldn't come amiss for Morton—say an hour a day. So Morton was detailed to parade on the gun-park with 'A' Troop the next morning. Morton told him flatly—young Paul is no respecter of persons!—that he had been mustered into the Battery as a clerk and he was damned if he was going to do any gun-drill. He didn't put it quite like that, of course, but his reply to the Captain was firm and to the point. So Blitz—short for Fitzgerald—referred the matter to the Old Lady, who supported him. 'Anything for a quiet life,' is the O.C.'s motto. Morton duly paraded with 'A' Troop the following morning and tried his hand at No 3. At the end of the hour, he went back to the office and diligently stuck in the mud for the rest of the day."

Johnny laughed at the recollection.

"By tea-time, Admin were purple with rage and were ringing up the Captain every five minutes about this, that or the other thing not having been done. Every time Blitz called Morton in for an explanation, Morton apologized politely and said the return—or whatever it was—would be ready for the Captain's signature within half an hour. It wasn't, of course. Morton saw to that! Since then, he hasn't done gun-drill."

"He certainly seems to have enough on his plate without that," I conceded. "I've never seen a more untidy desk in my life, except Robb Wilton's in his Police Station sketch."

"It may look a mess," Johnny said, "but it doesn't take Morton long to lay his hands on anything that's needed. He's an extraordinary lad. He runs Battery Office. He'd run the Q. side as well if there were twenty-five hours in a day. Everything passes through his hands, from training programmes to sick-reports; and he can quote A.C.Is. and King's Regs. by the yard. You'll usually find him in the office until ten o'clock at night; and even when he gets to bed he doesn't sleep, but reads murder mysteries well into the small hours. One of these days that young man will have a nervous breakdown."

"I like the look of him."

"Yes, he's popular in the Battery; and he's been the only one to get the better of Blitz Fitz. No, not the only one. Gianella was another. You remember Gianella at Burntash—the little Italian barber with the painted moustache and the swaggering walk? Gianella was too much for the sergeants, he was too much for the Ack-I.Gs. and he finished by being too much for Blitz.…'I can't do it, sir! Wiv the best will in the world, I just can't do it, sir.'" Johnny's imitation was lifelike. "And he got away with it."

I nodded. "He said he would."

Blitz took him off the guns and made him his batman. Now he spends half the day taking Scottie for little walks and the other half talking."

"Which reminds me," I said, looking at my watch. "We'd better be getting back."

"Plenty of time yet," said Johnny, settling his elbows more firmly on the table. "Up to now, I've answered all the questions. Now it's your turn."

Instinctively I knew what was coming.

"Some other time will do for—" I began.

"Did you see her?"

"Did I see who?" I asked without assurance or grammar.

"Hazel, of course."

"What, that At of yours at Burntash?" I played for time. "I—er—well I may have done, for all I know. There are a good few Ats in those parts, and as you never pointed her out to me, you can't really expect me—"

"No, I suppose not," he interrupted, much to my relief. "I wanted to know how she is. You might have had some little tit-bit of news for me. She hasn't written yet, but I expect the Admin Office keep her pretty busy.… I suppose I've just got to wait. I get excited round about mail-times, though!"

"Johnny," I said, "don't you think you're taking this affair too seriously? After all, you only saw her once."

"I saw her a lot of times," he contradicted. "She often came out of Admin Office when I was stooging around outside."

"Don't be dense! I mean that you only spoke to her— well, not more than twice. You can't expect a girl to write to an almost complete stranger."

"Stranger? But we were getting along splendidly, Peter! I think she—liked me a bit. If I hadn't got snatched away and bundled off up here..."

He left the sentence unfinished.

"All I say is, Johnny, don't be too disappointed if you don't get a letter from her. You know what women are."

He didn't. That was the trouble.

CHAPTER THIRTEEN

I

IT was eight o'clock the next morning. XYZ Battery was having its first parade of the day. Elsewhere around the Grand Wells other Batteries were also parading, but my concern is with XYZ.

The three troops fell in, each on its troop-sergeant, who acted as marker. I was in the front rank of "A" Troop. The Sergeant-major, looking no less seedy than when I had seen him the previous afternoon, brought the Battery to attention with a word of command that would have horrified the Cwmsamfach N.C.Os., then ordered:

"Call the roll!"

The troop-sergeants marched round to the front of their troops, stood them at ease and shouted the names from the lists they held. Each man came to attention as he answered to his name, then stood again at ease. When the last names had been called, the sergeants marched back to their positions on the right of their troops.

The B.S.M. brought the whole Battery to attention before ordering:

"Reports!"

The sergeants answered in turn:

"'A' Troop all present, sir!"

"'B' Troop all present, sir!"

"'C' Troop all present, sir!"

The B.S.M. stood us at ease, after which he walked—one cannot say that he marched—across to the orderly officer, halted, saluted and announced:

"XYZ Battery all present and correct, sir."

The orderly officer took his turn at bringing the Battery to attention, marched smartly up to the Major and passed on the glad tidings that the B.S.M. had imparted to him. The Major gave the order:

"Troop-sergeants take charge."

He and the orderly officer left the parade-ground together. The Sergeant-major waited a moment or two before following them. As he made for the steps leading up to the southern terrace of the Grand Wells, a voice full of hatred muttered sideways from next to me:

"That's *his* morning's work finished, the bone-idle———!"
I found the rhythm and alliteration of the epithet attractive.

The troop-sergeant of "A" came out in front of us with his papers clipped to a sheet of three-ply, on the back of which one or more hands had sketched in pencil a jumbled assortment of studies in the nude.

"Fall out the employed men!" was his first order.

When the employed men—that is, the men whose training in Ack-Ack gunnery had been abandoned as hopeless—had filed away to their sanitary and gardening duties, the Sergeant wrenched me out of my early-morning coma by saying:

"Gunner Bradfield, 254."

I stood to attention.

"Sergeant?"

"Fall out and report to Battery Office."

There is an unwritten law amongst gunners that, when ordered by a first authority to report to a second authority, the soldier will not proceed from Point A to Point B by the quickest and most direct route, but will quietly merge into the landscape for half an hour in the way that only a private soldier can. Authority No. 1 has forgotten him, Authority No. 2 is too busy to scan the horizon for him; and a man cannot for ever be considering others before self. So back in the Grand Wells I got hold of a morning paper and slid away, for a smoke and a read, to—well, it's no matter where I betook myself.

In not much more than ten minutes—certainly in less than three-quarters of an hour—I was knocking at the door of Battery Office.

The now familiar, clicking guttural of B.S.M. Yule instructed me to enter. He was in exactly the same posture as when I had last seen him at his desk. Nor was his desk less bare. Bombardier Morton was busy with his work at the second table.

You Gunner Bradfield?" the B.S.M. asked, without taking his cigarette from his mouth.

I agreed that I was, wondering what unpleasantness was to follow.

"Good at figures?"

I said I was. It doesn't do to be too modest.

"Use a typewriter?"

"Yes, sir."

He nodded towards the room's third table and chair.

"Sit over there," he said. "You're the pay-clerk."

II

The psychiatrists at Cwmsamfach—but enough of psychiatrists. I promise not to mention them again. On an earlier page, I gave it as my belief that a soldier will invariably finish up in the Army at the job for which he is best suited. I do not seek to quote myself as a distinguished exception, for I am still in the Royal Artillery and there is yet time for me to be transferred to another field of endeavour. Suffice it to say that from that morning in the autumn of 1942 until the present day, I have been the pay-wallah of XYZ Light Anti-Aircraft Battery, R.A.

The Sergeant-major went on:

"The bombardier will tell you what to do."

That was all he had to say. He did not address a further word to me during the rest of the day.

I went over to the third table. As I sat down, the Sergeant-major left his own seat and strolled out of the room with his

105

hands in his pockets. Up to then, Bombardier Morton had taken no notice of me, but as soon as the door had closed behind the B.S.M., he put down his pen and swung round towards me with a smile.

"Glad to have you in here," he said. "Admin, and pay are too much for one man. As a matter of fact, I marked you down as my prey when I saw you yesterday. I had a word with the O.C. last night—and here you are. I hope you don't mind?"

"Not a scrap," I hurried to assure him. "The switch-over from gun-park to pay-desk is somewhat sudden, but I'll be all right when I get my breath back! Anyway, it'll be more comfortable sitting in here." He offered me a cigarette.

"Now, Bombardier," I said briskly, when we had lighted up, "what can I do for you?"

"Firstly," he answered, "only call me 'Bombardier' when there are officers about. My name's Paul—Paul Morton. Yours is Peter, isn't it?"

"Yes," I smiled. "Peter and Paul should be a good combination!"

"Then that's settled. Secondly, if you're going to stop in Battery Office—and I hope you will—you've got to know the routine. That door there leads into the Major's room, which he shares with Captain Fitzgerald, the second-in-command of the Battery. When the O.C.—the Major—arrives in the mornings you jump up and stand to attention until he says, 'Good-morning.' Then, as far as he's concerned, you relax for the rest of the day. You don't play at soldiers every time he comes in or out, but if he speaks to you, you stand up before you answer. With the Captain, you keep your seat, though it's just as well to take the cigarette out of your mouth before you respond to his morning greeting!"

I smiled.

"As for the other officers—and they're always in and out of here—you stay put. Some of them don't like it, but they never mention it because they can't afford to fall out with you. You can take it from me that, unless the Major or the Captain have sent for them, they never come in here except on the scrounge. As a rule, it's a cigarette. I've never yet met a troop-officer with cigarettes of his own. And while I'm on the subject, if they come in here asking for any more pencils or notebooks, the answer's 'No.' I think they must send them home. Tell 'em we haven't any. If you want stuff like that for yourself, there's a good supply in that tin box under your table."

He flicked the ash from his cigarette.

"If there's anyone a bigger nuisance than the troop-officers," he continued, "it's the troop-sergeants. They're in and out of here all day. If it isn't one, it's another of them. Their excuses vary, but the two main motives behind their visits are either to dodge P.T. or to pick up scraps of information. They're always on the snoop; and if they're not asking you questions, they're having a stealthy glance at the papers on your table. It's not good for them when they know too much, so if they make themselves a nuisance, tell 'em to get to hell out of here."

"And me a gunner?"

"That makes no difference. They'll take it lying down. In their heart of hearts, all troop-sergeants are scared stiff of B.H.Q. They're never quite sure where they stand. The men in their own troops can't do them much harm, but a gunner in B.H.Q. might be able to do them a really bad turn. They never lose sight of that."

"Thanks for the advice," I smiled. "And now you've taught me Battery Office etiquette as relating to officers and sergeants, what about the B.S.M.?"

Paul shrugged his shoulders indifferently.

"The best thing to do," he answered with a frankness that surprised me, for we had not known each other long, "is to pretend he's not there. When I was in a civvy post, we had a joke about the three most useless things in the world. The third was the chairman's vote of thanks to the staff. Now, as far as this Battery's concerned, there's a fourth."

"I heard him described on parade this morning," I said, "as a bone-idle———."

"Quite right, too. He never does a stroke unless he's forced into it. Everything that comes out of the other room marked, 'B.S.M.—Action' is shunted over to my table. Just one word of warning about him, though: he can be dangerous, especially in the afternoon, after he's propped up the bar in the sergeants' mess for a couple of hours. Beer just makes him maudlin, but after whisky he's vicious and it's best to keep out of his way. But whether he's drunk or sober, never let him get the idea that you're afraid of him, or he'll play with you like a cat with a mouse. If you're firmly polite and make life easy for him by referring things to him only when it's absolutely necessary, he won't give you much trouble."

I was just about to speak when he resumed:

"There's a gunner—Owen, D., of 'C' Troop, a timid, harmless little Welshman, who used to be an elementary school-teacher in a village near Merthyr. He'd be quite useful at a desk job—something, anyway, that he could get on with quietly by himself, without being bullyragged. He might even make an efficient gun-number, provided he wasn't barked at too fiercely. Men like Owen, D. are the natural prey of the B.S.M. He's made the little fellow's life a misery since he came to Boxford. Every time Owen, D. is on gundrill—and he may be getting along quite nicely under the troop-sergeant or one of the Ack-I.Gs.—the B.S.M. strolls up. Owen, D. sees him out of the corner of his eye—and goes right to pieces. Then the B.S.M. gets cracking on him: gives him 'As far as detailed, go on' for a quarter of an hour, while the rest of the detachment stand round grinning."

I tut-tutted in sympathy with Gnr. Owen, D. I, too, had suffered from the infuriating, exhausting repetition of "As far as detailed, go on," which is, more or less, gun-drill by numbers, each stage being taken separately, without the swift, exciting sequence of the complete drill movement.

"By the end of it," Paul said, "Owen, D. doesn't know the gun from the predictor. The B.S.M.'s put him on fatigues every night since he first picked him out as a likely victim. I'm willing to bet you that Owen, D. will be having to report again to the orderly sergeant tonight."

He dropped his cigarette-end on the bare floor-boards and trod it out with his shoe.

"Between ourselves," he added, "the B.S.M.'s the foulest piece of work I've ever encountered."

"I arrived here only yesterday," I told him, "yet I've already heard some not very pleasant stories about him; tales concerning some of his private hobbies."

"Yes, it's curious how a man like that can succeed with women. A kind of hypnotism, I suppose.... 'Will you come into my parlour....'"

I said: "The stories I heard were not about women."

Paul had been looking at the floor, but now he jerked up his head and gave me a swift glance.

"No?" he said, but did not question me further.

III

We turned from gossip to Battery affairs. Pay was in a fearful mess, as Paul Morton readily admitted. That was the reason for my presence in the office, for pay, by itself, was a whole-time job and nobody, not even the industrious Paul, could run it as a sideline to Admin.

"You'll find," he said, "that the actual paying is child's play. You list the names on these long sheets, which are called acquittance rolls. Then you cast up the cash columns, work out how many pound notes, ten-shilling notes, half-crowns, florins and shillings you'll need, so that the paying officer can give each man the exact amount due. After pay parade—each troop has its own parade—you collect all the acquittance rolls together, get the grand total and agree it with the balance in the Imprest Account cash-book, which is kept by Captain Fitzgerald.

"Yes," Paul went on, "that part of it's easy. Queries are the real headache. Pay-day only comes once a week, but you get a pay query every ten minutes. Apart from the fan-mail from the Regimental Paymaster, which is considerable, there are the questions raised by the men themselves. They may want to increase their voluntary allotment to their wives, or to apply for a dependant's allowance for their recently widowed mothers, or to get a War Service Grant, or to claim travelling expenses to Timbuctoo and back. Then there is the perpetual pestering on the subject of Credits—with a capital 'C.' The chief thing to bear in mind about a Credit is that, in ninety-nine cases out of a hundred, it isn't."

He spread his hands and placed his fingers together, mock-judicially.

"Let me give you an example of the tangled messes into which men can get their personal affairs. A man married a woman who had already had three children by his brother-in-law—his sister's husband. In due course, he was called up and family allowance was granted to his wife and the three children. When he went home for his first leave, he found that his wife was living once again with his brother-in-law. He looked on this arrangement with an unkindly eye, principally because his brother-in-law was taking his whack out of the family allowance. On the grounds of serious misconduct on the part of his wife, he managed to get the family allowance discontinued. Six months or so later, he was back in the home town on another spell of leave and, quite by chance, fell in with his wife in a pub. She told him that she was on her own for the time being, as his brother-in-law was in gaol for forging a signature in a Savings Bank book. The conversation drifted from one thing to another—and the outcome was he went home with her and they spent the rest of his leave as man and wife."

"A reasonably happy end to the affair," I smiled.

"To the contrary. It was far from being the end of it. No sooner had he reported back to this unit, than his wife wrote to the Paymaster, claiming that a reconciliation had been effected and asking for a resumption of the family allowance. When asked for confirmation, the soldier very definitely disagreed. You can see his point of view, of course: immediately on release from prison, that wolf in sheep's clothing, the brother-in-law, would be up to his old tricks again and—if family allowance had been resumed meanwhile—they would all be back where they had started. Yet, on the other hand, going back to live with his wife was an implicit act of reconciliation by the soldier."

"A tricky point," I said.

"Don't think," said Paul, "that it's just a hypothetical case. The soldier is on the strength of this Battery and is, at the present moment—" he swung round to consult a sheet drawing-pinned to the wall—"listening to a lecture on 'Observation of Tracer.' His name is Jennings. There's a letter come in today from the Paymaster on the subject. It requires an answer."

I rose to my feet.

"If it's all the same to you," I said, with a smile to show that I didn't mean it, "I think I'll go back on the guns!"

IV

Without any prompting from me, Paul reverted again to the subject of the Sergeant-major before the morning was over.

"Remember this, Peter," he said. "As long as the B.S.M. treats you like a piece of the Battery Office furniture, you're safe. But when he starts getting over-friendly, beware. I'm only going on what I've heard about him, because I've only known him a few weeks, but they say that, once he gets a grievance against you—imaginary or otherwise—he immediately becomes extremely chummy. Then when you're preening yourself in the sunshine of his smile and telling yourself that all that had been needed was a strong hand, he strikes."

He gave this caution time to sink in before he went on: "This last week he's been showering his favours on a ginger-headed gunner in the Q. stores whose name is Fieldhouse. I've no idea how Fieldhouse overstepped the mark, but"—he flashed a glance at me—"if I were a friend of his, I'd warn him to look out for squalls."

I was afraid Paul was right. But I had tried warning Johnny before.

CHAPTER FOURTEEN

I

A FORTNIGHT after my arrival at Boxford, the Regiment proceeded—as Johnny's tobacconist had forecast that it would—to firing-camp.

It was situated on a desolate strip of the Norfolk coast and we christened it the Slough of Despond. From the other descriptions that our predecessors had scribbled on the walls of the latrines, we were not alone in our dislike of the place. We were there four weeks—four of the most uncomfortable weeks I have ever passed, Borstal, Mark II included. The rain fell steadily every day, the camp was a sea of mud and there were no duckboards. The nearest town was four miles away. There were no buses and Army transport was provided only on Sunday evenings. The Nissens were as watertight as colanders. Among the many other vexations of the place was a special blackout device fixed to the door of our Battery Office. It switched out all the lights in the hut whenever the door was opened; and as the days were dull, the evenings beginning to draw in, and men were passing in and out every two minutes or so, the result was nerve-racking. The remark most frequently heard in XYZ B.H.Q. during those four nightmare weeks was:

"Shut that——door!"

But for the gun-detachments, our stay in the Slough was invaluable. They were firing the guns for the first time in their lives. No longer did Nos. 5 and 6 scamper about like Egyptian dancers with imaginary clips of fairy ammunition held upright between their separated palms. The ammo. was now real and very heavy; it went off with a gratifying explosion when No. 4 brought his foot down on the pedal. The target (called a "sleeve") was of red silk and it was towed along by a plane. The cable was several hundred yards in length, yet I did not envy the pilot his job, for inexperienced gunners will have a crack at anything in the sky— even a seagull.

By the end of the four weeks, I had settled down in my new position. I had learnt the difference between a qualifying allotment and a contributory allotment. I knew the sinister meaning of "compulsory stoppage" and "5 days' ordinary pay and 2 days' pay by Royal Warrant." I could deal adequately with kit charges, travelling allowance, subsistence allowance and War Service Grants. I had even managed to get a grasp of double-entry book-keeping.

II

There was one tragic incident.

The Battery parade at 08.00 hours was continued at firing-camp. The ceremony has already been described fully, so there is no need to go into all the details of one Saturday-morning parade about a fortnight after we arrived in Norfolk. As B.H.Q. personnel were exempt from parades, I myself was not present, but I got the gen. afterwards from Chris Wilkinson, who had been in the front rank of "C" Troop, and Postbechild, who had been in the front rank of "A" Troop. This is what they told me, Chris over after-lunch coffee in the Naafi, and Postbechild later in the day.

Chris Wilkinson said: "When Sgt. Nelson called 'C' Troop roll, Gunner Owen didn't answer to his name. The B.S.M. called for the reports. 'A' and 'B' were all present. When it came to our turn, Sgt. Nelson shouted, 'One man absent, sir!'"

Sgt. Nelson was the most popular N.C.O. in the Battery. Young, tall and fair-haired, he combined a gay, carefree disposition with an alert brain. If we had a first-rate soldier in XYZ, it was Jack Nelson.

Postbechild said, in his normal death-warmed-up tone: "The B.S.M. stepped up to that red-nosed little rabbit, Bretherton, who was orderly officer, and reported, 'XYZ Battery all present and correct, sir.' Bretherton passed it on to the Captain, who gave the order for 'A' and 'B' Troop-sergeants to take charge, but 'C' Troop to stand fast."

Chris said: "The troop-sergeants marched 'A' and 'B' off the square. The Captain, with Mr. Bretherton and the B.S.M. trailing behind him, came up to us. We wondered what the trouble was. The Captain took the nominal roll from Sgt. Nelson and ran down the names with his finger. 'Why haven't you ticked Gunner Owen, D., Sergeant?' he asked. Nelson answered promptly in the tone of a man who's done his duty and knows it, 'He's not on parade, sir. I reported one man absent, sir.' The Captain asked, 'Is he sick?' and the Sergeant replied, 'Not as far as I know, sir.' The Captain told him to find out and report to him personally."

III

The Major was away for the week-end. Paul Morton and I were busy at our desks—knowing nothing, of course, of what had just happened on the square—when Blitzgerald came in from the parade, with anger in every stiff bristle of his magnificent moustache, and the B.S.M. at his heels. They swept past us through the general office into the part of the Nissen that had been partitioned off to form a room for the officers. When the door had closed behind them, Paul muttered with a pleased smile:

"Looks as if the B.S.M.'s on the carpet, I hope."

"He certainly looks sheepish," I agreed. "Wonder what he's been up to."

"I hope Blitz doesn't pull his punches," was Paul's fervent wish. "Listen..."

The partition was only of fibre-board, but the two men on the other side of it did not raise their voices sufficiently for us shameless eavesdroppers to hear more than an indistinct mumble of conversation. At last, after five minutes of tense listening, we caught the Captain's final words—and all that had been previously said became unimportant.

"You heard Sgt. Nelson report, 'One man absent' as clearly as I did, yet you were too lazy to find out who it was. All you wanted was to get back to your breakfast. You're the most unsatisfactory sergeant-major it's ever been my bad luck to come up against; and if you don't buck your ideas up, I'll find the means to make you. That is all I have to say. You may go."

We had heard all we wanted. I had the typewriter rattling merrily away when the B.S.M. came out. His expression was not pleasant.

IV

Paul Morton had spoken to me at Boxford of the Sergeant-major's persecution of Owen, D. Since then, I had come to know the man: an inoffensive little Welshman, with the high cheek-bones and curly hair of his race, a pair of pleading, pathetic eyes—like those of a bedraggled fox-terrier that seeks a friend—and a quick sing-song voice hard for an Englishman to follow. He was a bachelor and had been not quite old enough to escape conscription. I say "escape," for that is the only word to use. Had our country been facing the most deadly peril, they should not have called Owen, D. to the colours. They should have left him in his Welsh village—left him to carry on teaching the three R's to his beloved children. He could have done a hundred times more for his motherland in his poky schoolroom in the Rhondda valley than on any battle front.

Sgt. Nelson came into Battery Office fifteen minutes after the B.S.M. had been smartened up in so satisfactory a fashion by Blitz. He studiously ignored the B.S.M., who was moodily sketching squares and triangles on his blotting-paper, and addressed himself to Paul:

"Captain in, Bomb?" he asked.

Paul said: "Yes. Knock at the door and barge in."

The Sergeant was not long inside. When he came out, the Sergeant-major looked up from his doodling—and actually smiled.

"I'm sorry for what happened earlier on, Sergeant," he said. "It was my fault, but my mind was wandering. I've said, 'XYZ Battery all present and correct' so many times that it's become almost mechanical."

"That's all right, sir," said Sgt. Nelson shortly; and turned to leave the hut.

"They've laid on transport for the dance tonight," the B.S.M. told him. "Are you coming?"

"Probably not, sir," said Nelson; and the door of Battery Office slammed behind him.

The Captain emerged from the inner office.

"Bombardier," he said to Paul, "get me the camp commandant's office on the phone."

V

They found Owen, D. along the beach past the gun-park, but still within the boundaries of the camp. His little worn-out body, in soiled denims, lay alongside a breakwater, with his legs drawn up almost to his chin. His face and mouth were horribly swollen, his lips a dead white. And his lifeless hand, filthy from latrine fatigues, still gripped a rusty tin can, in which there lingered a few drops of undiluted disinfectant.

There was the inevitable inquiry. Paul was kept busy for a week typing letters and preparing forms for signature. But at the end of it all, nothing more was officially announced than the verdict of the coroner's jury: that Gnr. Owen, D. had taken his own life while the balance of his mind was disturbed.

A brother, his only relative, was serving with the Royal Artillery overseas. There was no one else to mourn the passing of the little schoolmaster who, with humane treatment—an ironic touch—might have turned into a fighting man.

VI

Within the Battery, of course, the tragedy was the subject of much speculation and argument. On one point, however, all parties were agreed: if Owen, D. had not drunk the disinfectant by accident, but had deliberately committed suicide, it had been B.S.M. Yule who had driven him to it. Even Johnny Fieldhouse and I, who could amicably differ over most things, were of one mind about that. He and I, although the Q. store was in a separate Nissen from Battery Office, were now once again sharing the same sleeping-hut. There were eight other men in with us. One of them was Gnr. Postbechild, who, by the way, was still alive, despite his unceasing assurances of imminent demise. He had been taken off the guns and was being trained as a telephonist, an exacting and important job in a Light Ack-Ack Battery.

Long after Lights Out on the evening that followed the discovery of the body, the discussion continued.

"I ask yer," said the shrill Cockney voice of Gnr. Jennings—he of the family allowance conundrum—from the darkness at the far end of the hut, "What's the two-faced——bin doin' to the poor little——ever since 'e first clapped 'is peepers on 'im at Boxford? Makin' 'is life a——burden, that's what. Owen only 'ad to breathe a bit noisy—and the B.S.M. turned rahnd and put 'im on——spud-bashing."

The melancholy voice of Postbechild was the next to be heard.

"It was murder," he announced. "Deliberate murder." Johnny, in the next bed to mine, took up the point.

"Murder's a strong word. We shouldn't go as far as that. I think myself—"

"Look 'ere, Ginger," the Cockney pulled him up, "just 'cause the B.S.M. treats you a——sight better'n what 'e does most of us, yer got the idea inter that carroty nob o' yours as what the B.S.M. ain't Public Enemy Number——One. Owen was the best-'earted, quietest, most 'armless little——in the Battery—in the 'ole Regiment, if yer like. 'E never turned rahnd and give no trouble ter nobody. For all that, the B.S.M.—"

"I know all that," Johnny interrupted in protest. "The only thing I don't agree with is your suggestion that the B.S.M. murdered Owen. To prove murder, you must first prove intention to kill. Did the B.S.M. intend to kill Owen?"

"Whether he did or not," said Postbechild, who had caused the argument, "he must have known something was wrong on parade this morning, or he wouldn't have done what he did. Cor starve a crow! Can you see the B.S.M. in the ordinary way covering up a——who's missing off parade? If he didn't actually know, he probably guessed that Owen had given himself the works, and was just playing for time, because he could see he was due for a rocket and wanted to think out a way of dodging it."

A new voice broke in on the conversation. It belonged to a gunner who was acting waiter in the W.O.s' and sergeants' mess.

"The Sergeant-major," he told us, "was up at the bar in the mess this evening, when in comes Sgt. Nelson. 'Evenin', Nelson,' says the Sergeant-major. ''Avin' one with me?' Nelson looks 'im up and down cool-like and says, 'No, thanks, sir—I'm not *that* thirsty.'"

"Good fer Nelson!" applauded the Cockney at the far end. "The only sergeant in the Battery worth a tinker's——! What did the B.S.M. 'ave ter say ter that, Nobby?"

"Oh, 'e just said, 'Please yerself,' and went on with 'is own pint."

Another man addressed a question to me:

"Brad, you was in the office, wasn't you, when Blitz marched the B.S.M. off parade? Did 'e smarten 'im up?"

"I didn't hear what was said," I lied; "but the B.S.M. wasn't looking too happy when he came out of the O.C.'s room."

"Blitz don't stand no 'anky-panky," chimed in the irrepressible Cockney. "The Old Lady's dead scared of the

B.S.M., but you see if Blitz doesn't force 'im into getting the B.S.M. posted."

He proved to be wrong. The Sergeant-major was not posted. He remained with XYZ Battery until the day—night, rather—of his death. Owen, D. was soon to be cast out of our minds—not for ever, for some of us were to have occasion to remember him again—because, a fortnight after the Welshman's death, our term in the Slough of Despond came to an end; and the whole Battery went on twelve days' leave.

It was the first leave I had had for four long eventful months, but I did not go home without some visible evidence of military advancement, for I bore, somewhat self-consciously, on my sleeves the single stripes of a lance-bombardier in the Royal Regiment of Artillery. Gnr. Fieldhouse, J. sought permission to travel to London in the same compartment. I was graciously pleased to agree.

CHAPTER FIFTEEN

I

ON a dull, bleak afternoon in late November, 1942, Johnny and I descended from the train at the railway terminus, Stalcote-on-Sea.

Our twelve days' leave was over. A good many other XYZ men had come down by the same train, and our noisy greetings on the platform reminded me of the first day back at school after the holidays. Johnny and I fell in with Chris Wilkinson before we had reached the barrier; and I noticed the spruce little figure of Gnr. Gianella a few yards ahead.

Stalcote-on-Sea was in Suffolk, one of those East Anglian towns that had suffered grievously—and continued to suffer—from air-raids. The principal thoroughfare, which was long and straight, was Corporation Hill. The sea-front was at its eastern foot, and the railway terminus was across the top of it, so that when one emerged from the station into the yard, one looked over the low wall that bounded the yard, straight down Corporation Hill to the sea.

I followed Johnny and Chris out into the yard. XYZ men were wandering about, looking, as gunners do, for someone to tell them where to go, what to do and how to do it; and others, with a sprinkling of civilian passengers, were pressing out behind us.

The cheerless day did nothing to soften the harsh outlines of wrecked buildings, shattered by high explosives or gutted by incendiaries. Away to the left was a church, with only the pitiful stump of what must have been a magnificent spire. As far as the eye could see down Corporation Hill, shop-fronts were boarded up; and in the station behind us, few of the glass roof-panes were still intact.

I saw no traffic in Corporation Hill. Council employees were sweeping the pavements clear of splintered glass; and, further down the hill, the front of a building had collapsed. The whole roadway was piled with bricks, plasterwork and jagged floor-joists. A gang of men was working on it; some on top of the pile, others shovelling the debris on a couple of motor-lorries. The pavement opposite the bombed building had already been cleared, and a policeman was posted there to direct the pedestrian traffic.

"Pretty recent," I said to Johnny and Chris. "We must have just missed it."

"Looks as if we're going to have a lively time here," grunted Johnny. "Why didn't they start us off in some quiet place where they have raids just occasionally—say the third Saturday in every month? Then the detachments could get their hands in before taking on the big stuff."

"Don't ask me," Chris Wilkinson answered, somewhat impatiently for him. "I didn't arrange—"

He stopped in mid-sentence. The sirens were beginning to wail.

Almost before the nearest of them had reached its crescendo, Jerry was on us—a single Focke-Wulfe that zoomed down out of the seaward clouds and roared the length of Corporation Hill at roof-top level, with its machine-guns chattering viciously.

It was coming straight at us. Soldiers, civilians, women and children were scattered about the station yard. The first instinct was to run—to get somewhere else; somewhere out of the way of those death-spitting guns.

I saw the policeman go down with his hands clutching his stomach. Two of the workmen pitched from the top of the rubble and lay sprawled on the roadway.

In the station yard, there was a mad dive for the low boundary wall. Those too far away from it threw themselves flat on the ground.

Johnny was sprawled beside me behind the frail brickwork.

"A nice state of affairs!" he grumbled.

The shrill, terrified voice of a child slewed us round. A little girl of five was standing alone, crying, "Mummy!"

Johnny was before me. In a flash he was up and running.

But another gunner got to her first, whisked her off her feet and was down on the ground with her beneath him.

It was the little barber, Gianella.

II

Such was our introduction to East Anglia. Besides the civilian casualties, three XYZ men finished their lives that November afternoon in the station yard at Stalcote. One of them was Gnr. Jennings, whose Family Allowance conundrum thereby found an answer.

Gianella got a bullet through the shoulder, but his charge was unharmed. Chris and I came through without a scratch—and so did Johnny, although he had been still running when the guns had sprayed the yard and bullets had ricocheted with a wicked whine off the flagstones.

It was quite a normal occurrence in Stalcote. The inhabitants claimed to have got used to it. If they had, they were made of sterner stuff than I. Jerry was over at all hours of the day and night, and it was seldom that a day passed without XYZ's guns joining their big brothers, the Heavies, in pumping shells into the sky. The unrepentant Hun's favourite time for a social call was early in the morning, when he could swoop down, with the sun behind him, and raise half a minute's hell before the guns could get at him. When the brief engagement was over and the D.Cs. gave the "Stand by direction ..." order, the guns were always laid on the sun.

All the advantages were on Jerry's side, yet he did not always get away. In fact, we had not been two days in Stalcote before two of our guns caught a Dornier in cross-fire and sent him blazing into the sea. That was on the 24th November, 1942. The date is worthy of particular mention because a year later, to the day, B.S.M. Yule met his death at the hands of a member of the Battery.

III

I did not enjoy those six months at Stalcote-on-Sea. The Regimental Paymaster's letters still had to be answered, even though it was hellzapoppin' around B.H.Q. Johnny had said that the Captain put Brens before pens. Before we left Stalcote I was fully in agreement with Blitzgerald, the fire-eater. Against a Dornier or a Focke-Wulfe there is not much defensive merit in a typewriter or the Royal Warrant For Pay.

There were disasters at Stalcote. The first of them was in the early spring of 1943, when an enemy bomb utterly destroyed a detachment of "C" Troop—gun, men, huts, everything. As far as this is a chronicle of the events that culminated in the ghastly death of the Sergeant-major, there were two others.

The first concerned Sgt. Nelson, the innocent cause of the Captain's blunt warning to the Sergeant-major. That Jack Nelson was innocent there can be no disputing. Two hundred men could bear witness to his having reported one man as absent that Saturday morning on the square in the Slough of Despond; and many of those same two hundred could testify that the B.S.M. had failed—whether deliberately or not—to pass on the information to the orderly officer.

That was Nelson's only crime. There was no other discoverable reason for the B.S.M.'s subsequent treatment of Nelson. I had mentioned to Paul Morton the morning after the incident that, in fairness to the B.S.M., I had felt that Nelson could have responded with a better grace to the B.S.M.'s undeniably complete apology. Paul had answered:

"Do you remember I once told you that when the B.S.M. goes out gunning, his first precaution is to make friends with the prospective victim?"

I had nodded.

"And do you remember I explained that I was only passing on the information; that I had had no first-hand experience?"

"Yes."

"Well, one of the men who had given me the warning was Sgt. Nelson. Now do you understand?"

So Jack Nelson was on the Sergeant-major's list. He was an eminently efficient troop-sergeant; his record was without blemish; and he was the best instructor in Ack-Ack gunnery that the Battery possessed. But he had given Blitz Fitz an excuse to rap the knuckles of the B.S.M.; and Yule was a man who did not readily forget.

The power invested in a sergeant-major is formidable. Within certain wide limits, his authority cannot be challenged, even by those who are his senior in rank. And when that power and authority are used without scruple to achieve a contemptible and petty revenge, what hope can there be for the victim?

The plan was carried out very cleverly, not too hurriedly. Paul Morton and I, who liked Nelson, were helpless onlookers, noting every move, but without being able to do more than drop a hint to Nelson when duty brought him to B.H.Q. With a grim smile on his handsome young face, he agreed with us that the storm-clouds were gathering.

The very nature of an Ack-Ack Battery deprives it of one valuable characteristic: compactness. Unlike the Army unit known in R.A. circles as an infantry mob, the men that go to make up a Battery are never congregated on one spot; they are dispersed over a considerable area. Some gun-sites may be twenty miles or more away from B.H.Q.; and the personnel of "A" Troop may not see their friends in "C" Troop for months, sometimes not from one main operational move to the next.

With this scattered distribution, efficiently administered local centres of control are of the greatest importance. That is the function of a troop headquarters—or, more usually, T.H.Q.—with its quota of officers and its troop-sergeant. A troop-sergeant's task is no sinecure. He must be a Jack-of-all-trades, equally expert at gunnery, pay and welfare problems, the tracing of missing laundry, the identification of aircraft and the preparation of a nominal roll of all left-handed Presbyterians born on a Tuesday—or any other return for which an inventive and capricious higher formation may call. Such a man, with a finger in so many military pies, will, not unnaturally, make a mistake now and again. The error may be small and unimportant, but a wily sergeant-major at the elbow of the O.C. can make a Star Chamber matter of it.

Week after week, Sgt. Nelson's stock gradually went down.

The B.S.M.'s pally attitude towards him never altered. Always he was assuring Nelson (I heard him) that he himself had done his very utmost to temper the wind to the shorn lamb; to put in a good word for Nelson with the Old Lady. The Sergeant listened obediently—and waited for the climax.

The first main event was when Nelson was removed from T.H.Q. and put in charge of a gun-site. The Captain stood out against it with all the power of his healthy lungs (I heard *him*, too), but the B.S.M. had such ascendancy over Major Mellis that he got his own way. B.Q.M.S. Ackroyd, that outspoken Yorkshireman, shared the Captain's opinion and did not hesitate to tell the Sergeant-major so.

But that was not the climax. Nelson had been discredited. The next step was to see that he was disgraced. Paul Morton and I waited apprehensively. We did not have to wait long.

There is no need to go into all the details of the final treachery. It is enough to say that, as a result of misleading orders by telephone, the gun for which Sgt. Nelson was wholly responsible was stripped down for cleaning and oiling at a time when readiness for action was vital.

There was no evidence to show that the instructions had been deliberately misleading. There was only Nelson's word against the Sergeant-major's that they had even been misleading. The High-Ups appeared to take the view that if Sgt. Nelson could not be depended upon to act correctly on a simple telephone message, he was no use as a D.C. The outcome of the miserable affair was that Nelson, the Battery's smartest sergeant, reverted to the rank of gunner and was cross-posted to XYY, another Battery in our Regiment, thirty miles along the coast.

Paul heard the B.S.M.'s last words to Nelson on the morning that he left.

"I'm b——sorry about this, Nelson," he said, "but you can see how I was placed."

IV

That was serious enough; the second affair was even more unpleasant. It happened in May, 1943, just after I had been made up to full bombardier.

Our B.H.Q. at Stalcote-on-Sea was in the residential district of the town; three detached houses in a row. The owners had fled from the air-raids in the early days of the war, leaving their homes at the mercy of the bombs, the elements and—an even greater menace—the requisitioning authorities. "Derwent" was the Battery Office, "Clovelly" the officers' mess and "Sea View," the largest of the three, was used for sleeping and feeding other ranks. The intervening garden fencing had been pulled down, and on the plot so formed huts had been erected to house the Battery's transport and motor-cycles, the quartermaster's store and the overflow of beds from "Sea View."

On that night in May, Chris Wilkinson, now a lance-bombardier and B.H.Q.'s mail-cum-medical orderly, was orderly N.C.O. It was his duty to be on hand should anything arise, and to do a turn at the switchboard between 20.00 and 21.00 hours, while the telephonist went to supper. Johnny was on fire picquet—one of the three gunners whose movements were restricted for twenty-four hours to the immediate neighbourhood of B.H.Q. and who reported to the orderly N.C.O. as soon as the sirens wailed.

The general office was in the front room of "Derwent"—probably the dining-room of its peace-time residents. The back room, with its french windows, contained the elaborate switchboard that connected B.H.Q. with the complicated network of air-defence communication.

At 20.00 hours to the tick—Chris was always punctual—Postbechild handed over the switchboard and went off to the Y.M.C.A. at the end of the road for a snack and a couple of games of table-tennis. Chris Wilkinson was left alone in "Derwent"

At 20.15 hours, he heard footsteps in the uncarpeted hall. The door of the telephone-room opened and the Sergeant-major poked in his head.

"Who's on fire picquet, Bombardier?" he asked.

"Mullins, Fieldhouse and Lloyd, sir," Chris told him.

"Go and find Mullins—no, Fieldhouse. Fetch Fieldhouse. There's a job I want done at once. I'll look after the box of tricks till you get back."

Chris hurried off to the Y.M.C.A., where he knew Johnny was to be found. There was no wrong in Johnny's being there, for the fire picquet were allowed as far as that, provided they doubled back to B.H.Q. immediately they heard sirens or gun-fire.

Johnny was playing table-tennis. He had beaten Postbechild in their first game, and they were half-way through the second when Chris intervened with:

"B.S.M. wants you, Fieldhouse."

Johnny threw his bat on the table.

"Blast the B.S.M.!" he said, but obediently returned with Chris to B.H.Q.

The Sergeant-major was waiting for them in the hall, with the inevitable cigarette between his nicotine-stained lips, and his hands in his pockets. Chris went back into the telephone-room, closing the door behind him, while Johnny followed the Sergeant-major into the general office.

Less than two minutes later, as Chris testified at the court-martial, the Sergeant-major shouted angrily:

"Keep your hands off me!"

Chris rushed out into the hall. The door of the front room was open. Johnny and the Sergeant-major were struggling together in the centre of the office.

"Get hold of him, Wilkinson!" the B.S.M. panted. "He went for me!"

V

Johnny was held in close arrest until the court-martial. On the charge of threatening and striking a warrant officer, he was sentenced to one hundred and fifty-six days' detention.

Little Johnny Fieldhouse, with his eager, freckled face.... One hundred and fifty-six days in the glasshouse.... Twenty-two weeks of hell for hitting that slinking, sadistic rat....

The previous evening, Johnny and I had gone to a dance.

They still held dances, even in bomb-blasted Stalcote. I had great difficulty in getting Johnny to accompany me, for he was still immensely girl-shy; and even though he did eventually come, he did no more than sit out watching.

We walked back together afterwards. The sirens had gone half an hour before, but nothing had happened. As we strolled along, with that curious sensation of a general silent awareness that possesses one during an alert without gun-fire or bombs, I gently pulled his leg over having been a masculine wallflower all the evening.

"In the first place, Peter," he replied, "I can't dance; in the second place, I don't want to learn. Dancing is the capering of imbeciles or savages. Cannibals dance round the stew-pot while the missionary's being brought to the boil."

"I'd like to see the B.S.M. simmering gently over a slow fire," was my unchristian wish.

"Why bring that up?" Johnny complained. "He gives me the creeps. Getting behind those dead eyes of his would be like turning over a stone in the back garden—all crawly. He worries me, you know, Peter. He's too darned fulsome. I'm always being reminded of the last line of that Limerick, 'The smile on the face of the tiger.' I do wish he'd leave me alone, because the outlook for me in the Battery is pretty promising. The Q. told me the other day that the O.C.'s considering making me up to quartermaster's-bombardier."

"Good luck to you!" I said. "It's about time they gave you a stripe or two."

"It'd be fine, wouldn't it?" he said. "Yours make me green with envy, but you're always the type that succeeds, while I'm the poor devil who, with the best intentions in the world, invariably fails. But let's talk about something else, Peter."

"What shall it be—'a love-song or a song of good life'?"

He capped the quotation rather too readily for my taste.

"'A love-song; a love-song!' But I don't think you'd be really interested in my serenade, Peter, because you've never met the lady on the balcony."

"I told you to forget her," I reminded him with unnecessary roughness. Hazel Marjoram was an unwelcome topic with me.

"I'll never do that, Peter. She's the only girl who ever meant anything to me—or ever will. When I get back to Civvy Street, I'm going to hunt her down and marry her."

"Cave-man," I murmured.

"I didn't tell you," he went on, disregarding my taunt, "because if I had, you'd have called me all kinds of a fool; but when we had leave from the Slough of Despond, I went down to Burntash every—I went several times. I was hoping to catch sight of her, even if we couldn't speak. On the last day of my—that is, the last time I went, I took my courage in both hands and stopped another At as she was coming away from camp. She remembered Hazel and told me that she'd been posted away from Burntash a couple of months after we left. She thought it was to Ipswich...."

We walked on in silence until he added:

"Funny how a night like this, when the stars seem twice as big as usual—more like silver globes than bright pin-points—you get a feeling of—longing. There's something terribly important to you—and it's not there. Oh, I know it sounds like a popular song, Peter, but that's the way I feel about Hazel. One of these days I shall find her...."

I asked after a space: "Do you remember the verse you marked in the *Omar* you gave me?"

"Did I? It's a dreadful habit to get into—scribbling in margins. I've tried to cure myself. What did I mark?"

"The verse that begins, 'There was a Door to which I found no Key.'"

"Oh, that was nothing to do with Hazel—except indirectly. I marked it a long time ago. It was really only the first two lines that struck me: 'There was a Door to which I found no Key; There was a Veil past which I could not see....' I've found the key now, Peter."

We turned the corner by the Y.M.C.A.

"I bought another *Rubaiyat*," he said, "but it's a different verse that I've bracketed this time—

Ah, Love! could thou and I with Fate conspire
To grasp this sorry Scheme of Things entire,
Would not we shatter it to bits—and then
Re-mould it nearer to the Heart's Desire!"

At the gate of "Sea View" we paused, for I slept in the house while Johnny had his bed in one of the huts at the rear.

"The B.S.M.'s got me a pass for next week-end," Johnny told me before we parted for the night. "I'm going to—to Ipswich."

It was on the tip of my tongue to reply: "'Beware of the Greeks when they bring gifts.'" But I forbore.

The next evening, in its shadowy, blood-spattered parlour, the spider struck.

CHAPTER SIXTEEN

I

SITTING at lunch with my mother, towards the end of my second spell of leave from Stalcote-on-Sea, I heard the crash of a bicycle flung to rest against the garden fence, the shuddering thud of the front gate as it hit the wooden border of the lawn, and the shrill whistling of "On the Road to Morocco" as the siffleur marched noisily up the garden path.

I swallowed back an Army phrase. If I read the evidence aright, the sounds meant only one thing: a telegram. Certainly I had but two more days of freedom, but every moment of leave is precious. I did not want to be dragged back before my time.

The wire, however, contained no curt recall. There was to be no shortening of my leave. Instead of reporting back to Stalcote by 23.59 hours on the next day but one, I was to rejoin the Battery at Cowfold Camp, Sheep.

"So XYZ have left Stalcote?" said my mother when I had read the message aloud.

It was one of those questions that mothers—the dear creatures—are forever asking, yet had it even called for a reply I should not have given it just then, for I was sitting dumbfounded at my good fortune.

Sheep, of all places! North Wales, Surrey, Derbyshire, Norfolk, Suffolk—and now Sheep. Right on my very door-step—well not exactly, for my doorstep was, by rights, at Hampstead; but on my adopted doorstep. Sheep, that most delectable of all villages, a few miles from Lulverton, where I had pursued the calling of detective-constable and had passed five happy years. Now I was going back there, not as a plain-clothes man, but as a Battery pay-wallah. Inspector Charlton and Sgt. Bert Martin were going to get a surprise when I called in at Divisional Headquarters to announce myself as a new neighbour. There would be plenty to talk about. I had not seen either of them for—how long was it? It was now early June.... Just over eleven months.

"Why are you smiling to yourself?" enquired my mother.

This time I answered.

II

Lulverton, on the seaward side of the South Downs, looked much the same as when I had left it; still as ugly and bustling and as intent on its own affairs as ever; still with the tall red chimney of its rubber-heel factory belching black smoke. Despite its nearness to the coast the town remained, as far as I could see, undamaged by enemy bombs. When I heard later of the V.P. that it was the Battery's duty to defend, I was even more surprised at the tolerance of the foe.

The anticipation of renewing old friendships had brought me down from Waterloo long before the 23.59 hours recorded on my leave pass. There was plenty of time for social calls in Lulverton before catching the bus to Sheep.

Inspector Charlton and Sgt. Martin were taking a cup of afternoon tea together when I breezed into the Inspector's room. A broad smile spread over the Sergeant's cheery, red face.

"Well, I'll be blowed!" was his welcome. "If it isn't a soldier!"

Martin, at fifty-two, had lost none of his old vigour. His sandy hair was thinner, perhaps, than when I had first met him, but he was the same old humorous fellow—a Camberwell Cockney and proud of it. I noticed that he had got himself a new blue suit.

"Hullo, you old sinner!" I grinned back; then turned to the Inspector: "Good afternoon, sir."

One would not have imagined that he, too, was over fifty. Admitted that his thick, brushed-back hair was grey, but there was still a youthful vitality about every movement of his well-built frame and a controlled power beneath the deep well-modulated voice. Wrongdoers did well to beware of that voice; it had in it a comforting, reassuring, almost hypnotic note, lulling the hearer so easily into a sense of false security. It was little wonder that they called him the "Doctor"—his bedside manner was perfect.

He had laid his cup and saucer on the desk when I came in. Now he got up and came across the room to shake me by the hand.

"Glad to see you, Peter," he smiled. "You're looking very fit."

"And a couple of stripes, eh?" said the Sergeant. "They make 'em up to corporal pretty quick in this war!"

"Bombardier, please," I corrected him. "Call a bombardier, 'Corporal'—and you've made an enemy for life."

"Sorry," said Martin with a wink at the Inspector, "but in the last scrap I was in the *Army*. The Boche never put the fear of death in us 'alf so much as what our own gunners did. P'raps it's different this time. Which mob are you in—Field, Coast or what?"

"Light Ack-Ack," I told him. "One of Mrs. Bofors' little boys."

I passed a pleasant hour with my two old friends. Our talk was largely concerned with local gossip and personal news. There was only one part of it that I afterwards had cause to recall. I had been telling them something of my duties in Battery Office.

"Funny thing!" chuckled Martin. "You saw more active service before you was called up than you did after!"

"How is crime?" I asked him.

"Pretty steady. Not much of the big stuff. They're all too busy on war work to find time for murder. Murder's a peace-time 'obby."

"I don't agree with you, Martin," the Inspector said. "War plays the devil with people's nerves—and with their morals. The newspaper headlines are not so charged with homicide as in pre-war days, but if you read the papers thoroughly you'll find scores of references to sudden death not caused by enemy action. Things have been quiet around Lulverton this last month or two, but that's not to say that they'll continue so. There's more than one powder-keg just waiting for a spark. I know of one case, for instance..."

We waited for him to go on.

"She's a very lovely girl. She lives at—well, not very far away from here. Her husband's a prisoner of war in Italy. ... One of these days—and that day may not be very far distant—he's going to come back home, to find that the wife he adores has..." He shrugged his broad shoulders. "She's pretty blatant about it, too. Can you imagine his reactions, Peter? After dreams in a concentration-camp of a loving, faithful wife, loyally—what does the song say?—'carrying the torch,' there comes blessed freedom.... The voyage to an English port.... The train that doesn't go fast enough.... The reunion, ecstatic on one side, guiltily reserved on the other.... And finally—what?"

"'E goes out gunning for the other fellow," said Martin, "and there's another little job for us."

The Inspector said, "There's been more than one other fellow."

"In that case," Martin decided briskly, "we'll call it a contract."

"What's her name?" I asked.

He shook his head.

"Then do I know her?" I persisted, for all this mystery was tantalizing.

"No, Peter," he answered, "I think not. For your sake, I hope you never do."

III

I caught a bus outside the public library. It took me eastward, along the Eastbourne road, through Etchworth, the ugliest village in southern England, and on to Sheep, where, after I had followed the other passengers out, it swung round for the return journey to Lulverton.

"Sheep village"—the quotation marks should be sufficient indication that this description is borrowed from another source—"had been enriched by civilization, but, unlike Etchworth, it had not fallen victim to the jerry builder. There is probably no other hamlet like it in England. As one came into it from the direction of Etchworth, the village green, with its lovely old chestnut trees, spread out on either side of the road in two almost perfect half-circles. Separated from the grass by curving pathways, just wide enough for a grocer's van, were the two rows of thatched, half-timbered cottages. The last on the right, before the road went on to Eastbourne, was the 'Sun in the Sands,' outside which the two buses, red and blue, turned round to go back to Lulverton. Each half of the green, with the cottages skirting it, was independently named. As one faced east, with one's back to Etchworth, to the left was Plestrium Sinister and to the right, Plestrium Dexter. Because of these names, scholars have tried to prove that Sheep is a survival of the Roman occupation of Britain; but although their Latin dictionaries are clear about Sinister and Dexter, none of them has ever traced Plestrium. Maybe it was born in the mind of an idle monk upon some sleepy mediaeval afternoon."

There were two buses when those lines were written. Now there was only one. It had once been blue.

Had I known the exact location of Cowfold Camp I could have saved myself a walk, for it was the best part of half a mile back towards Etchworth. Not that it troubled me. Blackout time was still a long way off; and I had only my small pack, steel helmet and respirator to carry. The rest of my kit had been left behind at Stalcote and had been transported to Sheep—or so I hoped—with the remainder of the Battery's equipment.

Cowfold Camp lay a hundred yards back from the road, from which it was hidden by a clump of beeches. It was reached by a track—one could hardly call it a lane—between two hedges; and it was composed, as I had feared, of Nissen huts. The modern wash-basins and bath in "Sea View" and the solid homeliness of the building had spoilt me for a bedroom of corrugated iron. The beech clump was roughly L-shaped and bounded the southern and western sides of the camp. Between the huts and the western trees was a football field; and in the north-west corner, a hundred yards from the main camp and at the foot of the smooth, steep slope of the Downs, was the officers' mess—a newly painted wooden building, adjoined by the Nissen that housed the two batmen and the mess cook.

The first man I met was B.Q.M.S. Ackroyd, he of the Yorkshire accent and the Cyrano nose. He was standing alone outside the Q. stores, which was the first hut one came to on entering the camp. He gave a broad smile of welcome when he caught sight of me.

"Hullo, Bomb!" he said. "Had a good leaf?"

Most soldiers, for some reason or other, say, "leaf."

"Fine, thanks, Q.," I replied. "So this is where they've brought us, is it? Moves and rumours of moves were in the air when I left Stalcote, but I didn't think it would happen quite so abruptly."

"Aye," he grinned. "We moved out as quick as if th' rent were owing. And did we bustle! Even th' B.S.M. were lending a hand."

Q. Ackroyd and I had got to know each other well at Stalcote. He disliked Yule as much as I did—more, perhaps, for he had been thrown into closer personal contact with him—and being a forthright man and direct of speech, he did not hesitate to air his views about the Sergeant-major, not only behind his back, but also to his face. Yule did not appear to resent it, because, by knowing his job inside out, Q. Ackroyd considerably relieved the burden that a less competent quartermaster would have thrown on the shoulders of the Sergeant-major. If there was one thing that Yule detested above all others, it was work.

We stood chatting for a few minutes, then the Q. suggested showing me round our new home. It was compactly arranged and promised to be quite comfortable—except, maybe, in the winter, when the mud would be likely to rival the Slough of Despond.

Cowfold Camp, as far as this story is concerned, was the end of my Army journeyings; and, as the tale centres around it, I have drawn a rough plan to show the distribution of the huts. It will be noticed that there were no guns. B.H.Q. was entirely administrative and none of its personnel had any direct dealings with gunnery. The nearest gun-site, the Q. told me, was half a mile away, off to the left of the road that led back to Etchworth and Lulverton. It was known officially as A.R. 4 and it was manned by a detachment of "A" Troop. The headquarters of "A" Troop were in Etchworth; a requisitioned house, one of the rough-cast horrors that flanked the long High Street of that unlovely village.

"B.S.M. were saying," the Q. added, "that we could have done with 'A' T.H.Q. ourselves, but there's too many of us."

He was right. It takes a lot of men behind the scenes to keep an Ack-Ack Battery operational. General administration, equipment, clothing, pay, leave, transport, food—all had to be dealt with by B.H.Q.; and its personnel was necessarily too numerous for anything less commodious than Cowfold Camp. Even at Stalcote, with three houses at our disposal, it had been a tight squeeze.

We had not gone far on our tour of inspection, which included a short chat with Scottie, the Captain's Cairn terrier, when Paul Morton sought us out. He was in search of the Q., who was wanted by "B" Troop on the telephone. The Q. hurried off to Battery Office, leaving Paul to ask me all the questions that one has to answer, sometimes untruthfully, on return from leave. Then he said:

"You and I are sitting pretty here, Peter. The Sergeant-

major decided—or the Q. decided for him, more probably—
that you and I should be taken into the sergeants' mess. It was
silly having a mess for just the Sergeant-major and the Q., so
you and I—the only full bombardiers at B.H.Q.—are going
to swell the numbers. We ought to be very comfortable. We've
got half a sleeping-hut between us. Come on, I'll show you."

The sleeping quarters to which he conducted me are
marked 6A on the plan. 6B, as Paul explained on the way,
was used by the Sergeant-major and the Quartermaster, The
Nissen was divided into two by a fibre-board partition. When
we went into 6A, I noticed my kit-bag standing alongside one
of the two beds.

"Glad to see my stuff wasn't left behind," I said.

"We only forgot the stuff that was better lost," Paul smiled.
"You can get rid of a lot of awkward things in an operational
move. The only thing we couldn't lose was the Sergeant-
major."

With eyebrows raised enquiringly, I nodded towards the
partition. It looked flimsy and none too soundproof.

"That's all right," he grinned. "The odious Yule went out
directly after tea and won't be back for hours yet. We'll have
to be careful, though, when he's in; you can hear every word
through that partition."

"Any office changes while I've been away?" I asked with
some diffidence.

One always returns from leave with a nasty premonition
that something unpleasant has happened. Whenever there are
changes to one's disadvantage, they are always arranged during
one's absence, so that one is confronted on one's return with
that most difficult of all situations, a *fait accompli*.

"Nothing that really affects you," Paul said to my relief.
"Regiment sent us along another clerk yesterday. Only a kid
of nineteen and a half." Paul, under the weight of his twenty-
two years, smiled indulgently. A real mother's darling, by the
look of him. Fair, curly hair, a baby face and a rose-bud mouth.

He'd look more at home in a velvet suit than a battledress."

"Appearances don't matter," I said. "The important thing is, will he be any good in the office?"

"Useless," answered Paul with decision. "Beautiful, but dumb. The O.C. asked Regiment for another clerk and they sent us that—that"—exasperation made him blurt the epithet—"that daffodil."

"What's his name?"

"It fits him. Aubrey Lovelock. He's going to be more trouble than he's worth. I gave him a stencil to run off, and he kicked up such a devil of a fuss about dirtying his lily-white hands with the ink that it brought the Sergeant-major out from the other room."

"Was the child suitably admonished?"

"No, he got away with it. The B.S.M. told me to do it myself." Paul shook his head sorrowfully. "It's a bad show when a thing like that happens. It undermines authority."

He had a good deal of authority in B.H.Q., had young Paul Morton. I was responsible for everything to do with pay and leave. Paul did the rest: Part II Orders, the never-ending flood of returns required by Regiment, documentation, general correspondence on anything from Secret to pig-swill; training programmes and A.C.I.'s. Apart from my own section, the only things he did not have a hand in were Q. matters, rations and transport, each of which last two had its own lance-bombardier in charge. It was an open secret at B.H.Q. that Paul and the Q. shared out the bulk of the Sergeant-major's work between them. The only responsibility that Yule never tried to dodge was marching men who were on a charge into the Major's office. The vicious flick with which he first knocked off their caps, and the gusto with which he gave the order, "Accused, evidence and escort, right *turn!*—Quick *march!*" showed that he was enjoying every moment of it. And the stiffer the punishment meted out, the more it pleased cruel Yule.

Paul Morton was looking much better by the time we

moved to Sheep. I remembered him as I had seen him that first afternoon at Boxford: pale, with dark rings under his eyes and a perpetual worried frown. He had worked too hard at Boxford. With the lessening of office drudgery in which my assistance had resulted he had lost his worried expression, and in the seven months that had passed had filled out into a healthy youngster (I can call him that, for I was nearly ten years his senior), more interested in having a good time than spending his evenings grappling with military bumph in Battery Office.

We talked in the hut until it was time for a bite of supper in the mess. The Q. was already there, eating bread and cheese and listening to the radio.

I shared Paul's pleasure in having been taken into the sergeants' mess. It was going to make camp life much more bearable. The mess was partitioned in the same way as our sleeping-hut. The smaller of the rooms so formed had been fitted with a bath, wash-basin and so forth—a great improvement on the primitive sanitary arrangements that prevailed in the rest of the camp.

We got to bed about eleven o'clock and lay talking for some time, part of the conversation being with the Q., whose boisterous tones carried easily through the fibre-board. Eventually we drifted off to sleep. Two hours later I was awakened abruptly, probably by the slamming of the door of 6B. There followed sounds that seemed—in my half-dreaming state—like the opening of the Second Front. Further consideration convinced me that the furniture in 6B was being broken up for firewood.

"What the hell's going on?" I grumbled sleepily.

Paul's voice answered calmly in the darkness:

"The B.S.M.'s come home plastered."

We heard the voice of Q. Ackroyd raised in pardonable annoyance.

"Tha clumsy lout! Don't kick up such a row!"

The Sergeant-major mumbled something that I did not catch.

"I'll talk to tha as I like!" retorted the Q. "Get to bed, tha kalied fat'ead!"

There was another crash; another angry protest from the Q. From the noises and remarks that followed, I gathered that the Q. was forced to get out and help the Sergeant-major to bed. The assistance was resented and strenuously opposed; and it was some time before peace was restored in 6B. We heard the Q.'s wooden bedstead creak complainingly as he climbed back between the blankets. Our quartermaster was a heavy man and I think his bed must have been the noisiest in Cowfold Camp.

Paul called out: "Did you kiss him good-night, Q.?"

"Aye," was the Quartermaster's reply; and the bedstead groaned again as he settled down for the night.

CHAPTER SEVENTEEN

I

THE Battery soon settled down at Sheep and for two months life went on in much the same fashion as it had at Stalcote, except that in Downshire we were comparatively free from air-raids. Jerry came over a good deal at night, but he seldom bothered to unload any of his cargo in the neighbourhood of Lulverton. The Battery's guns lay idle and the detachments began to get browned off—a type of boredom from which they had never suffered at Stalcote. It is a curious twist in human nature that, whereas at Stalcote we had yearned for a less disturbed existence, we now cried out against the peaceful tedium of Downshire. How was it Shakespeare put it? "...they surfeited with honey and began to loathe the taste of sweetness, whereof a little more than a little is by much too much." A stimulating spot of enemy action now and again would have made all the difference. Not too often, of course. To quote Johnny Fieldhouse, say the third Saturday in every month.

Johnny was no longer in the glasshouse. We had had official notification that he had been transferred from the detention barracks to hospital. No other information was forthcoming and, though I wrote to him several times, I received no word from him in return.

Although activity on the gun-sites was negligible, business in Battery Office was brisker than it had been at Stalcote. I cannot speak for other branches of the armed forces of the Crown, but in Light Ack-Ack, no sooner have enemy bombs cease to vex than rockets from Regiment and Brigade begin to burst around you.

In addition to the paper war, there were men posted in, men to be posted out, men to be relegated to Reserve, men to be despatched on courses. There was 927 Jones, C.J., whose mother was complaining of not receiving her dependant's allowance. There was 542 Jones, C. H., who vociferously continued to claim long service and good conduct pay, despite the assurance of both the Regimental Paymaster and the Officer i/c Records that the service of 542 Jones, C. H. had not been long enough, nor his conduct good enough to justify the award. There was 273 Jones, S., who was borne off in an ambulance with a dangerous appendix. Purists will instantly whinny that ambulances do not normally suffer from dangerous appendixes. In this instance, neither did 273 Jones, S. It was 148 Jones, S. who should have been whisked away. In XYZ Battery, it was a full-time job keeping up with the Joneses, to say nothing of the multitude of other affairs to which Bombardiers Morton and Bradfield had to attend.

To begin this chapter, I stated that for two months, existence at Sheep was little different from Stalcote. I put a period to this similarity because, eight weeks after we arrived at Sheep—that is, in early August—life for me underwent a radical change.

Her name was Susan Carmichael.

It is no figure of speech to say that I bumped into her in a Lulverton cafeteria. I did more; I knocked her off a high chromium-plated stool with a red leather seat. The delinquency was not mine. The place was always crowded in the evenings and there was much jostling and elbow-work. I had been sitting next to her and, having finished my sandwich and coffee, was getting off my stool, when some clumsy idiot cannoned into me, caught me off my balance and sent me lurching into her.

The epithet is withdrawn. That burly R.A.F. flight-sergeant shall be the last to be called a clumsy idiot by me, for was it not he—again no metaphor is intended—who threw Susan Carmichael and Peter Bradfield together?

The stool fell sideways on to the floor, but she managed to avoid falling with it by grabbing at the counter. Muttering apologies, I retrieved the stool and set it up again.

"It's quite all right," she smiled, climbing back on to her high perch.

Seeing that no blood was being spilt, the other customers lost interest in us. I looked round for the flight-sergeant and was glad to find that he had peeled off. When it comes to apologizing to gorgeous blondes, we Bradfields need no collaborators.

For she was a blonde. And she was gorgeous. Never in the annals of blondes (which, be it added, are neither short nor simple) was there ever such an exemplar as Susan Carmichael. Earlier in these pages, I confessed to a natural leaning towards blondes. I can claim, therefore, to be something of a judge of them. Yet there I had sat in that Lulverton cafeteria, munching a spam sandwich, while next to me had been sitting the quintessence of fair-haired comeliness!

"I'm awfully sorry!" I said again. "I do hope you're not hurt?"

"Not a bit," she assured me. "It wasn't your fault, anyway. The Air Force sergeant pushed you into me."

"One of those offensive sweeps we read about," I suggested.

To the ill-concealed irritation of several prospective snack-takers who were eyeing it jealously, I got back on to my stool.

"Whoever was responsible," I went on, "your coffee got spilt. Let me get you another."

"But it wasn't spilt!" she smiled. "I'd already finished it."

"If you hadn't," I pointed out, "it would undoubtedly have been upset, so it's only fair that I should replace it."

"There's a flaw somewhere in that argument," she said.

"All the nicest arguments have flaws in them," was my reply.

What was the advice I had given to Johnny at Burntash? It was that the average girl does not much care for sparkling dialogue. For all that, there was I talking like somebody in the first act of "Lady Windermere's Fan." I must alter the wavelength.

But she was laughing. Not just a weak titter. A real laugh.

"You're something quite new!" she said. "Most soldiers can't think of anything better than, 'Hullo, angel!' You begin with an epigram." She looked at me searchingly. "You're not a Nazi spy, are you?"

I exhausted my whole German vocabulary in one extravagant go.

"*Nein,*" I said.

She was not in uniform. She was wearing what is called, I believe, a blue tailor-made. Her hat—well, it was one of those little skull-cap things that give the impression of having been inadvertently sold as finished articles while the needlewomen who had just started on them were away answering the phone. Nevertheless, it was most effective. I was enthralled by the manner in which her hair curled up from under it. Poor Johnny Fieldhouse would have called her too tall. I found no blemish. A short blonde is a mistake.

Over two fresh cups of coffee, the delightful *tête-à-tête* continued, so that when the time arrived when we could not decently prolong our tenancy of the chromium-plated stools with red leather seats, we left the cafeteria as if we had known each other for hours.

With a wealth of experience in such matters, I saw to it that there was no standing about on the pavement outside, saying, "Well..." As the door swung shut behind me, I said in a tone that brooked no dispute:

"Which is it going to be: Greer Garson and Ronald Colman in 'Random Harvest' or Bob Hope in 'They Got Me Covered'?"

"I haven't seen either of them," she admitted.

"One this evening, the other on Saturday," I announced briskly. "I shall be orderly N.C.O. tomorrow. Which one tonight?"

"'Random Harvest,' if you please, kind Corporal," she answered meekly.

"Bombardier," I rasped, and bore her off to the *Odeon*.

II

It was not very late when we came out, but:

"I must run," she said.

"Let's run together," I suggested. "It'll get our circulation back. Which way?"

"No," she said. "Let me go by myself. I—I'd rather."

"Some uncouth fellow might pop his head out from somewhere and say, 'Hullo, angel!'" I warned her.

"I'll risk that. You've given me a lovely evening and now we must say good-night."

"But," I protested, "you can't go wandering round the streets of Darkest Lulverton alone! I ought to see you safely home."

She looked up at me—I was just tall enough for that— and asked softly:

"Are we going to see Bob Hope on Saturday?"

"Why, of course."

And am I going to meet you at seven o'clock?"

"By all means."

"In the cafeteria?"

"Indubitably."

"Well, then," she said; and glided off into the August night before I could even ask her name.

III

Lights Out at Cowfold was at 23.00 hours. For all that, it did not much matter what time we got in, provided it was done with discretion. So, as there was no particular hurry for me to get back, I decided to walk. It was a good distance, but the exercise would do me good. Besides, I wanted to think.

I had always had a fondness for girls. The pretty little things attracted me, much as a Camberwell Beauty or a Painted Lady will enchant a collector of butterflies. There had been scores of girls in my life. I take no shame in the admission, for there was

147

not a mite of harm in any of the dalliance. The affairs were, to quote again from Johnny's No. I poet, "Like Snow upon the Desert's dusty face, lighting a little Hour or two...." No more than that.

Marriage had not appealed to me. I was frankly afraid of it; not of its inevitable responsibilities, but of the unnerving possibility that I might choose the wrong girl and live in misery for the unexpired portion of my three score years and ten. A supper table, with subdued lighting and the lilting strains of balalaikas, was one thing; a breakfast table, with the watery rays of daybreak struggling through the dingy curtains and the strident radio of the people downstairs, was another. For the first, a pretty face and bright small-talk were enough. For the second, something more was needed. Much more.

The question I asked myself as I strode along, with lovely High Down looming under the night sky on my left, was simply this: had I found that which I had been seeking so long? Seeking is too determinate a word. It had not been a planned quest. Rather it had been a subconscious longing for the perfect companion. Had I found her?

Just under four hours.... It was not long to get to know a person. I had been very scornful about Johnny's infatuation. Now I was in much the same position. When it came to the point, I demanded sternly of myself, what was the sum of my knowledge? Her name? I had omitted to enquire. Married or engaged? She wore no ring, which was only circumstantial evidence. Likelihood that such a lovely thing had no ghastly male encumbrance? Microscopic. Would she make a good wife? Undoubtedly. Why? Because of the delightful way she wrinkled her nose. Was that strong enough evidence? Yes (defensively). Further outlook? She had agreed to meet me on Saturday. But would she turn up? How the devil did I know?

I reached camp in a most unsettled frame of mind. I decided that I would lie wakeful and brooding throughout the night. I was asleep within five minutes of getting to bed.

CHAPTER EIGHTEEN

I

Midnight, the little black kitten that the mess had adopted, was wildly chasing a screwed ball of paper round the linoleum when I went into breakfast the next morning. Paul Morton, who was passionately fond of animals, had got him from a Sheep cottager the week before.

The Sergeant-major, the Q. and Paul had already started on their porridge. Gunner Regan from Bootle—surely the most bungling orderly from which any mess had to suffer—had gone off to the cookhouse to fetch the tea, which he had forgotten.

I wished them all good-morning, served myself to porridge from the side table and took my accustomed place. Paul and the Q. were talking shop—all about some kit that one of our men had left in a train. The Sergeant-major, with his back to the door, was at the head of the long table—far too long for just the four of us. The Q's position was at the other end, while Paul and I sat one on each side. The Sergeant-major was eating his porridge in silence and had not troubled to respond to my salutation. He looked very much the worse for wear that morning. His return the previous night, so Paul had told me, had been late and turbulent.

Before I could start my porridge, he took the last mouthful of his, threw the spoon with a clatter into the plate, shoved the plate away from him across the table's bare boards, lowered at me and said:

"Go and find Regan. Tell him if he's not back soon with the——tea, I'll wring his neck."

Obediently I jumped up. Paul was standing at the side table helping himself to bacon and fried bread.

"I'll go, sir," he offered; and was on his way out before the B.S.M. could think of an objection.

The Q. smiled broadly in my direction.

"Who were th' blonde, Bomb?" he asked.

It was futile to hedge.

"What, last night?" I said easily. "Oh, an old flame of mine. I used to work in Lulverton, you know. Where did you see us—at the flicks?"

He rose from his seat to get bacon and fried bread.

"Aye," he agreed. "Good film it were, too. Yours were a nifty piece, though on th' skinny side. I like 'em better plump myself. Not that I wouldn't 'ave taken her on."

"A respectable married man like you!" I chided him. "You ought not to be interested in women."

He speared a rasher with his fork.

"No harm in lookin' 'em over," he grinned.

The Sergeant-major's breakfast had ended with the porridge. He had lighted a cigarette. As the Quartermaster resumed his seat, Yule left his and slumped down in one of the two easy-chairs. He was sitting with his chin sunk in fleshy folds on the collar of his battledress.

Paul came back.

"Regan's on the way with the tea, sir," he said.

A grunt was the only acknowledgment.

Regan, a stumpy dwarf of a fellow with close-cropped hair, large clumping feet and a wrinkled face that always seemed to need a shave, followed Paul into the mess. He was carrying a large tea-pail, filled almost to the brim. He came up behind Yule and dumped the pail alongside the Sergeant-major's chair in such a clumsy fashion that the steaming liquid slopped over on to the floor. The Sergeant-major turned his head.

"You damn fool!" he said. "This is a sergeants' mess, not a soup kitchen. What d'you think there's a teapot for?"

I had been startled myself when Regan had appeared with enough refreshment for twenty men. We had a big teapot for the mess; and Regan usually filled it in the cookhouse. It was the same tea as they had in the other ranks' mess and came out of the pot ready for drinking—that is, with milk and sugar added. The teapot was just a touch of civilization that gratified everyone but Regan.

"Not washed out, sor," said Regan.

"Why not?"

"Homitted to do it, sor."

"Well, go and do it now."

The hut shook as Regan tramped out in his heavy boots.

Q. Ackroyd had brought his plate back to the table.

"Art tha going to A.R. 4 today, Sar'nt-major?" he asked with his mouth full.

Without speaking, Yule shook his head.

"Then it's high time tha did," the Q. informed him with cool rudeness.

The Sergeant-major decided to break his silence.

"I'd thought of going," he said, "but I think I'll go to Lulverton instead. A.R. 4 can wait."

"Tha spends too much time in Lulverton to my way o' thinking," said the Q. "Tha should be taking gun-drill, not wasting time in th' pubs."

A.R. 4 will be remembered as the gun-position nearest to B.H.Q. One of a sergeant-major's duties is to visit detachments at regular intervals, to ensure that all is well with the gun and the site in general. The only means of transport for Yule was a bicycle. The neighbourhood was hilly, the weather hot; and our sergeant-major's excursions from Cowfold Camp were to Lulverton on the bus that had once been blue.

He took no notice of the sharp rebuke. I have already mentioned that he seemed to submit without ill-feeling to Ackroyd's hectoring.

I lighted a cigarette and got up from the table. It would be some time before Regan came back with the clean teapot. Regan would see to that. I looked with longing eyes at the steaming brew beside the Sergeant-major's chair, but I dared not scoop out a cupful. I must wait until it had been transferred to the teapot and thence into my cup.

I strolled to the window alongside the door. Midnight had tired of his ball of paper and was excitedly chasing an invisible prey on the seat and back of the second easy-chair. Through the window, I saw the tall, ungainly figure of Postbechild slouch across the open space on his way to Battery Office. Another gunner was pushing a wheel-barrow-load of coal towards the cookhouse. L/Bdr. Wilkinson was standing by the corner of Battery Office, lighting his pipe. Postbechild paused to exchange a word with him. Chris threw away the spent match.

Behind me the Sergeant-major said suddenly:

"Get off me, you little———!"

Q. Ackroyd laughed in his boisterous way. Midnight had no respect for Army rank.

"Fancy making friends wit' tha!" the Q. jeered; then his voice rose warningly: "*Look out!*"

I whirled round from the window.

But Midnight was in the pail of scalding tea.

II

One man—and one man alone—could say with certainty whether the little black kitten's death was an accident or a foul, deliberate act of cruelty. That man was Yule himself. The only witness was Q. Ackroyd. All he could testify was that Midnight had jumped on to the Sergeant-major's knee and had been caught by the scruff of its neck, to be dropped over the arm of the chair, straight into the tea-pail. The Q. admitted to Paul and me later in the morning, when we fell in with him outside his office, that the Sergeant-major had not turned his head before releasing hold of Midnight; and that had it been any other man than cruel Yule, he would have been the first to recognize it as a pure mishap.

"P'raps he forgot th' bucket were alongside th' chair," he growled, "and then again, p'raps he didn't. Th' merriest, gamest little cat I ever set eyes on. Snuffed out in a———bucket o' boiling char by that—that… One o' these days I'll take a runnin' kick at that fish-eyed Nero!"

To give point to the threat, he drove his heavy boot against the corrugated sheeting with such force that something fell with a crash inside the hut.

Midday dinner was an ordeal. The wistful shadow of Midnight hung over it. The ball of paper with which he had romped while we breakfasted was still lying on the floor. It was strange that three grown men should grieve for a kitten. It was not so much that he was dead that upset us as the manner in which he had died. I was glad that I had not caught the last look of agony in the eyes that, a moment or two before, had gleamed with mischief.

Yule was talkative, with the tense garrulity of one who knows he is in disgrace and endeavours to make amends.

"Q.," he said at one point in his monologue, "I think I'll take your advice and run over to A.R. 4 this afternoon. The Skipper was there on Monday. He told the O.C. that A.R. 4's a bad case of gun-site rot."

The Skipper was Captain Fitzgerald. Gun-site rot is a demoralizing and very serious mental complaint that attacks isolated detachments.

The Q. grunted some sort of reply and got on with his meal. Eventually, as I felt he would, the B.S.M, referred to the death of Midnight.

"Poor little devil!" he said in his loathsome guttural. "He would have been a fine mouser in a month or so. I could kick myself."

I seemed to hear the metallic thud of the Quartermaster's boot against the side of the Nissen.

"That fool, Regan, shouldn't have left the pail where he did," Yule went on, despite our discouraging silence. "I forgot it was there." He gave a forced laugh. "A bit of a hang-over this morning! I'm sorry it happened. I can't say more than that." He looked at each of us in turn before adding defensively, "Can I?"

"I wouldn't have fretted if tha'd said less," was the Quartermaster's uncompromising response.

The Sergeant-major half shrugged his shoulders and filled his mouth with food.

"Accidents happen every day," he declared after an interval of noisy mastication. "A chum of mine in Civvy Street— fellow in the works, as a matter of fact—ran a small car. One morning in the winter he was tinkering with the engine. He had the bonnet up, with the engine running, and as he bent over it the end of his woollen scarf got caught in the fan-belt. The poor chap was strangled."

"Aye," grunted the Q.; "and I'll wager tha were brokenhearted, not bein' there to watch it."

Yule took no notice of the gibe.

"He'd have gone far in the works," he said. "Brilliant, in his own way, was young Templeton."

The Q. paused with his laden fork half-way to his mouth. In spite of himself, he was interested.

"What were his name, did tha say?" he asked.

"Templeton," the Sergeant-major told him. "Alexander Templeton. Why? Did you know him?"

Q. Ackroyd finished the interrupted journey of his fork before shaking his head.

"Wouldn't be th' same chap," he answered. "Th' chap I knew were a tram-driver in Sheffield."

Now that the Quartermaster had broken down the barriers that the three of us had tacitly erected against the B.S.M., Paul and I took up the conversation. In a mess of four members there is nothing between surface friendliness and open, unsustainable war.

CHAPTER NINETEEN

I

SATURDAY began badly.

It was largely the fault of Master Aubrey Lovelock. His official position in Battery Office corresponded to that of an office boy in a civilian business. There was need of a bright, willing youth for all the little tasks that cropped up: to go and tell the Quartermaster that the Captain wanted him; to slip down to the village for paper-clips, or tobacco for the Major; to run off copies on the duplicating machine; to empty the filing-trays on the officers' desks.

Master Aubrey, however, accounted himself above such trifling employment. In fact, he accounted himself above any employment at all. His self-appointed mission in life was to be spotless and beautiful. In my attempt to describe him and his attitude towards the war, I am reminded of the subject of that magnificent outburst of Hotspur's in Shakespeare's *Henry IV*: "...a certain lord, neat and trimly dress'd, fresh as a bridegroom; and his chin new reap'd show'd like a stubble-land at harvest-home; he was perfumed like a milliner; and 'twixt his finger and his thumb he held a pouncet-box... he made me mad to see him shine so brisk, and smell so sweet, and talk so like a waiting-gentlewoman of guns and drums and wounds,—God save the mark!... and but for these vile guns, he would himself have been a soldier."

The blank verse is wrecked by my brutal abstract, but it is hardly necessary to quote the whole long speech.

Sweet Aubrey, loveliest gunner of XYZ, had passed his trade test and had been mustered as an Army clerk, so it was evident that he did have ability and could have shown it had he so desired. But all he wished was to be a graceful parasite. His favourite manœuvre was to play one of us off against another. If Paul needed him for some small task, he was just about to do something for me; if I attempted to enlist his aid, he was on the point of carrying out an order given by the Battery subaltern, Mr. Bretherton. When cornered, he appealed to the Sergeant-major. I cannot recall a single occasion when Yule failed to uphold him.

On the Saturday morning in question, things were brought to a head. One way and another, Paul and I had had a hectic month. Demands on us had been heavy and arrears were beginning to pile up. Soon after the morning's work had begun, Paul called Lovelock over to his desk. Lovelock rose from his place, which was just inside the main entrance door to Battery Office, lounged languidly across the hut, to stand by Paul with his hand on his hip. Paul held out a sheaf of amendments to be pasted in the relative sections of the unit's reference library— King's Regulations and the like. Lovelock took one look at them and backed away with a shocked whinny, explaining that he was looking through the 1941 A.C.Is. for the Captain.

Without a word, Paul got up from his chair, went through the Sergeant-major's empty room and into the office shared by the Captain and the O.C. Paul asked the Captain whether Lovelock was doing a job for him. The Captain shook his head and Paul came out again, to find that Lovelock had made a strategic withdrawal from Battery Office.

Paul was looking round for someone to send after him, when the Sergeant-major entered. He walked straight up to Paul.

"What've you been doing to Lovelock?" he asked, not loudly, but without troubling which of us others heard.

The answer was frigidly polite.

"I asked him to paste some amendments in K.Rs. and, while my back was turned for a moment, he slipped away. I'm sending out to find him."

"Oh no, you're not," said Yule with dangerous calm. "The kid's just come to me. He was nearly blubbing. It's time this persecution stopped, Morton. You'll not give him any further orders till the whole case has been laid before the Major."

"Captain Fitzgerald's in there now," suggested Paul coolly. "The Major's O.C. this Battery," scowled Yule, and slouched into his own room.

As he pulled the door to behind him, the grave-yard voice of Postbechild muttered from the telephone-desk:

"Bit O' luck for you, you two-timing——!"

II

For the rest of the story, I must rely on the Army equivalent of servants'-hall gossip. It is undoubtedly authentic, for if there is one non-commissioned rank in a Battery who knows *le dessous des cartes*, it is an officers' batman. A gentleman has no secrets from his valet; an officer, however much he may deceive himself to the contrary, has no secrets from his batman or, if the batman be of the garrulous type, from the rest of B.H.Q. personnel.

The batman in this instance was Gianella. The wound in his shoulder had healed long since and he now spent his days in a little white jacket, razor-edged trousers and rubber gym-shoes, polishing the officers' belts, serving at table and prattling continuously, like the sleek little magpie that—if any credence is to be placed in the opinions of Pythagoras concerning wild-fowl—in some former existence he must surely have been.

Before retelling Gianella's report, I must write a few lines about Lt. Bretherton. He has been mentioned already as the orderly officer on the morning at firing-camp when the B.S.M. failed in his duty and made an enemy for life of Sgt. Nelson. Mr. Bretherton had, at that time, been a single-pipper (popularly described as the lowest rank in the British Army); but time had passed and he had sprouted another pip on each shoulder. He was young, shy and as harmless as a babe in arms. Unremarkable in appearance—except for the damp redness of his nose, which was more the sign of dyspepsia than the oriflamme of past magnificent excesses—he had been brought in from Troop to B.H.Q. because, having been an accountant, he was sufficiently good at figures to maintain the unit's three accounts—Imprest, Battery Funds and Officers' Mess—in good enough shape to keep the Major and Captain Fitzgerald—a couple of appalling arithmeticians—out of trouble with the Regimental Paymaster and the periodical Audit Boards. His nickname in B.H.Q. was "Mr. Why." It originated from his disinclination to put his signature to anything, however trivial, without first making exhaustive enquiries.

This, in more or less his own words, was Gianella's statement. It was given direct to me that same evening, while the two of us stood waiting in the small bus-queue outside Sheep's only hostelry, the "Sun in the Sands."

"After lunch, it was, Bomb. All three of 'em was in; the Old Lady, my bloke and Mrs. Bretherton's little boy. Scottie was there as well, but 'e didn't 'ave much to say, being a sensible dog and knowing when to 'old 'is tongue. I'd given 'em cawfee, Bomb, and left 'em to it, but it so 'appened that I wasn't fur enough away to miss much of what was said. I wasn't listening deliberate, Bomb, but you can't 'elp *earing*, can you? The Old Lady, 'e was a bit picky. Lunch 'adn't bin all it might 'ave bin; and before that 'e'd bin playing abaht wiv 'is toy windmill— and it always gets 'is goat when that don't work."

I must interrupt Gianella at this point, to throw some light on the piece of electrical apparatus described by Gianella as a toy windmill. It was fixed outside the officers' mess: a tall pole stuck into the ground, with a propeller fixed, on the weather-vane principle, to the top of it. The theory was that the wind turned the propeller, which worked a dynamo, which charged a storage battery, which supplied interior lighting for the mess. That was the theory—and, admittedly, a very sound one; but in practice, the installation was not quite so satisfactory. The trouble was wind—or rather, lack of it. In the long periods between stiff breezes, the storage battery ran down and the officers' mess had to fall back on the ordinary paraffin-filled appliances known in the Services as tilly-lamps, by which all the other huts in the camp were illuminated. But the Major was a man who loved to tinker and was often to be seen perched with a screwdriver and a pair of pliers on the top of the ladder that he had rested against the pole. Not that many of us objected to his innocent hobby; it kept his mind off reorganizing the Battery.

But to return to Gianella.

"'Fitz,' says the Old Lady to my bloke, 'the Sergeant-major 'as mentioned to me the subject concerning Lovelock. It appears from the Sergeant-major's relative remarks regarding the matter as what the boy is being overworked in the office.'

"My bloke snorts like a nasty-tempered 'orse. You could see 'is moustosh bristling up wiv anger. Only in me mind's eye, that was, Bomb.

"'Lovelock,' 'e says in that Bren-gun voice of 'is, 'Lovelock's an idle, entirely useless young'—well, I won't soil me——lips wiv the word 'e used, but you could tell 'oo's side my bloke was on.

"Then the Old Lady turns rahnd and says, 'Be that as it may—'" (I smiled at Gianella's attempt to imitate the quiet, cultured tones of Major Mellis) "'Be that as it may, Fitz,' 'e says, Lovelock's made an official complaint to the Sergeant-major abaht the treatment vetoed aht to 'im by Bombardier Morton and Bombardier Bradfield.' Yes, you was both on Little Lord Fortescue's blacklist, Bomb—and jolly good luck to you, is what I say! Well, the Old Lady says, 'What am I going to do abaht it, Fitz?'

"My bloke laughs scoffin'.

"'*Do?*' 'e says, just like that, like somebody rammin' dahn a gun-picket wiv a ten-pahnd sledge. '*Do?*' 'e says. 'Why, get young Lovelock posted, er course! 'E's nothink but a plebiscite. What we want's a clurk, not a—' I can't repeat the word in mixed comp'ny, but it shows my bloke's got young Lovelock weighed up.

"'I know Morton,' 'e says, 'and I know Bradfield. Two of the nicest, straightest chaps as ever walked.' Yes, that's what 'e said abaht you, Bomb. 'And you're not goin' ter make me believe,' 'e says, 'as what they've bin taking the mike ahter young Lovelock.' 'As Lovelock,' 'e says, 'ever done anythink what you told 'im? First go off, I mean, wivaht you 'avin' ter jog 'is mem'ry?'

"'No,' says the Old Lady, doubtful like, 'p'raps 'e 'asn't.'

"Then my bloke turns rahnd triumphant and says:

"'My advice to you, Major,' 'e says, 'is get 'im posted. And while we're on the subject of unsuitable personnel,' 'e goes on in an o-minious voice, 'what abaht makin' a double event of it and kicking aht Yule at the same time?'

"'What, the Sergeant-major,' says the Old Lady in an 'ushed tone, as if my bloke 'ad suggested getting rid of the Church of England. 'That's rather astringent, ain't it?'

"'It's 'igh time there was a show-dahn,' snorts my bloke. 'The feller's incomparable'—meaning u/s, Bomb. 'E turns rahnd to Bretherton and says, 'Don't you agree, Percy?' Breth chokes over a marthful er cawfee, then manages to say as what my bloke 'as rung the bell; that the B.S.M.'d be in 'is sediment be'ind the bar of a boozer. 'E called it a 'poblic horse,' as if 'e was 'olding it up between 'is fingers.

"Then my bloke chimes in with: "E's u/s on the guns. 'Is knowledge of admensuration is nil, 'e's no idea of discipline and all the men 'ate 'im like——poison.' 'E don't mince 'is words, don't my bloke, Bomb!

"The Old Lady turns rahnd and says, quite uppy for 'im:

"'I ain't prepared to disgust the matter any further. Maybe there's better sergeant-majors than what Yule is, but I'm satisfied wiv 'im. I'll 'ave a word wiv Bombardier Morton this afternoon.'

"'All right!' my bloke turns rahnd and snaps at 'im. ''Ave it yer own way, Major, but don't say I didn't give yer the tip. One of these fine mornings, somebody in this Battery's goin' ter get a nasty surprise.' 'Ere comes the bus."

The last observation was Gianella's own.

III

I reached the cafeteria at ten minutes to seven. It being Saturday evening, the place was jammed. From near the doorway, I scanned the chattering crowd of civvies, soldiers, sailors and airmen, in search of my gorgeous blonde.

A masculine voice behind me said:

"Still carrying on the old trade, Peter?"

I turned to see who it was.

"Hullo, Jack!" I smiled. "Glad to see your ugly old phiz again! No, for the time being, I'm no longer a bloodhound of the law. How's the world using you?"

He gave the reply that nine out of ten always give.

"Mustn't grumble, you know."

Jack Nightingale was an old acquaintance of mine. A farmer of some importance in the neighbourhood, he was a square-built, good-natured, florid man in the late forties, very much under the thumb of his angular wife.

"Times are difficult," he went on, "but things may pick up. Where are you stationed?"

"Cowfold Camp."

"What, XYZ? That's a coincidence! Your Battery's by way of being tenants of mine. One of your guns is on my land, 'way up past the farmhouse. A.R. 4 they call it, don't they?"

He saw from my expression that I was not anxious for a session of careless talk and changed the subject by asking:

"Meeting somebody?"

"Yes," I replied.

"A wench, I'll be bound!" he chuckled. "I remember a thing or two about you in the old days."

"Well, try not to remember them aloud, Jack," I urged him.

"I'll keep mum," he promised. "I'm meeting the missus in half an hour. Thought I'd drop in here for a snack, to fill in the time. I've got some tickets for the *Empire*. You

161

and your lady friend any plans? I've a couple of spares. The Richardsons were going to make a four, but they let us down. How about it?"

"That's nice of you, Jack," I said, not quite knowing whether to say yes or no. "As a matter of fact we hadn't fixed anything definite and—"

I broke off; my gorgeous blonde had come in behind him.

"Hullo!" I smiled a welcome at her over his shoulder.

"You're well on time!"

"I'm always punctual," she said.

Jack Nightingale turned.

"Well," he said, "I must be getting along. Glad to have seen you again, Peter."

And he pushed past her out of the cafeteria.

IV

Susan and I went to the *Plaza* to see Bob Hope in "They Got Me Covered." As we came out, I said:

"Let's not have any of that running-off nonsense this time. The night is yet young, so what about a nibble at a spam sandwich?"

"Lovely idea," she agreed.

So we went in search of food. We did not go to the cafeteria. Somehow, I had lost my liking for the place.

Over our second cups of coffee I said:

"My name's Peter Bradfield. Is yours a secret?"

"No," she laughed. "All my friends know it. It's Susan Carmichael."

"It suits you perf—"

I pulled up dead. I had said that to Hazel Marjoram.

It was developing into a routine.

"Why did you stop so suddenly?" Susan wanted to know.

"I was rendered speechless by the truth of what I was about to say. Susan Carmichael fits you like a pre-war glove. I'm glad we know each other's names now. It would have been awkward, in the long, happy years ahead, to call each other Miss A. and Mr. B. I suppose you are Miss A.?"

My heart sank into my civvy shoes when she answered: "No."

"Why's that?" I managed to enquire.

"I'd be Miss C.," she told me. "'B' for Bradfield, 'C' for Carmichael."

My laugh was far louder than her little joke demanded. "Have you lived in Lulverton long?" was my next question. "You mustn't mind me firing a string of quizzes at you. It's force of habit. I was a detective before I was called up."

She wrinkled her nose at me. "As a matter of fact, Mr. Holmes, I don't live in Lulverton."

"I knew it!" I said. "You're not human. You live in Fairyland and when the clock strikes seven—"

"Five to," she corrected me.

"Clocks," I retorted, "don't strike five to. When the clock strikes seven, you lay aside your wand and—er—gossamer attire, pop on that fetching little hat and—"

"Do I have anything to replace the gossamer attire?"

"Oh, yes," I hastened to assure her. "It's getting nippy in the evenings, even though we're not out of August yet. Of course, if we had a real heat-wave..."

"Go on..." she provoked me.

"You could come bareheaded," I finished. "But joking apart, wherever you live, may I take you home tonight?"

"On one-condition."

It was my turn to say, "Go on...."

"That you don't take me right home, but leave me when— when I ask you to. Will you do that?"

I held my hand aloft.

"You have my word on it," I said solemnly.

"I live," she told me, "at Sheep."

V

There was still time to catch the last bus, but Susan insisted on walking. It was well after midnight before we reached Sheep village.

The moon was up, but from under the chestnut trees on Plestrium Dexter, cool shadows beckoned us. The night was beautiful and there was bewitchment in the air....The minutes flew by, never to return—and with them went the memory of all the other soft lips I had kissed....

At last I had to leave her—alone under the chestnut tree. As I set off along the road back to camp, one clear conviction emerged from the tangled disorder of my mind. For the first time in my life, I was wholeheartedly in love.

Yet my last waking thought was not of Susan, but of Jack Nightingale. Why had he left us so suddenly?

CHAPTER TWENTY

I

"MY friend, Alexander Templeton," remarked Battery Sergeant-major Yule, helping himself to another cup from the pot, "was always one for the women. Couldn't keep away from them."

Two months had gone by. It was a glorious afternoon towards the end of October, 1943, and the usual four of us were having five-o'clock tea in the mess. Yule had been jovial to the point of nausea during the previous weeks. I preferred him when he was moody; it was not such a strain on my powers of dissembling my dislike of him. On that autumn afternoon, his life had just under a month to run.

"Alex—we all used to call him Alex," he went on, "got himself into one scrape after another; but finally he found a good, plain, stay-at-home girl. He married her and settled down in Welwyn Garden City to a life of complete respectability."

We had given up speculating about Yule's odd friend, Alexander Templeton. The first time Yule had mentioned him in my hearing, the unfortunate Alex had been strangled by the fan-belt of his car. From subsequent references by the Sergeant-major, it seemed that Alex had recovered from this fatal accident and had lived on to have adventures whose dullness and lack of point were equalled only by the Sergeant-major's obvious relish in retailing them.

"If Alex had gone on the way he was going," he continued, "God knows where he would have finished up. Yes, he was wild in his youth, was Alexander Templeton."

He turned to B.Q.M.S. Ackroyd.

"Q.," he said, "I was in your stores this afternoon. Everything's a long way from ship-shape. Get the place straightened up, will you? The new Brig. may be around any day now."

"Aye, tha's right," the Q. nodded, reaching for the jam. "'Tis time it were done. I'll see to it, Sar'nt-major. Trouble is I've never had a storekeeper a tenth so good as were young Fieldhouse."

"Fieldhouse..." mused the B.S.M. "Fieldhouse... With so many men passing through the Battery, I don't remember him."

"He was ginger-headed, sir," Paul Morton explained crisply, "and he went to detention for hitting you."

Light dawned on Yule; it was an unconvincing performance.

"Of course! Memory plays some funny tricks, doesn't it? A wicked-tempered young——. Went for me like a mad dog."

"Regiment were on the phone to us about him this afternoon," Paul told him. "They've had word that he'll be reporting back to us from Convalescent Depot within a fortnight."

"B——hell!" burst out Yule. "Why send him back here?"

Paul made no attempt to keep the satisfaction out of his voice when he answered:

"Regiment didn't say, sir."

The Sergeant-major was manifestly shaken. When he spoke again, it was to the Q. on the subject of the untidy stores. A few minutes later, the two of them left the hut together, giving Paul and me an opportunity to settle down for a quarter of an hour in the easy-chairs, which, with one or both of our seniors usually in the mess, we seldom enjoyed simultaneously. For a while we smoked in silence, each busy with his thoughts. Mine were about Johnny.

Then Paul said casually:

"Peter, I'm thinking of getting married."

"Splendid!" I said heartily. "Who's the unfortunate female? Anyone I know?"

"No. She lives at Etchworth and she's perfectly marvellous, Peter!"

"What's her name?"

"Fay Gilbert."

"First I've heard of this," I complained. "You've managed to keep your amours a secret! How long has it been going on?"

"Nearly a month."

"I was beginning to wonder where you sloped off to, four nights out of five."

"She has a widowed mother to look after—a permanent invalid. I met Fay in a café in Lulverton, when I was mooning around by myself one evening."

"You didn't knock her off her stool, by any chance?"

When he shook his head, I was not surprised; the arm of coincidence is not as long as that.

"No," he replied. "It so happened that she couldn't get her cigarette-lighter to work. It needed filling."

"Or a new flint?" I suggested with bright ingenuousness.

"Whatever it was, it was a good enough introduction. Now. I'm trying to pluck up enough courage to propose to her."

"Don't forget the ailing mater," I cautioned him. "If you marry the girl, you'll probably get Mum thrown in. Is the old lady one of the nagging kind?"

"I don't know. I've never seen her. She's always been upstairs in bed when I've gone in with Fay. I—I've never fallen with such a crash for any girl before, Peter. There's a well-paid job for me to go back to after the war. Would you advise me to—"

I raised a detaining hand.

"Oh, no!" I said firmly. "I never give advice in such matters. Whichever way the thing went, you'd blame me. All I'm ready to do is help you drown your sorrows if she won't marry you, or save up to buy you a set of fish-knives if she will. I'll accept no other responsibility."

Paul grinned and was about to reply when the mess waiter came in to clear away the tea-things.

Regan of Bootle had been replaced long since. He had become intolerable. Being an awkward, slovenly fellow was bad enough, but when he decided to work his ticket by embarking on the twitching-face racket in a big way, out he

167

had gone. Now he was jakes-wallah and had plenty of leisure to work out new tricks with his countenance in the seclusion of the boiler-house.

His successor was a Welshman. The attendance he gave us was a vast improvement on Regan's take-it-or-leave-it and— in the later stages—convulsive service. He had two great drawbacks. First, he fussed around the Sergeant-major like an old hen with her sole surviving chick. There was always enough food at Cowfold Camp, but there was far from an abundance, so that when a quartette of hungry men sat down to the amount sufficient for four dinners that had been brought in from the cookhouse, it was irritating to see an undue proportion of it heaped on one plate. Second, his speech was, for the most part, unintelligible. I usually had to ask him to repeat his remarks two or three times before I could get at his meaning. He was tall for a Welshman, gaunt and ugly, a hard and uncomplaining worker and as strong as a horse. His name was Owen.

II

As Paul had informed the Sergeant-major, Johnny Field-house duly reported back for duty. A spell of detention will have its effect on any man; it had had its effect on Johnny. It had aged him. And it had turned him into a soldier. He had lost his youthful appearance. No longer was his uniform worn like a costume for a fancy-dress ball. His movements were drilled, composed and precise. The temperamental, disputatious, fey boy had been changed, it seemed, into a grave, submissive man. The authorities would argue that detention had knocked the nonsense out of him. My own first impression was that it had knocked Johnny Fieldhouse out of him.

There was something wrong with his face. His jaw looked lop-sided, and he scarcely moved his lips when he spoke.

He was put back on his old job of quartermaster's storekeeper. It was not until the next evening that I found the chance of a confidential chat with him. I was setting out to keep an appointment with Susan. As I passed the Q. stores, Johnny came out. We had, of course, exchanged greetings the previous day, so now I merely said:

"Coming for a stroll?"

He nodded and fell in beside me.

I had intended to catch the bus from Sheep, but it was a fine light evening, and if Johnny had anything to confide in me the open road was the best place to avoid eavesdroppers. If we were to walk as far as Etchworth and I caught the bus there, I should still not be late for my date with Susan.

"Bad time, Johnny?" I asked, as we turned into the main road.

His reply was in a dull monotone.

"Yes, for the first month. At the beginning of July I went to hospital. I was three months in hospital, then I went to a Convalescent Depot."

"We heard that you'd been transferred from D.B. Did you get my letters?"

"Yes, thank you." There was no warmth in his tone.

We strode on abreast in silence for a while, with Johnny easily keeping pace with me. There was no need now to suit my stride to his. As we neared the lane that led off to the left to Jack Nightingale's farmhouse and A.R. 4 gun-site, he asked:

"Have you noticed anything wrong with my face?"

"Yes. Was that why you went to hospital?"

The question remained unanswered. When he spoke again, it was almost the voice of a stranger, not the clear, eager, boyish tones that I remembered so well. He seemed to choose his phrases with care, as if he were using a foreign tongue. As the dreadful tale proceeded, he talked with increasing speed, yet not until the end did a passionate resentment colour his words. He began as if he were reading aloud from a book—a book that he did not understand.

"There were five floors. On each floor there were five cages and in each cage there were twenty men. The cages were breast-

169

high brick, then steel-mesh. They were joined together like a row of cages at the Zoo and right round them was a wide space for the staff-sergeants to patrol. I was in the middle cage on the fourth floor. Our food came up in a lift outside the cages and they let us out to sit at tables for meals. There was a large lavatory on each floor. It had no partitions in it. We weren't allowed to talk to each—"

He broke off. We were just passing the end of the lane and I saw that Johnny had turned his head and was looking along it. I followed his gaze.

Coming towards us from the farmhouse was the familiar solid, leather-gaitered figure of Jack Nightingale. He was leading two horses.

Johnny drew in his breath sharply and stopped dead. Then he startled me by turning without warning into the lane.

Taken by surprise, I followed him. Jack Nightingale had paused when he saw us, and stood waiting between the horses, with a bridle in each hand. I managed to catch Johnny up and we reached Jack side by side.

"Good evening, Jack," I said somewhat awkwardly.

He returned my greeting with a dour grunt of which I did not like the sound. He and I had not met since the evening in the Lulverton cafeteria. I was thinking desperately of something else to say, when Johnny asked in a voice that had something in it of the old animation:

"If you don't mind my asking, sir, what kind of horses are these?"

I was obviously out of favour with Jack, but Johnny was evidently not included, for his question was pleasantly received.

"They're a couple of hunters, though there's not much of it to be done these days." He jerked his head to the left. "The mare here, she's Etchworth Lass, and the gelding goes by the name of Etchworth Lad. They're both by Burgeston Boy out of Etchworth Beauty."

"I suppose hunters are much more highly strung than ordinary farm horses?"

"Naturally. You can't have class without the temperament that goes with it."

"Which of these two is the more excitable?"

Jack Nightingale looked at him curiously.

"The Lass. You'll find it's the general way with females."

"Yes, I suppose it is," Johnny agreed seriously. "Is she easy to manage? Doesn't bite or anything?"

"She's docile enough unless she gets a sudden fright. Slow movements and gentle handling—that's the treatment for the Lass—or for any horse, if it comes to that."

"Where do you keep them—in a field?"

Jack jerked his head again, this time to the right.

"In there," he said.

We were all standing near the gate of the field indicated by his nod.

Johnny said with a smile that seemed to cost him an effort:

"Thank you, sir. I'm very much obliged to you for answering my questions so patiently. Good-evening."

He turned abruptly and retraced his steps down the lane, leaving me to take an embarrassed farewell of Jack, who grunted at me for the second time.

When Johnny and I got back into the road and had turned to the left for Etchworth, he resumed his story as if there had been no queer interruption.

"On the last Sunday in June, the staff-sergeant on duty took me off the O-eight-fifty church parade, so that I could help scrub out the lavatory on our floor. There were three other men on the fatigue; two hulking brutes and a spineless little man called Simpson, who was in for desertion.

"Most of the staff-sergeants were on the church parade. The two louts—both long-term men—took advantage of it by leaving Simpson and me to do all the work. I wasn't looking for any trouble, so I said nothing, but Simpson whined a complaint and the bigger of the two knocked him down.

"...Then I went for the swine. I got one in on his ugly face, but he put his twelve stone behind a swipe at me. It caught me on the shoulder. I slipped on the wet floor and fell. As I was scrambling up again, I got a frightful blow on the side of the face. He must have lashed out at me with his boot.

"I didn't pass out, but everything went back like a receding wave and stopped there, as if somebody had suddenly checked the movement of a film-projector. I can remember getting to my feet after a minute or two. My head felt soft and dead, like a lump of putty, and I couldn't get a grasp on what was going on round me.

"That was soon after nine o'clock in the morning. My next conscious thought was at noon, when the staff-sergeant blew his whistle for dinner. I found myself sitting on my bed, holding a towel to my mouth.... I couldn't work out why the towel was soaked in blood....

"As we were filing put of the cages for the food, a staff-sergeant asked me what had happened. I heard my own voice telling him that I had tripped and caught my face against the bed.... I couldn't eat my dinner. It was snatched up by the man next to me.

"Sunday afternoons were always spent cleaning kit and washing oddments in cold water. We each had a bucket that had to be kept so polished and shining that it looked silver-plated. After dinner that Sunday we all filled our buckets and were then locked in our cages until tea-time. Every moment we were watched by the staff-sergeants and we had to work at something all the time, cleaning and cleaning the same few things over and over again....

"I sat on the three-legged stool by the side of my bed, with my head pressed back against the wall. It steadied me. A towel soaked in water from my bucket was against my jaw. I had a boot on my knee and tried to look as if I was cleaning it with the cloth in my other hand.

"A staff-sergeant who had been watching me called me over to the steel-mesh and told me to get on with my work.

But when he saw my face, which was beginning to swell up to a great size, he let me go back and sit on my stool. I didn't have to go on polishing the boot, but just kept it on my knee.

"When tea-time came at four o'clock, I managed to stand up. I don't know how, but I did. I tried to sip some tea, but the blood that got mixed with the first mouthful made me feel too sick to swallow any more.

"We were locked back in the cages after tea and I sat with the boot on my knee until eight o'clock, when we were allowed to stop work.

"I try not to remember those hours, Peter—or the night that followed.... As I was getting out of bed at O-five-thirty Reveille, I just folded up on the floor. They took me off to hospital with comminuted fracture of the jaw...."

For twenty yards, he said no more. Then he went on:

"Sergeant-major Yule sent me into that hell. With no more excuse than that I stopped him once from torturing a mouse, he deliberately did that to me."

"You lost your temper and hit him," I reminded him gently.

There was impatience rather than protest in his reply.

"I didn't lay a finger on him. He told me he wanted a little job done. I said, 'Yes, sir?' and waited to hear what it was. Then he suddenly shouted at the top of his voice, 'Keep your hands off me!' and flung his arms round me, so that when Wilkinson came in from the other room we were standing like boxers in a clinch."

He gave me no time to speak, but went straight on:

"The blackest horror of the weeks in D.B., Peter, was that I was all alone. There was no friend left. I used to lie awake with the dreadful thought that wouldn't leave me, that you— even you—had let me go to... *that*. You couldn't have done anything—I know that now. I knew it all along, but a fellow's not normal in D.B.... I wanted to pound on the wire-mesh and scream till I went mad. They might have taken me away if I went mad.... The only thing I thanked God for was that it was Wilkinson, and not you, who had to give evidence at the court-martial.... I had a fair trial, but they wouldn't believe me. They preferred to believe Yule.... I have now two aims in life, Peter. One of them is to find to be my wife.... The other is... 'An eye for an eye, a tooth for—'"

"Johnny, for God's sake—"

"I'm not asking you to help," he told me calmly. "I've got used to being alone."

III

We reached the bus stop in Etchworth.

"I've brought you on a fool's errand, Johnny," I told him. "I've a date in Lulverton this evening and—well, I can't very well ask you to come along. You see..."

"Another blonde?" he asked, and I caught a flash of his old smile.

"Yes. Dead serious this time, though. Are you going back to camp or will you come on with me into Lulverton and then drift off on your own? I can recommend the film at the *Plaza.*"

He nodded agreement and we waited for the bus together.

It was over-long in arriving, and night had fallen before we reached Lulverton. I could have found my way about the town blindfolded, but Johnny lacked my experience and local knowledge. He switched on his torch. We had not gone far towards the centre of the town, when two pairs of khaki-trousered legs came into the down-directed beam. We might never have known to whom the legs belonged had Johnny not missed his footing on the kerb. The beam jerked upwards and, for an instant, spotlighted two faces.

"Switch that thing off!" said a guttural voice that I knew only too well.

Johnny immediately obeyed and stumbled on in the darkness as if some evil thing was at his heels. Out of earshot of Yule and his companion, he asked in a low tone:

"Who was that with him?"

"Lovelock," I grunted. "Known as Little Aubrey. And if you were to ask me why a B.S.M. of the Royal Artillery spends his evenings with a gunner, I wouldn't know."

IV

The *Palace* was a modern cinema and had a café. Susan would never let me call for her at Sheep and we had fallen into the habit of forgathering in the *Palace* café. Then, if one of us were late, the other could while away the time with a cup of coffee, listening to the little orchestra playing popular classics on the daïs in one corner of the spacious room.

Like a belated chamois, I leapt up the thickly carpeted stairs—cinemas built and furnished in the middle thirties always evoke a feeling of guilt in me; they seem too lavish for these stark war years—and went into the café. It was comfortably full. To my relief, I saw no sign of Susan, for, despite my confidence on setting out from Cowfold, I was ten minutes late.

Our usual table was disengaged. I threaded my way towards it and had nearly reached it when a voice made me pause. It said with a clarity that took it high above the music of the orchestra, the clatter of the cups and trays, the hum of fifty conversations—and sent a cold shiver down my spine:

"Peter, *darling*!"

At a table that I had just passed were two Ats and a staff-sergeant in the Engineers. One of the Ats was Hazel Marjoram.

V

The situation was delicate—decidedly delicate. Susan might arrive at any moment—might even be sitting unespied at another table—and here was one of my old flames burning with disconcertingly public vigour in the *Palace* café.

I screwed my face into a smile of welcome. Regan, the ticket-worker, might have got a tip or two from the performance.

"Why, Hazel!" I said in a tone that didn't sound the least bit cordial from where I was. "Fancy meeting you!"

Yes, I thought, just fancy! How one's little peccadilloes do follow one around!

There was a fourth chair at the table. It was empty. Life is like that. Had I wished for nothing better than to sit down beside Hazel, there would have been a thin-lipped disapproving maiden lady poised primly on that chair.

I stood awkwardly by the table. Hazel said:

"Mary, this is a very old friend of mine—Peter. Peter, this is Mary, and this is her fiancé, Bill. Now you all know each other." She looked up at me. "Sit down, silly!" she ordered in that delightful, imperious manner that I knew so well.

Trapped....

"As a matter of fact," I began, as one does when it is really a matter of fiction, "I'm looking for my side-kick. I arranged to meet him in here, but he said that if he wasn't here when I arrived, he'd be waiting outside the public library. So I'm afraid I must dash along. Awfully nice to have seen you again, Hazel."

And I bolted. I incontinently fled. There might just be time to shunt Susan in another direction before she got into the cafe.

But it was not Susan I met on my precipitant descent. It was Johnny. As I flashed past, I fired at him:

"She's up there!"

I was at the foot of the stairs before he had collected his wits enough to ask, "Who?"

"Your At."

There was no time to observe his reactions. By a narrow margin, I intercepted a breathless and apologetic Susan in the booking-hall, and shepherded her out of the Restricted Area.

It was not until later that I recalled that I was not meant to know Hazel, as far as Johnny was concerned.

CHAPTER TWENTY-ONE

I

I LIFTED up my voice and swore bitterly.

It was the next morning. I had typed, "SUBJECT: Pay" in the top left-hand corner and below it, the address of the Regimental Paymaster. I had begun the letter thus: "Ref your LAA/PW10/732/S dtd 8 Nov 43 relating to a/n NCO with encl AFN 1483 showing Dr balce of 14s 5d as at 24 Sep 43. Dr condition of the a/c is not understood by this unti..."

Reversions are a typing weakness of mine (even when the "a/n NCO" was that important personage, W/Bdr. Bradfield, P.) but I had not lifted up my voice and sworn bitterly until I had turned up the paper in the machine to erase "unti" on the duplicate—and found that the carbon paper was also reversed.

The celebrated sweet disposition of the Bradfields was not much in evidence that morning. I had had a tiff with Susan over some trifle the night before, I had cut myself shaving, there had been a loathsome slab of tubey liver for breakfast and I had received a rocket from Blitz Fitz for arriving at the office five minutes late.

My mood was not improved by a remark by Master Lovelock that followed my outburst. He was busily writing in an exercise book, but he stopped his work to call from the far end of the hut:

"Touchy this morning! That's the worst of these late nights."

I snapped back at him: "That's enough of your funny cracks, Gunner Lovelock. You can keep your humour for your friends!"

He looked at me for a moment, as if considering further impertinence, then lowered his glance, took up his pen again and said no more.

A couple of chapters back, I retold Gianella's report of a conversation between Major Mellis and Captain Fitzgerald, at the end of which the Major announced that he proposed to reprove Paul Morton for his alleged harsh treatment of Lovelock. But since then, he had said nothing to Paul—or to me. It is possible that Yule had taken this reticence as a danger signal, for he had been much less blatant in his championship of Little Aubrey. Apart from other considerations, Paul, as Battery clerk, was in a unique position to make things uncomfortable for his superiors. I was not so happily placed, nor had I his audacious talent for deliberately sticking in the mud.

After my short exchange with Lovelock, the morning's work went quietly on. I inserted fresh sheets in the typewriter and began again with, "Subject: Pay." All Army correspondence has, "Subject: This," "Subject: That," or "Subject: The Other" in the top left-hand corner. It is also full of contractions and all the nouns begin with capital letters, as in German or the *Rubaiyat* of Omar Khayyám. Chris Wilkinson sorted out the inward mail, to be distributed to troops later in the morning by Don-R. Lovelock continued writing in his exercise book with such industry that it was patently not Army business on which he was engaged. At the telephone-desk in the corner, Gunner Postbechild, in a torn and stained leather jerkin, with his long body draped untidily on a chair, was mumbling a message into the transmitter in the *argot* of his craft:

"...Brackets off. Blocks on. Benders. Beer-Easy-Nuts-Donald-Easy-Ronald-Sugar. Blocks off. By twelve-hundred hours. Message ends. Your initials? ...Easy Love. Mine are Sugar Peter...."

A gunner brought in a bucket of coke and carried it through to stoke up the fire in the officers' room. The stove in the middle of the general office needed attention and, as he passed me on his way out with the empty bucket, I told him to fetch some more. In a Nissen hut in winter, it doesn't do to let the fires get too low.

Postbechild called the number of another T.H.Q. and started off again with his phonogram:

"Message for you. From X-Ray-Yorker-Zebra-Love-Ack-Ack Battery, R.A., to Troop Commander, 'B' Troop. Message: Blocks on. Charley-Sugar-Baker. Blocks off. Brackets on...."

The Major came in by the end door. It was his first appearance and, with one accord, we jumped up and stood to attention—all except Postbechild, whose voice droned on, and Little Aubrey, at his table behind the door through which the Old Lady had come, who went on busily scribbling away in his exercise book.

It was the Old Lady's normal custom, on arriving for the day's work, not to use the door at his end of the long, partitioned hut, but to make a formal entrance through the eastern door and walk through to his own room, past his assembled clerks, all rigidly to attention. It was, admittedly, Bullsh, but it pleased the Old Lady and caused us little inconvenience. Had it not been for that daily reminder, we might have forgotten that we were soldiers.

That morning he did not go straight through the general office, but paused, turned and walked back to Lovelock's table. Aubrey was still intent on his work. He glanced up sharply, however, when the Old Lady said:

"Lovelock!"

Aubrey jumped to his feet, looking apprehensive.

"Didn't you see me come in, Lovelock?"

"No, sir. I'm sorry, sir."

The rest of us resumed our seats.

"What work were you doing, Lovelock?"

"I was just going to find out some home addresses for Bombardier Wilkinson, sir."

"I asked what you were doing, Lovelock, not what you are about to do. Let me see that book you were writing in."

"It's—it's private, sir."

The situation was developing on satisfactory lines. Personal work during office hours was much frowned upon at XYZ B.H.Q.

179

"I wish to see it, Lovelock."

The unhappy Aubrey had no recourse but to hand over the exercise book. The gunner came back with the coke-bucket refilled. The Old Lady went through the performance of changing his spectacles; then began to glance through the pages of the book. For two or three minutes he stood by Lovelock's table. Then, with a stern expression on his usually benevolent face, he folded the book into two and took it to the circular stove, into which the gunner was about to shoot fresh fuel.

"Wait," he said; and dropped the book in on to the glowing coke. Not until the book had been burnt to ashes did he allow the stove to be filled.

He said: "Bombardier Morton, who is orderly N.C.O. tonight?"

"The Quartermaster, sir."

"Get someone to fetch him."

It looked as though the "waiting-gentlewoman" was due for some fatigues that evening. I was glad the Q. was orderly N.C.O.; he could be depended upon to find something disagreeable for Aubrey to do.

II

Later in the morning, with my bad temper dissipated by Aubrey's discomfiture, I went into the Q. stores in search of Johnny. He was alone, and stopped work when he saw me.

"Morning, Johnny," I greeted him. "Just dropped in for a moment to ask how you got on."

He was a very different young man from the previous evening. When I came in, he was humming gaily to himself; and it was with his old infectious grin that he replied to my question.

"Wizard, old boy! Absolutely wizard! I'm meeting her again tonight."

"That's fine!" I smiled. "Where?"

"In the *Palace* café."

Which made it awkward; I had a date with Susan there myself, and there was already one tiff to be made up.

"It was a miracle finding her again like that," Johnny went on. "When you told me she was there, I thought you must be joking. Then I realized that you wouldn't do a filthy thing like that. I leapt up the rest of the stairs and—" He stopped suddenly to ask: "How did you know it was Hazel? You'd never seen her before."

I had been expecting it. I recalled something about tangled webs.

"I—er—well, it was a sheer coincidence, really. I was just pushing my way between a couple of tables, when I heard a girl's voice say, 'It's going to rain tonight, as sure as my name's Hazel Marjoram.' Hazel Marjoram, I said to myself; surely that was the girl Johnny had a crush on? That's how it happened."

I looked at him doubtfully, waiting for his verdict, like a snide-carrier waiting for the Bank cashier to give him change for a dud half-crown. But Johnny swallowed it whole. I think, with a sufficiency of suitable opportunities for practice, I might become an accomplished liar.

"What a stroke of luck," Johnny said without a trace of suspicion in his tone. "Actually, it didn't matter much, because I should have caught sight of her in any case. I was on my way up for a coffee when you came flashing past me. I went along to the *Plaza* first, but they were showing a film about espionage in Occupied Europe—and I loathe war films."

"What did you do when you got in the café?" I asked with curiosity.

"Looked round for Hazel, spotted her at a table with another At and an R.E. staff-sergeant and bore down on them. After D.B., the very sight of three stripes and a crown makes my blood run cold—even when it's only the dear old Q.—but I pretended the Engineer fellow wasn't there. I smiled at Hazel

181

and said in a way that was friendly, but firm: 'Good-evening. I expect you remember me. I'm John Fieldhouse and we met at Burntash.' Then I sat down next to her, and after that, it was roses, roses all the way."

Now I come to consider it, that was probably the right way to woo Hazel. How had she described him?... "He was only a nervous little scrap of a soldier. All he wanted was mothering." As a vest-pocket Lothario, he was far more likely to succeed. Perhaps it was not to be in vain that Johnny had spent those weeks of purgatory in the glasshouse.

"What did you do?"

"Oh, shook the others off," he answered with a careless wave of his hand. "Hazel and I went downstairs into the cinema."

"But I thought you didn't like war films. It was all to do with fighting the Japs in the Pacific."

He looked surprised.

"Was it?" he said.

III

Before the day was out, I had news concerning another love affair. After Johnny's happy tidings, it made unpleasant hearing.

It was getting on for 23.00 hours. I was lying in bed reading when Paul Morton came into the hut. I greeted him with a grunt and went on reading. He took off his overcoat, threw it across the table and sat down on his bed. He stayed there quietly for so long that I looked across at him. His thin, sensitive features were white and set, and he was *staring* at the floor. I laid down my book.

"What's the trouble, Paul?" I asked.

"Everything," he answered without shifting his gaze.

"Don't let it get you down," I advised him. "I had a row with Susan last night and it was great fun making it up this evening."

"We didn't have a row," he said dully. "It's far worse than that. She's married."

"What, Fay Gilbert?"

"Yes.... I proposed to her this evening and she laughed at me. The horrible part of it is that her husband's a—" He moistened his dry lips with his tongue. "He's a prisoner of war. When she last heard of him, he was in Italy."

Paul went on talking, but my attention strayed to the conversation I had had with Inspector Charlton on the day of my arrival in Lulverton.

Paul was saying: "The invalid mother doesn't exist. Fay invented her, so as not to frighten me away.... Night after night, Peter, I've been alone with her in that house—making love to another man's wife... 'Fay' is her stage name. She was an actress before her—marriage."

In 6B the Quartermaster's bed creaked impatiently.

"This evening she suggested that we should—go on. But that's impossible."

His romance was over. He was, I knew, too honourable to continue a furtive affair with Fay Gilbert.

He looked up at me and said passionately:

"Married women should be forced to wear their wedding-rings!"

From the other half of the hut, the Q.'s voice complained:

"Stop gabbing, you two! I want to get to sleep."

We finished the conversation in undertones.

Lying in bed after Paul had turned out the tilly-lamp, I tried to recall the exact words the Inspector had used.... She's a very lovely girl. She lives at—well, not very far away from here.... One of these days—and that day may not be very far distant—he's going to come back home.... She's pretty blatant about it, too...."

Poor Paul.... It was tragic that his first real love affair should end so unhappily.... I sympathized greatly with him in his disillusion.... But deep down in my heart there was a selfish relief. Charlton had spoken of a beautiful young wife who had proved faithless to a husband in enemy hands. He had refused to tell me her name. For weeks I had been wondering about Susan. All I knew of her was that she acted as secretary to the almoner of the Lulverton War Memorial Hospital and that she lived in one of the cottages in Sheep village. Even of those two facts, I had only her own assurance. Now, however, one thing seemed reasonably certain: that Susan had no husband in an Italian prison camp.

But that was not the entire answer to the riddle.

CHAPTER TWENTY-TWO

I

OF all the many vexations of a Battery Office, perhaps the worst are courses. A course is a period of instruction in some specific subject. Its duration varies from a single day to several months and it may take the soldier to the nearest town for Gunnery, or to the North Pole for Handicrafts. The Powers That Be have no conception of distance.

The first difficulty is to find your man. The preliminary notification reads: "One N.C.O. will be nominated from your unit." Then the fun begins, somewhat in this fashion:

"Who shall we send, sir?"

"Lance-bombardier Jones of 'B' Troop is the very man. Send him."

"He's on leave, sir."

"Then Bombardier Smith of 'A' Troop."

"Went to hospital yesterday, sir."

"Lance-sergeant Robinson?"

"He can't be spared from the site, sir, with the D.C. on leave."

"Who else is there?"

"Gunner Brown, sir."

"Brown? He seems to spend his whole time on courses."

"He's the only man we can spare, sir."

"But he's completely useless."

"That's why we can spare him, sir."

The inevitable outcome is that poor old Brown packs his small kit and goes off on another course, this time with a local lance stripe that will come down as soon as he returns. Brown will come back as ignorant as when he departed, but the instructions of the higher formation have been obeyed. One N.C.O. has been nominated.

Before he is despatched, there are all the formalities of the Joining Instructions to be complied with: advance of pay, travelling allowance, haversack rations, regimental route, medical inspection and the rest.

We of XYZ got it both ways. We not only sent men on courses; we also received them, for Cowfold Camp, with its considerable accommodation, was a favourite point of assembly. And so we had not been surprised to hear that a regimental gunnery course was due to commence at Cowfold on Saturday, the 13th November—the day following the events I have recorded in the previous chapter.

The course was regimental—that is, it was composed of men from the Batteries that went to make up our Regiment. A training gun had been brought into B.H.Q. and an Ack-I.G. from Lulverton was due to attend daily for the period of the course, which was scheduled to last a fortnight.

Early on the Friday evening, the men began to arrive. One of the four from XYY Battery was Gunner Nelson, J. He was once a troop-sergeant in our own Battery.

II

Little reference has been made in recent pages to Chris Wilkinson. That does not mean that he was not playing his part in the affairs of the unit. There was much to be done on the medical side: sick parades twice a week, when the M.O. visited Cowfold; urgent cases to be sent direct to hospital; appointments to be fixed for men to see the medical or surgical specialists, or to be fitted with new dentures, or to go before a Medical Board. Besides this, Chris had to be always on hand to attend to cuts and bruises, to dispense pills and cough-mixture and to ensure that Gunner Snooks swallowed two tablets three times a day.

Apart from all this, Chris had the added duties of mail orderly. He dealt not only with official mail, but also with the men's personal letters and parcels. If I was pestered twenty times a week by the question, "What about my Credits, Bomb?" Chris was pestered twenty times a day by the question, "Anything for me, Bomb?"

Yet surrounded by pills and parcels, messages and massages, Chris never lost his head. He was still the same placid old fellow of P.T.C. days, with, as I have already portrayed him, his heavy sandy moustache clipped clear of his mouth, gold-rimmed spectacles and observant, twinkling eyes. Since Cwmsamfach, he had become the proud parent of another child.

I had expected strained relations between Johnny and Chris, when Johnny came out of detention. I was pleased, however, to find them meeting each other again as old friends. Johnny seemed to bear Chris no ill-will; and, after all, Chris had done no more and no less than his duty in the evidence that he had given at the court-martial. If anything, they were more cordial than they had ever been before.

It was Chris, usually not given to gossip, who told me about Fay Gilbert and the Sergeant-major.

Our conversation took place a couple of days after Paul Morton had made his heart-breaking discovery. Chris had no direct evidence, having got the story from L/Bdr. Lomas, Troop clerk of "A" Troop, whose headquarters were, as I have already explained, in a requisitioned house in Etchworth village.

"Lomas told me," said Chris, "that the B.S.M. has been hanging round her for some time past. He's been noticed slipping in and out of the house after dark. Lomas says that another young gentleman of our mutual acquaintance has also been frequently observed on the same errand, but not on the same nights. Miss Gilbert evidently runs a shuttle service on the same lines as Box and Cox's landlady. I hope, for somebody's sake, that neither Box nor Cox ever finds out."

"I don't think such a situation will arise now," I said. "Our mutual acquaintance has discovered that she's married, and is therefore giving Etchworth a wide berth."

"There are such things as sour grapes," Chris reminded me, and plodded off to the M.I. room.

III

Four days before the Sergeant-major died—on Saturday, the 20th November—Scottie, the Captain's Cairn, disappeared.

Briefly, the circumstances were these:

On evenings when it was not convenient for Captain Fitzgerald to do so, Gianella took Scottie for his evening run. On the Saturday evening in question, Blitz was out visiting in Lulverton. At half-past eight, Gianella and Scottie, who were great friends, set off for their walk. Because of the danger from passing cars, Scottie was on his lead—a strong leather affair.

They had not gone far along the road towards Sheep, where Gianella proposed to have a pint in the "Sun in the Sands," when they met the Sergeant-major hurrying back to camp. He flashed on a torch.

"Ah, Gianella!" he said genially. "You're just the very man! I went off to catch the bus and left a parcel behind. Slip back for it, will you? It's a small, brown-paper parcel and it's on the table alongside my bed. Give me the lead. I'll look after the dog."

Gianella had no liking for the turn of events, but there was no alternative but to obey. He handed Scottie over to the Sergeant-major and ran back to camp as fast as his short legs would take him. In less than five minutes, he was back again with the parcel. The Sergeant-major had walked on slowly towards Sheep, but Scottie was no longer with him.

"Did he catch you up?" he asked Gianella.

"I ain't seen 'im, sir," Gianella replied.

"He took me by surprise. He jerked the lead out of my hand and was off after you before I could stop him."

At that stage Gianella was not really anxious, expecting to find Scottie waiting outside the officers' mess when he got back. He said as much to the Sergeant-major, who agreed, took his parcel and went off to catch the bus.

But Scottie was not waiting outside the mess. The little batman spent an hour wandering round the camp locality, calling the terrier's name with growing anxiety; and was finally forced to report the loss to the Major, orderly officer for the day, who was reading in the mess.

Knowing the Captain's fondness for his pet, the Major called out every available man to join in the search. It was of no avail. Scottie, with his lead still attached to his collar, was nowhere to be found. The Old Lady rang the police.

Captain Fitzgerald returned at midnight and was out for two hours, roaming the neighbourhood. When he eventually went to bed, he could not have slept, for he was sufficiently awake at three o'clock to hear Scottie's weak scratching at the front door of the mess. He reached for his flash-lamp and got out of bed.

When he saw the condition of the little Cairn, who, now without his leather lead, had managed, by some miracle, to crawl back to his master, he fetched his revolver and shot him.

IV

There was a full inquiry next day. Gianella described how he had met the Sergeant-major and, on his instructions— Gianella stressed that—had passed Scottie into his care. The Sergeant-major fully accepted the responsibility imputed to him by Gianella, and told how Scottie had leapt suddenly forward in an attempt to run after the batman.

The Major mentioned a point that had already occurred to most of us: that Scottie could run a good deal faster than Gianella and should have caught him up long before he reached the officers' mess. The Sergeant-major's reply was that such would certainly have been the case had Scottie freed himself soon after Gianella's departure for the parcel; but although Scottie had strained at his lead at first, he had soon quietened down and had walked docilely along beside the Sergeant-major. Then, when Yule paused to light a cigarette, he wrenched the lead from the Sergeant-major's partially relaxed grip, and headed back the way they had come.

"The only thing I can suggest, sir," Yule ended his statement, "is that somebody caught him by the lead before he reached the camp entrance, and took him on in the direction of Lulverton."

The hypothesis was too reasonable to be ignored. There was no question of the Sergeant-major standing trial for inflicting such terrible injuries on Scottie, but if there had been, there was Gianella's evidence to support him.

As I said to Johnny privately afterwards:

"It's a question of fact. If Yule had made off with the poor little devil, there would be something more than flimsy suspicion to work on, but Scottie wasn't with him when Gianella came back with the parcel. What do you imagine Yule had done with Scottie?"

"Tied him up, to go back for him afterwards."

I shook my head. "It's not reasonable, Johnny. There simply wasn't time to get very far from the road. Can you picture Scottie not yapping his head off as Gianella went by? No, I believe we can rule the Sergeant-major right out of that piece of beastliness."

"I think you're right," said Johnny, "but I wish you were wrong."

CHAPTER TWENTY-THREE

I

LANCE-BOMBARDIER Lomas, the clerk of "A" Troop, was a babbler, constitutionally incapable of keeping his mouth shut. One of the silliest things he ever did was to tell Paul Morton that Sergeant-major Yule was calling on Fay Gilbert. That it was Lomas who let the cat out of the bag, I learnt from Paul himself—but not until after he, also, had committed his crowning folly.

It was early on the Wednesday morning—the last morning that Yule ever saw. The officers had not arrived in Battery Office. Yule was by himself in his own room and the rest of us were unlocking our boxes in the general office, and getting out our papers for the day.

Paul went into the Sergeant-major's room, closing the door behind him. Had I tried to overhear what followed, I should have failed. The partitions in Battery Office were of stouter stuff than those in our sleeping quarters.

The conversation was short. In less than three minutes the door opened again, just soon enough for me to hear Yule's concluding words:

"You can take it from me, Morton, that wild horses won't drag me away from her."

Paul was white with anger.

"We shall see," he answered as he closed the door.

II

That day, Wednesday, the 24th November, 1943, was the anniversary of XYZ Battery's first success against enemy aircraft. To mark the occasion, the Major invited B.H.Q.'s senior N.C.Os.—the Sergeant-major, the Quartermaster, Paul and myself—to take a drink with the officers in their mess. The time fixed for the ceremony was 18.00 hours.

As the four of us left the main camp and made for the officers' mess, the keen north-west wind stung our faces. The ground was frozen hard and there was no fear of mud, so we took the short cut across the football field. I was thinking that there was something of an ordeal before us. Paul had maintained a frigid silence towards the Sergeant-major throughout the day. Since the loss of Scottie, Captain Fitzgerald had been moody and even more unapproachable than usual. At the best of times, he treated the Sergeant-major with scant courtesy. Now that Scottie had lost his life as a direct result of Yule's negligence, even a formal show of amity seemed unlikely.

Apart from Scottie, there was another bone of contention between them. On the day following Master Aubrey Lovelock's defeat at the hands of the Old Lady, the Captain had thrown Lovelock out of the office into the outer darkness of the quartermaster's stores. In the presence of Aubrey, Blitz had instructed the Q. to see that he was kept healthily employed on manual labour for every minute of the working day. The Sergeant-major had taken a hand, protesting that Lovelock was a clerk and should not be used for rough work. The Captain had replied, "Then we'll de-muster him," and consequently Aubrey had left his comfortable chair in Battery Office and was handed over to the tender mercies of the Q., who set himself with relish to find tasks that would leave Aubrey, at the end of each day, dirty, exhausted and extremely bad-tempered.

Neither the Q. nor I was a ray of sunshine that evening.

I was worried about Paul—and Johnny. Now that the gauntlet had been thrown down by Paul, Yule was certain to embark on a campaign against him. That Yule could be successful in such enterprises was manifested by the misfortunes that had overtaken Johnny Fieldhouse, ex-sergeant Nelson and Gunner Owen, the little Welshman who had committed suicide in the

Slough of Despond. And Johnny.... I was not happy about that phrase of his, "An eye for an eye...."

Q. Ackroyd had lost, of late, much of his old boisterousness. To add to his other anxieties, his wife's mental condition had taken a turn for the worse.

In contrast to the rest of us, Yule was in the best of spirits. Even at tea-time, when Regan of Bootle—acting as mess waiter in the absence on leave of his far more satisfactory successor—had spilt a cup of tea over him, he had dismissed the matter with a laugh; and his "You clumsy——" seemed to have no more behind it than good-tempered exasperation at Regan's general ineptitude.

The Major, the Captain and puny Mr. Bretherton, with his damp, red nose, were waiting to receive us in the mess. Gianella was in attendance.

Drinks were poured. The Old Lady, exuding liberality and goodwill, made a little speech. Then, when we had drunk to the past and future glories of XYZ, conversation became general. There was a fine big fire in the open grate and Gianella did not stint the whisky. As he replenished my glass beyond the point where hospitality ends and prodigality begins, he muttered in my ear:

"Yer won't fergit me Credits when I go on leaf, will yer, Bomb?"

The Major was on one side of the fireplace, looking very small in the big easy-chair. Yule had the chair on the other side of the fireplace. Between the two of them, on seats of less splendour, were Mr. Bretherton, the Q., Paul and I; and behind the Major—with us, but somehow not of us—was Captain Fitzgerald, sitting on the corner of a table, swinging his leg and flicking the ash from his cigarette on to the carpet. His good-looking young face, with its heavy black "Anton" moustache, was sombre, and he spoke only when directly addressed.

We discussed the history of XYZ Battery, of its formation at Boxford and subsequent activities in the Slough of Despond,

Stalcote-on-Sea and Sheep. We spoke of the men who had been killed by the bomb that had hit their gun-site at Stalcote. It was the Major who struck a lighter note by recalling an incident at Boxford, when, during fire-fighting drill, a canister of tear-gas had been released in mistake for a smoke-generator. This was a cue for Mr. Bretherton to leap into the saddle of his hobby-horse.

"I am very—very—I am somewhat disturbed, sir," he said in his repetitive mode of speech, "to notice the—the—the— to observe the very low standard of—of—of gas-preparedness in this unit. During gas-drill last Saturday afternoon, some of the men were not—not—not—had very little conception of the dangers we run from—from—from surprise attack with poison-gas by the enemy."

I stole a glance at Paul, who tossed his head in mute exasperation. We had had more than enough of Mr. Bretherton and his anti-gas antics: personal decontamination, cotton-waste, ointment, gas-capes, eye-shields, sleeve-detectors and all the rest of the boring business. There are no intermediate feelings in gas-training: either one thinks gas, talks gas and dreams gas, or one loathes the very mention of the word. "Mr. Why" was an enthusiast. The previous Saturday afternoon he had been in his element, having had the whole of B.H.Q. personnel, except the duty telephonist, on an hour's gas-drill that included a drop of liquid mustard on our wrists (during which Mr. Bretherton took care to wear a pair of the official green-rubber anti-gas gloves); and culminated in our being incarcerated in batches in the gas-chamber with our respirators on, while Mr. Bretherton, having laid his rubber gloves aside, heated tear-gas capsules over a little spirit-lamp.

The gas-chamber—known locally as "Bretherton's Folly"— was a square building of brick with a flat concrete roof. It stood among the trees to the west of the football field and had "DANGER. KEEP OUT" painted on its heavy teak door. We of XYZ needed no such warning.

Little "Mr. Why's" monologue continued until the Sergeant-major coolly interrupted him by addressing a question to the Old Lady.

"Do you remember, sir," he asked, "that man we had at Stalcote? What was his name, now?... Began with a 'T'."

He sat in thought for a moment, then his brow cleared. Intuitively, I knew what was coming.

"Templeton," he said. "Yes, that was it: Templeton. Always getting himself into trouble over women."

"No," was the Major's decisive answer, "I don't recall the man."

"Surely, sir!" Yule persisted. "Have you forgotten how he was carrying on an affair with a young married woman whose husband, he thought, was a prisoner of war in Italy; and how the husband suddenly turned up? At Stalcote, it was."

The Old Lady smiled indulgently and struck a match.

"Extremely embarrassing for him," he said when he had relighted his pipe and thrown the spent match into the fire, "but I imagine you are becoming confused, Sergeant-major. I don't pride myself on many virtues, but I can claim a retentive memory for names and faces. I remember the name of every man who has passed through this Battery, and I have a mind-picture of all their faces. We have never had a man called Templeton in this Battery."

"I don't like contradicting you, sir," the Sergeant-major pursued the point with an ingratiating smile that I should have delighted in removing with some such missile as a well-aimed Army boot, "but Templeton *was* on our strength. Not for long, I'll admit. Templeton.... Templeton.... Doesn't the name strike a chord, sir. As far as I can remember his appearance—"

The Major swung round in his chair.

"Captain Fitzgerald," he said, "can you call this man Templeton to mind?"

"No," was Fitz's blunt retort. "I suggest that the Sergeant-major drops the subject."

Pointedly, with his right forefinger, he pushed the sleeve of his battledress from the face of his wrist-watch. Yule had sufficient tact to take the hint. He was levering himself awkwardly out of his chair, and we others were getting to our feet and pulling down the waistbands of our blouses, when the lights went out.

The Captain's forthright tones came out of the darkness.

"I thought you'd mended that contraption, Major?" he said with a short laugh with not much humour in it. "There should be wind enough to work the propeller tonight."

The Old Lady's apologetic voice replied:

"It has probably disturbed the wiring."

He escorted us to the front door. We thanked him for his hospitality and followed the Sergeant-major out on to the macadamed roadway. As we walked off towards the main camp, the Old Lady called after us:

"Bombardier Morton, please get someone to bring the typewriter up from the office. I have some work to do on it tonight."

"Very good, sir," Paul shouted back.

III

We left just before seven-thirty. Half an hour later, Battery Sergeant-major Yule walked out of Cowfold Camp for the last time.

His bloody, shattered, almost unrecognizable body was found next daybreak in one of Jack Nightingale's meadows. His wrists were lashed together behind his back by a leather dog-lead; and he was roped by his ankles to foam-flecked, wild-eyed, utterly exhausted Etchworth Lass.

How many times the mare had dragged him, feet first and face downward—a ghastly human harrow—around the iron-hard, frozen field, and how many times she had reared back on him with trampling, grinding hooves, it was impossible to tell.

It was not from the rope or the thing at her heels that she had tried to escape, for she was accustomed to harness. It was from the thistle that had been thrust under the dock of her tail.

Part IV

Subject—C.I.D.*

CHAPTER TWENTY-FOUR

I

"BY the law of England," reads the second paragraph on page I of the *Manual of Military Law*, "a man who joins the Army, whether as an officer or as a soldier, does not cease to be a citizen. With a few exceptions, his position under the ordinary law of the land remains unaffected. If he commits an offence against the criminal law, he can be tried and punished for it as if he were a civilian."

Consequently, one of the first things that the Army authorities do when faced by a case of death not caused by the King's enemies, is to wash their hands of it.

At this point in my story, therefore, the focus shifts. Murder had been done—and overnight the officers and soldiers of XYZ Light Anti-Aircraft Battery became citizens, answerable, in so far as the death of Yule was concerned, not to the military authority as represented by their commanding officer, a colonel of the Royal Artillery, but to the civil authority as represented by Harry Charlton, an inspector of the Criminal Investigation Department.

II

It was John Nightingale himself who discovered, still hitched to Etchworth Lass, the bloody remains of our Sergeant-major.

---

*. NOTE.—For the details of many of the incidents that follow, I am indebted to Inspector Charlton.—P.B.

He hobbled the mare and stood guard over her, while the Land Army girl who was with him ran off to telephone the police.

Detective-sergeant Martin received the call at Lulverton Police Station and, immediately afterwards, rang first the Divisional Superintendent, whose name was Kingsley, and next Inspector Charlton at his home in Southmouth-by-the-Sea, three miles to the south of Lulverton. Martin then put through calls to the police surgeon, the ambulance station, the police photographer and finally the Army authorities. Then—and not until then—he replaced his feet on the Inspector's desk, helped himself to a cigarette from the Inspector's box, lighted it with one of the Inspector's matches, and relaxed.

Within three-quarters of an hour, all the parties so summoned—except Supt. Kingsley, who had been unable to attend—were assembled in the lane by Farmer Nightingale's meadow. The ambulance and cars were left in charge of their drivers in the main road.

Charlton and his assistant, a detective-constable, got busy. The ground had been frozen hard for several days and there was little chance of finding any useful footprints. Nevertheless, Charlton allowed nobody to enter the meadow until he had made a survey of it.

The field was skirted on its northern side by the road that ran from Lulverton, via Etchworth, to Sheep. It was bordered on each of its four sides by a high quick-set hedge of hawthorn. Along its western side ran the lane leading to Nightingale's farmhouse, and further along, A.R. 4 gun-site, where it petered out. A gate, about fifty yards from the main road, gave access from the lane into the field. It was by this gate that Johnny had chatted with Nightingale, while I had stood awkwardly by. In the south-west corner of the field was an open-fronted lean-to.

When the M.O. and the police surgeon had confirmed that life was extinct, the photographer made his exposures. The medical men conferred and decided that death had occurred at some time between midnight and 2 a.m.

As he put his thermometer away, the M.O., Capt. Bell, said to Charlton:

"I know the man well, Inspector. His name's Yule— Sergeant-major Yule of XYZ Light Ack-Ack Battery. Cowfold Camp, their B.H.Q., is just off to the left of the road, about half a mile this side of Sheep. Will you leave it to me to inform the O.C.?"

"If you wish, sir," Charlton agreed. "Will you please ask him to arrange for the whole Battery to be confined to camp until further notice. I'll follow you later."

Capt. Bell accepted the implicit dismissal with a nod and went off to his car. With nothing further to detain them, the police surgeon and photographer also departed.

III

Yule had been harnessed to Etchworth Lass by means of a single length of rope, which, by being doubled and knotted into a loop, had been made to form a primitive neckband, breast-strap and traces. The ends of the traces had been secured to the victim's ankles.

The rope—hawserlaid white hemp cordage—was twenty-six feet in length and an inch and a half in circumference. When Charlton examined it, he found that it was not merely an odd length cut from a coil, but had all the appearance of an article of equipment. One end of it was whipped with twine and the other neatly finished with a loop.

The body was clad in the ripped remnants of a battledress. On the feet were brown civilian shoes. An Army greatcoat with a sergeant-major's brass crown-and-wreath badges on the sleeves, and a field-service cap with a Royal Artillery badge, had been thrown down against the hedge, a few yards to one side of the gate.

Hanging loosely round the neck of the dead man was a khaki handkerchief, torn and caked with frozen blood. Two corners were knotted together as if, before it had slipped down from the wearer's face, it had been used in fun for blind-man's-buff, or in deadly earnest for a gag. In one corner, in marking-ink, was the laundry number LY 207.

The dog-lead was of stout leather, half an inch in width. The clip for attachment to the animal's collar was missing. The lead had originally been passed through the clip, folded back on itself and fastened by two nickel-plated bifurcated rivets. As a result of tension—or so it appeared to Charlton—the rivets had been dragged through the short end of the loop. One was still in its second hole, but of the other there was no sign. In spite of the rough treatment the lead had received, it still showed evidence of conscientious polishing, and Charlton was hopeful that Sgt. Peters, the finger-print man at Police Headquarters in the County town of Whitchester, would be able to make something of it.

The lean-to in the corner of the field was an ancient structure of bricks, with a tiled roof. Etchworth Lad, the gelding, was just outside it, placidly breakfasting off the fodder that the Land Army girl had strewn there earlier that morning. The building supplied Charlton with no helpful clues.

A list was made of the articles in the dead man's pockets. The body was placed on a stretcher and transferred to the ambulance for conveyance to the mortuary. The dog-lead, greatcoat, field-service cap and handkerchief were passed into the care of the detective-constable, who travelled in the ambulance back to Lulverton, then on in a police car to Whitchester, with the dog-lead in a cardboard box. The Inspector retained the rope.

IV

Charlton and John Nightingale were well known to each other. They left Etchworth Lass in the soothing hands of the Land Army girl and went along to the farmhouse, where easy-chairs and hot coffee enabled the conversation to be more comfortably conducted. After hearing a full account of how and when the body had been discovered, Charlton said:

"Those horses, Mr. Nightingale—are they usually to be found in that particular field?"

"Yes," nodded the farmer. "They're a pair of half-bred hunters. Not much opportunity for that sort of thing these days, but the Missus is fond of 'em and..."

In his grimace there was a wealth of husbandly resignation. Mrs. Nightingale was, by repute, something of a Xanthippe.

"What kind of disposition has Etchworth Lass?"

"Nervy, you know, but not more so than most mares. Easy enough to handle, if you don't treat her too roughly."

"And with a stranger?"

"That's another matter. Horses don't care much for strangers. I wouldn't say, though, that it couldn't have been done. Some folks have a way of their own with horses." He leant forward to put his empty cup on the table. "Let's say the chap you're after lullabied the Sergeant-major to sleep with—well, with a sandbag, say; then gagged him, doubled the rope, looped it, for passing over the mare's head, with a harness-hitch—"

"So you noticed that?" Charlton interrupted with a slight smile.

"Couldn't miss it! Make a note of that, Charlton: your murdering friend knew something about knots. Tom, Dick or Harry would've made an ordinary loop-knot, but this chap went one better....Where was I? Oh, yes. The Sergeant-major is face downward on the ground. The ends of the rope are fixed—ordinary clove-hitches, this time—to his ankles. The murderer spends a minute or two with the Lass, getting her in a quiet frame of mind, then leads her out. He slips the halter over the mare's head. A tricky little job, especially in the dark—always got to start from the front of a horse, you know—but not too difficult for anyone with a sound knowledge of the beasts. Then lift the dock. A handful of thistles—and off she goes like a frightened comet...."

"Put yourself in the murderer's place for a moment, Mr. Nightingale. Last night in that field there were two horses, both readily accessible....Which would you have chosen?"

The answering tone was dubious.

"Depends which way you look at it. The mare would be a bigger handful to manage than the gelding, but you could rely on her to give a—how shall I put it?—a more violent performance." He ran his fingers through his hair. "You can't have it both ways, you see. Geldings are placid—they're not as Nature made them. The Lad would have given less trouble in the preliminaries, but he might not—I only say he *might* not—have acted lively enough for the job. Not that the murderer took any chances; the time-worn thistle trick made certain of a sticky finish for Yule."

"So given a choice between a gelding and a mare—and assuming that you had enough experience to cope with her—you'd select the mare?"

The farmer smiled and shook his head slowly. "Put me in the witness-box, Charlton, and you'll not get a plain 'yes' or 'no' to that question. There's no hard-and-fast rule. Horses are like men and women—they vary."

"But," persisted Charlton, "if you'd to choose between Etchworth Lass and Etchworth Lad...?"

"I'd pick the Lass every time." He shot a shrewd glance at Charlton. "I see what you're getting at," he added.

"One other thing," the Inspector said. "The gate into the field was open when I arrived this morning."

"That was my doing. I unlatched it to get into the field and didn't close it again."

"It's not fastened at night? I noticed that the other gate on the east side of the field is padlocked."

Nightingale shrugged his shoulders.

"Women at war," he said. "Time was when both gates were kept locked, but Miss Perkins—my Land Army girl—she found it easier without the chain and padlock, so..."

The sentence was left unfinished.

Charlton asked: "Did you know Yule at all?"

"Not to speak to. Only by sight. One of the Battery's guns is on my land"—he jerked his thumb southward over his shoulder—"down the lane. The lads are always in and out of here for eggs and a bit of butter on the q.t. Yule never looked much like a soldier to me. One of the Citizen Army, I'd say."

"Have the men ever referred to him?"

"According to them, there's only one thing in his favour—he leaves 'em alone. Never goes near the gun-site. But that aside, they haven't a good word to say for him. Not the usual complaints about slave-driving and spit-and-polish—good, healthy grouses deserved by any sergeant-major worth his salt—but different, more personal things, if you follow me. 'Slimy,' 'sly,' 'vicious,' 'tricky' are just a few of the words the lads have used about him."

"A married man?"

Again the farmer shrugged his shoulders.

"So they say. It didn't seem to handicap him much, though. D'you know the Saunders woman at Etchworth?"

"Fay Gilbert, the actress?"

"Fat lot of acting she ever did," grunted Nightingale, "Fan dancer or some such tarradiddle, wasn't she? They say this Yule chap's been—well, let's call it friendly with her for some time past." He relighted his pipe before adding from behind a cloud of smoke, "He was there last night."

Charlton looked interested. Nightingale went on:

"I didn't see him myself, but Miss Perkins did. Come to that, there's precious little that Miss Perkins doesn't see! She's got an eye like a hawk. She's billeted in Etchworth and, from what she told me this morning, she was—"

"Perhaps she'd better tell me herself," Charlton suggested. "May I have a word with her?"

The girl was fetched. She was sandy-haired, plain-featured and forthright, with a dumpy figure that breeches and thick stockings did nothing to enhance.

At a few minutes after 8.30 the previous evening, she told Charlton, she had been walking past Mrs. Saunders' house, "Lyme Regis," which was at the eastern end of Etchworth's long, unattractive High Street; and had caught sight of Mrs. Saunders admitting Yule.

"Are you sure it was he?" Charlton asked her.

"Oh, certain. I've seen him lots of times before and he's been pointed out to me as Sergeant-major Yule of Cowfold Camp. Mrs. Saunders—or Miss Gilbert, whichever she likes to call herself"—her sniff was eloquent of disapproval—"didn't switch off the hall light before letting him in, and I saw him perfectly."

The Inspector thanked her with a smile and was just about to mention another matter when she said:

"There's another soldier from the same camp who goes to see Mrs. Saunders a good deal. A young corporal—or bombardier, isn't it, in the Artillery? Somebody once told me his name's Morton. Rather thin-faced, with a sharp nose. Very intellectual he looks—like Leslie Howard." Again her sniff was censorious. "She's fond of variety."

"I gather, Miss Perkins, that you are concerned with looking after Etchworth Lass and Etchworth Lad?"

"That *poor* dear! She must have been simply mad with terror. I've had an awful job pacifying her. Why on earth they couldn't have killed him without disturbing Etchworth Lass, I simply can't think. Why couldn't they have shot him or had an accident with a hand-grenade or—"

"Have you noticed anyone recently, Miss Perkins, who's shown an unusual interest in the field or the horses?"

The farmer gave an ejaculation and was about to speak when Charlton stopped him with:

"Just a moment, Mr. Nightingale. Let Miss Perkins answer first."

"Not as far as I can remember," she replied. "I've mentioned them to various people and talked about them quite a lot, but I've never been deliberately questioned."

"Now, Mr. Nightingale, you were going to say...?"

"I can tell you something. It struck me as queer at the time. Now it strikes me as even queerer." He puffed at his pipe while he assembled the facts. "It was—yes, it was last Thursday week, a fortnight ago. It was in the evening just before dusk and I was leading the mare and gelding back from here to the field. I was drawing near to the gate when I saw two soldiers coming towards me. One of 'em was your friend, Bradfield, and t'other was a thin, little, ginger-headed gunner."

The Inspector rose to his feet.

"I'm obliged to you, Miss Perkins," he smiled down at her. "I think that will be all for the moment."

She was reluctant to go, but he had left her no option.

Alone again with Mr. Nightingale, he said:

"Please go on."

"The gunner did all the talking. He'd evidently left the main road and come along the lane for the one purpose of questioning me. He put very much the same questions as you've put to me this morning: Which of the two was the more excitable? Was the Lass easy to manage? Did she bite? And he finished up by wanting to know where they were kept. After what's happened today, Charlton, you'd do well to have a chat with that young man."

The Inspector agreed and turned to another matter.

"The field is not far from this house. Did you hear anything abnormal last night? Any shouting—any sounds of a quarrel?"

"All I caught," the farmer answered, "was a snatch of singing as some of the lads went past on their way back to the gun-site, after their evening off duty. That would have been a minute or two before eleven o'clock. I was abed myself by then and dropped off to sleep soon afterwards."

Thank you, Mr. Nightingale. Now may I speak to your wife and anyone else who slept here last night?"

The subsequent questioning revealed one significant fact. The information came from an ancient labourer by the name of Doggett, who was in Farmer Nightingale's employ.

"It were a soldier," said Doggett, with toothless gums. "'E were leanin' on the gate, puffin' at 'is pipe, 'e were. The mare and the gelding were grazin'. Then 'e bends down an' pulls an 'andful o' grass, 'e does, and 'olds it acrarst the gate to the mare, which was nearest. The Lass she takes no 'eed, she don't, for all 'is whistlin' and wheedlin'. After a while, 'e looks up and down the lane, e' does, then opens the gate and steps—soft and gentle like—up to the mare, makin little coaxin' noises. She lifts 'er 'ead and looks at 'im, she does. 'E gets right up to 'er. She stands there quiet. 'E puts up 'is 'and—nervous like—and strokes 'er muzzle. Then 'e offers 'er grass on 'is flat palm, 'e does—and she takes it. 'E gives 'er a few more friendly pats afore 'e comes away."

"When did this happen?"

"Sunday afternoon, it were—four days ago. Round about three o'clock."

"Can you describe the man?"

"Young feller, 'e were, sir. Bit undersized. 'Air were red as a carrot."

V

Charlton came out of the farmhouse and walked along the lane towards the main road. At the gate he paused and, after a moment's hesitation, lifted the wooden latch and entered the field. Around the perimeter he went with busy eyes, and backwards and forwards across it. But nowhere did he find what he sought.

Back in the main road, he unlocked the door of his car, slipped into his seat and pressed the starter. But the big black

Vauxhall had moved only a few yards towards Cowfold Camp when he changed his mind, backed the car into the lane and made for Etchworth.

As the car purred along, there persisted in his thoughts an idea that eventually brought a smile to his lips.... One might as well search for a needle in a haystack, yet it would be interesting to discover, somewhere in that Downland countryside, a thing that he had failed to find in Farmer Nightingale's meadow: a clump of spear plume-thistle with one spiny stem snapped off some eight inches from its prickly head.

CHAPTER TWENTY-FIVE

"IT was poor Trilby's sad distinction," wrote George Du Maurier, "that she surpassed all other models as Calypso surpassed her nymphs; and whether by long habit, or through some obtuseness in her nature, or lack of imagination, she was equally unconscious of self with her clothes on or without!

"She would have ridden through Coventry," Du Maurier went on, "like Lady Godiva—but without giving it a thought beyond wondering why the streets were empty and the shops closed and the blinds pulled down—would even have looked up to Peeping Tom's shutter with a friendly nod, had she known he was behind it."

From Fay Gilbert, whom he had met before, the Inspector had never received an impression of the adorable Trilby's artlessness. Certainly, he imagined, Fay would have been as much at her ease in the altogether, but there would be nothing ingenuous in the undraping. She would have been vexed, he felt, by the deserted thoroughfares and angry had Tom not peeped.

Fay was a lovely creature. Charlton had said as much to me. Had he told me that her hair had the chestnut lustre of polished mahogany, he would have saved me much anxiety.

There seemed no uneasiness in her manner when she opened the front door to him.

"Why, Inspector!" she smiled gaily. "This *is* a pleasant surprise! Won't you come in?"

She was dressed in an ankle-length house-coat of green corduroy velvet, zip-fastened decorously up to the neck. He followed her into the french-windowed lounge at the rear of the house and accepted the easy-chair, but not the cigarette, that she offered him. She switched on the electric fire in the grate.

"It's months since I last saw you," she smiled again—and Charlton felt something of the personal magnetism of her. "Not since you got my handbag back for me. What is it brings the great detective once more to my little home?"

Still there was no tremor in her voice; nothing more than playful curiosity in her expression.

"I'm afraid it's something rather serious, Miss Gilbert," he answered. "I have grave news for you of Sergeant-major Yule."

The smile faded naturally, as if with conventional concern. Her glance was level as she asked, quite simply:

"Is he dead?"

"Yes."

She drew a sharp breath, which, when she expelled it, sounded to the quietly watchful detective like a sigh of release from emotional tension.

She asked: "Why do you come to me?"

"He met his death last night, Miss Gilbert. I am given to understand that he spent a part of the evening in this house. Perhaps you will tell me what time he left here?"

Flat denial seemed on the tip of her tongue, but finally she replied:

"About half-past eleven."

"Did he tell you where he was going?"

"No. Straight back to camp, I should imagine. How did he die?"

"Have you known him long, Miss Gilbert?"

"About six weeks." Suddenly she flared up: "Tell me it was an accident—that somebody didn't kill him!"

Charlton shook his head.

"I can't do that," he told her softly.

"Murder," she said dully; then burst out: "Oh, my God!"

With her elbow on the arm of the chair, she buried her face in her hand. Charlton rose from his seat, stepped to the french windows, one of the foot-square panes of which was filled by a sheet of cardboard, and stood there for a moment or two, looking out at the short, neglected, weed-choked garden. When, at length, he turned and went back to stand on the hearthrug, she was lying back in the chair with her eyes closed.

211

"I'm sorry," he murmured with a gentleness not entirely feigned, "that I have had to cause you so much distress.... It is a sad thing to lose a friend."

Her head still resting on the back of the chair, she opened her eyes and looked up at him. Her tight lips bared her splendid teeth as she answered:

"If you mean William Yule, I hope his soul burns in hell for ever."

With a swift, lithe movement, she sat up straight and motioned him back into his chair with an imperious wave of the hand.

"I'll tell you something," she said, but paused to light a cigarette from the packet on the table by her side before going on: "I first met him at an Officers' and W.O.s' dance in the Drill Hall at Lulverton. He brought me home. He'd had a good many drinks—and—so had I. I asked him in for a nightcap. I'm a bit hazy about it now, but I don't think he stayed very long. What I do remember is arranging to meet him in Lulverton later in the week.

"When I woke up the next morning, I decided he was quite the most repulsive man I'd ever met." She looked at him with wide, innocent eyes. "Have you ever found drink do that to you—make you believe you like the people you really loathe?... I didn't keep the appointment. Later the same evening, he called here. He was in a wicked temper and would have made a scene on the doorstep if I hadn't let him in."

She flicked the ash from her cigarette into the fireplace. He waited for her to go on, but it took time to arrange her thoughts.

"The war," she said at length, "has altered a lot of things. Some of us are beginning to look at life in a different way. ...Perhaps it's the wrong way.... But we're all of us clinging on the edge of a volcano that's more than likely to bubble over at any minute.... We live for the moment.... And there are thoughts that we want to keep out of our—"

"You were going to tell me about Sergeant-major Yule," he interrupted, sharply for him.

"I wanted you to understand," she told him plaintively.

"There was a young officer—a staff-officer for P.T.—who I... used to know. Then he went overseas. There'd been no harm in it—just dances and things; but people must have talked, because Sergeant-major Yule had heard all about it. That evening he told me he knew. And he pulled a piece of paper from his pocket to read out an address."

The hand that held the cigarette shook slightly.

"It was the address of a prison camp in Italy where my husband is.... He said that if I tried to keep him away from me—those were the words he used—he would see to it that my husband got to know about... the other business. Can you imagine what that would have meant?"

"There is a simple remedy for blackmail, Miss Gilbert. You should have gone at once to the police."

"But the awful publicity! The newspapers—"

"There would have been no publicity. The Courts take an extremely severe view of blackmail. Every adult person in this country should be aware of that."

"*I* wasn't. Well, I suppose I was, really; but this didn't seem like ordinary blackmail. There was nothing definite—nothing *real* about it. He didn't demand money or... anything. All he did was to come in here—in this room—and sit with me, just as you and I are sitting now, one on each side of the fireplace, for hours on end. After the evening of the dance, he never touched me—never laid a finger on me. ...More than once he spoke of 'unendurable pleasure indefinitely prolonged.' I think it's a quotation from somewhere. He nearly drove me crazy, sitting there like a potbellied heathen idol, with his hands clasped across the stretched, crumpled, cigarette-ashy waistband of his battle-dress and his top lip stained a dirty yellow with nicotine...."

She squirmed as if a chilling hand had stroked her spine.

"Sometimes he fetched books along for me to read aloud to him.... Disgusting, beastly books. But I think he got his chief enjoyment out of my loathing for him—the sickening horror of being anywhere near him. I suppose it was a sort of revenge for the way I had more or less run away from him.... One book—the most revolting of them all—was a very bad translation of a story called "Juliette" by a Frenchman whose name was—I've forgotten it."

He did not think it necessary to refresh her memory. He said instead:

"How did Yule get to know your husband's address?"

"I had had a letter from Italy on the morning of the Drill Hall dance. It was lying on the back of the settee when I brought the Sergeant-major in. While I was out of the room, he read it. He was that kind of man."

"Can you give me the details of what happened last night, Miss Gilbert?"

"Yes. He got here about half-past eight. He brought with him another horrible book of the sort he gloried in. It was all about—well, you can see for yourself."

She reached behind her and produced from under the chair cushion a book with a tattered paper cover, once brightly coloured, but now soiled and stained. Without further comment, she passed it over to him. It bore the title, "The Bloodhound of Valladolid."

Chapter I began:

> "Some time during the year 1420—the exact date is not known to us—there was born in Valladolid in Old Castile a boy whose very name was destined to strike terror in hundreds of thousands of hearts and was to be passed down from generation to generation as synonymous with cruelty; the name of one of the most callous exponents of man's inhumanity to man that this world has ever known.

"Tomas de Torquemada, infamous son of a saintly father, contrived, during his seventy-eight years of existence, to smirch the fair name—not only of Spain, but also of the Roman Catholic Church. Entering as a boy the Dominican Order, in which he might have lived an austere and useful life, his unbounded ambition ultimately gained him the important appointment of confessor to the Infanta Isabella.

"His domination over the young princess was soon absolute; and, on her marriage with Ferdinand of Aragon, with whom she was eventually to rule over all Spain, his control extended to her husband. With so much power in his unscrupulous hands, it was an easy task for Torquemada to persuade his royal puppets to give formal sanction to his life-long dream, the pitiless persecution of heretics and Jews.

"Such were the beginnings of the diabolical tribunal that even today, after four and a half centuries, stops the breath and makes the blood run cold: the Spanish Inquisition."

After these turgid, not strictly accurate, yet harmless opening paragraphs, the anonymous author wasted no time in getting down to business, which was a minute account, extending over three hundred pages, of every conceivable (and inconceivable) method of causing physical discomfort to heretics, Jews and all others whose religious or political views ran contrary to those of the inquisitor-general. The iron maiden, the thumbscrew, the boot, the stake, the pincers—those and many more were described and illustrated by harrowing pictures. It was an exhaustive survey, yet its real purpose was manifest on every page. The author was no diligent historian. The book was not intended for the earnest student; it was to satisfy the sadist—

and, by correlation, the masochist—which, though it seldom finds outward physical expression, lurks in the margin of consciousness of the mass of mankind.

Charlton's lip curled with distaste; it was not pleasant to think of a girl reading of such atrocities aloud. He almost hoped that it might not be his duty to lay hands on Yule's murderer, who had displayed such a precise awareness of the fitness of things, such a sense of poetic justice.

He laid the book on the arm of the chair.

"Not very pretty," he said. "How did that window-pane get smashed, Miss Gilbert?"

The sudden question caught her unprepared, as was intended.

"The window-pane?" She turned in her chair. "Oh, that. I—I did it myself. I had to break into my own house, if you can imagine anything quite so silly! I went out without my key and had to come along the side passage, climb over the back-garden wall and break the glass, to get at the latch inside the door."

"When did this happen?"

"Some weeks ago."

"If you have a vacuum-cleaner," he suggested dryly, "I recommend you to use it. Even after this lapse of time, there are still some dangerous splinters of glass on the carpet."

"It's the terrible problem of servants. You simply can't *get* a girl. I'm afraid I'm not the truly domesticated type of—"

"Was there any incident last night, Miss Gilbert, that you would not describe as a normal part of your evenings together?"

The question was answered with reluctance and only after long hesitation.

"Yes.... It was after eleven o'clock before he let me stop reading. For about ten minutes, he sat slumped in his chair and not saying anything. I was practically on the point of screaming when he suddenly jumped up and began to shout horrible threats at me—all the things he'd do if I didn't stop treating him so coldly.

"Did he attack you?"

"No. I believe he would have done, but fortunately he was interrupted."

"By what?"

She bit her lip.

"Oh, we were just interrupted. Something happened. Yes, it was the phone. A wrong number. But it was providential, because when I came out of the front room, where the telephone is, he was in the hall, putting on his greatcoat. He left without saying another word to me."

"He was the only visitor here last night?"

"Yes. After he'd gone, I made up my mind never to let him in the house again, whatever he might threaten to do."

"Was there any regularity in his visits?"

"Oh, yes—that was one of the worst parts of it. He used to come every Wednesday evening. He would arrive at half-past eight and leave at half-past eleven. It never varied. My first thought when I woke up on Wednesday morning was—"

The front door bell was ringing. With a word of apology, she got up and left the room. Absentmindedly, for his brain was busy with other things, Charlton picked up "The Bloodhound of Valladolid" and idly ran through it. Just as he was about to throw it aside, something caught his eye.

"Lopez de Gonzala, Marquis of Santagena, was taken to the place of execution. His legs and arms were lashed separately to four great white stallions, which were then urged with whips, each in a different direction."

It was not by chance that he had noticed the paragraph. His attention was drawn to it by the two parallel brackets that had been pencilled down the margin.

Fay Gilbert came back with the remark that tradespeople always seemed to call at the wrong moment.

Charlton asked: "Where did the Sergeant-major get this book, Miss Gilbert?"

"Where he got all the others, I suppose. I really don't know."

He concluded the interview and, with "The Bloodhound of Valladolid" in his pocket, went out to his car.

The visit to Fay Gilbert had been far from unprofitable, he felt, even though he was not quite certain whether to believe a single word she had said. He had no knowledge of her merit as a fan-dancer, yet he could not share Jack Nightingale's poor opinion of her acting ability.

CHAPTER TWENTY-SIX

I

MAJOR T. W. MELLIS, R.A., did not rise from his chair, but remained seated behind the plain deal table.

In the first moment of meeting, Charlton's brain registered the impression of a retiring, unpretentious, small, grey-haired man in tortoiseshell-rimmed spectacles, who would have appeared more at home surrounded by dusty, taped bundles of conveyances and wayleave agreements; and whose pacific, mild demeanour seemed a repudiation of the cloth crowns on the shoulders of his battledress.

The horizontally fluted interior of that end of the long, partitioned Nissen was painted green to waist level and finished off in cream. In the centre was a circular stove, from which ash and coke cinders had spilled untidily on to the concrete floor. Unplaned planks laid on iron brackets bolted to the curved wall-stanchions formed primitive shelves, on which were disorderly piles of Army publications—A.B.C.A. Bulletins, "The British Way and Purpose" and training handbooks—and, immediately behind the Major's sparsely covered head, a tilting row of reference books, among which Charlton was surprised to notice Moriarty's *Police Law* and Lombroso's *The Female Criminal*.

On the end wall were boards carrying dozens of different-coloured, metal-rimmed cardboard discs, each on its separate nail. On the other wall were drawing-pinned silhouettes of German and Allied aircraft; and to the side of the door leading into the late Sergeant-major's room was another board that permanently required answers to the two questions, one below the other: "Where are you going, sir?..." and "When will you be back?..." Chalked against the first was, "Leave" and against the second, "16 Jun," which information struck Charlton as only of historic interest.

219

"Good morning, Inspector," was the Major's unsmiling greeting. "Please sit down."

Charlton laid his black homburg on the corner of the table and took his seat on the yellow-varnished folding chair. The Major went on: "Captain Bell, the medical officer, has told me what has happened. I understand from him that the police investigation is in your hands; and have given instructions for the whole personnel of this Battery to be confined to camp or gun-site, as the case may be. You can safely rely on my full co-operation—as far, of course, as my position permits."

"Thank you, sir. First of all, what was Sergeant-major Yule's laundry number?"

The telephone was on the shelf behind the Major. He reached round for the hand-microphone, waited until the duty telephonist in the general office answered and said:

"Go and ask the Quartermaster to tell you the Sergeant-major's laundry number." He placed his hand over the transmitter and invited Charlton to continue.

"Captain Bell will probably have told you, sir, that death took place late last night or in the early hours of this morning. I have already established that Sergeant-major Yule left Etchworth, after visiting an acquaintance, at approximately eleven-thirty, presumably with the intention of returning to camp. The circumstances suggest that he was intercepted before he reached here. What are the camp standing orders, sir, about reporting in at night?"

"As a warrant officer, the Sergeant-major had full liberty of action on such nights as he was not acting as orderly officer."

"And the rest of the men?"

"Lights Out is at twenty-three hundred hours. It is the duty of the orderly N.C.O. to go round the sleeping-huts and ensure, before turning out the lights, that all personnel not issued with a late pass are in camp."

"Is this rule rigidly enforced, sir?"

"As far as I am officially aware. I have confidence in the good sense of the men in my charge." Charlton thought he detected a twinkle in the kindly grey eyes. "It is not always desirable for a unit commander to question the discretion of his N.C.Os."

The Inspector smiled comprehension and tactfully changed the subject.

"There's nothing to suggest, sir—as far as my enquiries have gone at the moment—that the Sergeant-major was killed in hot blood. The affair was premeditated. It might possibly be that the intention was to give the Sergeant-major no more than an uncomfortable quarter of an hour; and that murder was not contemplated. But it wasn't done on the spur of the moment. The rope used for the crime—"

The Major cut him short.

"I can help you there. Captain Bell mentioned the point to me. I've not seen it, of course, but Captain Bell's description leaves little doubt that it is the forward brake-rope of a Light Anti-Aircraft gun. One end is looped for attachment to the metal toggle of the rear brake-rope, which forms a part of the brake mechanism. When the gun is mobile, the free end of the forward brake-rope is held in the hand of a member of the gun detachment, travelling in the tractor that draws the gun along. When the gun is static, the rope is detached and wound round a pair of hooks on the platform of the gun."

"Are you able to tell me yet, sir, whether any of the Battery's brake-ropes are missing this morning?"

"Yes. In the ordinary way—"

He stopped speaking, removed his hand from the telephone transmitter and said, "Yes?"

When he had rung off, he turned back to the Inspector.

"The Sergeant-major's laundry number—that is, the one he has used since we moved into this area—is LY 207."

Charlton thanked him. He had feared as much.

"Now," said Major Mellis, "where was I? Oh, yes... In the normal way, there is no gun at B.H.Q., but during the last ten days or so we have had one here for training purposes. Yesterday it became operationally necessary to move the gun elsewhere and I—or rather, my Battery Captain—gave instructions in the afternoon for it to be sent away from here at O-seven-thirty hours this morning. A quarter of an hour before that time, my quartermaster reported to me that the despatch of the gun would be delayed until a forward brake-rope could be obtained.

"Naturally, I asked the Q. why such an important detail had been left until the last minute. His reply was that, a week ago, a gun on one of the Battery's sites had to be sent to R.E.M.E. workshops for overhaul and, as it was found that the brake-rope was unserviceable, Captain Fitzgerald—the Battery Captain had given instructions for it to be replaced by the rope from the training gun at B.H.Q.

"What should have happened, of course, when the gun was returned to site from R.E.M.E., was for the brake-rope to be sent back immediately to B.H.Q. Human nature being what it is, however, the matter was deferred. When he heard that the training gun had to be urgently despatched, the Quartermaster gave instructions for the rope to be retrieved from the gun-site. An indent for a new rope had, of course, been put through, but it had not arrived. The gunner to whom the Quartermaster gave this order—"

"Just a moment, sir. Where is this gun-site you mention? Is it the one on Mr. Nightingale's land?"

"Yes. I hardly think I am betraying a military confidence in telling you that it is known as A.R. 4. As I was about to say, the gunner who received the instructions from the Quartermaster—the man's name is Fieldhouse asserted, first to the Q. and later to me, that he duly collected the rope from A.R. 4, brought it back to B.H.Q. and wound it on the hooks of the training gun. Fieldhouse admits that he did not carry out the order until last night, his excuse being that he forgot. He reported to the Quartermaster before he went to bed that the rope was in position on the training gun; but it was not there when the Quartermaster examined it a few minutes after seven o'clock this morning. I took the precaution—this, of course, was before we had heard the grave news about the Sergeant-major or even realized that he was not in camp—I took the precaution of ringing up the Sergeant in charge of A.R. 4. He confirmed that the brake-rope was handed by himself to Fieldhouse at eleven o'clock last night."

"Have you any reason, sir, to doubt the word of Gunner Fieldhouse?"

The Major stroked his chin.

Well, he said after a thoughtful pause, "I have never found him untruthful in my direct dealings with him. If anything, his failing lies in the other direction. As is frequently the case with ginger-headed persons"—(Charlton's interest in Fieldhouse quickened)—"he is a most outspoken young man—and something of a stormy petrel. An ungovernable temper has got him into serious trouble in the past; he served a period of detention earlier in this year for striking the Sergeant-major."

"Sergeant-major Yule?"

"Yes. At the court-martial, the boy flatly denied having made the attack, but the evidence against him was too strong. A warrant officer is not likely to charge an—er—unimportant member of the rank and file with assault, if such were not the case. And in addition, the sounds of the struggle were heard in the next room by one of my N.C.Os., Lance-bombardier Wilkinson, a very dependable and trustworthy man."

"Where did this happen, sir?"

"At Stalcote-on-Sea, our previous station. Whilst Fieldhouse was in detention barracks, he met with an accident—a fractured jaw. I say an 'accident'; and so it is described in the records." He shook his head sadly. "I suspect that it was more likely the result of a brawl. The injury considerably delayed Fieldhouse's return, and it was not until the tenth of this month—a fortnight ago yesterday—that he reported back to this unit."

"What has been his general manner since?"

"Subdued without being sulky. I was beginning to hope that he had at last learnt his lesson and had decided to turn himself into an efficient soldier. I am bound; to say in Fieldhouse's defence that, apart from striking the Sergeant-major, he has never given any trouble during his service with this Battery, although his primary and corps training units gave a very unfavourable account of him. I believe myself that his greatest shortcoming is that he is not, by nature, amenable to discipline; he is resentful of any interference with his freedom of action." Once more he shook his head. "The Army has little patience with such men. My own view, as a student of psychology—not a very brilliant one, I'm afraid!—is that you cannot turn a man into a good soldier by force. And that you cannot treat them all alike. Men of Fieldhouse's temperament need individual attention; no bullying or shouting—just a quiet word of praise now and again." Charlton nodded agreement.

"Upbringing has a lot to do with it," he said. "Squalid homes; insipid, uninspired methods of school-teaching; spare time divided between the dance-hall and the dog-track; the—"

"That is hardly the case with Fieldhouse," the Major threw in. "He is a well-educated and widely read young man."

"A lively imagination?"

"Undoubtedly." He shot the Inspector a shrewd glance. "To employ the jargon of the neuro-psychiatrists, I should class him as an introvert; a dreamer, a dreamer, shall we say, with a grievance—rather than a man of action. In Fieldhouse, there are the makings of a good novelist. Following what I take to be your line of thought, Inspector, I'd say that Fieldhouse would have been capable of planning this murder in every detail, but would not have put it into practice. Any intelligent man can commit murder—on paper. If Fieldhouse had killed the Sergeant-major, he would have done it, I feel certain, not by careful, prearranged plotting, but on the impulse of the moment, in blind rage and with the nearest weapon."

"Thank you, sir. That's very helpful.... Now, there are one or two other questions I must ask you. The first is, what are the arrangements for guarding this camp at night? Are sentries posted?"

"No. The functions of a B.H.Q. are largely administrative; it is of no vital military importance. Besides, one would need a hundred sentries for this camp. You will have seen that it's as open as a native village. Of course we have certain safety precautions. A fire-picquet composed of one N.C.O. and three men is posted every night. Their whole period of duty is from six o'clock one evening until six o'clock the next. Naturally, their fire-watching responsibilites are restricted to the hours of darkness—or, to be more exact, from Lights Out to Reveille. During the day-time they carry on their normal work, undertaking, in addition, any camp-maintenance fatigues that may be necessary. They are confined to camp during the hours of blackout. They periodically tour the camp throughout the night, to ensure that all is well; and whichever of them may have that particular turn of duty gets the cookhouse fires going and rouses the duty cook at O-six-hundred hours."

"May I have the names of last night's fire-picquet?"

The Major reached forward to a filing-tray on the table, ran through the papers and extracted a sheet.

"This is a copy of yesterday's Daily Orders," he said, and, after changing his spectacles, consulted the sheet and went on: "The orderly N.C.O. was Lance-bombardier Wilkinson; the three men, Gunners Nelson, Regan and Lovelock. Gunner Nelson is not on the establishment of this unit. He forms one of a small party of men from other Batteries who are here on a gun-drill course. It was on account of the course that the training gun I have mentioned was brought to B.H.Q."

Charlton jotted down the names and glanced up to find the little Major looking at him rather speculatively, like a sparrow with its head on one side.

"It is not for me, Inspector," he said, as if doubtful how the remark would be received, "to do more than answer your questions and tell you the facts as I know them. I'm a trifle hesitant, therefore, in giving you one or two details about Gunner Nelson."

"Please go on, sir."

"At one time, this man Nelson was a war-substantive sergeant on the strength of this unit. He was, in fact, a troop-sergeant, holding a more responsible position than an ordinary detachment-commander. He was a most competent soldier, thoroughly acquainted with his duties—and I considered him to be one of the best men under my command. Then suddenly, for no apparent reason, he began to go to pieces, until finally he was guilty of an act of such gross negligence that he was asked to relinquish his stripes. He reverted to the rank of gunner and was cross-posted to another Battery."

The Major paused.

"It may be only a coincidence," he continued, "but nevertheless, it is curious that the Sergeant-major should meet his death during Nelson's short stay in this camp."

"But why the Sergeant-major? From what you tell me, he doesn't seem to have been concerned in Nelson's relegation."

"I should have added," the Major hastened to enlighten him, "that in the last stormy interview I had with Nelson, he placed the entire blame for his alleged deterioration—which he stoutly denied—on the Sergeant-major, even going so far as to describe the Sergeant-major's treatment of him as calculated, cold-blooded victimization."

"I take it, sir, that you supported the Sergeant-major?"

"Yes. It was a serious decision and not reached without weighty consideration. The Colonel of the Regiment accepted my recommendations. What gives added point to these remarks of mine was a casual comment passed to me by the Sergeant-major only the day before yesterday. His actual words, as I remember them, were, 'I'm warning you, sir, to expect trouble with Nelson. I've caught him looking at me once or twice in a very strange manner and he's quite likely to start something.'"

He sat back in his chair with a look of mild triumph on his face.

"Discover the motive, Inspector," he said, "and you are half-way to discovering the murderer."

Charlton smiled sweetly.

"I always find it quicker," he said, "to discover the murderer first."

He was afterwards to remember that sweeping dictum.

II

He referred again to the training gun.

"Is it," he asked, "locked up at night? It may become necessary to corroborate Gunner Fieldhouse's story."

"The gun is housed in a shed normally used for M.T.—that is, motor transport. The shed is kept padlocked at night and the key is hung on the key-board over the telephonist's desk in the general office. I have not questioned Fieldhouse on the point, but if he did, in fact, bring the brake-rope back from A.R. 4, he would have had to obtain the key from the office and would, presumably, have returned the key to the office after relocking the shed."

"Is the Battery Office empty at night?"

"No. It is occupied by a duty telephonist every minute of the twenty-four hours. There are three telephonists—Gunners Postbechild, Allman and McFinnon. There is a bed and mattress kept in the general office for the night telephonist. By sleeping alongside the phone, he need not stay awake all night. There is a loud bell fitted to the instrument. The telephonists have instructions to lock themselves in the office before settling down for the night."

"Which of the three was on duty last night?"

"That I must find out for you. Telephonists do not appear on Battery Orders. I shall have to refer to—just a moment, though. It was Gunner Postbechild."

Charlton, with pencil poised, made a humorous grimace.

"Will you spell it, please?"

The Major did so, adding:

"A singular name for a very singular young man. I recall that he was on duty last night, because I telephoned from the mess—there is an extension through from the office to the mess—to ask for the correct time; and it was Postbechild who told me—with some annoyance; I imagine I had interrupted his slumbers!—that it was 23.45 hours—a quarter to twelve."

"Is there a duplicate of the key to the shed, sir?"

"Duplicates of all the keys in the camp are held in a strong-box, which I keep for safety in the mess. Captain Fitzgerald and I are the only holders of keys of the strong-box."

"No other key will open the gun-shed padlock?"

"Not as far as I know. They are all strong padlocks of the most reliable manufacture."

"And all the keys, including the gun-shed key, are kept hung on a board in Battery Office."

"Yes. They are obtained from there as and when required. I need hardly say that the telephonists have strict instructions not to hand them to unauthorized persons."

The Inspector restrained his satisfaction; the position was beginning to clarify. If the rope that he himself had removed from the mangled body of Sergeant-major Yule was identical with the rope handed over by the A.R. 4 detachment-commander to Fieldhouse, the *prima facie* evidence strongly suggested that if Fieldhouse had not used the rope on Yule, but had brought it back and locked it away in the temporary gun-shed, then the murder could have been done only by someone who had access to the gun-shed—i.e. a member of XYZ B.H.Q. personnel. It seemed inconceivable that any other person would endanger his safety by entering the camp in order to steal the forward brake-rope of the training gun. It was not the only length of cordage available in Downshire. The murderer, he thought with a grim inward smile, would one day find that out.

"I have one last question, sir. When we found the Sergeant-major's body this morning, his hands were lashed behind his back with a dog-lead. Does any man in the camp keep—"

He stopped short when he saw the expression on the Major's face.

"Was it of flat, reddish-brown leather, about half an inch wide, with the clip missing?" the Major demanded.

Charlton nodded and the Major went on, with gathering excitement:

"That is a very remarkable thing! Let me give you the facts. Until recently, Captain Fitzgerald had a little Cairn terrier, of which he was extremely fond. Last Saturday evening, his batman, whose name is Gianella and who was also devoted to Scottie, took the dog for its evening walk. Because of the danger from traffic in the blackout, Scottie was kept on the lead. They had not gone far towards Sheep village when they met the Sergeant-major, retracing his steps from the bus-stop. He sent Gianella back to camp for a parcel he had left behind, and meanwhile took charge of Scottie. But the dog jerked the lead out of his hand and went running off after Gianella, with the lead trailing behind him. In spite of—"

"One moment, sir. Are there any witnesses to the fact that the lead was still attached to the dog's collar when he broke loose?"

"Only the Sergeant-major. In spite of protracted search, Scottie was neither seen nor heard again until three o'clock in the morning, when he awakened Captain Fitzgerald by scratching at the outer door of the mess. The Captain found the poor little fellow in such a terrible state—he looked as if he had been kicked hard, persistently and without mercy— that he put him out of his agony by shooting him. The clip of the lead was still attached to the collar, but the lead itself was nowhere to be found. It is astonishing that—"

"Is Captain Fitzgerald in at the moment, sir?"

"I'm afraid not. I expect him back early this evening."

"I'll see him then, if it's convenient. Now I'd like, if I may—"

The telephone was ringing again. The Major reached round for the hand-microphone and said into it:

"Battery Commander.... Yes, he's here. One moment, please."

He passed the instrument over to Charlton. The caller was Sgt. Peters from Whitchester.

"About that dog-lead," he said. "Thought you'd like to know as soon as possible. There's some good, clear prints on it. Two of them were made by the deceased, but not the others."

"That's a good start," Charlton approved, "and it means some more work for you. I want the apparatus—plate, squeegee, ink and so forth.... Yes, I want them here. If you can't come yourself, send someone else along.... No, this afternoon would do.... That will be soon enough. And bring plenty of paper, Peters—it's a wholesale job.... Right. Goodbye."

He hung up and said to the Major:

"I've a rather large request to make, sir. It's necessary to take the finger-prints of every man in this camp."

The Major smiled: "That can be easily arranged, Inspector. I'll get one of my clerks to prepare a nominal roll of B.H.Q. and attached personnel; and I'll call a muster parade for—what time will suit you?"

"Two o'clock, sir?"

"Very good. Now, do you wish to speak to anyone else?"

"I'll want to question everybody eventually, sir."

"Then I have a suggestion to make to you, Inspector. Bombardier Bradfield told me this morning that he was your assistant before he was called to the colours. Would it be of any help to you if I released him from his duties for a day or two?"

"That's very kind of you," Charlton said gratefully.

"You will have to regard it," was the Major's warning, "as having effect only within this camp and, if you find it necessary to go there, A.R. 4 gun-site. We will define Bradfield's status as 'N.C.O. Conducting Visitor.'"

Thus, to my astonishment, did I get my old job back.

CHAPTER TWENTY-SEVEN

I

I REQUISITIONED the lecture-hut, arranged a table and chairs, supplied paper, pens, ink and blotting-paper, and got the stove going.

"Now, sir," I asked the Inspector briskly, "which men do you want to see—and in what order?"

Sitting at the table, he consulted the nominal roll that I had typed for him. He looked up at me.

"Is this the whole boiling?" he enquired.

"It includes everyone who was—or should have been—in camp last night: officers, N.C.Os. and men. It includes ten men temporarily attached to us on a gunnery course, but it doesn't include a man who's on leave, Gunner Owen, the sergeants' mess orderly. He's due back by 23.59 hours today."

With the nominal roll in front of him, he took a sheet of paper and wrote down a list of names. He handed it across to me with the remark:

"Those will do for a start."

I raised my eyebrows when I saw the men he had chosen.

"You've not been wasting your time," I told him, and went off to fetch the first of them.

I was not present at the interviews that followed. I was stamping up and down outside in the cold.

II

No. I was the lugubrious Gunner Postbechild....

"What was your period of duty?"

"Twenty-three hundred yesterday till O-seven hundred today."

It was one of Postbechild's periods of dudgeon. There were days when he was convinced that every man's hand was against him. This was one of them.

"Who was on duty before you?"

"Gunner McFinnon."

"Did anyone come into Battery Office after you had taken over from McFinnon?"

"Yes."

"Who was it?"

Postbechild took his time to answer; there is a loyalty among gunners. Finally he blurted:

"Gunner Fieldhouse."

"What did he want?"

"The key of one of the M.T. sheds. It was Okay for him to have it, 'cause—"

"Yes," Charlton soothed him. "Just answer my questions. What time was this?"

"'Bout eleven-twenty."

"Why did he want the key?"

"To put away a brake-rope that he'd just fetched from site."

"Had he the rope with him?"

"Yes."

"You're sure it was a *brake*-rope?"

"I know a brake-rope when I see one."

"When did he return the key?"

"Three or four minutes after."

"What did he say?"

Postbechild's expression showed all the bottled-up impatience of a child-plagued parent.

"Something about having wound the rope on the gun, ready for the morning."

"That was all he said?"

"Yes—except 'good-night.' I put the key back on its hook and tried to get some sleep."

"You'd locked yourself in?"

"Yes. Standing orders."

"And you had no further interruptions?"

233

The lanky telephonist glowered at him with a splenetic eye.

"Interruptions? On this job, it's nothing else but. Just dropping off, I was, when the O.C. was on the blower, wanting to know the time. As if *he* should worry."

"When was that?"

"23.45. Time he ought to've been in bed."

"Nobody else came into the office?"

"Not last night."

"And this morning?"

"Cor starve a crow! You keep at it, don't you? I was sweeping out the office—it was about quarter to seven—when the Q. knocked on the door to come in. The conversation was as follows: 'Good morning, Postbechild.' 'Good morning, Q.' Conversation ends. He took the key of the gun-shed and went out again. I went off duty at seven."

His manner defied Charlton to think of any further questions. Charlton had one ready:

"You're quite certain that nobody besides Gunner Fieldhouse had access to that key last night?"

"I don't know about access," said the singular young man, "but no one else got at it."

III

No. 2 was stolid, sandy-moustached, spectacled L/Bdr. Wilkinson....

"You were N.C.O. in charge of fire-picquet last night?"

"Yes, sir."

"Who were the men on with you?"

"Gunner Nelson, Gunner Lovelock and Gunner Regan."

"How was the duty divided last night?"

"Each of the three men did two hours and forty minutes. Lovelock from eleven till twenty to two; Nelson till twenty past four; then Regan till seven o'clock."

"The N.C.O. doesn't take a turn?"

"No, sir. He stays in the fire-picquet hut. There are four bedsteads in it. We take our own blankets round. The N.C.O. fixes the spells of duty, gives the men any special instruction there may be about particular people to be wakened, and then gets to bed. The man on last turn calls him at quarter to seven, and he goes round rousing the camp at seven o'clock."

"Did anything out of the ordinary happen last night?"

"Nothing, as far as I was concerned, sir. I went round at about five past eleven, to make sure that all lights were out."

"Was there any roll-call?"

"There was no actual shouting out of the names, sir, but I ran an eye over the beds."

"Any absentees?"

"One, sir. Gunner Fieldhouse. He was out on duty. He had reported to me before he went."

"Did he report to you when he came back?"

"No, sir."

"What about the senior N.C.Os.? Did you visit their huts?"

Wilkinson's eyes twinkled humorously.

"No, sir. They were outside my province. When I got back to the fire-picquet hut, Lovelock was waiting for me in the regulation dress—greatcoat, respirator and steel helmet. The three of them had fixed it amongst themselves that he should go on first. Nelson and Regan were already in bed. I sent Lovelock off on his patrol and went to bed myself."

"And at twenty to two, you changed the picquet?"

The eyes behind the gold rims gleamed again.

"I'm afraid I didn't have much to do with it, sir. Theoretically, the orderly N.C.O. should make certain that the men are relieved at the correct intervals, but in practice, a man can be depended upon to call out the next man at the proper time."

"You yourself, then, were not aroused throughout the night?"

"No, sir. I slept right through from—well, I suppose it was somewhere between eleven-thirty and quarter to twelve that

I got to sleep—until Regan shook me at six-forty-five this morning."

"You weren't disturbed when Lovelock came in to wake Nelson?"

"No. I'd had a long, busy day and I slept like a log."

IV

No. 3 was languid, wavy-haired, cherub-faced Gunner Lovelock....

"What time did you leave the fire-picquet hut?"

"I really don't remember exactly. Somewhere round ten past eleven, I expect."

"Where did you go when you left the fire-picquet hut?"

"Oh, we wander about for two hours and forty minutes, then we go and dig the next fellow out."

"When I said *you*, Lovelock, I meant *you*. Where did you go?"

"Just on a general stooge round the camp. Here and there, you know. Along the paths between the huts and down as far as the main road once or twice. Anything to keep awake and pass the time. Fire-picquet's a crashing bore and you feel like *death* the next day."

"On leaving the fire-picquet hut, did you go anywhere near the M.T. sheds?"

"Look here!" said Lovelock grandly. "I don't know anything about this murder. I don't know anything at all. I didn't touch the rope and nobody's going to—"

"Which rope, Lovelock?"

"Why, the one on the training gun that everybody's discussing, of course. If you want to know anything about that, go and ask Fieldhouse!"

This dramatic announcement was taken calmly.

"Did you go anywhere near the M.T. sheds?" Charlton asked again.

"Yes, I did! And I caught Fieldhouse trying to pinch the rope!"

"Really?" said Charlton, raising his eyebrows. "Did you catch him in the act, with the rope in his hand?"

The reply was a mixture of defiance and regret.

"No."

Charlton's impassive face masked his feelings. If Lovelock was trying to injure Fieldhouse, he obviously had not a proper knowledge of the facts.

"He was unlocking the door when I first noticed him," Lovelock went on. "He had a torch, so I saw him perfectly. When he heard me coming, he pretended to be locking it, and had the sauce to expect me to believe that he'd brought the brake-rope from A.R. 4 and had just put it away. Of course, I didn't know then that it was important—or I should certainly have reported it to an officer."

"Did you see the rope?"

"No. He went off towards Battery Office, saying he was going to return the key—and that was the last I saw of him."

"You met nobody else in or around the camp?"

Lovelock shook his curls.

"There's another thing you may care to know," he drawled. "Make what you like out of it. Yesterday morning in the office, Bombardier Morton threatened to tear the Sergeant-major apart with wild horses."

V

No. 4 was tall, healthy, intelligent Gunner Nelson....

"You had the middle period of duty, I believe?"

"Yes, sir."

"So that Gunner Lovelock awakened you at 1.40?"

"Er—no, sir."

"Why was that, Nelson?"

"I don't want to get the kid into trouble, sir—I've had trouble enough of my own in the Army—but I've got to tell you this, because murder's a serious matter. What actually happened, sir, was that, knowing I was to do the middle turn, I bedded down in the fire-picquet hut well before ten o'clock. I woke up later of my own accord and struck a match to see the time. I was surprised to find that it was ten to three. I saw that Lovelock's bed was empty, so I scrambled into my kit and went off to look for him. He was sound asleep in the cookhouse. I sent him off to bed and took over until it was time to wake Gunner Regan."

VI

No. 5 was stumpy, wrinkled-faced, close-cropped Liverpool-Irishman from Bootle, Gunner Regan....

"Yes, sor, I was on t'ird. Gonner Nelson 'e gives me a shake at twenty past four. At five-t'irty, I starts the foires in the coo-k'ouse and at six o'clock, I wakes op the coo-ks. At quarter to seven, sor, I was on the way round to the foire-picquet hot, to call Bombardier Wilkinson, the orderly N.C.O., and I'm jost passing the M.T. hot, where the training gon is kept, when the Q. calls out to me from the door of the hot, where he's standing. 'E shoines a torch to see who I am, sor, and sends me off for Gonner Field'ouse. The Q., sor, 'e was in a bloody bad temper, sor."

"Bombardier Wilkinson has told me, Regan, that you were already in bed when he got to the fire-picquet hut last night. Were you awake when he came in?"

"Yes, sor, I was still awake, but I dropped off, sor, a minute or two after. I don't remimber northing till Gonner Nelson gets me out of bed."

VII

No. 6 was aesthetic, thin-nostrilled Bdr. Morton, with a bandaged right hand....

The Inspector went straight to the point.

"Where were you between eleven o'clock and midnight yesterday, Bombardier?" he asked briskly.

"I was out of camp, sir. I went for a walk."

"What time did you get back here?"

"Soon after half-past twelve."

"Did you meet anyone during your walk?"

"No, sir."

"Did you call anywhere?"

"No, sir."

"How did you injure your hand, Bombardier?"

"I cut it rather badly last night. I was on the way to clean my teeth, when I slipped on the duckboards and fell forward with the glass in my hand. The glass broke and—"

"Bombardier Morton"—there was a sharp note in the deep voice—"you will save a great deal of my time if you will keep to the truth. I suggest to you that you damaged your hand on the french window at the rear of a house called 'Lyme Regis' in Etchworth village. Am I right?"

Morton licked dry lips.

"Yes," he admitted after a pause.

"Why did you go there?"

"I know the people."

"Mr. and Mrs. Saunders?"

"Yes."

"Mr. Saunders—that is, Lieutenant Saunders—has been in enemy hands for some time. Were you acquainted with him before he became a prisoner?"

"I suppose," Morton said drearily, "I'd better tell you the whole story. I got to know Mrs. Saunders. She called herself Miss Fay Gilbert and she didn't wear a wedding-ring. One evening, I proposed to her. She told me that she was already married and that her husband was a prisoner of war in Italy. I kept away from her after that. Then I heard that Sergeant-major Yule was making himself a nuisance to her."

"Who told you?"

"Lance-bombardier Lomas, one of the N.C.Os. at our T.H.Q. in Etchworth. He said that the Sergeant-major had been seen coming in and out of 'Lyme Regis.'"

"And last night...?"

"You'll understand, Inspector, that I haven't been very cheerful recently, especially as I knew that Sergeant-major Yule—a particularly unpleasant type of man—was thrusting his company on Mrs. Saunders, whose safety and happiness meant—and still mean—a lot to me. Yesterday evening I was very restless. Early in the evening, we had a small party in the officers' mess to celebrate the anniversary of the first Jerry plane brought down by this Battery. It broke up in the region of seven-thirty; and half an hour later, I noticed the Sergeant-major leaving camp. I guessed where he was going. .....Do you mind if I smoke?"

"Of course not. Have one of these."

"As I said," Morton resumed when their cigarettes were lighted, "I was restless. Around ten o'clock, I decided to go for a walk, to make myself tired enough to sleep. Almost in spite of myself, I drifted in the direction of Etchworth. I went through the village and on towards Lulverton. Then I turned back.... On my way past 'Lyme Regis,' I slowed down and stopped."

"What time was that?"

"I don't know exactly. Somewhere round quarter past eleven, I think.... I don't really know what made me do it, but, after listening to hear whether anyone was coming along the road, I slipped down the passageway between 'Lyme Regis' and the next house and climbed the back-garden wall.... I couldn't see anything through the french windows because of the blackout curtains, but I heard enough to make me ram my fist through the glass, feel for the catch and pull open the door."

"What did you hear?"

"It was the Sergeant-major. He was threatening Mrs. Saunders. That was enough for me. I saw red. I burst into the room and told him to get out or I'd throw him out."

"Did he go?"

"Not at first. He smiled at me in that oily, ingratiating way of his and told me not to be a damn fool. He sat down in a chair and lighted a cigarette. He said, 'I don't recommend you to try anything so silly, Morton. You'll remember what happened to Gunner Fieldhouse.' I shouted back at him, 'Yes—and I haven't forgotten what happened to Owen and Nelson, either. If you're not away from this house in less than a minute, I'll give you the biggest hiding you've ever had in your disgusting, useless life!'"

He was breathing heavily, as if at the recollection of the scene. Then he smiled apologetically at Charlton.

"I got a bit worked up. I should have hit him, but he didn't give me a chance. The man was an utter coward at heart. He got out of his chair without a word and went across the room. He stopped at the door and said to me, with another of his nasty smirks, 'I hope you enjoy your chat with Captain Fitzgerald. He's looking for someone like you.'"

"Do you know what he meant?"

Morton shrugged his shoulders.

"The only thing I could think of at the time was that he was going to report me to the Captain for threatening him. On thinking it over, though, I can't see why. Things like that are done normally through the Battery Commander. In any case, the B.S.M. was far from popular with the Captain. Besides, I don't see how he could have put me on a charge; he wouldn't have shown up very well himself. The only witness was Mrs. Saunders."

"A day or two ago," Charlton said casually, "Captain Fitzgerald's Cairn terrier was kicked nearly to death."

Bombardier Morton looked at him steadily. Comprehension slowly dawned.

"You mean that he was going to frame me? It's the sort of thing to be expected of him, the septic swine! Good God, I hadn't thought of that! But how could you have—anyway, he didn't get time to do it, because Captain Fitzgerald was quite friendly with me this morning."

"No," the Inspector agreed, "he didn't get time to do it." Morton looked at him sharply, but he went serenely on: "Last night's quarrel was not the first you've had with the Sergeant-major, was it?"

The question was answered with a bleak smile.

"Somebody's been talking, I see! Yes, we've had several rows about one thing or another. That was the first major engagement. The others were only local skirmishes."

"One of them being yesterday morning, I take it, when some reference was made to wild horses?"

Morton jumped with surprise.

"But that was only—I mean, they weren't real horses. I'd been asking the Sergeant-major to stop visiting Mrs. Saunders and his only reply was that wild horses wouldn't drag him away from her."

"And your answer was—"

"Yes, I know what I said! I said, 'We shall see,' but that was only a vague sort of threat, sir, because there didn't seem to be much else to say. Who's been telling you these rotten things about me?"

He received no reply. As an alternative, Charlton said:

"After his remarks about Captain Fitzgerald, did the Sergeant-major leave 'Lyme Regis'?"

"Yes. He put on his greatcoat in the hall and went without saying another word to either of us."

"What did you do?"

"I stopped for a few minutes, to try and reassure Mrs. Saunders. I asked her, for her own sake, not to let him in the house again; and after she'd promised she wouldn't, I came away."

"What time did you leave?"

"Questions about exact times are always difficult to answer, sir. I imagine it was in the region of twenty to twelve."

"Did you come straight back to camp?"

"Well, not exactly. The B.S.M. had something like ten minutes' start of me, but I was the faster walker and I didn't want to catch him up. I had a feeling there'd be trouble in the morning, but I wasn't anxious for any more just then.

"I got to the entrance to the camp without seeing him. I can tell you what time that was, because I stopped and looked at my watch. It was two minutes past twelve. I decided to give him half an hour to get to bed; and walked on into Sheep. It was half-past twelve when I eventually got back into camp. Bombardier Bradfield will be able to confirm that, because he was still awake when I got in."

"The road from Etchworth took you past the field in which the Sergeant-major's body was found this morning. Did you notice anything unusual as you went by? Any shouts or sounds of a struggle or the noise of galloping hooves?"

"No, sir."

"And you met nobody between Etchworth and this camp?"

"Nobody at all."

"When you reached here, was there anyone about?"

"Everything was quiet. The only person I saw or spoke to was Bombardier Bradfield, when I got back into our hut."

Charlton, who had been idly scribbling on his blotting-pad, now laid his pencil down.

"Thank you, he said. "That's the end of my questions."

Morton rose to his feet.

"I'm sorry, sir," he said, "that I started off by lying to you. It had nothing to do with the murder, It was because..."

His voice trailed off and he looked unhappy.

"I understand," Charlton said, with a smile that might have meant anything.

CHAPTER TWENTY-EIGHT

I

NO. 7 was loose-limbed, black crinkly-haired, big-nosed Battery Quartermaster-sergeant Ackroyd....

"Aye, I told young Fieldhouse to fetch th' brake-rope from A.R. 4. When I went round to th' gun-shed first thing this morning, to make sure everything were ready for th' gun to be despatched, the brake-rope weren't on its 'ooks."

"Was it there last night?"

The Quartermaster shook his head regretfully.

"I don't know," he admitted. "I give Fieldhouse orders to fetch it, then it went out of my mind till he reported that he'd brought it in."

"What time was that?"

"Late. Very late it were. It should have been done hours before. I'd say it were nigh on eleven-thirty when Fieldhouse came round to my hut to report."

"And this morning the rope was missing."

"Aye. I sent th' nearest man off to—"

"Gunner Regan?"

The Quartermaster nodded.

"I sent him off to fetch Fieldhouse. I raised hell with Fieldhouse, but he stuck to his story that he'd brought th' rope from A.R. 4 and put it to bed on th' gun. But that didn't help to get th' gun away by O-seven-thirty-hours, so I reported th' facts to th' Battery Commander and we sent off to A.R. 3 gun-site for another rope."

"I understand that you collected the key of the gun-shed from the Battery Office this morning. Was the padlock properly secured?"

"Oh, aye. It were all in order. I undid th' lock and went in. First thing I looked for was th' brake-rope, but it weren't where it ought to've been. I looked round to see if

Fieldhouse'd slung it on th' floor, but it weren't anywhere about th' place."

The Inspector rose from his chair, walked to the end of the Nissen and came back with the rope that he had removed from the body. He threw it on the table and invited the Quartermaster to examine it.

"That's a forward brake-rope, all right," the Quartermaster said without hesitation, "but I can't say whether it's th' one we've just been talking about."

Charlton pushed the rope to one end of the table. He said, as he resumed his seat:

"When did you first discover that the Sergeant-major was missing?"

"Him and me share a half-hut. I saw when I'd got th' light on this morning that his bed hadn't been slept in, but I didn't think much to it. It wouldn't have been th' first time he'd not come in till Reveille. Later in th' morning, we all began to wonder a bit, for 'e were always careful to get back in camp before th' officers began asking for 'm." He gave a crooked smile as he added: "That's off the record."

"You've known the Sergeant-major for some time, haven't you?"

"Fifteen months or so. We were on th' same cadre together and were posted into this Battery at th' same time."

"So you got to know him pretty well."

"We've been in each other's pockets morning, noon and night; and if one man ever knew another man down to th' bottom of his soul, I knew Bill Yule."

The tone was bitter and full of unconcealed dislike.

Further patient questioning brought out, amongst other things, a second account of the downfall of Sgt. Nelson, a description of the scalding to death of Midnight, our mess kitten, the Quartermaster's version of the ill-treatment of Scottie— the blame for which he attributed entirely to Yule— and a reference to Fieldhouse's court-martial and detention.

Charlton said:"He was found guilty. What are your own views?"

"I reckon it were a put-up job. Fieldhouse is a hot-tempered young——, but he's no liar. Right from th' start, 'e swore he'd never laid a finger on th' B.S.M. and I were one that believed him. Likely as not you're extra interested in Fieldhouse, but you can take it from me that if he *did* do it, it weren't like him. Th' nearest pick-helve would come more natural to Fieldhouse than ——ing around with horses and brake-ropes."

"During the last few days, Q., have you noticed the Sergeant-major with a paper-covered book? It was called 'The Bloodhound of Valladolid.'"

"Oh, aye, I've seen it. It was lying on his table in th' hut last evening. All about torture and th' like. Sort of thing that were right up his street. Last thing I saw him do was slip it in his greatcoat pocket just before he went out."

"Where did he get it?"

"It's been kicking round camp for some time. A boy by th' name of Lovelock were reading it t'other day. Maybe Lovelock passed it over to Yule."

"Did you read it yourself?"

"I picked it up and glanced through it in th' hut last night, but it's not my notion of entertainment."

"Did you catch sight of any passages marked in pencil?"

The Quartermaster shook his head. Charlton asked his next question:

"Who is Owen?"

"Th' sergeants' mess waiter. He's on leave."

"Has he any serious grievance against the Sergeant-major?"

"Not so far as I know."

"The Sergeant-major never treated him badly?"

"No. Th' B.S.M. knew enough to keep on th' right side of folks like Owen. Make an enemy of th' mess waiter and, sure as Fate, there'll be paraffin in th' porridge!"

"But I've heard Owen's name coupled with Nelson's as fellow victims."

"Ah," said the Q., his brow clearing, "I've got it now. Th' chap you mean is not th' same Owen. T'other Owen was with this Battery till we got to firing-camp, where he committed suicide. There's not much doubt but that Yule drove 'im to it. Gave 'im a——dog's life."

"How did you spend yesterday evening, Q.?"

Ackroyd's mouth twisted in a wry grin.

"Reckoned you'd be coming round to that before long," he said. "After th' do up at th' mess, I went back and did a couple of hours' work in th' Q. office. Then I wrote a letter to th' Missus and went to bed. That would have been about ten o'clock. I read for a while before putting out th' light. Bombardier Bradfield were fiddling around in t'other half of th' 'ut, where him and young Morton sleep. We chin-wagged through th' partition for a time. Then I tried to get to sleep, though Bradfield've gone on talking all night if I'd given 'im th' chance. I'd just dropped off when young Fieldhouse came knocking at th' door. When he'd gone, I couldn't get to sleep again and was tossin' and turnin' a long time. But I did drop off at last—but couldn't 'ave been asleep for above a minute or two, when I was wakened up by Morton arriving back."

"What time would you say that was?"

"Can't tell exactly. Must 'ave been well after midnight. Morton and Bradfield started chewing th' rag, and not being in th' best of tempers by then, I told 'em to shut up."

He shrugged his shoulders.

"Not p'raps what you'd call a watertight alibi. I'd 'ave fixed something better if I'd guessed it were going to be necessary!"

The Inspector smiled, as he had smiled at Morton.

"There are few things more suspicious," he said, "than a perfect alibi."

II

No. 8 was small, dapper, gym-shoed and white-jacketed Gunner Gianella....

247

"Yessir. Almost the last thing I done before taking Scottie for 'is walk was to polish up the lead. I liked the poor little devil to look smart, sir, and be a credit to me—and to Captain Fitzgerald, er course. The two of us 'adn't got very far along towards Sheep, where a nice pint er you-know-what was waiting for us, when we met the B.S.M."

Garrulous little Gianella then went on to tell, at great length, all he knew and much of what he merely surmised about the loss of the Cairn terrier. He had just worked his story round for the fourth time to his departure with Scottie from the officers' mess, when Charlton cut him short.

"When," he asked, "did you last see the Sergeant-major alive?"

"'Arpar seven yes'dy evening, sir," was the prompt reply. "The officers and the N.C.Os. from the sergeants' mess 'ad a short session up at our place, to celebrate the adversary of the first Jerry plane brought dahn by the Battery. It finished at 'arpar seven to the tick, just in time for me to serve up their nibses' dinner wivaht it spoiling."

"What is the staff in the officers' mess?"

"Free of us, sir; me, the other batman and the cook. We all sleep in a Nissen 'ut adjourning the mess, wiv a passage to link it up."

"When did you get to bed last night?"

"Late, sir————late, if I may say so. Officers' batman 'ave to learn to live wivaht shut-eye."

"How late?"

"Must 'ave bin coming up to quarter to one, sir, before I really kipped dahn. The Captain was away and—"

"When did he get back?"

"'E ain't back yet, sir. 'E went up to London, sir. So wiv 'im aht, that left the Major and Mr. Bretherton. Mr. Bretherton, 'e went to bed early—rahnd abaht ten o'clock. The Major stayed readin' in front of the fire for 'alf an hour or so, then went along to 'is own room, where 'e shut 'imself in and got dahn to a bit of typin'. At quarter to twelve 'e went back into the lahnge and I 'eard 'im ring up Battery Office to ask the time. 'Quarter to twelve,' 'e says. 'Late as that, eh? Thanks, Postbechild. Goodnight,' 'e says. Then 'e calls aht fer me. 'Gianella,' 'e says, 'be a pal—' well, 'e didn't put it as nice as that, but the long and short of it was that 'e wanted 'is service-dress pressed. Nice time o' the night, you'll say, fer such an underrating, but that's batting all over. So I says, 'Yessir.' 'E goes to 'is room, 'ands aht the uniform to me and closes the door wiv the obscuration, 'If I want you again I'll call you.' Anyone'd think I was a twenty-four-hour Valet Service! 'E settles down again at 'is typewriter, while I goes and gets on wiv pressin' the uniform."

"Where were you?"

"In the Nissen, sir. There was a fire in there, for the iron."

"What about the cook and the other batman?"

"They were already in bed and asleep, sir; and all the noise in the world wouldn't wake them two when they get going. It takes me the best part of 'alf an hour to finish the job. Just as I'm getting ready ter crawl inter bed, the Major opens the door of 'is room and calls aht fer a cupper cocoa. A cupper cocoa, if you please, as if I was running an all-night snack-bar! 'Yessir. Very good, sir,' I says, keeping me feelings in jeopardy; and I sets abaht boiling some water. It couldn't 'ave bin a minute before quarter to one that me weary 'ead touched the piller, sir—and then up agine at arpars——six, to go through the 'ole——performance agine. Sometimes I wish, sir, as what I was back on the guns, which I shouldn't 'ave bin taken orf if the detachment N.C.Os. 'adn't got jealous of me. There's more jockeying fer positions, sir, in a—"

"Let's leave that," Charlton interrupted hastily. "Now, I want you to tell me again—and be quite certain before you do so—that no one but yourself touched that dog-lead before you handed Scottie over to the Sergeant-major."

"Bible honour, sir. As I said just now, polishing it up so as you could 'ave seen yer fice in it was the last thing what I done. Scottie and I 'adn't gone more than a matter of— well, put it at a coupler hundred yards, sir, when aht of the gloom suddenly appears—"

"Thank you," said Charlton firmly. "That will be all."

Gianella's expression suggested that the subject had been no more than touched upon.

III

No. 9 was small, freckled, ginger-headed Gunner Fieldhouse....

"Before you say anything, Fieldhouse, I want to warn you that I am going to write down your answers to my questions and that they may be used in evidence." He smiled, reassuringly. "So don't be in too much of a hurry, and think before you speak."

"Thank you, sir," answered Fieldhouse gratefully.

He had not expected so gentle a reception. Other men in the past had been similarly surprised—and ultimately disillusioned.

"I want you to tell me in your own words, Fieldhouse, precisely what happened last night, giving the times as nearly as you can remember them."

"The B.Q.M.S., sir—that's the Battery Quartermaster-sergeant—instructed me yesterday afternoon to fetch a brake-rope from one of the gun-sites. I'm afraid I forgot about it and didn't remember until late in the evening. I left here at twenty to eleven and—you know the gun-site, I suppose, sir?" Charlton nodded. "As I reached the lane, I met two gunners on their way back to the site and went along the lane with them. They had had a good evening and were singing. I collected the rope from the D.C. and, at about five minutes past eleven, started back for this camp. When I arrived here, I got the key of the gun-shed from the telephonist—it was then twenty-past eleven by the watch hanging over his desk— and took it out to get the rope put away. I went along to the M.T.

shed, undid the padlock, wound the rope on the hooks on the gun platform, and took the key back to Battery Office. It must have been five-and-twenty past eleven by then."

"You're quite satisfied that you fastened the padlock correctly?"

"Absolutely, sir."

"Did anyone see you put the rope away?"

"I don't think anyone actually saw me do it, sir, but one of the fire-picquet—Gunner Lovelock—came up just as I'd finished relocking the shed. I give you my word, sir, that I did exactly as I have said, and that I didn't touch the rope again after I had replaced it on the gun."

The unforced earnestness of the assurance impressed the Inspector.

"And when you had returned the key to the office, what did you do?"

"I reported at once to the B.Q.M.S. that the rope was ready for the morning, then went to bed."

"Was anyone in your hut awake?"

"I don't think so, sir. I'd got my bed down before I went out, so I didn't have to disturb anyone by switching on the light. Besides, it was getting late."

"You didn't leave camp again?"

"I haven't been out since, sir."

"Thank you, Fieldhouse. Now cast your mind back to last Sunday afternoon." Fieldhouse raised his eyebrows in mild surprise. "Where were you at three o'clock?"

"Out for a walk, sir. We have Sunday afternoons off and I went for a stroll."

"Which took you, I believe, in the direction of the lane leading to the gun-site?"

Fieldhouse nodded without speaking.

"When you reached the gate into the field, you pulled a handful of grass and offered it to a mare that was grazing in the field." His tone was one of gentle enquiry as he asked, "Why did you do that, Fieldhouse?"

"I wanted to make friends with her."

"Why?"

"Because—oh, it's jolly difficult to explain, sir."

"Please try. I needn't tell you that the question is important."

"I—er—well, as a matter of fact, sir, ever since I was a kid, I've been frightened sick at the very sight of a horse. Recently I've been psycho-analysing myself, and decided that it was high time I—er—got to grips with my inhibitions. I knew there were a couple of horses in that field because I'd noticed them during a previous walk."

"And also discussed them with Mr. Nightingale, the farmer."

"Yes, sir. I made a few preliminary enquiries before beginning on the horses themselves. I didn't want to start on anything too difficult. Bombardier Bradfield was with me when I spoke to the farmer. Last Sunday afternoon, I started off on my own, with the single intention of proving to myself that a horse is nothing to be scared of. I succeeded, sir, but it looks as if I got myself out of the frying-pan into the fire."

He looked at Charlton with steady eyes.

"I hope, sir," he said, "that you will believe all I have told you. I give you my word of honour that, whatever he did to me—you will probably have heard all about it—I had nothing to do with the death of the Sergeant-major. I have had a bad time, sir, and I've managed to stand up to it, but now I..."

He bit his lip and was unable to continue.

IV

That was the end of the list drawn up for me by Inspector Charlton. When Johnny had left him, he called me into the hut. I was glad of the chance; even with a greatcoat, it was cold walking up and down outside, trying not to eavesdrop.

"That's the first lot," he smiled, taking a cigarette from the packet on the table. "I've just time to do a few more before lunch."

"Oh, yes?" I replied without zest.

"I want to see Gunner McFinnon and also all the men who slept last night in the same hut as Gunner Fieldhouse."

"About Fieldhouse, sir—" I began, but he stopped me.

"You'll have your little say in due course," I was assured.

Nine men shared Johnny's hut with him. All save one affirmed that they had gone early to bed and could tell him nothing about Johnny's movements during the previous evening, or of the hour of his retirement for the night.

The exception was the telephonist, Gunner McFinnon.

V

No. 10, then, was Gunner McFinnon; twenty-two, pale, round-faced, Army-spectacled, unsmiling and a Scot of Scots.

"You're a telephonist, I believe, McFinnon?"

"Aye, Ah am that."

"What were your hours of duty yesterday?"

"Three o'clock in the afternoon to eleven o'clock at nicht."

"You were relieved by whom?"

"Gunner Postbecheel'."

"Punctually?"

"Twenta-three hunner oors tae the meenit."

"I have been told that the key of the hut in which the training gun is being temporarily housed is kept at night on a board over the telephonist's desk in Battery Office. Is that so?"

"Aye, whoaever locks the dour at the aind o' the day brings back the key."

"What time was it returned yesterday?"

"Roon' aboot five o'clock, nigh afoor tea."

"Who brought it in?"

"The Q."

"And afterwards—that is, from five o'clock until you went off duty, the key did not leave the board?"

"Naw, sir."

"Thank you, McFinnon. Now there's just one other thing. When you went off duty, did you go straight to bed?"

"Aye, Ah wus daid bate."

"Did anyone else come in after you?"

"Oh, aye. Gunner Fiel'hoose. He woke me up."

"What time was that?"

"Tain meenits tae yin."

"Ten minutes to *one*?" Charlton was startled.

"Tain meenits tae yin," McFinnon repeated doggedly.

"Are you sure of that?"

There was a big difference between 12.50 and Johnny's 11.30.

"Ah'm share enough. Ah had ma lumeenous watch on ma wreest, so Ah wus een a poseetion tae ken. He woke me up an' Ah telt h'm no' tae mack sich a bloody din."

The Inspector repressed a smile. Gunner McFinnon, as unit telephonist, must have caused many a Sassenach at the other end of the line to scratch his head.

"Did he get into bed in the dark?"

"Aye, he did that, but Ah kent it was h'm aw richt, for Ah kent hees vice when he spake back."

"What did he say?"

"He wus verra rude tae me. Aye, verra rude he wus. He says, 'Gang awa' tae sleep, ye heelan' heathen.'"

Charlton was trying not to laugh at the grieved expression on the round, earnest face, when McFinnon spoke again:

"Are ye eenterested in keys?"

"Yes, very. Why?"

"There's anither key that's been meesin' fra eet's hook in the office seence Sa'urday. Eeet's the key o' the gas-chamber."

But Charlton was not much concerned with the gas-chamber. He said:

"Let me see your watch, please."

The young Scot stretched his left arm across the table. Charlton noticed that the face was luminous and that the hands indicated, to within a minute, the same time as his own watch.

CHAPTER TWENTY-NINE

I

THERE was a muster parade of the Battery at 14.00 hours. All ranks—officers, N.C.Os., clerks, cooks, M.T. personnel, batmen, quartermaster's assistants, fatigue men and the rest—were present, with but three exceptions.

At 14.10 hours Sgt. Peters arrived in a police car with his helper; and one by one, from the Major down to the jakes-wallah, XYZ B.H.Q. personnel registered their finger-prints.

The three exceptions were Captain Fitzgerald, who had still not returned, Gunner Owen, who was not due back from leave until 23.59 hours, and the duty telephonist, Gunner Allman, whose prints were taken in Battery Office immediately after the parade.

At one point there was a slight delay, while Paul Morton removed the bandage from his damaged right hand. I noticed Chris Wilkinson replacing it for him afterwards.

At 15.15 hours, Peters and his assistant departed, taking with them the sheaf of finger-prints, but leaving the dog-lead behind. Charlton's first care was to obtain Gianella's confirmation that it was Scottie's missing lead.

"And now, Peter," he said to me, "we'll adjourn the court of inquiry and have a quiet little snoop round. I believe it's known in your curious Army vocabulary as a 'recce.'"

I took him on a tour of the camp. He poked his head into every hut, wanted to know who slept where, and plied me with many other questions.

A building that received his particular attention was the temporary gun-shed. It was, like all the other camp buildings except the officers' mess, a Nissen. The only thing inside it was the training gun on its wheeled mounting, with its fully depressed barrel pointing straight at the large double doors, which formed the sole entrance into the windowless hut.

When we came to examine them, the doors were pushed to, but not locked. When fully secured, one of them was kept in position by bolts at top and bottom, while the other was fixed to it by means of a stout hasp and staple of galvanized iron and a heavy padlock of far from inexpensive make. The hasp and staple were attached by bolts that passed through the thickness of the doors and were firmly held by washered nuts. The hinges were similarly fastened, so that, without a key to the padlock, nothing short of a crowbar could have opened the door from the outside. Of such rough treatment we detected no sign, nor was there any suggestion that the lock had been picked.

"It seems to me," said Charlton, "that if the brake-rope was removed from here last night, it was done by somebody who had a key of the padlock." He paused before adding significantly, "*If* it was taken."

I tried to change the direction of his thoughts.

"Are you satisfied," I asked him, "that the rope used for the murder was the one from A.R. 4? There's more than one Bofors brake-rope in the neighbourhood, you know."

"I've not got as far as proving it yet," he admitted, "but take a look at the supporting evidence, Peter. You can see for yourself that the rope isn't on the gun now. Quartermaster Ackroyd says it wasn't there first thing this morning. Fieldhouse says he put it away at 11.20 last night. If he didn't commit the murder, it's a reasonable assumption that Fieldhouse was telling the truth. Can you advance any reason—assuming that he didn't kill Yule—any reason at all why he should have lied to Lovelock, Postbechild and the Quartermaster last night about having put the rope away?"

"No," I grudgingly conceded.

"And if Fieldhouse did the murder, why did he change the ropes?"

"I don't know."

"And if the rope from the body is not the rope from A.R. 4, then where is the rope from A.R. 4?"

"All right," I growled. "You win. What do you want to do next?"

"Satisfy myself," he informed me blandly, "that the rope used for the murder was the one from A.R. 4."

We walked. It took us thirteen minutes. I was carrying the rope. As we went along, Charlton gave me a rough outline of his investigations thus far.

II

A.R. 4 was a typical Light Ack-Ack gun-site. It consisted of two Nissen huts, newly tarred and with green window-frames, and, some twenty yards away, at the end of the vegetable plot, the gun in its sand-bagged pit.

Charlton questioned the sergeant in charge and the members of the detachment. Two of the gunners confirmed that Fieldhouse had joined them at the end of the lane at a few minutes before eleven o'clock on the previous evening; and the Sergeant attested that it was he who had handed over the brake-rope to Fieldhouse.

"I had it all ready for him," he added. "I'd been told on the phone by the Q. to expect him hours before. Fieldhouse left here with it—well, it must have been still on the right side of five past eleven."

At Charlton's request, he and his second man, a lance-bombardier, examined the rope. I doubted, myself, whether they would be able to identify it with certainty. They showed no indecision, however, expressing the confident conviction that it was the same rope.

"I'd know it anywhere," the Sergeant said, "by those tar splashes. We tarred the site last week and"—he smiled ruefully—"not all the tar went on the huts. We tried to clean it off the rope, but weren't very successful. See those three blobs in a row? I'd go into the witness-box over those."

"And so would I," the lance-bombardier supported him.

Neither they nor any of the gunners could throw further light on the crime; and their mutual alibis were unshakeable.

III

Darkness was still some way off. As we left A.R. 4, Charlton said:

"You take one side of the lane and I'll take the other. Look out for a snapped-off thistle stem."

All along both sides, we scanned the hedges and ditches, but without result. When we reached the main road, Charlton paused.

"It's a curious thing about that thistle, Peter," he pondered. "We ought to be able to find the plant from which it came."

"Is it important?" I asked him.

He shook his head. "I don't imagine so, but the question teases me. I went over the field pretty thoroughly this morning, and kept my eyes open as we came along the road from the camp earlier on. The thistle plants we've come across have all been intact. If we could find a headless stem, it might give us a line on the direction from which the murderer came."

"Perhaps," I suggested, "he picked it one day last week in Northumberland."

He seemed not to be listening. He had turned and was looking along the road towards Etchworth. I waited with some apprehension, not being anxious to inch my way along another mile of hedgerow. But after a moment or two, he swung round in the opposite direction, shifting his speculative gaze to the clump of beeches that hid Cowfold Camp from view.

"If you wanted to slip out of camp at night without being seen," he asked, "which way would you go?"

"An awkward question," I replied. "It depends on several factors. As you've seen for yourself, the camp's not wired or fenced in any way, so it's possible to leave it at any point of the compass. Assuming that your destination was that field there—" I jerked my thumb in the direction of the meadow in which the body had been found—"you could avoid the main road by coming across country. You see those trees?" (Suddenly remembering my field-craft training at P.T.C., I did not point again). "They run from the road up to the foot of the downs and, being L-shaped, they form a natural boundary to the western and southern sides of the camp. If you wished to get from the camp to here, you could come through the coppice, get through the hedge that borders it on this side— see it?—and finish the rest of the distance across that field. You can't quite see it from here, but there's a gate out of the field into the road. As for the coppice, it wouldn't be too easy to negotiate in the dark, particularly if you didn't fancy flashing a torch. The alternative would be to by-pass it, but it would be a somewhat long way round. The main disadvantage, as I see it, is that the gun-shed's on the far side of the camp. To get the brake-rope from there to here via the coppice, you'd have to walk right through the camp. You'd stand far less chance of being caught, by using the quickest and easiest route—that is, the main entrance."

"Sound enough reasoning," Charlton said, "provided your point of departure was the gun-shed."

"That's where the rope was taken from, wasn't it?" I demanded.

"An assumption," he said, starting back towards the camp, "based solely on the testimony of Gunner Fieldhouse."

IV

A hundred and fifty yards from where we had stood talking was the gate I had mentioned. We stopped, by tacit consent, when we reached it.

Charlton lifted the wooden latch and I followed him into the field. As we walked, one behind the other and keeping close to the hedge, we carefully examined each thistle plant we encountered. It was not until we had turned left at the corner of the field and had gone twenty yards or so along the hedge that bordered the coppice that we found the clue that Charlton had been seeking: a healthy clump of spear plume-thistle with one of its spiny stems headless. Near by it in the hedge was a gap through which, after he had examined the thistle, Charlton led me.

There was no footpath to guide us through the trees. Charlton chose a course that would bring us out eventually on to the football field. But before we got as far as that, we came upon the flat-roofed, red-bricked building that was known in XYZ as Bretherton's Folly.

"What's that?" asked Charlton when he first caught sight of it between the trees.

"It's a gas-chamber," I told him; "one of the many horrors for which we have to thank the unrepentant Hun. We use it, from time to time, to test respirators."

"'There's anither key," Charlton murmured in broad Scots for which I could detect no reason, "'that's been meesin' fra eet's hook in the office seence Sa'urday.'"

We walked round to the front of the building. The key was in the lock of the heavy door—and the door was slightly ajar.

Disregarding the "Danger. Keep Out" notice, Charlton pushed open the door. It was too dark inside to see very much. He pulled an electric torch from his overcoat pocket. The only furniture was a trestle table on which were a candle stuck by its own grease to a cracked Naafi plate, the small spirit lamp over which little "Mr. Why" heated his tear-gas capsules in the lid of a tobacco tin, a tube or two of gas ointment and a pair of green-rubber anti-gas gloves.

The beam from the torch stayed fixed on the gloves for some moments before it was directed elsewhere. The next thing it picked out was something on the floor in a far corner—something that reflected back the light in a gleaming pin-point. It was a plated metal bifurcated rivet.

He told me to light the candle. While I did so, he produced the dog-lead from his overcoat pocket. With his handkerchief, he retrieved the rivet from the floor and, bringing it to the table, compared it with the rivet that remained in the lead.

"Identical," he said at last, with a note of deep satisfaction in his voice.

V

There was a well-worn path from Bretherton's Folly out of the coppice. As we walked along it, I said—in a low tone, for fear we might be overheard:

"The business of Scottie is obviously tangled up in this murder. Something I haven't been able to understand up to now was, how was it possible to ill-treat the dog without anyone hearing the hullaballoo? The gas-chamber seems to supply the answer. Once Scottie had been dragged inside and the door closed, very little would be heard outside. Then, when the swine had done all he wanted to the poor little brute, he left Scottie lying on the floor and came away, forgetting to close the door. Scottie must have recovered sufficiently to crawl back to the officers' mess. But how the devil did the lead find its way on to the Sergeant-major's wrists?"

The Inspector's only response to my query was to turn without warning in his tracks and retrace his steps towards Bretherton's Folly.

Buried in the palm of the right-hand green-rubber anti-gas glove, he found a thistle spine.

CHAPTER THIRTY

I

O N our way back to camp, I told the Inspector all I could remember about the period of gas-drill that we had had the previous Saturday afternoon. I was glad to be able to do so, for I felt that it would take his mind off Johnny. Yet, at his seat again in the interview hut, he said curtly:

"Get Fieldhouse."

I went off in search of Johnny with feelings of deep misgiving, having no liking for the way in which the evidence had piled up against him. Frankly, I was beginning to suspect him myself.

He was in Battery Office. I sent him off to the interview hut. Postbechild, who had duly taken over the telephone from Allman, took the opportunity to tell me that Police Sgt. Peters had been on the line for Inspector Charlton, and would the Inspector please ring him back.

"Was it urgent?" I asked.

"Didn't sound so," was Postbechild's indifferent reply, and I decided it could wait for another ten minutes.

Meanwhile Johnny was having his second interview with Charlton....

"You told me this morning, Fieldhouse, that you were in bed last night by half-past eleven. That was so, I think?"

"Yes, sir."

"Did you leave the hut again after that?"

"Yes, sir, I did."

"Why?"

"I went to the lavatory."

"How long were you out of the hut?"

"About ten minutes."

"What time was it?"

"I don't know, sir. I didn't look at my watch."

"Why wasn't I told this when I questioned you this morning, Fieldhouse?"

"You didn't ask me, sir; and I thought I'd better not say anything about it, as it wouldn't make things any better for me and might make them worse."

"Did you dress before you left the hut?"

"I just slipped my trousers on over my pyjamas and put on my greatcoat."

"Can you name anybody who heard or saw you leave the hut?"

"Gunner McFinnon spoke to me when I came back. The high wind made the door slam and it woke McFinnon up. He told me not to make so much noise and I—"

"But you can't produce any witness to prove your statement that you were only out of the hut for ten minutes?"

"No, sir, I'm afraid not."

"Thank you, Fieldhouse. That will be all. Please ask Bombardier Bradfield to come in."

But I was snatching a quick snack. A man's got to look after himself in the Army. Nobody else will.

II

I made amends for my dereliction of duty by bringing back with me a mug of tea and some hefty slices of bread and suspiciously pippy jam. Then I told him that Sgt. Peters wished to speak to him, and we went along to Battery Office for Postbechild to put through the call. Peters must also have been having his tea, for it was a long time before Postbechild handed over to Charlton.

"Hullo, Peters. Yes, this is Charlton here.... Splendid!... Yule and Gianella?... Yes.... Who was the third?... Who was the third again?... Yes, I've got it now. Just those three.... Where?... Down near the clip. I see.... Thanks very much, Peters. You'll be getting the usual confirmation from the Bureau, I take it?... Good.... Cheerio!"

I followed him back to the interview hut. When I had closed the door, he sat down at the table and scribbled a few lines in his notebook. As he slipped the book back into his pocket, he said:

"Pop along, will you, and ask Mr. Bretherton to spare me a few minutes?"

"Was he the third?" I demanded rudely.

His sole response was a slight, irritating smile.

III

Lieutenant S. P. Bretherton, R.A., small, insignificant and with a damp red nose, had a curious trick of speech. He would, as it were, *vamp* on a word, almost as if his tongue had outstripped his brain and was marking time until his brain caught up.

"I'm sorry to bother you, sir," Charlton smiled politely, "but, purely as a matter of routine, I'm trying to check the movements of everyone who was in this camp last night. Will you please tell me how you spent the evening?"

"Yes, of course. I shall be only too glad to help you in every way—way—way—way I can, although I don't think I'll be of—of—of very great assistance. I spent most of the evening working on—on—on the Battery's accounts and went to bed at—at—at—and went to bed at ten o'clock almost to the minute. I was asleep in next to no time, having had a most—most—having had a most strenuous day. I remember nothing until my batman brought in my early morning cup of tea at—at—at seven o'clock."

"There was a small celebration in the mess last night, at which I understand you were present, sir. Did you find the Sergeant-major in his usual spirits?"

"Yes, Inspector, I think I can say—say—say—I think I can say that he was. Perhaps I shouldn't speak ill of the dead, but—but—but I'm forced to admit that the Sergeant-major's usual spirits did—did—did—his usual spirits did not always appeal to me."

"Turning to another question, Mr. Bretherton, have you ever seen in this camp a copy of a book called 'The Bloodhound of Valladolid'?"

"Yes, as a matter of fact, I have. One of my duties in this Battery, Inspector, is—is—is attending to welfare. Some weeks ago—ago—ago—some weeks ago, we received from a charitable source in Lulverton a collection of second-hand books and magazines of all—all—all kinds. I distributed most of them down to sites and kept the remainder for B.H.Q. Amongst those I retained was—was—was—among them was 'The Bloodhound of Valladolid.'"

"And it went with the others into the men's rest-room—or wherever the library is kept?"

"Er—eventually, yes. In the first instance, I withheld it. It was a book of unusual type and I was not too—too—too—I was not too sure that it came under the heading of—of—of Welfare! I was in two minds whether to—to—to—whether to put it on the fire. There is, I think you'll agree, more than enough cruelty these days for one to deliberately—for one deliberately to pander to it. But I decided, after glancing through it, that—that—that it was no part of my duties to censor the books of—of—of—to censor the reading matter of grown men. So I passed it out for—for general consumption."

"Were you the first person in the camp to see the book?"

"Undoubtedly. The parcel came addressed to the Welfare Officer and it was I who untied it."

"When you looked through it, sir, did you come across any paragraph marked in pencil?"

"No. I can assure you on that point. I should—should—should—I should have instantly noticed anything of the sort."

"You mentioned that you *glanced* through it."

Mr. Bretherton smiled shyly.

"A figure of speech! I must—must—must confess that I read the whole book from cover to cover. It was not—not— not— it was far from pleasant reading. I was—was—was repelled, yet

I could not tear myself away. I am being very frank with you, Inspector."

"And as soon as you had finished it, you handed it over to the rank and file?"

"Er—not exactly. There was no—no—no—there was no definite act of handing over. Candidly, the facts are—are—are—are somewhat obscure. You know how it is with books; they pass from—from hand to hand, until one loses—loses—loses—until one loses track of them. To the best of my recollection Captain Fitzgerald dipped into it after me and I seem to remember catching sight of it in the possession of—of—of the Captain's batman, Gunner Gianella."

Charlton sighed inwardly. The intimate biography of the infamous Torquemada was turning into a will-o'-the-wisp. It was not unlikely that the whole camp had read it. The most interesting thing was that, if Mr. Bretherton's evidence could be relied upon, the book had been marked since it had come into Cowfold Camp.

"When did this particular parcel of books arrive, sir?"

"If I remember rightly, in the region—region—about six weeks ago."

"Thanks very much, Mr. Bretherton. I have just one other question for you. I believe, that besides being the unit Welfare Officer, you are also Gas Officer?"

Mr. Why gave a thin smile.

"And the Entertainments Officer, the M.T. Officer, the Messing Officer, the—the—the—I think that is all."

"Last Saturday afternoon, during a period of gas-drill, you were using a pair of rubber gloves. Do you know what happened to them afterwards?"

"An—an—an—an unexpected enquiry, but I will do my best to answer it, as far as I myself was—was—was concerned. I left them on the table in the—the—the gas-chamber, after having decontaminated them with gas ointment. It is my— my—my—it is my custom to keep the gloves in the gas-chamber, ready for the next—next—next—ready for the next occasion. The door of the chamber is kept locked, so there is no possibility of—of—of—no possibility at all of unauthorized persons—"

"It wasn't locked this afternoon, sir. I pushed open the door and went straight in."

The Gas Officer's insipid face took on a shocked expression.

"That is—is—is extremely serious," he said. "I will make—make—make—I will make full enquiries and advise you of—of—of—and let you know the outcome."

"Thank you, sir," Charlton said mechanically.

He knew very well what that outcome would be: a Battery Order threatening condign punishment if such a thing happened again. His bet was that the gas-chamber door had not been secured because some careless idiot, commissioned or otherwise, had left it unlocked.

"Can you tell me, sir," he went on after a slight pause, "what happened to the collar of Captain Fitzgerald's terrier?"

"The Captain took the—the—the poor little chap's body away from the immediate neighbourhood of the mess and buried him. He and Gianella carried out the—the—the interment and, as far as—as—as—as far as I am aware, the collar was buried with Scottie."

Charlton rose to his feet. Following suit, Mr. Bretherton said:

"Am I right in thinking, Inspector, that you—as well as myself—found in—in—in that book a similarity between the—the—between the death of our Sergeant-major and that of the Marquis of Santagena?"

The Inspector saw no harm in saying:

"It was that particular passage that was marked."

"So I imagined. It is reasonable to—to—to surmise that had not 'The Bloodhound of—of—of—The Bloodhound of Valladolid' come into the camp, the Sergeant-major would have—have—have—would have come to his end in a different fashion."

He looked at Charlton queerly.

"But," he appended, "I doubt if—if—if—I doubt whether it would have been less sudden."

"Can you amplify that statement, sir?"

But little Mr. Why took fright, and hedged.

IV

I was told to fetch Little Aubrey. He came with reluctance, complaining bitterly in his high treble....

"Lovelock," Charlton began in a tone that meant business, "I want you to answer some more questions."

"*More?*" was the impudent retort. "I thought you'd asked them all last time. What do you want now—my mother's maiden name?"

"When did you last take the Captain's dog for a walk?"

The boy's slim body stiffened with a jerk and he drew a sharp breath.

"Never," he said. "Never in my life. He was Captain Fitzgerald's—not mine."

"Then when did you last have hold of the terrier's lead?"

"I told you, never. Gianella used to take him out. It was Gianella who lost him. Gianella or the Sergeant-major. Ask Gianella. I don't know anything about it."

Charlton fixed him with grave grey eyes, in which there was no sympathetic light.

"When the Sergeant-major's body was found this morning, Lovelock, his wrists were tied behind his back with Scottie's lead."

"Well, that's nothing! It got lost the other night; somebody must have picked it up."

"Before you answer any more questions, Lovelock, I'm going to warn you that I shall write down anything you say and it may be used in evidence."

He gave point to the words by pulling a sheet of paper towards him.

"Since tea-time last Saturday," he went on, "have you touched that dog-lead?"

"*No*, I keep on telling you, no. The blasted brute was Gianella's pigeon."

"The dog-lead, Lovelock, has been examined by an expert, who will go into the witness-box and testify that he found your finger-prints on it."

"It's a——lie!"

"Don't talk to me like that!" There was a dangerous rasp in Charlton's deep voice. "Your finger-prints were on that lead—and you're going to explain how they got there! If you don't tell *me*, then you'll have to tell the Court."

"It's a trick!" said Lovelock wildly. "You're trying to catch me! Finger-prints don't prove anything!"

"This is a case of murder, Lovelock. Men have been hanged on the evidence of finger-prints alone. How did yours get on the terrier's lead?"

Master Lovelock had had enough. Quelled and very badly frightened, he said:

"Because I was holding it—but not last night. I didn't touch it last night—I swear I didn't! I haven't seen it since Saturday."

"Tell me the facts—and just in case you try any more fairy tales, young man, you may as well know that I have heard Gianella's evidence. Now let me have your version."

"I—er—I was leaving the camp, on my way out for a walk, when the dog came running along from Sheep with the lead trailing behind it." Charlton noted a gathering confidence, and prepared for further falsehoods. "I managed to snatch at the loop, but before I could get a firm grip on it, the brute gave a furious tug that jerked it out of my hand and ran off towards Etchworth. I never saw either the dog or the lead again."

"You caught at the loop, but it was instantly snatched away from you?"

"Yes, I didn't get a chance to—"

He looked up. Charlton was on his feet.

"I'll give you five minutes to get your small kit ready," the Inspector told him.

"Why?"

"You're coming along to Police Headquarters with me. I've heard enough of your lies."

"It's the truth, I tell you!"

"Finger-prints of yours were found not only on the loop, but also on the other end of the lead. I'll give you one last chance, Lovelock—and to keep you from any further flights of fancy, I'll tell you what you did last Saturday evening."

He sat down again.

"Last Saturday evening," he repeated, "you did, as you have just told me, intercept the terrier on his way back to camp, but he didn't get away from you. You took him to the gas-chamber. You closed the door, so that nobody would hear, then kicked him—or so you thought—to death. In his early struggles to avoid your boot, the lead was wrenched away from the clip on his collar. Not content with more kicking, you also thrashed him with the lead, holding it by the lower end because the loop would deal heavier blows. When you imagined that no life remained in him, you left him there and sneaked back to camp."

He stopped speaking. With hung head, Lovelock stayed silent.

"Was that how it happened?" Charlton asked, then snapped, *"Answer me!"*

"Yes."

"What did you do with the lead?"

"Threw it on the floor. I suddenly got the breeze up and made a bolt for it."

"Leaving the door ajar?"

"Yes, I believe so."

"How did you know, when you took the dog there, that you would be able to get in?"

"We'd been using the place that afternoon. We came away for tea and afterwards the Sergeant-major told me to go back and lock it up. But I didn't go."

"Purposely?"

"No. I forgot."

"Why did you hurt the dog?"

"Because it was the only way I could think of to get my own back on Captain Fitzgerald. He's been bullying me ever since I came into the Battery."

Charlton unclipped his fountain-pen and wrote speedily until the sheet before him was nearly filled. Then he passed the paper across to Lovelock.

"Read it and sign it," he ordered.

The thoroughly subdued young man obeyed without a word, and handed the sheet back to him.

The Inspector jerked his head towards the door.

"Now get out," he said briefly.

V

He wanted to see the Major again. The Old Lady was in the mess. I got through on the extension from Battery Office and was told to bring the Inspector along. So Mahomet had to go to the mountain.

"I'm sorry to bother you again, sir," Charlton smiled apologetically when they were alone together, "but there are one or two things I must refer to you. First, I should like to have the services of Bombardier Bradfield at Police Headquarters this evening. His knowledge of local conditions will greatly assist me in assembling the evidence."

"By all means. Do you wish the remainder of the Battery to continue to be confined to camp?"

"If you please, sir. Secondly, have you any news of Captain Fitzgerald's return?"

"It has been delayed, I'm afraid. I have received a telegram, saying that he expects to be back tomorrow."

"May I ask where he has gone, sir?"

"To London. He went there for a War Office interview." He smiled benign apologies as he added, "Please do not press me for further details. And now, Inspector, what is your third question?"

"In the course of my inquiries today, sir, I have obtained certain information that I feel it my duty to pass on to you. It concerns the ill-treatment last Saturday evening of Captain Fitzgerald's Cairn terrier. I have found out who was responsible for it."

The Major stroked his face with his hand.

"I was afraid you would," he said.

"Then you knew it was Lovelock, sir?"

"*Lovelock?* Good God! But I thought it was—"

He stopped dead.

Charlton asked: "You were going to say, sir...?"

"I think I had better not. Can you give me any details?" The Inspector recounted as much of his investigations as concerned the death of Scottie. When he stopped speaking, the Major said:

"May I ask you to keep this matter a secret for the time being, Inspector? Captain Fitzgerald was deeply attached to little Scottie and he is—well, let me put it that he has an impulsive disposition."

"I understand, sir," said Charlton, and rose to go.

CHAPTER THIRTY-ONE

I

I was glad the C.B. ban had been lifted for my benefit, because I had a date with Susan that evening. Apart from other items on the agenda, I had the useful sum of a penny to collect from her as the result of a wager. She had said on our previous meeting that the quotation beginning, "And the night shall be filled with music" and finishing with a reference to a strategic withdrawal on the part of the Arabs, was from the *Rubaiyat*, while I had argued that it was the work of Longfellow. The penny bet had followed, so before I set out for Lulverton Police Station—Charlton had gone on ahead—I slipped the little book that had once been Johnny's into my greatcoat pocket.

II

There were four of us in the Inspector's room, It was not the first occasion that we same four had sat in conference there. This time I was in battledress, with two stripes on my arms, but the others looked much the same as ever: Inspector Charlton, Sergeant Martin and Superintendent Kingsley. The Super was in the early fifties; a big, breezy, matter-of-fact son of Downshire, with none of Charlton's finesse and subtlety, but nevertheless, much solid merit. To the lesser breeds without the law, he was known as "old Carthorse"; to his friends, far more affectionately, as "Tiny." That evening he was wearing mufti; a thick, rust-coloured, hairy sports-coat, flannel trousers and brown golfing shoes. He had nominal authority over Charlton and the other C.I.D. men attached to his Division.

"Now, Harry," he said, puffing at his ancient curved-stemmed pipe, "let's have the gen."

Charlton began with a description of the finding of the body, and went on to tell of Yule's last visit to "Lyme Regis."

He then turned to the two chief clues, the rope and the dog-lead.

"The rope," he said, "was the forward brake-rope of a Bofors Anti-Aircraft gun. At eleven o'clock last night, it was on A.R. 4 gun-site. At a minute or two after eleven, it was handed over by the detachment sergeant to a gunner named Fieldhouse. Fieldhouse says that he took it straight back to Battery headquarters at Cowfold Camp, wound it in position on a gun that was standing in a hut, locked up the hut and took the key to the Battery Office.

"Any witnesses?" asked the Super.

"Yes. The evidence comes from a young gunner called Lovelock. He says that he found Fieldhouse opening the door of the hut. Personally, I don't believe him; it's far more likely that Fieldhouse was locking the hut, after having put the rope away. The other witness was the duty telephonist, Gunner Postbechild. He confirms that Fieldhouse had the rope with him when he called in at the Battery Office for the key at eleven-twenty. He also confirms that the key was returned by Fieldhouse within five minutes. Fieldhouse told him that he had put the rope away for the night."

So nobody besides Fieldhouse can say that the rope was in the hut when he locked it up. Then what was to stop Fieldhouse—"

Charlton held up his hand.

"Not so fast, Tiny," he smiled. "Let's keep to the sequence of events. We'll come to Fieldhouse later. Postbechild, the telephonist, states definitely that after Fieldhouse had returned it, the key did not leave the Battery Office until the next morning. I have examined the hut in which the gun was kept overnight. There are no windows. The only entrance are the double doors at one end of the hut. The hinges are bolted to the frames and the doors are fixed by strong door-bolts, a hasp and staple bolted through the thickness of the doors, and a hefty padlock. If the padlock was fastened in the correct manner, nobody without a key could have got into the hut except by force. I found not the slightest trace of any attempt to break in."

"Then either this Fieldhouse fellow didn't fix the padlock properly, or he's lying when he says—"

"At a quarter to seven this morning," Charlton coolly interrupted him, "Battery Quartermaster-sergeant Ackroyd collected the key from Postbechild and took it round to the gun-shed. He has told me that he found the padlock correctly secured, and that when he pulled open the doors and went into the hut the brake-rope wasn't there."

"Of course it wasn't! Field—"

"That disposes of the rope, for the time being. Next we come to the dog-lead. The facts about the dog-lead are rather curious. The Battery's second-in-command, Captain Fitzgerald, had a Cairn terrier. On the evidence of his batman, Gunner Gianella, the dog-lead I found on Yule's wrists was used, until last Saturday, for the terrier. I won't bother with all the details now, but this, briefly, is the recent history of the lead: Last Saturday evening, Gianella—a man who obviously likes to have everything spick and span—polished the lead and took the terrier for a stroll. They hadn't gone far when they met Yule, who took over the lead and sent Gianella running back to camp on an errand. The Sergeant-major said afterwards that, while he was lighting a cigarette, the dog jerked the lead out of his hand and went pelting off after the batman."

He turned to me.

"It's an interesting point, that. The lighting of the cigarette explains how Yule's finger-prints got on to the lead. The nights are cold and it's a hundred to one chance that he was wearing gloves; and another hundred to one chance that he took them off to light the cigarette. If he'd not decided to have a smoke, his prints would probably not have—"

It was the Super's turn to cut in.

"This is the first time you've mentioned finger-prints," he complained.

"Sorry," Charlton grinned. "That was just an aside to Bradfield. As I was saying, the dog ran after Gianella with the lead trailing behind it. At the entrance to the camp, the lead was caught by a soldier I've mentioned before, Gunner Lovelock. Lovelock apparently has no love for the dog's owner, so he took the unfortunate little tyke off to a quiet spot and nearly kicked him to death."

I smothered an exclamation; this was new to me. The Super muttered a word or two under his breath.

"The quiet spot in question was a brick-built gas-chamber that is a part of the camp and stands among the trees adjoining. Lovelock shut himself in with the terrier—he's admitted all this in a signed confession, by the way—and started on him with his boot. The lead got pulled away from the clip fixed to the dog's collar; and after he'd had enough fun and games, Lovelock left the dog—and the lead—in the gas-chamber. The dog had sufficient life left in him to crawl back to his master, who shot him. The lead was removed later from the gas-chamber by some person as yet unknown, and used—by him or somebody else—to strap Yule's hands behind his back."

"Damn curious," mused Kingsley, stroking his strong chin.

"Peters has run the yardstick over the dog-lead and has reached the definite conclusion that the only finger-prints on the lead were those of Gianella, who was the first to hold the lead after it had been polished, Yule, who was the second, and that nice young gentleman, Mr. Lovelock, who was the third. If neither Lovelock nor Gianella did the murder—and I can't see either of them doing it myself—then the murderer must have taken precautions—"

"Rubber gloves," threw in the Super, as if only he could have thought of them.

"Precisely," agreed Charlton, "and that brings me to the thistles."

"Am I intended to see the connection?" asked the Super with heavy irony.

"I should have told you. In order to liven up the mare, the murderer played the old horse-fair thistle trick. Bradfield and I discovered a thistle plant this afternoon. It had one stem missing and was in a more or less direct line from the gas-chamber to the scene of the crime. On a table in the gas-chamber, I found a pair of rubber gloves. They are always kept in there and everyone in B.H.Q. probably knew it. Still stuck in the palm of the right-hand glove was a thistle spine."

He lighted a cigarette while the Super digested these facts. The Super said at length:

"That connects up all right with Fieldhouse. It wouldn't have done to take the rope straight from the gun-site and use it on Yule. Too damned obvious. So he brought it back to Battery headquarters, made sure that somebody saw him there with it, pretended to stow it away in the shed, then slipped out of camp again with it. On the way, he called at the gas-chamber to get the rubber gloves, saw the lead and took it with him, thinking it might come in handy to tie up Yule. He slipped on the gloves and, on his way to the field, he picked a thistle—and the rest of it speaks for itself."

He sat back in his chair with a smile of triumph, but leant forward again almost at once.

"Any witnesses to prove he didn't sneak out of camp again, after leaving the key with the telephonist?"

"No," Charlton answered, I thought reluctantly. "I found a gunner who said Fieldhouse came into the sleeping-hut at ten minutes to one."

"There you are, then! That would have given him all the time he needed."

"Fieldhouse's story was that he actually went to bed at half-past eleven, but had to leave the hut later, to go to the latrines."

"Can he prove it?"

"No."

"Any motive for murder?"

"A strong one. Earlier this year, Yule got him sent to detention. The rights and wrongs of it aren't too clear, but Fieldhouse reported back to the unit a fortnight ago."

"Any other evidence against him?"

"Of a sort. Last Sunday afternoon, he was observed trying to make friends with Etchworth Lass."

It seemed high time to take a hand in defence of Johnny. So I ventured:

"I think I can throw some light on that, sir. I've known Fieldhouse since July of last year and he's always been frightened of horses. There was an occasion during our P.T.C. days together, when he flatly refused, even when told by an N.C.O., to go into a field where a harmless old mare was grazing. Fieldhouse was very worried about his weakness in that direction; and I'm sure he must have been making chummy overtures to Etchworth Lass, just to overcome his complex."

"That's what he told me when I asked for an explanation," Charlton said; and I smiled at him gratefully.

"Complex, my aunt!" snorted the Super, who was a most downright man. "He was obviously getting on good terms with the nag, so that he wouldn't have any trouble with her when the big moment came. Clearest case I've met in years. Any jury would convict."

"Care to hear the rest of the story," Charlton enquired casually, "before you finally decide?"

The Super struck a match.

"Carry on," he said between puffs at his pipe. "I've an open mind."

"You'll agree with me, I think," Charlton began, "that if Fieldhouse didn't murder Yule, his evidence can be accepted as reliable? that when he said he locked the rope away in the gun-shed, he did, in fact, do so?"

"Very likely," the Super conceded grudgingly.

"You don't sound very convinced!" Charlton smiled. "Let's follow it through from the beginning. Will you accept the testimony of the A.R. 4 detachment sergeant and his lance-bombardier that the rope I removed from the body with my own hands this morning was the same rope as he handed to Fieldhouse last night?"

The Super's agreement was immediate; the whole case against Johnny depended upon it.

"Right," Charlton went on. "Now will you accept the testimony of Gunner Postbechild that Fieldhouse was carrying a brake-rope when he went into the Battery Office at 11.20 last night?"

"Yes."

"We're still assuming, remember, that Fieldhouse wasn't the murderer. Can you think of any convincing reason why that rope should not have been the rope from A.R. 4?"

"No, I can't," the Super had to admit.

"And can you think of any convincing reason why, having got so far with it, Fieldhouse should not lock it away and bring back the key to Postbechild?"

"No, but that's only if he didn't—"

"So far, so good, then. We agree that if Fieldhouse didn't kill Yule, the brake-rope was, by 11.25 last night, safely locked away in a shed in Cowfold Camp?"

The Super nodded.

"Let us suppose for a moment that the murder of Yule was planned by some person not normally resident in Cowfold Camp—in other words, somebody who hadn't a reasonable excuse for being in the camp lines after 11.25 last night. If you were such a person, Tiny, and needed some rope for an experiment in homicide—any length of stout rope would have sufficed—would you have risked getting caught in Cowfold Camp when you could have procured rope elsewhere?"

"Perhaps I couldn't have laid my hands on any," suggested the Super.

"Not many people knew, don't forget, that the rope was in the gun-shed or even in Cowfold Camp. The men on A.R. 4

were aware of it, but I'm confident that none of them left the site last night. If one of them murdered the Sergeant-major, the rest of them must have been accomplice to it."

"Somebody might have noticed Fieldhouse carrying the rope back to the main camp, followed him and stolen it from the shed."

"Which was locked and showed no signs of unlawful entry."

"And so proves my argument," said the Super, poking the stem of his pipe towards the Inspector. "If the doors were locked and the key in good hands, how the devil could the rope have been pinched? I stick to my opinion that Fieldhouse—"

"There's no disagreement, then, with my argument that the crime was done by someone from Cowfold Camp? It's no use sitting there looking stubborn, Tiny! You're going to hear the rest of the evidence, if I have to talk till breakfast time."

For my own personal reasons, I hoped it would not be later than 8.45. Amongst other things, I wanted to collect that penny from Susan.

"I have questioned today," Charlton continued, "most of the men at the B.H.Q. There was not enough time for the rest; I must see them tomorrow. For what the information is worth, the orderly N.C.O., Lance-bombardier Wilkinson, states that, apart from the officers' mess staff, every man below the rank of bombardier was in camp by eleven o'clock—except, of course, Fieldhouse." He shot a mischievous glance at me. "The august quarters of the full bombardiers were immune from visitation."

I grinned: "One of us was in."

"Which reminds me," he said, "that so far you've dodged a catechism. Can you produce any sort of alibi, or must I take you into custody on suspicion?"

There was a smile on his lips, but I knew that his question was more serious than it sounded. He was thorough in his methods.

"My alibi relies on the Quartermaster," I answered. "You know we have a hut partitioned across the middle, with the Sergeant-major and the Q. on one side and Morton and myself on the other? Well, I don't know whether the Q. mentioned it to you this morning—I expect he did, because our alibis are inter-dependent—but after ten o'clock the Q. was in his half and I was in mine. The partition's only a couple of fibre-boards nailed one on each side of a wooden framework, so conversation's not very difficult. We chatted on this and that until, round about eleven o'clock, the Q. decided on some shut-eye. He's an early-to-bed-and-early-to-rise addict."

"Eleven o'clock's late enough for anyone," said the Super, whose habit was to sit up yarning till two.

"We didn't speak to each other again and I don't think he got to sleep very quickly. He was tossing and turning for quite a time. Poor old Q.'s not very happy these days. I don't know all the facts, but his wife's in pretty poor shape. Some nervous complaint, I believe. He hardly ever mentions it. At half-past eleven there was a knock on the door of 6B, and I heard Fieldhouse's voice telling the Q. that the brake-rope had been put to bed in the gun-shed. The Q. answered something like, 'And about time, too,' and Fieldhouse closed the door and went away. The Q.'s bed went on creaking for some time, until eventually he must have dropped off to sleep. Bombardier Morton, my side-kick, came in at half-past twelve—he probably told you all about that—and between us we managed to disturb the Q., who told us to make a little less noise. His exact words were—"

"We can guess them," Charlton assured me quickly. "What time did you yourself get to bed?"

"Soon after eleven o'clock. I wasn't at all sleepy and was still reading when Morton arrived."

"What did he say when he came in?"

"He came straight across to my bed and asked me in a low tone whether the Sergeant-major was back. We have to be careful what we say in that hut, believe me! I told him I hadn't heard the B.S.M. come in. He sat down on my bed and went on to tell me the events of the evening. Did he mention them to you?"

"Go on," he said, refusing to be sounded.

"There's a young woman in Etchworth that Morton was friendly with until he found out that she was married. The Sergeant-major was also running after her. Before I go any further, sir, will you answer a question?"

"Depends what it is."

"Was she the girl you spoke of, that first day I got here?"

"Yes, she was. Now carry on...."

"Sitting on my bed, Morton described to me how he had suspected that the Sergeant-major had gone to see the girl, and how he had followed him to the house and been silly enough to burst in on them through the french windows. He told me about the row that had followed between him and the B.S.M. and asked my advice on what he should do about it. I suggested that he should sit tight and wait for the Sergeant-major to make the first move. He was worried at the prospect of going the same way as Fieldhouse, who was handed out a hundred and fifty-six days' detention for doing much the same thing. I did the best I could to reassure him with the argument that the B.S.M. would have to face a good deal of awkward questioning if he tried to pin anything on him, but I'm sure I didn't convince him at all. Then he pulled his hand out of his pocket. It was wrapped in a blood-stained handkerchief. I got out of bed, ripped open a field-dressing and bandaged it up for him as best I could."

"Where were the injuries, Peter?" Charlton asked.

"On the knuckles mostly."

"Would you say they were caused entirely by broken glass?"

"Yes, by the look of them."

The Super spoke again.

"Coming back to the brake-rope, what kind of knots did the fellow use? Knots are good clues sometimes."

The Inspector answered: "Clove-hitches for Yule's ankles and a harness-hitch for the mare."

"A harness-hitch, eh? The common-or-garden loop-knot

wasn't good enough for him. He obviously knew something about knots."

"Nightingale used those same words this morning, but because the murderer knew something about knots, it doesn't follow that he knew his stable-procedure. A harness-hitch isn't a horseman's knot. It's used for tow-lines, where a series of loops is needed for slipping over the shoulders of the men hauling on the rope. A harness-hitch is much easier to undo than a loop-knot, which binds like the devil under tension."

He switched the conversation back to the point where he had begun to question me, and went on to summarize for the Superintendent the evidence that he had so far accumulated. At quarter to nine, just as I was thinking of an excuse to slip away, he mentioned "The Bloodhound of Valladolid."

"It's turned out to be something of a dead end," he said regretfully. "Somebody in Cowfold Camp marked the passage concerning the Marquis of Santagena, but I'm doubtful if I shall ever find out who it was."

"How was it marked?" the Super asked idly.

"With two square-ended brackets, one inside the other, rather like a side and two corners of a photo-frame."

I drew in a sharp breath. In my overcoat pocket was the *Rubaiyat* that had once been Johnny's; and the verse on page 42 had been marked by two square-ended brackets.

There was a struggle within me between duty and friendship. Duty won. I got to my feet and walked across to where my greatcoat hung....

CHAPTER THIRTY-TWO

I

SUSAN was already in the cafeteria when I arrived. We pecked together at some light refreshments, to the accompaniment of small-talk that was not, as far as I was concerned, so bright as usual; then started on the long walk back to Sheep—exercise of which I had become not a little weary during the weeks previous.

My worst enemy cannot say that I am, by nature, a gloomy fellow. Yet that evening I was melancholy. I will not pretend that I mourned the sudden passing of a fellow creature; I grieved more for Johnny's participation in it. Johnny was one of my closest friends and I do not like to see my friends in deadly danger of the hangman. My conscience was pricking me, too, over my treachery with the *Rubaiyat*. Every human instinct told me that I should have held my tongue. Charlton had said, after examining the two books together—and using the word for the second time that day:

"Identical."

I, Johnny's friend, had been responsible for that.

It may have been because my mind was so disturbed that, walking along with Susan's arm in mine, I resolved on a show-down; to demand answers to all the questions that I had never before presumed to ask.

"Why," was my first enquiry, "do you always insist on foot-slogging back when there's a perfectly good bus?"

"Because I like the walk, Grumpy," she answered.

"That's not the real reason. Don't you want to be seen with me on the bus?"

"Oh, do let's talk about something else," she begged. "What's the matter with you this evening, Peter? You're like a bear with a—"

"It's not my head that's sore. I don't like mysteries."

"Don't you? I thought all great detectives thrived on them."

The little pleasantry found no responsive chord in me and we walked for fifty yards in silence, beyond which distance I could not sustain my role. I have said already that I cannot stand on my dignity for long without wanting to laugh. On this occasion, I was in no mood for merriment, yet it was in much less uncouth fashion that my next remark was made.

"We've known each other now, dear, for—how long is it?—over three months. We reached the conclusion a long while ago—I did, at any rate, and I believe you did, too—that we... get along pretty well together. I'm never very happy when you're out of my sight and I earnestly hope that *you* are as miserable as sin."

She squeezed my arm.

"Worse than that."

"We Bradfields," I said, with a flippancy that did little to mask the gravity of my thoughts, "have been renowned right through history for the openness—one might almost say the flagrant publicity—of our love affairs. Ever since the first Bradfield made known his intentions by snatching the girl of his dreams from the bosom of her family and dragging her by the hair to his cave away up the cliffside, the male members of my family have announced their affairs of the heart to a wondering world with flourish of trumpet and beat of drum. Yet here am I, the last of the Bradfields—or in danger of being so—pursuing a courtship in a manner that is, to say the least, furtive. I've told you all about myself. I've admitted to a selected few of my previous expeditions along the primrose path. I am, to the best of my knowledge and belief, a bachelor. I am A1 at Lloyd's and well fancied for the Centenary Stakes."

We walked on. Susan was content to wait for my next remark.

"In return for this frankness," I resumed, "I have been put in possession of the following facts: One, you are Susan Carmichael, spinster of this parish. Two, you are employed by the Lulverton War Memorial Hospital in the capacity of almoner's secretary. Three, you live in the village of Sheep. Four, you are the loveliest creature I have ever met. Five, and the most adorable."

I came to the end of my list.

"And six?" Susan asked.

"There is no six."

"The other night it was Heart's Desire."

"Well, six, Heart's Desire, if you're really set on it; but beyond that I have no data. Joking apart, darling, why must there be all this mystery? Why can't we go on the bus, like Jack Citizen and Jill Citizen? Why can't I call for you, instead of meeting you in back-street teashops in Lulverton? Why can't I take you right home to your door—or at least to the garden gate?"

There were other questions needing answers, but I stopped there. The rest would come after. We had gone some distance before she replied, slowly at first:

"My father was killed in France at the beginning of 1918, when I was two months old. I was the only child. My parents had been married a little over a year. My mother had loved my father very dearly, and when he died I was all she had to live for. I can only guess at how she must have scraped and saved to bring me up, to send me to a good school—and all the other sweet, wonderful things that she managed to do for me. So you see, Peter dear, that I would rather do *anything* than cause her sadness or pain."

I grunted my sympathetic understanding, though wondering where these opening remarks were leading.

"My mother had a sister who loved another man almost as much as my mother loved my father. He was a soldier, too. He was stationed at Whitchester, where my aunt was living then with my grandmother. That was in 1916. They—had to get married. Then he was drafted overseas at a time when she—when she had most need of him. He left her without saying goodbye. She waited for many weeks, but no news came. She wrote to him care of his unit, but her letter was sent back marked 'Not Known.' She wrote to the Regimental Paymaster. It was found that he already had a wife and that he had married my aunt under a false name. They caught him and he was punished; but a week before the baby was due to arrive, my aunt's body was found in the canal."

"But, my darling thing!" I began to protest. "You're not suggesting for a single moment, are you, that—"

"Let me say the rest of it, now I've started," she begged. "It's not very easy, dear.... My father's best friend was with him when he was killed. He says my father saved his life. They were in the same shell-hole with two or three other men. The Germans threw over a hand-grenade. They couldn't get to it in time to throw it back, so my father... flung himself on top of it. That same friend, Peter, came back to Lulverton when he was demobilized in 1919. By then, his son was nearly two and just as much the apple of his parents' eye as I was of my mother's. We two war babies grew up together and, long before either of us had had a single idea on the subject, it was an understood thing between our parents that one day we would marry each other. As is often the way, we drifted into accepting the arrangement and—are you listening, dear?"

"Yes."

"Tommy and I were never officially engaged. They wanted us to be—and so did Tommy; but I managed to put them off. I couldn't go on in that way indefinitely and would have had to say 'yes' eventually. If I hadn't, it would have broken the old people's hearts. Then the war came. Tommy rushed off and joined the R.A.F. He came out of the Battle of Britain with the D.F.M. with bar. He's out in Africa now. His father and mother are so proud of him.... My mother is, too. I can see it always in her eyes. She nearly bursts sometimes with happiness at the thought that one day—if Tommy gets through—he'll be her son-in-law, and all the sacrifices she has made for me will not have been made... in vain. Tommy's a darling and I'm very fond of him. But I don't love him—I never shall love him—as I do you."

She pulled me to a stop and swung herself round in front of me. In the darkness, her face was close to mine.

"Sometimes in these last months," she breathed with a depth of passion in the lovely undertone, "I've almost wished that he'd be—"

"Please don't say it."

She buried her head in my shoulder and burst into tears.

II

Our mood changed. We talked with something of our usual gaiety until we reached our friendly old chestnut tree on Plestrium Dexter.

"Darling," I murmured, "I started out by being a brutal cad this evening. May I tell you how sorry I am?"

"It's I who should be repentant," she whispered back. "I've been a selfish little beast, not just this evening, but for weeks and weeks. But you do see why, don't you? I wanted to be with you every possible moment, but I dared not let Mother get to hear about it. It was risky being out together so much in Lulverton; but coming home on the same bus as half the inhabitants of Sheep would have been simply fatal. I don't think Mother suspects anything. I've told her they've been keeping me late at the hospital. Oh, Peter, my darling, what are we going to *do*?"

I kissed her before I told her.

"The solution is simple," I said, "but it all depends on one thing."

"And that is...?"

"Will you marry me?"

"Yes, of course I will," she said carelessly, "but that doesn't—"

I interrupted her with gentle firmness.

"You might," I suggested, "give my important enquiry a less indifferent reception. I invited you to marry me, not to come and have a Cup of tea somewhere."

Instantly she was full of remorse.

"I thought," she explained, "that that was all fixed."

The way of a maid with a man, I pondered. Shall we simple males, I asked myself, ever understand them?

"It won't be fixed," I reminded her, "with this Tommy fellow hovering round in his Spitfire. You'll have to finish with him first. What's the position? Do you correspond much?"

"Not so much as we used to. The last letter I had from him was about three weeks ago."

I seized the opportunity thus offered.

"Shameful!" I muttered. "Unforgivable neglect. He must have found somebody else. What was the tone of the letter—friendly, but stilted?"

"I suppose it was, really," Susan agreed doubtfully.

"Well, that simplifies things considerably," I said, brightening up. "Tomorrow you can write a letter saying how sorry you are—no, you needn't be too sorry, because you're not engaged or anything tiresome like that. You can say that you're sure that he'll be pleased to hear that you've met the most wonderful man in all the world. You can put it in your own words, of course," I conceded generously. "I'm just giving you the gist of the thing. Do that tomorrow."

"Yes, dear," she said with a dutifulness that I noticed with no little satisfaction.

"Next," I went on in a businesslike, if lowered, tone, "your mother."

"Yes," she said, "Mother."

The impression she gave was that here was a greater obstacle than Tommy.

"There seem to be two main difficulties: firstly, it's her dearest wish that you should marry this other fellow; and secondly, she has a natural dislike and suspicion of soldiers with no—er—respectable civilian background. To me, the second appears the more serious."

"Yes, if only we could lessen the first shock. Do you think I could take you home in—"

"I was coming to that," I said. "In a fortnight's time, I start my next leave, when I shall be able to wear civvies for nine days with impunity. Wouldn't that be a good time to spring me on the parent? Then, when my natty gent's suiting has had the inevitable reassuring effect and the winsomeness of my character begins to make its mark on her, the splendours of Tommy would begin to fade."

Susan agreed: "That's a lovely idea! I could tell her—at first—that you're on important work in Lulverton for one of the Ministries."

"That's right," I grumbled, but only half-humorously, "wrench me out of uniform and then manufacture an excuse for my not being in it!"

"I should have to say *something*, darling; otherwise she might think you were an enemy agent."

"For Pete's sake!" I protested. "First I'm a seducer of innocent womanhood and now I'm a blasted spy! Anyone would think that you were introducing a case of scarlet fever into the house."

"Darling," she said, so tenderly that I was busy for some minutes.

"Anyway," I said at length, "I shall be glad when this hole-in-corner nonsense is done with."

"Yes," she agreed, "but I couldn't do anything else, could I? If I'd told you, you would have been miserable and would probably have stopped away from me.... We had some narrow squeaks, though. The worst moment was when Mr. Nightingale nearly caught us together in the cafeteria."

"Nearly?" I said. "It was more than that; it was a fair cop. Yes, I remember it. I remember it only too well. Is Mr. Nightingale a friend of the family?"

Susan said: "He's Tommy's father."

CHAPTER THIRTY-THREE

I

IT was left at that. On the morrow, Susan would write to Tommy Nightingale; and in a fortnight's time, a handsome civilian stranger—albeit with a nose too wide and flat—would be introduced into the Carmichael household.

"After all," I said to her, just before the final good-night, "it isn't as though I were a pauper. I've anything up to five pounds Post War Credit, a couple of fifteen-shilling War Savings Certificates and another book more than half full of stamps."

"We shall be rich," she said, with a contented sigh that had in it no love of money.

"Rich," I agreed. "Rich beyond the dreams of munition workers."

II

Paul Morton was lying wide awake in bed when I got back into the hut.

"Well?" was his greeting. "What's the news?"

"Nothing much," I answered with a shrug of my shoulders. "The police are following up an assorted handful of clues. No startling announcement yet."

"I'm worried sick, Peter," he confessed. "I'm properly in a jam."

"I wouldn't go as far as that," I tried to hearten him. "The evidence against you is, at the best, wildly circumstantial."

I felt it hardly prudent to tell him that nearly all felons are convicted on circumstantial evidence alone.

"I'm not bothered so much about myself, Peter, as about Fay. Think of the headlines when the Sunday papers get hold of it. Columns and columns of tripe, with 'Morton Pleads Innocent' in the stop-press. What's going to happen when Fay's husband finds out?"

291

I hung my greatcoat on the hook behind the door and began to undress.

"'Sufficient unto the day...'" I said. "Very probably it won't get as far as that. Your name—or hers—may not even be mentioned. Anything been cooking in camp while I've been out?"

"Yes. They've taken young Lovelock off to hospital in an ambulance."

"Have they, though? What was it—an accident?"

"He was beaten up."

There flashed through my mind a picture of Blitz Fitz.

"Who by?"

"Gianella."

Of course. Charlton must have passed on the information to the Old Lady in the officers' mess; and batmen are quick of hearing.

Paul said: "He caught Lovelock alone in his sleeping-hut and nearly battered the life out of him. Everyone's highly delighted, though nobody seems to know why Gianella did it. The Old Lady put him under close arrest."

"He could hardly do anything else," I said, pulling back the mattress and laying my trousers on the plywood base of the bed.

III

The next morning, Johnny Fieldhouse was taken into custody.

Charlton arrived early, accompanied by Sgt. Martin and a plain-clothes constable. They were shown by Paul into the Major's room. In a few moments, Johnny was sent for. They were all inside together for a quarter of an hour. When Johnny emerged again, Sgt. Martin was on one side of him and the police constable on the other.

As he walked between them past my desk, I got up from my chair. He turned his head towards me. Horror and fear were in his eyes.

"Peter!" he shouted wildly. "For God's sake get me out of this!"

Before they reached the end door, I had time to reply:

"Don't worry, Johnny! Leave it to me!"

Then they took him away. It was the blackest moment of my life.

IV

Charlton seemed disinclined to follow. He came out of the Major's room a minute or two later, summoned me away from my desk and bore me off to the hut that had been placed at his disposal. He sat down at the table and motioned me to take the other chair. I slumped down miserably.

"Don't get too worked up over it, Peter," he urged me. "He's only been taken into custody on suspicion of being concerned in the murder."

"You wouldn't have gone as far as that," I retorted bitterly, "if you hadn't been sure of your ground."

"In your heart of hearts, Peter, don't you believe that he did it?"

I said flatly: "No, I don't! Do you?"

"During my whole life, I have met few people who gave an impression of such transparent honesty as Fieldhouse. I'm not easy to convince, Peter, but truth seemed to shine out of every word he said to me yesterday. Yet the evidence is damning. He admitted in the Major's room this morning that he marked that paragraph in 'The Bloodhound of Valladolid.' He even admitted that, when he marked it, he put the Sergeant-major in the position of the Marquis of Santagena. He told us all quite openly just now that, of all the atrocities described in that book, there was none that he would have been more delighted to see perpetrated on the Sergeant-major. That was why he marked the passage.... How he must have hated Yule!"

"He had every reason to. Whatever happens, I don't think

293

I shall ever forget the part I played when I showed you the *Rubaiyat.*"

"You did your duty. It's no fun, sometimes, being a policeman. You'd put up an honest fight for Fieldhouse—and you were as straightforward with me when the evidence went against him. I admire you for it, Peter."

"That smacks of sophistry," I growled. "But the honest fight I've already put up for Johnny is only the beginning. From now on, it's tooth and nail!"

"Good for you," he smiled slightly. "Let's see what we can do about it, shall we? I like the look of Fieldhouse and I'd be very glad to see him cleared. But the evidence against him is strong"—he shook his head slowly—"very strong indeed."

"The only way to free him," I asserted with no great discernment, "is to find the man who really did it."

"Easier said than done, Peter." He felt in his pocket and pulled out his notebook. "Let me give you the details of my investigation so far...."

He spoke for half an hour, glancing at his notes from time to time. He finished by saying:

"There is only one small point in Fieldhouse's favour: an intending murderer with any intelligence at all would have faked some sort of clue to suggest that the gun-shed had been broken into. It would have given strong support to a defence on his behalf that the brake-rope was stolen after he had put it away."

He closed the book and laid it on the table.

"Now you know as much as I do," he said. "Any suggestions?"

I pondered for a while before I began to speak.

"If the gun-shed doors," I said, "had been left open, or the rope allowed to lie loose somewhere around the camp, there were several B.H.Q. men with ample opportunity to slip out of camp via the gas-chamber, intercept the B.S.M. on his way back from 'Lyme Regis,' knock him unconscious, rope him to Etchworth Lass, and be back in camp—once again via the gas-chamber, to replace the rubber gloves—all in less than three-quarters of an hour. The B.S.M. was anything but an energetic walker. It would probably have taken him all of twenty minutes to get from 'Lyme Regis' to the point where the lane leads off to A.R. 4."

I grabbed a sheet of paper and took a pencil from my pocket.

"Say the murderer met him there at 11.50. Give him two minutes to lure the B.S.M. off the main road; four minutes to get him as far as the gate, knock him unconscious with a sand-filled sock and drag him into the field; six minutes, say, to lead the mare out of the lean-to, hitch her to the B.S.M. and set her running. That brings us to two minutes after midnight. Allow ten minutes—no, make it twelve—and there he is, back in camp by 12.14. Give him twenty minutes for the outward trip, because he couldn't bank on the B.S.M. arriving at a given moment—and there you have the whole expedition completed in just under three-quarters of an hour."

"You've raised an interesting point," Charlton said. "Miss Gilbert told me yesterday that Yule's invariable practice was to leave at 11.30 and that he visited her only on Wednesday evenings. I wonder how many men in camp were aware of that?"

"You'd probably be amazed if you knew. In a place like this, there's not much that isn't common knowledge."

"Maybe you're right," he agreed. "Now, you said just now that the murderer lured the Sergeant-major off the main road. How?"

"It was late. All the evening-outers would be back on A.R. 4. Farming folk can be depended upon to get to bed early, so it was heavy odds in the murderer's favour that nobody would be using the lane in the region of midnight. We'll take it that the murderer was a B.H.Q. man. He reached the lane junction and waited for the B.S.M. When the B.S.M. eventually strolled up, our homicidal friend told him that something had happened at A.R. 4 and would the B.S.M. get along there *pronto*. We needn't bother about the reason; one story would have been as good as another. Then, when the two of them got safely away from the main road and near the gate, the murderer carried out the next step in his plan by slugging the B.S.M. with a sandbag."

"Was he still wearing the rubber gloves? or hadn't he yet put them on?"

"It's a small point. We don't know when the thistle spine got planted in the palm. If he had been wearing the gloves when he met the B.S.M., it's unlikely that the B.S.M. would have noticed them."

"And the thistle?"

"Tucked away somewhere. Very likely in his greatcoat pocket, with the dog-lead."

"The rope?"

"He would have dumped it in the field as soon as he arrived—and, of course, before the B.S.M. turned up. He might even have kept it and fitted it into the yarn he pitched to the Sergeant-major."

The Inspector nodded several times.

"All quite feasible," he said. "The trouble is that it fits Fieldhouse as neatly as anyone else."

He rose to his feet and began pacing up and down the long hut, with his hands clasped behind his back. I sprawled in my chair, my hands pushed into my trouser-pockets, and puffing viciously at my cigarette. He paused in his stride and looked down at me.

"I'm sorry, Peter," he said gently, "but it's a cast-iron case. *Motive:* Yule sent him to detention. From what we know of Yule, the alleged assault was a frame-up, which makes the motive stronger. *Alibi:* none. *Opportunity:* everything in his favour. *Method:* highly unusual, entirely in keeping with his temperament. *Witnesses:* heavily against."

"And not a penn'orth of direct evidence amongst 'em! Bring me the man who saw him do it—and I'll believe he murdered Yule! If that's a cast-iron case, it's due for an almighty wallop that will crack it right open!"

He listened without interruption to my tirade. When I reached the end of it, he said:

"Long after you left us last night, the Super and I continued our discussion. You'll remember his creed of old: that the most obvious suspect is almost invariably the criminal; that the 'least likely' murderer is found only in fiction. In the main, I agree with him, just as I also agree with his other dictum, 'Facts, nothing but facts.' Yet there are times, Peter, when, however loudly the facts cry out, I am more ready to listen to the quiet little voice of intuition. The facts tell me that Fieldhouse murdered Sergeant-major Yule; intuition tells me that he did no such thing. But intuition takes me no further than that blind belief; and the Central Criminal Court will listen to nothing but facts. Crack my cast-iron case wide open, Peter; it is more than I can do."

And he resumed his restless pacing of the hut.

V

It is an odd characteristic of the human mind that it is never completely logical; that, whatever its owner's powers of concentration, the thought-sequence is always interrupted by irrelevant, and usually fantastic, intrusions. One ponders, for example, on patriotism and suddenly, in one's mind's eye, there is a cat sitting on a pile of firewood. One meditates on the wonders of the Universe and there drifts into one's consciousness the image of a tapioca pudding. One seeks to recapture a memory and recalls only Brighton Pier. Then, when one has given up trying to remember and has philosophically transferred one's attention to Brighton Pier, only to have that structure superseded by the foolish face of the cherished teddybear of one's childhood, up pops the long-sought memory as if it had been waiting to catch one unawares.

In just that inconsequential fashion, I reached my objective that morning. While Charlton loped up and down the Nissen, as busy with his thoughts as I, I endeavoured to fix my mind on the problem that confronted us. But my brain was skittish. It would not concern itself exclusively with brake-ropes, alibis and rubber gloves, preferring to trifle with the Eiffel Tower and a bus-conductor's ticket-puncher. It must have been a full five minutes later, when I was engrossed with two rabbits and a bright new penny, that there dropped into my mind a name that found involuntary utterance from my lips:

"Alexander Templeton."

CHAPTER THIRTY-FOUR

I

THE sequel to my involuntary mention of Alexander Templeton was that the Q. and Paul Morton were summoned to the conference.

"Now," said Charlton, when chairs had been fetched for the others and we were all seated round the table, "tell me everything you know about this fellow, Templeton. Bombardier Morton, let's hear you first."

"Do you remember," Paul began, "when Clapham & Dwyer used to broadcast in the old days, how Clapham was always mentioning a man he called, 'My pal, Spiegel'? Perhaps you don't, but the B.S.M. had a similar stooge whose name was Alexander Templeton. The first time I heard the B.S.M. mention the name was in the early part of last August. It was, now I come to think of it, during lunch on the same morning as Midnight, our mess kitten, was drowned in a pail of tea. The B.S.M. got on to the subject of accidents and described Alexander Templeton as a young motorist friend of his who had been strangled by his woollen scarf getting caught in the fan-belt of his car. From that day forward, the B.S.M. was always dragging Templeton's name into the conversation. There didn't seem to be any rhyme or reason in it. The second time he spoke of him as an old man who lived entirely on goats' milk. After that, we came to accept it as a ponderous and not very funny form of joke, but recently we've come to the conclusion that there was something more sinister behind it."

"Who are 'we'?"

"The Q., Bombardier Bradfield and I. There were only the four of us in the mess. I've never heard the B.S.M. mention Templeton outside the mess—until Wednesday night.

I don't remember quite how it cropped up, but we were all sitting round the fire with the three officers, and the B.S.M. found some sort of opportunity to mention Templeton. He referred to him as a gunner who was once in this Battery. The Major replied that he didn't recall the name, and everything would have passed off all right if the B.S.M. hadn't pressed the point. The Major got somewhat huffy and said that there never had been a man called Templeton in XYZ Battery, whatever the B.S.M. cared to say about it. I quite agree with the Major. I'm in close touch with things and I'm ready to swear that no Templeton—Alexander or otherwise—has ever been on the strength of this unit."

Charlton turned to the Quartermaster.

"What do you know about Templeton, Q.?"

"Nowt at all, except what I heard from th' Sergeant-major. 'E were always cracking th' bloodyfool joke. 'My friend Templeton did this' and, 'My friend Templeton did t'other Me, I'd say Templeton never existed—like Jack, th' Giant Killer!"

Charlton smiled.

"Yet," he said, "it seems that he must have had a good reason for mentioning Templeton. Why do you suppose he spoke of him in the officers' mess on Wednesday?"

"I think 'e were getting at—"

He pulled up short.

"Yes?" Charlton prompted.

"It's not worth bothering about," growled the Q. "What a chap does with his spare time is no business of mine—and it weren't no business of th' Sergeant-major's, either."

"I don't quite follow you," Charlton said.

"Let me explain, sir," suggested Paul. "The Q. doesn't like to mention it, because he doesn't think you know about Mrs. Saunders. On Wednesday evening, the B.S.M. described Templeton as having played around with a young woman whose husband was a prisoner of war in Italy. That couldn't have been anything but a stab at me. He pretended to jog the Major's memory about what had happened to Templeton when the husband had suddenly put in an appearance. But the Major's memory wasn't to be jogged. Then Captain Fitzgerald took a hand in the conversation and told the B.S.M., in no uncertain terms, to pipe down."

II

The others went, leaving the Inspector and me alone together.

"Peter," he said, "you've given me an idea. Let us approach this murder from a new direction, having Alexander Templeton as our starting-point. Our first question is, does Alexander Templeton exist—is he a man of flesh and blood?"

"I should say not."

"Then it's a name without a body. A fictitious name. As the Q. said, 'Jack, th' Giant-Killer.' In other words, it's a pseudonym. What does that suggest to us?"

There flashed into my mind the recollection of Susan's aunt, who had gone to the Registry Office with a man who had used a name that was not his own. I said, almost without thinking:

"Bigamy."

"Hypothetical," was his verdict, "but we'll pursue it by enquiring, What is the most obvious link between bigamy and murder?"

I answered without hesitation: "Blackmail."

"Precisely. Consider this thesis, Peter. At some time before your Battery came to this neighbourhood—perhaps before the war, or when the man in question was still in Civvy Street—a member of your B.H.Q. got into deep water with a woman and only managed to struggle out of it by marrying her at a Registry Office under the name of Alexander Templeton. A splendid opportunity for blackmail, you'll agree, especially if the fellow already possessed one wife. Imagine Yule discovering this closely guarded secret—a Battery Sergeant-major is in a very favourable position to pick up such tit-bits—and putting on the screw tightly and still more tightly, until the victim decided that he'd had enough and made away with his Jonah. Does that explain Alexander Templeton?"

I readily agreed with him. It was Johnny's only chance.

"Bombardier Morton told us," he said, "that the Sergeant-major never mentioned Templeton until you came to Cowfold Camp. Do you agree?"

"Yes, definitely. Our previous station was at Stalcote-on-Sea—which reminds me that on Wednesday evening, the Sergeant-major particularly mentioned that 'Gunner' Templeton had his affair with the P.O.W.'s wife at Stalcote."

He rose to his feet.

"I think," he said, "that we will follow our intuition and send a telegram to Stalcote."

III

It was not until the afternoon, just after Mr. Bretherton and I had finished the pay parade, that I saw the Inspector again. He took me outside, where we should not be overheard.

"We've had a nibble," he murmured. "The Registry Office at Stalcote confirm that Alexander Templeton was married to a Miss Angela Lang in May last. That's all I know at the moment, but I've sent Martin off to Stalcote.

All we can hope is that he brings back something useful in. the way of information and something identifiable in the way of a photograph."

Sgt. Martin returned that night with both. At eleven o'clock, just as I was going to bed, I received a telephone-call from Charlton, calling me to another conference; and a few minutes later, a police car picked me up at the camp entrance and whisked me off to Lulverton.

The Inspector was waiting in his room with Martin and Supt. Kingsley. When I had found a chair and lighted a cigarette, Charlton slid a postcard-size photograph from an envelope and passed it across to me with the words:

"Alexander Templeton."

I needed no more than a single glance at it.

"Good Lord!" I said in a small, hushed voice, "*Him.*"

"Yes, Peter, him. Our theorizing this morning has produced something tangible. Martin's inquiries have been highly successful." The Sergeant beamed happily at this praise. "After making contact with the local police, he went along with an inspector to the home of old Mr. and Mrs. Lang, where the so-called Mrs. Templeton is living with her infant child. The old people were out at the time, so Martin and the inspector were able to have a confidential chat with the young woman. She guessed at once what they'd come about, and took it quite calmly—almost with relief. When they questioned her—they made no mention of the murder, of course—she admitted that she had known, right from the start of their association, that he was already married; and that when she had discovered that she was going to have a child, she had insisted on his going through a form of marriage with her, having been ready to risk the penalties of bigamy, rather than face the reproaches of her parents and the tittle-tattle of the neighbours. She told Martin that she had been expecting exposure for some time past; her parents were beginning to ask too many awkward questions about the Army allowances that hadn't materialized."

"But," I burst out, "if he committed the murder, how the hell did he manage it?"

"At tain meenits tae yin," Charlton answered in Mc-Finnon's dialect, "Fieldhouse returned from the latrines and would not have roused the 'heelan' heathen' had not the door of the hut been slammed shut by the wind."

"What of it?" I demanded.

"I'll leave you to work it out for yourself," he answered with that irritating smile of his. "I have also hit on a method," he added, "by which the gun-shed could be opened without a key."

"Yes?" I said eagerly.

"You may care," he smiled once more, "to exercise your brains on that as well."

CHAPTER THIRTY-FIVE

THE gun-shed conundrum beat me, but I solved the other riddle before I went to sleep that night.

In the morning, events moved swiftly. Charlton arrived before nine o'clock. With him were Martin and the plainclothes man who had accompanied him the previous day. Something big, I saw, was afoot.

He was closeted alone with the Major for ten minutes. They came out together into the general office and the Old Lady sent me off to fetch the Q., who was acting-B.S.M. When I came back with him, the Old Lady instructed him to the effect that the whole of B.H.Q. personnel, including cooks and batmen, would parade at once in the lecture-hut.

The only permissible exception was the duty telephonist, Gunner Allman.

Ten minutes later, all were assembled: The Major, the Captain (back from London the previous afternoon), Mr. Bretherton, Q. Ackroyd, Paul Morton, Chris Wilkinson with Gianella, remanded in close arrest for the C.O., in his charge, Postbechild, Nelson, Regan, Owen (back from leave) and all the others. The only absentees were Lovelock (in hospital), Johnny Fieldhouse (in custody), Allman (on duty) and myself. I had received murmured instructions from Charlton immediately before the meeting began; and Sgt. Martin and I had a job to do.

The door of the lecture-hut was closed and Charlton, standing before the seated officers, N.C.Os. and men of XYZ B.H.Q., began to talk to them in the deep soothing voice that had lulled so many malefactors into an ill-advised sense of well-being.

"As all of you will know by now," he said, "your Battery Sergeant-major met his end the night before last, by being tied to a horse and subsequently dragged and trampled to death by the maddened animal. Some of you will also have heard that one of your number, Gunner Fieldhouse, has been taken into custody on suspicion of having been concerned in the crime."

(Martin and I got the doors of the gun-shed open. Following Charlton's suggestion—I could have kicked myself for not having thought of it—I took a spanner and removed the nuts and washers that secured the hasp-staple to the right-hand door. Then leaving the staple still in position, with the bolts through the woodwork, we closed the doors, slipped the hasp over the staple and fixed the padlock. The gun-shed had all the appearance of being safe from casual intruders. But when I pulled on the padlock, the bolts of the staple, freed of their nuts, were drawn through the woodwork; and all that was left in the right-hand door were the two holes through which the bolts had passed, not loosely, but tightly enough not to arouse Johnny's suspicions when he had closed up the gun-shed.)

"Yesterday," Charlton went on, "I had a few minutes' talk with most of you, from which I gained a great deal of information, some of it of little use, but a certain amount of it of real value in my investigation. Nothing that I learned justified me in refraining to take a step that I was most anxious to avoid—the apprehending of Gunner Fieldhouse. When I say that I was anxious to avoid it, it was for this reason: that I was convinced in my own mind that it was not Gunner Fieldhouse who had murdered your Sergeant-major, but"—his gaze travelled from face to face—"somebody now in this hut."

(I replaced the washers and nuts on the staple-bolts, and Martin and I swiftly proceeded to another part of the camp. The Inspector could not be expected to talk all the morning.)

"Today I have conferred with your Battery Commander, Major Mellis, and he has kindly consented to the calling of this unconventional muster parade. By no other means could I make known to you, all at the same time, that the circumstantial evidence against Gunner Fieldhouse is so overwhelmingly strong that if something is not done quickly to prevent such a calamity, he will be sentenced to death for another's crime. I therefore address a plea to all of you except one guilty man. Is there anyone here this morning who has held back evidence, however trivial it may seem, that may have some bearing on the murder? Can any of you give me one single fact that will enable me to go to my superiors and say to them, 'I have failed to find the murderer, but Fieldhouse can be released from custody'?"

He paused impressively, but there was no response to his appeal.

"Then I ask the murderer, if he has any sentiments of humanity and pity, to save Fieldhouse from the hangman's rope."

Again his eye travelled round the hut, row by row, from the officers in the front, to the gunners in soiled denims at the back.

Not a man spoke or stirred.

With a shrug of his broad shoulders, he resumed his peroration and was still talking when there was a knock on the hut door behind him and Sgt. Martin appeared. Charlton turned and approached him. When he got close enough, Martin muttered:

"Okay, sir."

Charlton swung back and addressed himself direct to the Major.

"That is all I have to say, sir."

"Quartermaster," said the Old Lady, "dismiss the parade." With military smartness, the Q. was on his feet.

"To your duties, file out!" he ordered.

The Inspector stood just inside the door. As one of the men was about to pass him, he laid a restraining hand on his arm. The hut emptied rapidly until only the two of them remained.

The men were fanning out in all directions, on the way back to their tasks. Martin and I stayed where we were, ten yards from the door of the hut, with the two men in full view.

"'E's arrested 'im," Martin muttered in my ear. "Now 'e's giving 'im the caution. That's another one for the Old Bailey; and another notch in the Inspector's gun."

We stood waiting until the two men came out into the open. The prisoner at Charlton's side was the Q.

CHAPTER THIRTY-SIX

THERE is very little left to explain.

Battery Quartermaster-sergeant Ackroyd was Alexander Templeton. He admitted later that Yule had hit by accident on his secret and had made his life a hell by threatening him with exposure that would not only have sent him to gaol for nine months, but would also have deprived his wife of her already tottering reason.

Yule had not extorted a penny in blackmail, but had quietly gloated over his helpless misery, just as he had gloated over the dying agonies of the mouse under the glass at Boxford.

At last the Q. could stand it no longer, had plotted and killed him. Johnny had nearly wrecked the plan by forgetting to fetch the brake-rope from A.R. 4 until the last minute. The Q. had read the marked paragraph in "The Blood-hound of Valladolid" a week before he committed the crime; and had decided, in his own stolid way, that if Yule, was to die, there should be poetic justice and the punishment should fit the crime: Owen, the little Welshman; Nelson; Johnny Fieldhouse; Midnight, the mess kitten; Scottie—or so the Q. imagined; all had to be avenged in fitting fashion.

As for the details of the murder, they were as Charlton and I had already envisaged them. The only fresh thing was the method by which the Quartermaster had led me to believe that he was turning restlessly in his bed: a length of cord from the leg of the bed to the knob of the open door, so that when the door swung with the high wind, it tugged at the bed and made it creak. Martin and I reconstructed the simple apparatus and, though there was no wind that morning, I moved the door backwards and forwards and it caused the bed to creak most convincingly.

Pushed well down into the Quartermaster's kit-bag was a sock inside which there were enough particles of sand to leave little doubt of the purpose to which it had recently been put;

and in the right-hand pocket of his greatcoat, the shrivelled leaf of a spear plume-thistle.

In considering the possible murderers, I ought to have looked with a more suspicious eye at the Q. Johnny had told me that the Quartermaster had been a steeple-chaser. He was therefore well versed in the ways of horses. I should have remembered, too, the Q.'s reactions to Yule's first reference to Alexander Templeton; and how, from that day onward, he dropped his brusque manner towards the Sergeant-major and became his yes-man.

CHAPTER THIRTY-SEVEN

THE epilogue to my story concerns four people alone: Susan, Hazel Marjoram, Johnny and I.

It was three weeks later. Johnny and I were on embarkation leave, as XYZ Battery, with a new sergeant-major and a new quartermaster, was soon to be off for foreign parts. The four of us were in London, celebrating a double engagement, for Hazel had decided that Johnny needed somebody sensible to look after him; and Mrs. Carmichael, after the first shock of revelation, had reached the conclusion that Susan might, were she to search long enough, find a less suitable husband than I. The situation had been eased by the fact that Tommy Nightingale had replied to Susan's letter by sending news of his impending engagement to a Waaf.

In the cocktail bar before we dined, Johnny—in faultless civvies that made him almost imposing—raised his glass and said:

"Well, here's to all four of us! May we enjoy a happy future and forget all that has happened in the past!"

As we drank the toast, Hazel's mischievous eyes twinkled at me over the rim of her glass.

I drained my own glass and placed it on the counter. "Private Marjoram," I said courteously, "may I escort you in to dinner?"

"Of course, Corporal," she replied, and slipped her arm into mine.

If we were not to be joined in wedlock, we were, at any rate, united by a tacit bond of mutually advantageous silence.

Glossary

A.B. 64	Soldier's Service and Pay Book.
A.C.I.(s)	Arm Council Instructions.
Ack-Ack	Anti-Aircraft (A.A.).
Ack-I.G.	Assistant Instructor, Gunnery (Rank, W.O. II).
A.D.G.B.	Air Defence of Great Britain.
Admin.	Administration.
At(s)	A.T.S. Women's Auxiliary to Territorial Army.
B.H.Q.	Battery Headquarters.
B.Q.M.S.	Battery Quartermaster-sergeant. Three chevrons with gun and crown above.
B.S.M.	Battery Sergeant-major (Rank, W.O. II). Crown and Laurels on forearm.
Cadre	Nucleus of officers and N.C.Os. on formation of new Regiment, etc.
C.B.	Confined to Barracks.
C.M.P.	Corps of Military Police ("Red-caps").
C.O.	Commanding Officer.
D.B.	Detention Barracks.
D.C.	Detachment Commander (Rank, Sergeant).
Don-R.	Despatch Rider (D.R.).
F.S.	Field Service.
F.S.M.O.	Field Service Marching Order.
G.S.	General Service.
i/c.	In charge.
Jankers	Pack-drill.
L.A.A.	Light Anti-Aircraft.
L.M.G.	Light machine-gun.
M.I.	Medical Inspection.

M.O.	Medical Officer.
N.C.O.	Non-commissioned officer.
O.C.	Officer Commanding.
P.T.	Physical Training.
P.T.C.	Primary Training Centre.
Q..	Quartermaster.
R.A.	Royal Artillery.
R.E.	Royal Engineers.
Recce.	Reconnaissance.
Red-caps	See C.M.P.
R.E.M.E.	Royal Electrical and Mechanical Engineers.
R.P.	Regimental Police.
Stag	Watch. Look-out duties.
T.H.Q.	Troop Headquarters.
Ticket	Discharge.
Ticket, working	Gaining discharge by feigned illness, etc.
Tilly	Utility.
T.O.E.T.	Test(s) of Elementary Training.
u/s.	Unserviceable.
V.P.	Vulnerable Point.
Waaf	Women's Auxiliary Air Force (W.A.A.F.).
W.O. I.	Warrant Officer, Class I (Rank, Regimental Sergeant-major). Lion and Unicorn on forearm.
W.O. II.	Warrant Officer, Class II (see B.S.M. and Ack-I.G.).